THE FAMILY

They're rough, they're tough, and they're back...

Tilly, Alice and the rest of the Keiver clan are knuckling down to life on one of the toughest most villainous streets in London. But their world is rocked to its core when someone they thought, and hoped, was dead, turns up like the proverbial bad penny – Jimmy Wild – small time crook and big bully. Jimmy brings his beautiful step-daughter Faye, and his downtrodden wife, Edie, to live on the street, and while they do their best to scratch out a miserable existence, Jimmy barely lifts a finger to help. What devastating act was so bad that it drove them away from their home in Kent to this hovel?

THE FAMILY

THE FAMILY

by

Kay Brellend

Magna Large Print Books
Long Preston, North Yorkshire,
BD23 4ND, England.

British Library Cataloguing in Publication Data.

Brellend, Kay
The family.

A catalogue record of this book is available from the British Library

ISBN 978-0-7505-3693-6

First published in Great Britain in 2012 by HarperCollins*Publishers*

Published in Large Print 2013 by arrangement with HarperCollins Publishers

Magna Large Print is an imprint of Library Magna Books Ltd.

Printed and bound in Great Britain by T.J. (International) Ltd., Cornwall, PL28 8RW

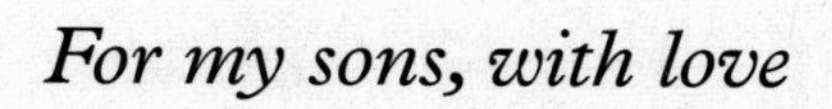

For my sons, with love

ACKNOWLEDGEMENTS

Big thanks are due to:
My agent, Juliet Burton – here's to the next 25 years! A great HarperCollins team – Sarah Ritherdon, Kate Bradley, Hana Osman and not forgetting Victoria Hughes-Williams and Amy Neilson who were in on the start.

PROLOGUE

November 1919

'Shut up making that racket, fer Gawd's sake, you're not a kid any more.'

Robert Wild glowered at his younger brother, who was cuffing tears and snot from his face, then snapped defiant eyes to a couple hovering close by. They were frowning in censure rather than sympathy as Stephen carried on sobbing his heart out. The bigger boy stared back belligerently until the woman gripped her companion's elbow, urging him to hurry on.

Yanking at his brother's arm, Robert steered him into the grimy corridor of the Duke of Edinburgh pub. From beyond the closed door of the saloon bar they could hear their kith and kin, voices raised in revelry; it served only to increase Stephen's misery.

'They ain't bothered she's dead, are they?' he hiccupped. 'Just us, ain't it, who's real upset?'

''Course they're bothered,' Robert muttered. 'Only it won't be till they've sobered up that they'll remember it.' From his superior height he cast a look at the top of his brother's wiry dark curls, glistening with droplets from the November night air. 'Want a drink?' he asked in an attempt to cheer Stephen up. 'I mean a proper drink, not another sup of shandy.'

Stephen shook his head then let his chin drop towards his chest. He stuffed his icy fingers into his pockets to warm them.

'I'm gettin' one,' Robert stated confidently. The door to the saloon bar was within arm's reach, but he stayed where he was. Much as he would have liked to enter and buy himself an ale, he wasn't old enough to be served; besides, he had no money. It would have been easy enough to cadge one off somebody, but right now he couldn't stir up the cheek to do it. Hearing his name called, he raised a lethargic hand in greeting as two young women emerged from the twilight, huddled in their coats. Alice and Bethany Keiver were their cousins, and their friends.

'Had enough in there with that rowdy lot?' Alice asked gently, putting an arm about Stevie's slumped shoulders. She offered no more words of sympathy; she and her sisters had given the boys enough support earlier that day. Having only recently lost people they loved to the Great War, the Keivers knew that pity, however well meant, should have its limits. But Alice's voice throbbed with emotion when she suggested, 'Why don't you both come up the station with us and see Sophy off?' She cocked her head, waiting for an answer. 'We're going to fetch little Luce and let her come with us. It's way past her bed-time.' She grinned, thinking how excited her seven-year-old sister would be about going out with the grown-ups so late at night. 'Come on,' Alice urged, 'Sophy's catching her train in about half an hour.'

Sophy, the eldest of the Keiver girls, was in

service in Essex. She'd travelled down yesterday, but her employer was not prepared to give her more than a day's leave to see her Aunt Fran laid to rest, so she had promised to return within hours of the funeral.

'Yeah, it'll give you both something to do. Take your minds off things. We can get some chips on the way back,' Bethany encouraged. 'You hungry, Stevie?' she asked brightly.

He shook his head, snorting back a sob.

'We're all right,' Robert said gruffly. 'Goin' off home soon in any case.' This was a lie. Neither he nor Stevie wanted to return to the dank, depressing room in Campbell Road where they lived. Better to loiter on the corner of Fonthill Road, breathing in air so cold it glassed their throats, than return to a place where their mum's whispering presence seemed to melt into every shadow.

'Best be off then,' Alice murmured and the two sisters walked on arm in arm in the direction of Campbell Road, heads down against the drifting mist.

Stephen raised his bloodshot eyes to Robert's face. 'What we gonna do now Mum's gone?' he croaked.

'Same as we did before,' Robert returned. 'No, that ain't right,' he corrected himself with a bleak smile. 'I'll be doin' the same as before, but you won't.' His tone grew bitterly ironic. 'Come Monday morning, you'll be out o' school and knockin' yer guts out down the market, same as me. I was thirteen when I started work, so it ain't gonna kill you, doin' the same. We're going to need every penny we can get to pay the rent and get fed now Mum's not around, so you've gotta do your bit.'

'But I ain't thirteen,' Stevie whimpered.

'Soon will be. You're close enough.'

At this, Stevie's fragile composure crumbled and he started sobbing again, head hanging between his hunched shoulders.

'Bawlin' ain't gonna help,' Robert said quietly. He'd learned young to control his tears. His lash-happy father had taught him that all crying got you was something else to howl about.

The saloon door suddenly swung outward and Robert dodged nimbly aside to avoid a blow from its iron handle.

'Wondered where the pair of you had got to. What you doing out here all on yer own?' Tilly Keiver asked in her whiskey-grizzled voice. 'Come back inside. It's bleedin' freezin' by this doorway.' She tilted her head to examine her youngest nephew's blotchy face. 'Come on, Stevie, mate,' she encouraged him, putting a red-raw hand on one of his shoulders. Through the rough fabric of his coat she gave his thin frame a squeeze. 'Yer mum's watchin' over you, y'know. She wouldn't want you so upset on her account.' Tilly's voice had thickened with emotion and she blinked as heat blurred her eyes. She'd been very close to her sister and had been distraught when the Spanish flu had finally overcome her. Fran had put up a fight for almost a month, but it had come as no surprise when she'd grown too weak to battle on. In a way it had been a blessing to see her suffering at an end.

Putting her lips close to Robert's ear, she whispered conspiratorially, 'Let's get the two of yers a little summat to warm the cockles, shall we?'

Robert recoiled slightly as her alcoholic breath wafted across his face. But he smiled. He could do with a bevy, all right. Despite being a good height and well built for his fourteen years, the publicans around the Islington area knew him and his family well; they knew how old he was and would only serve him on the sly now and again when they were feeling friendly. When he could afford it, Robert frequented hostelries further afield.

'Get yerselves sat down by the window, outta sight.' Tilly pointed to a bench and the two brothers slid obediently on to its smooth shiny surface and watched their aunt disappear into the thick atmosphere. The pub was packed with mourners, yet few had bothered to turn to acknowledge them this time. The wake had been going on for hours and most people were too far gone to remember the *poor orphan lads* they'd consoled at the cemetery that afternoon, then later when they'd all first filed soberly into the saloon bar. Robert had known what was behind their crooning voices and sad smiles as he received hugs and handshakes from one and all.

Poor sods, they'd all been thinking, they're orphans, even if they are almost grown and one of them already out earning. Stevie's going to be a burden on Rob if he don't toughen up. What a family! Their old man was a wrong 'un and did them all a turn by going missing during the war. But now Fran Wild's kids have got no mum, no money, and no nothing ... except one another.

As they'd offered up their pity, and their silent prayers that such bad luck might pass their own kids by, Robert had stared into their eyes, and known exactly what was going through their minds. He'd made himself a promise: by the time he was twenty, they'd be looking at him in a different light. And if there was an afterlife, and his mum was watching over him and Stevie, for the first time in her miserable existence she'd be feeling happy and proud. He'd make sure of that.

ONE

Early June 1927

'Gawd help us! Thought you was dead. Everybody thinks yer dead, y'know.'

'Well ... I ain't...' Teeth tightened against his lips, the sallow-faced fellow gestured that further explanation wasn't going to be forthcoming and yanked his arm free of the woman's restraint. He'd been on the point of buying a baked potato from a trader when she'd accosted him. Now he grabbed his thrupenny bit back from the merchant and dropped the hot tater on to the tray. Eyes darting to and fro, he retreated from the stall then turned to barge a path through the crowd thronging Dartford marketplace.

''Course you'd know yer wife got sick 'n' died, God rest her soul. Spanish flu, it was.' The woman doggedly pursued him, dodging past limbs in an attempt to catch up. 'But then the two of yers had been livin' apart for some while, hadn't you?' she shouted in his wake, puffing along with her shopping bag of vegetables banging against a stout leg. She angled her head to read his reaction. Her expression betrayed a mixture of fascination and horror as it clung to his back. In common with a lot of people, she'd been secretly pleased to assume that this nasty individual's disappearance had been due to him pushing up daisies.

'Nice to see you, Lou.' The remark was delivered over a shoulder in a scathing tone. 'But I've gotta be off.' He continued barging his way through the crowd, uncaring of the pained grunts of those he elbowed aside.

'Yer youngest lad's getting wed soon. Yer oldest boy's done all right fer himself.' Lou Perkins had given up the chase and stood wheezing and wondering how on earth she'd recognised him. It was close to ten years since she'd seen him, but he looked twenty years older and, from the crater in one of his cheeks, appeared to have been in the wars. But for having noticed the snake tattoo on one of his naked forearms, and thinking it looked familiar, she might not have bothered to peer again at his grizzled face. 'Got houses, 'n' a car too, he has...' Her voice tailed off as he vanished into the throng. She shook her head in mute amazement. She'd only made the trip to Dartford to give her sister a hand. The poor cow had knocked out five nippers in seven years and was due to drop the sixth at any moment. Lou was a dab hand at helping babies into the world. In fact, she recalled trying to help that fellow's wife give birth to her third child. It had been a tragedy when the little girl had finally been delivered stillborn after a long labour. She continued staring although he was lost to view. Had she been able to pursue him she'd have seen the fellow dodge down an alley and come to a stop, a decidedly foxy smile crinkling features that moments before had been resentfully set. Knowing him the way she did, she'd have realised that it was learning about Robert's flash lifestyle, rather than

Stephen's forthcoming wedding that had brought about the transformation.

Lou started to trudge back through the market place. She'd come out for a breather and to do a bit of shopping for the kids' teas. Now she wished she was heading back to Islington straight away instead of in a fortnight's time. She reckoned when she did return the tale she'd got to tell would keep her in drinks in the Pooles Park Tavern for a couple of months at least. Jimmy Wild might look like death warmed up, but he was definitely very much alive! What a turn-up!

Ten days later

'Coming back inside?'

'Just finish this and I will.' Robert Wild drew deeply on his cigarette. He turned to face his brother, head tilted back as a smoke ring escaped his lips to drift towards the sky. 'Happy?'

'Yeah, course ... me wedding night, ain't it?' Stevie grinned. 'Ain't a man alive who wouldn't be happy, knowing he's got that to look forward to.'

'Yeah...' Robert's smile was rather wry; they both knew the wedding night had come early. Robert hoped the kid wouldn't too. That'd give every gossiping old biddy a field day in around six months' time. He loosened his collar to let air to his damp throat. It was mid-June and despite the lateness of the hour the sultry heat felt as unbearable as it had at noon. The twilight had not properly descended and above their heads stars sparkled faintly in a sky still blue.

Robert extended the packet of Players that had been idly cradled in a fist. His brother withdrew one, stuck it between his lips and struck a match.

'Got to thank you for all this...' Stevie started gruffly, staring at the glowing ash between his fingers. 'Me 'n' Pam know we owe you a lot.' He shuffled and stuck his free hand in the pocket of his tailored jacket, ruining the lines of his smart bridegroom's outfit. 'She's sent me out to look for you and bring you back inside. She wants me to do a speech in there saying thanks and so on in front of everyone.' A backwards flick of his head indicated the Duke of Edinburgh pub, where his wedding reception had been underway for some time in a private room with trestle tables groaning under platters of delicious food and a free bar until ten o'clock.

There was more grub on display this evening than Stevie reckoned he'd put away over his twenty years. But then being hungry had been part and parcel of his and Robert's childhood, so at first he'd reasoned that he might not be qualified to judge whether it was a proper feast. He'd listened to his wife's parents – who claimed to be of good stock although they were so tight-fisted you'd think they didn't have a pot to piss in – gawping awestruck at the spread as though plucking up the courage to dive in. Stephen had smiled to himself and in a deliberately loud voice encouraged them to fill their boots.

Robert had paid for everything, right down to the bride and bridesmaid's dresses and the flowers. His in-laws might think they were a class above, but they'd never found the manners to offer a contribution to the cost of marrying off their daughter. Considering her condition, if they'd put off until her old man prised open his wallet they'd have been celebrating a christening before the wedding. Not, of course, that the old miser knew that his little princess was up the spout.

'Come back inside or she'll be nagging me for the rest of the night...'

'No need for any of that,' Robert cut him off. He ground the stub of his cigarette underfoot. 'You already thanked me enough, and I told you – you don't owe me. It's your wedding present.' He smiled. 'Saved me a job traipsing round in Gamages looking for a vase.' He strolled towards the pub entrance and raised his voice to be heard over the cacophony from within. 'Still time for a few bevvies before chucking-out time.'

The brightly lit pub seemed to rock on its foundations with the wedding guests' roistering. They'd been at it for several hours and would probably continue for several more before the landlord called time. A piano was being bashed fit to shatter the keys and a female voice was warbling at full volume. Beyond the frosted glass, the heads of dancing couples waltzed by.

'Ever think of Dad?'

Robert stopped dead and turned. Even though he'd been gone from their lives almost ten years now, the mention of Jimmy Wild had the power to tilt his guts. He came back towards Stevie so they could converse in a normal tone rather than holler at one another across the pavement.

'Never give the shit a thought,' he lied. 'You?'

'Dreamed of him last night,' Stevie said hoarsely. He smiled diffidently. 'Can't put it out of me mind. We was all back in The Bunk. You, me, Mum, all of us. Number twenty-seven, it was. It was morning and we was getting ready for school and he'd given Mum a good hiding over something; then he started on me 'cos he checked the sheets and knew I'd wet the bed.' He gave a self-conscious chuckle. 'Then Aunt Til come barging in, Uncle Jack 'n' all. Old Til started squaring up to Dad and he slunk off out, like he always did ... like butter wouldn't melt...'

For a moment there was a protracted quiet as both men recalled how often that scene had been played out in their early years. Robert slung an arm about Stevie's shoulders. 'That ain't a dream, mate, that's a nightmare. And it'll be down to the amount of booze you knocked back on your stag night.' With an attempt at drollery he added, 'But you're sober now. Sweet dreams from now on.'

'Yeah...' Stevie said, but he sounded unconvinced.

'Look, I know your wedding day's a time for reflecting. But there's better things to think about than getting a hidin' off that bastard 'cos you wet the bed when you was little.' Robert patted his brother's shoulder. 'If you've got to reminisce, think about how happy Mum'd be to see you togged out in all yer duds and how she'd love to know her first grandchild's on the way too.'

Stevie blinked in alarm. 'Not so loud! It's supposed to be a secret,' he muttered, glancing about for eavesdroppers. 'Pam's still not told her folks. Bleedin' good job she's not yet got a belly on her.'

'Now you done the right thing by her, they ain't going to care either way.' Robert took his brother's lapels between his fingers and straightened them. He re-pinned his carnation with deliberate slowness to allow his brother to blink the glistening tears from his eyes. 'Come on, you daft git, forget about the past. You got a future with Pam and a baby to think about now.' He gripped Stevie's shoulders in an encouraging way. 'Your wife ain't going to thank you for going soft on her tonight, you know,' he lewdly mocked.

Stevie sniffed a laugh, still blinking rapidly. 'I know you shouldn't say it about your own, but... God, am I glad he's six foot under.'

'Everyone's glad he's gone,' Robert said brusquely. 'Now that's enough about him; this is a day to enjoy and I ain't talking about any of it no more.'

'If you two don't come back in, I'll bring the party out here.' Silhouetted in the aperture of the pub doorway was a young woman dressed in a white silk sheath that stopped short of her knees and displayed her shapely legs. She sashayed forward a few steps then hopped and removed first one then the other of her shoes and carried them with her. 'Gawd, me dogs aren't half barking. Old uncle Ned must've trod on me feet a dozen times when we was doing the Charleston.' She slipped her arm through her husband's. 'What you two doing out here?' She gave her brother-in-law a meaningful look, whilst massaging sore toes. 'What've you been up to, Rob? Vicky's been looking for you. I reckon she thinks you've gone off her.' She paused, hoping for an answer but all she got was an indifferent shrug. 'We saw the way Gloria was making a play for you earlier.' Stevie's new wife slanted her sly eyes up at her brother-in-law. 'In case you don't know the rules, Robert Wild, the best man's supposed to get off with the bridesmaid, not the tart behind the bar.'

'I've been enjoying a smoke,' Robert explained smoothly and ignored the rest.

A subtle glance passed between the brothers.

An hour earlier Stevie had stepped into the Duke's corridor just in time to see his brother gliding downstairs shrugging on his jacket. Gloria had reappeared a moment or two later and taken up position behind the bar looking flushed and secretly pleased. Robert had made sure he'd timed it right: the drinking, by that time was well under way and the pair of them wouldn't have been absent long enough to arouse any suspicions. Stevie knew if he hadn't happened to nip out for a smoke and a breath of air, he'd have been none the wiser either. Robert didn't boast about his conquests, or anything else he had.

Gloria was a looker with a magnificent bust that magnetised a man's eyes from the moment he was over the Duke's threshold. Stevie wouldn't blame any bloke for taking off her what was offered on a plate, even if the chance had come up during his wedding reception and the girl with an ambition to become Robert's sweetheart was Pam's bridesmaid. Stevie knew his wife's friend was kidding herself. So did Robert, although he seemed in no hurry to shatter Vicky's illusions about hooking him. His brother wouldn't restrict himself to just one woman. Pam could matchmake all she liked, but Robert would take or leave Vicky Watson, just as he had all the others who'd believed they could rein him in and get his ring on their finger.

At that moment Vicky flounced out on to the pavement. 'So, where've you been?' she demanded of Robert, fanning her sulky face with a hand.

'I've been right here. Why d'you want to know?'

A sheepish smile was Vicky's apology and she fixed her eyes on the cigarette packet rotating idly in his hands. 'I wouldn't mind a fag.'

Robert offered her the cigarettes and once she'd taken one and he'd lit it, he started towards the pub. Vicky quickly slipped her arm through his and the newly married couple followed, locked in an embrace that made them stumble and giggle. Stevie swung his new bride into his arms and carried her wriggling over the threshold.

'That's you two sorted out for later. That's my boys.' The growling voice erupted in a lascivious chuckle.

Robert glanced over his shoulder to see a couple, half shadowed by a high wall, watching them.

'Piss off, mate. Private party.' Robert had already ejected several gatecrashers from the reception. The chance of a free feed and unlimited booze was too hard to resist for most people who lived around Campbell Road and struggled to put a plate of chips on the table. Once news of the wedding had got around, half of The Bunk's inhabitants had been angling for invitations to the reception.

'That's no way to speak to yer old dad, Bobbie.'

It was a moment before Robert pivoted about. Only a few people called him Bobbie now. Family, mostly.

'Remember me?'

Now the ribaldry was gone, Robert realised the voice was the same even if the man in front of him looked to be a pale imitation of his former self.

The father he remembered had been a muscled fellow with a dark head of hair and a lean face. The man sauntering towards them looked to have shrivelled in height and ballooned in weight. He appeared, too, to be fair-headed but was, Robert realised, almost completely grey. But his eyes, dark and sharp, were the same, pinning him down, still no escape.

For a moment Robert felt rooted to the spot, trapped in his brother's nightmare of last night. He licked his parched lips and shot a look at his brother. Stevie was gawping at him, slack-jawed, waiting for reassurance that it was just a phantom and everything was going to be all right.

'Go back inside.' It was a hoarse murmur as Robert disentangled his arm from Vicky's clutch and gave the middle of her back a little push to hurry her on her way.

She tottered forward with a mew of indignation.

'Go inside, Pam,' Robert ordered his sister-in-law, his voice strengthening.

She looked mutinous, but Stevie dropped her quickly to her feet, where she landed in an ungainly hobble. He nodded vigorously at her to do as she'd been told. His obvious agitation prompted her to obey, albeit with a sullen expression.

'What the fuck d'you want?' Robert spat through his teeth as soon as the two young women had disappeared into the pub.

'We thought you died in the war. We thought you was dead.' Stevie's words emerged in a strange, high-pitched whine.

'Ain't dead, son.'

It had been said in that gentle way Jimmy had that had always set Rob's teeth on edge. His crooning voice had been as deceitful as everything else about him. Robert took a step forward to put himself between his father and his brother.

'Just some real bad things was goin' on at the time and I had to get away,' Jimmy continued in his dreary drawl. 'Best thing for everyone, you see, for me to disappear fer a while.'

'Best thing now 'n' all,' Robert ejected through his teeth. 'So get goin' 'n' don't ever come back. There's nothing here for you. D'you understand? Nothing.'

'That ain't nice, Bobbie.' Jimmy sounded plaintive. 'I come to wish me son all the best for his future happiness, ain't I?'

'How d'you know I was getting wed?' Stevie had recovered a little from his shock. Although he was visibly shaking, he had a few questions ready. He grabbed the cigarettes from Rob and fumbled to get one lit then dragged deeply on it. 'You been spyin' on me? How d'you know anything about me now?'

'Just 'cos I ain't been around, don't mean I

ain't been keepin' a watchful eye on yers. You're me flesh 'n' blood.'

Robert threw back his head and roared out a vicious laugh. He took a menacing pace forward, stopping Jimmy from coming any closer to his brother. Their father had been edging forward one step at a time and Robert knew it was his intention to win them over with his wonky smile and weasel words. When they were kids it might have worked; just as a whipping with a belt had worked. But it was different now.

'This ain't the time fer none of yer lies,' Robert enunciated through stretched lips. 'If you care about Steve's future happiness you'll fuck off now and stay away from all of us.' He jabbed a finger close to Jimmy's chin. Now he was within striking distance he could see what the dusk had disguised. One side of his father's face now had a slightly concave shape as though, at some time during the last decade, his cheekbone had been smashed. 'So get going or there's gonna be blood 'n' guts all over the place.' Robert leaned forward. 'We ain't scared of you now. You're nothing to us and we ain't interested in any of yer threats or promises...'

'Bobbie ... hang on ... let's hear where he's been...' Stephen had reverted to using his childhood name, something he hadn't done in many years. Robert knew that hearing Jimmy use it had prompted him to do so and it enraged him. He swung about and glared at his brother.

'You're not wanted here.' Robert sent that over a shoulder at his father as he gripped Stephen's arm and shoved him towards the pub.

'We goin' in fer a drink, Jim? Could do with a drink, Jim.' The woman who'd been lurking quietly by the kerb took a pace forward. Her short, skinny body had easily been overlooked in the shadowy gloom. But now she nervously approached. Edie Greaves had need of a drink and Jimmy had promised her he knew of a place where they could go this evening and get treated handsomely for free. In fact, he'd been promising her many good things would come their way once they got to Islington. In Edie's eyes, the only benefit so far had been in managing to abscond and leave a pile of debts behind in Kent.

Robert turned back just in time to note the change in his father's attitude. He recognised the look gripping Jimmy's sagging face and it turned his guts. Jimmy sorely wanted to tell the woman to shut up or, as he'd frequently done with their mother, stop her complaints with his fist. But he couldn't because he was putting on an act for them all. The prodigal father had come to give his blessing to his son's marriage. Like fuck! Robert knew that if this miserable, cowardly excuse for a man had come to find them it was because he wanted something very badly. The crafty bastard had probably already made it his business to find out that Stephen had nothing to offer, so Robert knew it was him he was after. Somehow, Jimmy Wild had discovered he'd done all right for himself and had come back to Islington to see what was in it for him.

'What's goin' on?' Matilda Keiver came bursting out of the pub trailing people in her wake. 'Pam said there's a feller being a nuisance. Want him shifted, Rob?' The crowd behind her chortled and encouraged her playful belligerence. Everyone knew Tilly Keiver wasn't frightened of a fight. If a bloke needed a slap, she was the one to give it to him. And he'd come off worst. Her nephews knew her reputation too, and would usually have laughed along with the others.

But they didn't; and after a moment it penetrated Matilda's booze-fuddled brain that something wasn't right. She marched forward, whiskey glass in hand, squinting into the dusk to see who was causing a ruckus at her nephew's big day. After their mum had died, and when they were just starting out fending for themselves as young teenagers, Tilly had done what she could to help Rob and Steve even though money was tight for her too as a war widow. She still treated Fran's boys as an extension of her own family. Today she'd had the status of the groom's mother, and the bride's family were duly conscious of her role.

Tilly stopped and frowned at the man lounging against a wall a few feet away.

'Hello, Tilly. Remember me?'

At the sound of his voice, she froze, open-mouthed, her whiskey hovering by her lips. A moment later the glass slipped from her nerveless fingers and shattered on the ground, spattering her shins and the hem of her best dress.

'Jimmy?' she gasped, and tottered a step closer, her head leading the way as though she were trying to identify a deadly reptile without getting close enough for it to strike.

'Long time no see,' he murmured, grinning at her. 'Bet you missed me, ain't yer?'

At this she bounded forward, letting fly with her fists. 'You fuckin' bastard! You should be dead!' She sobbed in anguish.

Jimmy ducked easily out of the way of her assault. 'No need fer that, Til. I'd've got you another drink, gel, honest!' He hadn't lost the knack of winding her up in a way that only she could hear and understand. 'Still need the booze then, do yer?' he laughed, fending her off as her clawed fingers flew at his face.

And that was all the private chat they managed after not seeing one another for almost ten years. The next moment Edie Greaves had hold of Tilly's thick, fiery hair and was yanking back her head to slap her face. Robert landed a heavy hand on his father's chest and shoved him so hard he was freed from Tilly's grip and went tottering backwards until he collapsed on his backside on the pavement.

More people had come out of the pub to see what was going on. Alice Chaplin rushed to her mother's side and a moment later her sister Bethany joined her in trying to prise the two women apart. As Edie stumbled away, breathing hard, Tilly drew back her lips in a snarl and landed a final punch on the side of her opponent's head.

'Come back tomorrer and have some more,' Tilly spat at her, knuckling blood from her lips.

'For Gawd's sake! What's going on?' Alice demanded, gazing horrified at her mother's cut mouth.

Trying not to meet her eyes, Tilly put an arm round Alice's shoulders. 'Let's get back inside,' she muttered hoarsely, shrugging off concerned guests who'd come to her aid. Catching sight of Pam's mother, who was gawping at her with disgust, Tilly tilted up her chin and gave her such a fierce look the woman scuttled back through the Duke's doors.

'Little Alice ... you've grown, ain't yer?'

Alice looked about to see where the voice had come from. There was something horribly familiar about it, and instinctively her stomach had lurched. But her mother had hold of her arm and was forcefully steering her towards the pub. Breaking free of her mother's grip, she turned with an unaccountable feeling of dread. It was then that she saw him. He was still sitting on the pavement, but comfortably now, as though he liked it there, with his arms clasped about his knees. 'Did you marry the lanky git who lived next door?' Jimmy asked. 'Geoff Lovat, weren't it? He were right sweet on you, as I recall...'

Alice glanced over at her husband, her eyes wild with terror, her heart drumming so fast she feared it might burst from her chest. Josh Chaplin had their daughter in his arms. Lilian was still sleeping, undisturbed by the pandemonium. He quickly handed over his precious burden to a woman close by in readiness to rush to his wife's aid, but by the time he reached her she'd crumpled unconscious to the floor.

TWO

'I did feel a right fool, fainting like that.'

'All things considered, it's lucky you didn't have a bleedin' heart attack,' Tilly returned forcefully. 'Or me, fer that matter,' she continued in a mutter. Slanting a look at her daughter, she poured her a cup of tea then pulled out a chair opposite her at the table. A silence settled on the two women as they brooded on their own thoughts, elbows on the splintered tabletop, cups cradled in their palms.

A few days had passed since Stevie's wedding reception had been ruined by Jimmy Wild's reappearance in the land of the living. The party had broken up after the commotion, despite the newly wed couple's halfhearted attempt to persuade people to jolly up and stay a while longer. The bride's parents had been the first to leave. Mr and Mrs Plummer had scrambled to collect their coats and fled, relatives in tow. Tilly had felt like telling them that their daughter had a bun in the oven, just to wipe the contempt from their faces. But by then everyone had had enough. The festive atmosphere had vanished. The immediate family had been too preoccupied with the turbulent emotions and memories stirred up by Jimmy's resurfacing; the guests couldn't wait to get out and spread the gossip. Even for this neighbourhood, where calamity and drama were regular visitors, this was sensational news.

Tilly and Alice had not seen each other since that evening. Once Alice had revived from her faint, Robert had insisted on taking Alice, Josh and little Lilian home in his car. Today it was business as usual for those in employment, but Alice had taken a day off from her job as a charwoman. Abandoning her usual routine of taking Lilian with her to clients' houses, she had set out early and dropped her daughter off with her mother-in-law to be looked after for an hour or two whilst she visited Tilly. Normally she would have walked, but today she had caught the bus from Wood Green to Islington. There was an urgency about this visit that justified the fare being spent.

'He was dead!' Alice whispered, shaking her head in disbelief. 'He *was* dead, wasn't he, Mum?' she pleaded. 'All that blood...' Her voice tailed off.

'Seems he wasn't. He must've just been knocked unconscious after yer aunt Fran whacked him with that iron pot...' Tilly shuddered. 'Did you notice that dent in his cheek?' She clamped her lips together. 'No point in going over it now. I put it out me mind years ago and it's staying out.'

'Should we tell Rob and Steve what actually went on?' Alice asked with an apprehensive glance at her mother. 'I know we've never lied, rather just avoided the subject, but...'

'No!' Tilly harshly interrupted. 'Let sleeping dogs lie where they're concerned. No point in upsetting them more'n they are already. If they're interested in knowing where he's been, or why he disappeared, they'll have to ask Jimmy for answers.'

'Will he tell them the truth, d'you reckon?'

'If he does, it'll be the first time in his miserable life,' Tilly grimly replied. She pursed her lips. 'He won't want his sons, or anybody else for that matter, knowing he went on a rampage that night and we managed to turn the tables on him.' Matilda slid a look up at Alice. 'What did Josh have to say about it all?'

Alice shook her head in despair. 'He doesn't know what to think or to say, same as me.' Her dark eyes seemed huge in her pale face as she gazed at Tilly. She knew that the same dark thoughts and secrets were circling in both their minds, but that didn't make it any easier to speak about it. 'I can't stop thinking about Geoff. He was too young to fight, but he went to war anyway because of Jimmy's wickedness. He died thinking he'd killed him.' Tears of frustration glistened in Alice's eyes as she remembered the strong, handsome youth she'd considered to be her best friend a decade ago.

Geoff had saved her from being molested by her uncle and, during a vicious fight, and in self-defence, had stabbed Jimmy with his own knife. On that dreadful night she'd been out with Geoff and had returned home to discover her monster of an uncle battering and attempting to rape her mother. She'd never forget the sickening sight of her mum's bloodied face, or Jimmy's penis poking out of his dirty underclothes as he loomed over Tilly sprawled, semi-conscious, on the floor. Alice knew that harrowing scene would remain in her memory until she died. When she tried to flee to get help, Jimmy had turned his attention on her, forcing her down on to the bed. With her mother too badly injured to protect her, it had been sheer good luck that Geoff was still close by and had heard her scream. He'd raced to her aid, and in doing so had forfeited his life.

There wasn't a day went by that she didn't devote private minutes to Geoff's memory. Why would she not, when he'd sacrificed everything for her?

When she'd been growing up in Campbell Road the Lovat family had lived next door. Her big sister Sophy had married Danny Lovat, the eldest child of Bert and Margaret Lovat. The Lovats were still Tilly's neighbours although they'd moved to the better end of Campbell Road where they'd got more room for their brood, most of whom still lived at home. The Lovats had been guests at Stevie's wedding and had been as flabbergasted as everyone else to discover that Jimmy Wild was not dead.

But Bert and Margaret were not among the handful of people who knew why Jimmy had suddenly vanished from The Bunk. They would not have understood why his turning up alive was so devastating for Matilda and Alice. And they certainly had no idea that their son's abrupt decision to go to war had been prompted by his role in Jimmy's disappearance. At eighteen, Geoff had perished fighting in Flanders, as had Alice's father.

'Damn shame the swine ain't dead.' Tilly's

mouth pressed into a hard line. 'Still, it don't matter. Alive, dead – he's nothing to us now. He can crawl back under his stone and stay there. I'm just glad yer Aunt Fran ain't here to see the day.'

Tilly fingered her healing lip. She didn't bear a grudge against Jimmy's other half for clumping her. If the woman hadn't been with him for long she might not know better than to stick up for the evil git. It had taken her sister Fran fifteen years to finally turn her back on him. This new woman had shown her loyalty in public, but what went on behind their closed doors was anybody's guess. Tilly could guess. She knew Jimmy Wild would never change.

'That poor cow he's got in tow don't know what she's let herself in for. There's plenty of people round here could tell her her fortune if she sticks with him.' She grunted a sour laugh. 'Nellie'll give her a piece of advice,' she said, mentioning one of Jimmy's fancy women. Nellie Tucker had been a looker in her time and choosy in her punters, but now she'd grown blowsy and turned tuppenny tricks for drunks coming out of pubs. Tilly reckoned that every woman who came into contact with Jimmy Wild would be degraded by the experience. She'd fought hard to prevent it happening to her.

A knock on the door brought Tilly's reflections to an end and her on to her feet. 'Not expecting anyone.' She frowned at Alice, pushing her chair back from the table.

A neighbour, who'd had rooms in a house across the street for almost as long as Alice could remember, barged in before Tilly had the door properly open. Obviously Beattie Evans was bursting with news she wanted to get off her chest.

'Ain't sure how to tell you this, Til,' the woman wheezed out. It was always Beattie's way to draw out a drama if she could.

'Straight out'll do,' Tilly responded flatly, planting her hands on her hips.

'First off, I just seen Lou Perkins. She's back from Kent and ain't pleased to know Jimmy's arrived here before her. She reckoned she'd be the one breaking the news about him not being dead, 'cos she ran in to him in Dartford market.'

'That it?' Tilly barked.

Beattie shook her head. 'Jimmy and his woman are moving in up the road.'

Beattie had been expecting a fiery response to her news, but even so she jumped back in surprise at the force of it.

'What?' Tilly roared. 'Where? What number?' She was already rolling up her sleeves. 'If he thinks he can rub our noses in this, he can bleedin' think again.'

'Mum! Don't!' Alice shot up from the table to position herself between her mother and the door, blocking her way.

'He ain't moving back to Campbell Road!' Tilly thundered, swinging around to slam a fist on the table and send the cups crashing over. 'Ain't havin' the bastard livin' near me after what's gone on. I'll swing fer him, so help me Gawd. If he weren't dead before, he soon will be.'

Robert Wild was of the same opinion as his aunt about Jimmy returning to his old stamping ground. Not that Robert lived in Campbell Road any more. For fifteen months he'd been renting a smart townhouse in Tufnell Park and kept his new Sunbeam Tourer parked on a side driveway that used to lead to stables. His ambition was to buy the freehold of the property. But for now he was content to use his profits to expand the businesses he already had, and to invest in more. Robert had a wily head on his shoulders and knew acting flash with his cash could jeopardise his plans for his future security. He was twenty-three and intended to retire a millionaire when he was thirty-five. His only real luxuries were his house, his car, and a few decent suits. He had justified those purchases with the logic that an appearance of modest affluence was necessary when negotiating with people who had more money and experience than he did. Young he may be, but he was careful never to present himself as a chancer, or a threat. He knew he was a match for any of them. He also knew it was too soon to let them become aware of the fact.

He had bought property, but none that he'd consider residing in himself. He was the landlord of a shop in Queensland Road and three tenements in Campbell Road. He also had a nicer house in Playford Road, where his brother and sister-in-law now lived rent-free on the ground floor. He'd picked them up as a job lot for refurbishment three years back. Solly, who'd owned the secondhand shop in Queensland Road, had wanted to quickly offload all his premises and retire to the coast before the cancer eating away at his insides finished its work.

Robert had been twenty at the time. He'd used every penny he'd scrimped and saved from working his market stalls for six years to do the deal behind the back of old Mr Keane, who liked to think he was the wheeler-dealer landlord in Campbell Bunk. The sulky old git hadn't spoken to him since even though Robert had been at pains not to rub his nose in it because you never knew who you might need on side.

The deal had been struck with Solly because the old Jew liked him, and remembered a promise he'd made years before. When Rob had been at school he'd often run errands for Solly, and he'd done a bit of lifting and carrying the old boy couldn't manage to do himself. Solly had never paid him; at the time he was a regular tightfist, but he'd always told Rob he'd see him all right one day. And he'd been true to his word. Rob knew Solly could have got a better price for his properties from old man Keane, but he'd let him have them for what he could afford to pay. It had been the turning point in his career; from that point on he'd been resented and courted in equal measure. In the estimation of most of the folk in these parts, Rob Wild had hit the big time when he took on Solly's stock.

He had three men working for him, but Stevie was the only one of his employees he trusted to collect the rents from his tenants in Campbell Road. Today he had taken on the task himself as Stevie and a few of the boys were picking up a shipment of market stock.

He had just stopped to scrape the sole of his shoe on the kerb, having stepped in some slimy cabbage stalks in the hallway of one of his properties, when he looked up and saw Jimmy carrying sacks of possessions into a house a few doors down from the intersection with Paddington Street.

Robert's lips whitened over his teeth as he spat out a curse. He sprinted across the road and, grabbing his father by the shoulder, viciously spun him against the iron railings. 'No yer don't.' He thrust his face up close to Jimmy's concave, unshaven cheek. 'Wherever it was you've been hiding yerself all these years, you can piss off back there. I told you, you're not wanted round here.'

With a strength that belied his grizzled appearance, Jimmy pulled out of his son's grip. 'You don't own this house, Bobbie,' Jimmy sneered. 'I made sure of that.' He didn't look or sound so complaisant today. 'Old man Keane's still got this one, so you can't put me out. I'll live where I want. And I want right here.' He smiled slyly. 'Be nice 'n' close to yer aunt Til again. She'll like that.' A private joke caused him to smirk. He turned his head towards the junction with Seven Sisters Road where the Keivers had rooms. 'Be nice 'n' close to Stevie 'n' all. Lives just around the corner in Playford Road now, don't he?' He started to gather up his belongings and move again towards the door-less portal, beyond which was darkness and a stink of decay.

Robert took hold of his father's shirt collar and

hauled him backwards. He pushed him stumbling into the gutter and threw the bags he'd dropped after him. A few old clothes spewed on to the pavement as one of the bags gaped open.

'What's goin' on?' Edie's cry reached the two men as a faint wail. She had been proceeding down the road some way behind Jimmy. They'd turned the corner from Seven Sisters together but being relatively unencumbered, he had managed to pull away from her. With one hand Edie was pushing a pram filled to the brim with utensils; the other hand gripped the wrist of a small boy. The child was whimpering and dragging her back because his little legs couldn't keep up with her faster pace. Behind them, and obviously part of the family, trailed an older boy who looked to be about ten years old and a young woman. Both were carrying boxes. Although the girl was some years older than her brother the resemblance between them was striking. Both had fair complexions and thick blonde hair and eyes of a deep blue.

Seeing Jimmy on his knees, scrabbling with his clothes, Edie started to jog, pulling the toddler with her and making him cry. Despite her spindly limbs she put on a spurt that belied her frail appearance. The creases in her complexion deepened with her determination to find out what was going on. As the toddler stumbled to his knees she let go of his hand and rushed on, the pram bouncing in front of her, and one of her hands batting back pots trembling precariously close to the sides. The young woman immediately dropped her box and went to tend to the whimpering infant. The older boy shuffled close by, obviously preferring to wait for his big sister to accompany him into unknown territory.

If Robert had not been so het up at the sight of his father on Campbell Road he might sooner have spotted Edie and the children trailing in her wake. Having digested the scene he turned back. 'If you've knocked that lot out,' he snarled at his father, 'you must've started with that old bag before Mum was dead.' His eyes were redrawn to the young woman who was crouched by the sobbing child and dabbing at his grazed knee with a handkerchief. Robert guessed she was in her late teens. 'In fact, I'd say you must've been at it before we was hanging out the flags believing you was gone for good. Seems we were wrong about everything. We all thought Nellie Tucker was your tart.'

'Can't help being popular with the ladies, can I?' Jimmy grunted a chuckle, still stuffing clothes back into the bag. He seemed unflustered by his son's rough handling.

'No *lady* would have anything to do with you. No wonder we never had a decent meal inside us as kids. You'd have spent yer last fucking farthing keeping yer cock happy rather than us, wouldn't you?'

Jimmy sprung up, surprisingly agile all of a sudden, his eyes narrow slits in his puffy, sallow face. 'You want to learn a bit of respect. Who do you think you're talking to? I'm still yer father and can give you a wallop, y'know.'

'Don't I just wish you'd try,' Robert returned softly. ''Cos I'm itching for an excuse to lay you out ... just like you did to all of us.'

Jimmy slanted a look up the road. His scrawny wife was still haring towards him behind the bouncing pram.

'Edie's,' Jimmy said succinctly, ignoring the reference to the brutality he'd dealt out to his first family. 'All of 'em stepkids.' Noting the direction of his son's steady gaze, he pursed his mouth before a shrewd smile skewed a corner of it. 'Well, I never ... something about me yer like after all, eh, son?' he taunted. A glance slew to his step-daughter.

Faye was petite, like her mother, but there all similarity ended. Edie was shrunken and shape-less, and her once-fair hair had turned to an un-attractive salt-and-pepper hue. Faye's body was curvaceous and her shiny golden hair framed an extraordinarily pretty face. Jimmy liked to think he was a bit of a connoisseur when it came to women. He also liked to think that he appreciated the value of female allure. He'd been Nellie Tucker's pimp for some while, and they'd both profited from it. He reckoned touting the services of a cheap whore from a damp room justified his arrogance.

With his bags in his fists he pushed past Robert and entered the gloomy hallway of his new home, chuckling beneath his breath. His laughter in-creased when Robert made no move to stop him this time. But he wasn't feeling as smug as he'd sounded. Lou Perkins had recognised him in Dartford market and told him his eldest boy was flush with money. Jimmy had come to see for himself and work out a way he might benefit from an upturn in the Wild fortunes. He'd known his reappearance would cause a rumpus at first, but had counted on persuading his sons they should be pleased to have one of their parents still alive. Jimmy reckoned he'd manage to bring Stevie round to that way of thinking, but Stevie wasn't the one holding the purse strings. Bobbie had the cash, and he was extremely hostile.

Edie's face was scarlet as she skidded to a halt by Robert. Her lips, customarily puckered as though she was sucking on an invisible cigarette, suddenly sprang apart and words came tumbling out of them. 'So, it's you. Thought it were the other one, 'cos Jimmy told me he comes down here collecting the rents. Thought you were Stephen. Just leave us be. We need somewhere to live, same as other folk. You don't interfere with us, we don't interfere with you.' She turned and, having drawn in a lungful of air, yelled at the boy who was closest, 'Get in there and lend a hand to your dad.'

Casting a wary sideways look up at Robert, she manoeuvred the pram past the obstacle of his body, bumped it over the threshold of the house and started to unload it on to bare boards.

The toddler, obviously over his mishap, came tearing down the road at such a pace that it looked as though his momentum would send him hurtling past his destination or falling on to his face. At the last moment he saved himself by clinging to Robert's shins for support, offering up a shy smile before he scrambled on into the house. His older brother gave Robert a suspicious look before ducking his face behind his box and following on. Robert could hear their mother giving instructions to the boys on what to carry up the stairs. From those bawled commands Robert learned that one boy was named Michael and the other Adam. He wasn't interested enough to peer in to discover which face went with which name. But he was interested in the girl coming towards him. And she knew it, and was battling not to look uneasy because of it.

Having tilted up her chin and waited for Robert to move out of the way, the young woman turned sideways with her box to try to edge past him, muttering beneath her breath. He moved to block her path. Flicking her head aside in irritation, she stepped the other way to avoid him, her expression bored.

'Do you know who I am?'

''Course I know,' she said impatiently, setting her box down. 'You're one of his sons, me mum told me. She saw you just after we turned the corner and said there'd be trouble.' She glowered at him with large blue eyes. 'Are you going to get out of the way so I can go inside?'

'Yeah ... in a minute...'

'Me mum told me you wouldn't let them have a drink at your wedding reception and a ruckus started because of it. Tight-fisted git, are you, as well as having no manners?' With that she again picked up her box and glared at him to move.

'Well, if you'd've come along to the Duke that night, perhaps I might've thought twice about getting a round in,' Robert said. 'Or perhaps you're too young to have a drink?'

She blushed, but not because his subtle flattery pleased her, rather because he thought her a kid.

'Why don't you get off home to your wife so's I can get in there and give a hand before your father turns nasty.' She freed some fingers from beneath the box to give his arm a shove. Although her hand bounced off muscle, Robert relented and moved his fist from where it had enclosed a railing, effectively barring her entry.

'What's your name?'

'Faye! Get in here now and help, will you.' Edie's screech emerged from the bowels of the house.

The young woman gave him a sour look and took a step forward, trying to shake off his grip, which had transferred from the railing to her wrist.

'What's your name?' Robert asked again.

'You deaf as well as all the rest?' she cried out, yanking her arm free with such force that she dropped her box in the process. Cutlery and china scattered on the floor drawing a gasp of dismay from her. The ground was littered with blue-and-white shards that looked to have been a full tea service a moment ago, and not a bad one at that.

'All of your name... Faye...?' Robert insisted, idly scraping the debris to one side of the doorway with his foot.

'Greaves,' she shouted in exasperation. 'Faye Greaves! Look what you've done! Now what we gonna do? Can't even have a cup of tea – that'll set him off for sure.'

A note of real distress had entered her voice and Robert could guess why. His father now had an excuse to vent his anger on somebody. He wondered whether Edie Greaves would have the backbone to stand up to him and whack him back. Was she like his aunt or his mother? He'd seen Tilly knock Jimmy bandy for giving her sister a split lip. Rob reckoned Edie was more like his mother: she'd quake, but take the bruises so that her kids might escape the old man's fists. Then there'd be other times when, too ground down to resist, she'd pretend not to hear the sound of a leather belt cutting through the air, or the whimpers that went on all night.

He picked up the box and gave it to her. Then in a single scoop he collected the undamaged cutlery and chucked it in. He drew out a five-pound note and let it fall in as well. 'Should cover it,' he said. With that he walked off before Faye had a chance to recover sufficiently from his astonishing generosity to comment on it.

'Want a lift home?'

Alice had been walking with her head down, deep in thought, when she heard that tempting offer. 'No, it's all right, Rob,' she declined with a smile. 'It's kind of you, but I bet you're too busy to be running me about.'

'Nah ... I've got a bit of business Wood Green way in any case. Where's Lilian?'

'Josh's mum's looking after her.' Alice knew that his question about her daughter's whereabouts was just a way of avoiding talk of Jimmy. She wished she could cast the horrible spectre of her uncle out of their minds and out of this neighbourhood. 'I wish Jimmy hadn't turned up out of the blue like that,' Alice blurted. 'After all this time, it gave us such a turn.'

She watched for her cousin's reaction. Jimmy's disappearance had always been a taboo subject. Bobbie and Stevie must have realised a vicious argument had taken place between their parents just before Jimmy vanished. Their mother had been in a terrible state the morning after the fight, as had their Aunt Tilly. But the boys had grown used to seeing Fran Wild laid up after a beating from her husband. And if they'd suspected Tilly had come by her injuries in an unsuccessful attempt to protect her sister, they'd kept it to themselves. By that time, their parents had been separated for some years, following Jimmy walking out to shack up with Nellie Tucker. But it had been his habit to come back on odd visits ... usually when he was on the scrounge.

With a little shudder, Alice recalled the surprise visit from the police that had unnerved them just as they were struggling to get back to normal after that dreadful night. A body had been found floating in the Thames that'd had a similar tattoo to the one Jimmy sported on his left arm. As Jimmy Wild hadn't been seen in a while the police had put two and two together. Luckily, on the day of that shocking news, her cousins had been out so had not overheard talk of a headless corpse.

A couple of months later, when Robert realised his father's absence had been lengthier than usual, Alice had been present when he questioned his mother over it. Her aunt's mumbled response that Jimmy had probably gone to France to do his duty, and not before time, had seemed to satisfy the boys. For the first time in their young lives they'd probably believed they had a reason to feel proud of him.

But neither of her cousins had spoken much about him and not once had Alice heard them bemoan the loss of their father. However they'd been distraught to lose their mum eight years ago during the flu epidemic that had decimated the population. An abrupt question from Robert put an end to her melancholy reflection.

'Did you know Jimmy's moved in up the road?' He took Alice's elbow and steered her towards his car, which was parked close to the junction with Seven Sisters Road.

Alice nodded and let out a dejected sigh. 'Old Beattie came in and gave us the news. Mum's gone mad. I told her to ignore him. I bet she doesn't. I bet she'll be up the road after him as soon as she's had a few...' She tailed off. As soon as her mother hit the whiskey she'd get reckless and belligerent. Rob knew as well as she did what Tilly was like. Their two families had lived cheek by jowl for too long not to know each other's habits. 'Glad I'm not living round here now,' Alice said vehemently. 'Bet you are, too...'

'Yeah... But not because of him. He's not going to affect my life ever again. I won't let him.' Rob opened the car door and helped Alice in, then tossed a coin to the young lad who'd been charged with keeping an eye on the vehicle while he went about his business. Despite Rob's reputation as a hound you didn't mess with, some of the local lads were sufficiently desperate to risk the consequences and try to steal the hubcaps or anything else they could prise free and sell.

'Ta, mister.' The boy beamed at the thrupence on his palm and hared off.

Robert put the car in gear and headed up the road. As they passed the house where Jimmy and his family had just moved in, he didn't even turn his head. But a muscle contracted spasmodically in his cheek.

Alice glanced at her grim-faced cousin and wondered how to lighten the atmosphere. Getting a ride in a car was a treat for her, especially when she'd been expecting a long walk home. The last thing she wanted was to spoil a pleasant drive with more depressing talk about rotten Jimmy Wild. 'So ... what's this I hear about you getting engaged to Vicky Watson?' she teased him. Alice had already guessed it was more gossip than truth. Vicky had probably started the rumour in hope rather than expectation of it becoming fact.

Robert smiled. 'First I've heard about it!'

Faye Greaves was standing close to the window when the open-top car and its laughing occupants sailed into view. She felt an illogical little pang tighten her insides as she watched the pretty dark-haired young woman enjoying her husband's company. He obviously had a better side to him. She'd been on the point of moving away to avoid observing their contentment when her mother looked over her shoulder and also saw Robert and Alice drive past.

'So, he's off is he,' Edie muttered, keeping her voice low so Jimmy didn't hear. 'I'll have him next time he's about. He owes us for a tea-set, and I'll have the money off him for it, you wait and see. Tight-fisted git,' she spat.

Faye chewed her lip, feeling guilty. She'd called him a tight-fisted git, too, and to his face, but she'd discovered that Stephen Wild was anything but mean with money. He'd handed over far more than was necessary to replace the broken china. But she wasn't about to let on that she'd been compensated. If they'd had any inkling of it, her mother and Jimmy – especially Jimmy – would have had the cash off her.

She had said nothing to Jimmy about the loss of the crockery, and she knew her mother would keep quiet about it. Angry as she was about the damage, Edie didn't want any more trouble with Jimmy's sons; she was relieved just to have a roof over their heads after they'd absconded from Kent.

Their old place, a poky, spartanly furnished terraced house in Dartford, now seemed a palace compared to the two squalid rooms that had replaced it. Faye would have returned there in a flash if she could. Not that there was any possibility of that.

She thought back to the times their landlord, Mr Mackinley, had come battering on the door on rent-collection day. Rather than open the door to him, her mother would holler out of a bedroom window that Jimmy had sworn he'd paid everything up to date. Mr Mackinley would bawl back up at her in his guttural Scottish accent, telling her that she was a stupid woman who should know by now that she was saddled with a donkey. Through it all, Faye would sit on the bed, listening dejectedly to their raucous shouting and muttering her agreement with the landlord's opinion.

Faye had known for some time that, with Mackinley threatening to send in the bailiffs, a flit was imminent, but it had never occurred to her that they'd be dragged as far away as North London. Then one evening Jimmy had come home from the market empty-handed but with a sly smile that'd prompted Edie to demand why he was looking so pleased with himself when there was no food for their supper. Faye now knew that had been one of the rare occasions he'd given her mother a truthful answer. He'd run into someone from the old days, and they'd given him some right good news about how well one of his sons was doing.

Faye's eyes slipped sideways. Jimmy probably wasn't feeling quite so chipper now the reunion had taken place and his sons had made it clear they wanted nothing to do with him. She turned to focus properly on Jimmy, who was frowning at the newspaper pinned beneath his elbows, tapping his teeth with a pencil. He'd been sitting like that for some time, leaving Faye and her mother to bring some sort of order to their seedy home. Faye turned away from the front-room window and swept the room with her gaze, taking in the stained and sagging flock mattress that covered the bed, which had been pushed against the wall to make room for the rest of the furniture, all of it shabby and clearly on its last legs. In the back room, where she would sleep with Michael and Adam, there was a tiny iron bed for her and a large flock mattress on the floor for the boys. All the bedding was in a similar sorry state with springs and wadding exposed in places.

Faye's eyes returned to Jimmy, who was squinting fixedly at the racing pages, sucking on his pencil. Luckily it seemed he hadn't been eavesdropping on her conversation with Edie. A five-pound note was rare treasure and she wasn't going to let anyone deprive her of it. She could get a decent secondhand tea service for a few shillings, perhaps some dinner plates as well to sweeten her mother and make her forget about bringing up the subject with Jimmy's son when next their paths crossed. Faye would tell Edie she'd treat her to the new set from her wages. Fortunately she'd already found a job.

Earlier that day, as they'd made their way along Blackstock Road towards The Bunk, she'd seen an advert for an assistant being placed in the window of a baker's shop. The fellow had noticed her looking at it and had smiled and jerked his head, inviting her in. She'd smiled right back, knowing even before she pushed open the door that the job was hers if she wanted it. She'd told Michael to wait outside with their boxes and a few minutes later she'd emerged with a position that paid fourteen shillings a week. It wasn't much, considering the long hours. She'd wanted more, but having seen her family go by carrying boxes of possessions the old miser had put two and two together and come up with somebody desperately in need of a job. So on Friday she'd buy the crockery for her mother and put the fiver in a hiding place.

She wasn't being greedy or selfish, Faye told herself; she just wanted to start a little nest egg that someday soon would take her and Adam – Michael, too, if he wanted to come – a million miles away from her rotten stepfather ... and her pathetically weak mother.

THREE

'Wait a moment, for Heaven's sake,' Faye hissed as her mother attempted to delve into her bag before she was completely out of the shop. 'At least let's get up the road in case he sees and gets suspicious.' She slung a glance over her shoulder at the bakery whilst walking swiftly away from it. But her boss, Mr Travis, was busy pulling down the shop blinds in the window furthest away from them.

'Didn't you get a pie?' Edie moaned, peering in and poking at the contents of her daughter's canvas bag. 'You know your dad'll be expecting a meat pie.'

'They were all sold by this afternoon.'

'Couldn't you've put one by early on?' Edie huffed.

'No, I couldn't,' Faye snapped in exasperation. 'Getting loaves or buns out is bad enough. Are you trying to lose me me job when I've only had it a short while?'

'That's nothing fer his dinner then ... 'cept a bit of bread and dripping,' Edie whined as she again poked about in the bag that held two small white loaves.

'Well, bread and dripping it is then, for him same as the rest of us for a change,' Faye responded tersely. 'And it's the last time I'm pinching anything at all. Old Mr Travis ain't stupid. I'll get the sack and no reference either. Might even end up in court. Then what we going to do? It's only us two earning; what's he doing, apart from sitting on his backside reading the paper, or leaning on the railing outside, watching the world go by? Let him buy his own bloody meat pie!'

'You watch yer tongue,' Edie hissed, thrusting a finger under her daughter's nose. 'Your dad's looking fer work. Ain't much about for men his age. And you know he's got bad knees.'

'Doesn't afflict him when he's charging up to the pub at opening time, does it?' Faye snapped. 'And I suppose there wasn't much about a year 'n' a half ago when you took up with him, was there?' Faye pointed out fiercely. 'In fact, what's he ever done except live off us?'

Edie turned red and gawped at her daughter. She knew that Faye didn't like Jimmy and never had, but until now she'd kept her tongue in check, just letting slip the occasional hint that she considered Jimmy a lazy, bullying bugger. Considering the trouble she'd caused, you'd think the little madam would toe the line! If it hadn't been for Faye, she might never have got involved with Jimmy Wild in the first place.

Edie was also coming to the conclusion that Jimmy was a wrong 'un, but now that he had her pinned under his thumb, she despaired of ever ridding herself of him. The charmer with the soppy smile who'd won her over and gained her trust had long since disappeared. But not before he'd moved in with her and got his boots well and truly under her bed. Any hint from her that she'd had enough of him and he'd come back with threats to tell her kids a tale about the time he'd first met their ma, years ago, when he was working in that hospital in Kent... And Edie couldn't bear to let them suffer hearing those ghastly details.

Besides, Edie had learned some painful lessons about the consequences of telling Jimmy Wild to sling his hook. Best not to rile him, he always said, stroking the place he'd struck. Edie had to agree, especially on that occasion when his eyes had travelled until they landed on little Adam, grizzling on the floor. He didn't like whining kids, he'd told her, and she'd scooped the boy up and got him quickly out of sight. So far she was sure he saved his temper for her. But Faye was starting to rock the boat and that made Edie fearful. 'What's brought this on with you?' Edie cried, angry now. 'You've always got to be contrary, ain't you, and cause trouble. And you got no right to, considering what I've had to put up with from you, miss!'

Faye looked at her mother, startled by her ferocity. 'If you're that bothered, I'll buy a bloody meat pie and fetch it in with me later.'

'Bakers'll all be sold out by now,' Edie grumbled.

'Corner shop might have one.'

'He'll want a nice fresh one ... out o' Travis's.

Anyhow, why lay out good money on what you should've got fer nuthin'?'

'I'm going for a walk; I'll be back later,' Faye muttered, exasperated, and started to move away. Her mother darted after her, tugging on her arm. 'You'd best come home and explain to yer dad. He's expecting something more'n bread for his tea.'

'I wish I'd never brought a damned pie home last week,' Faye shouted, swinging about. 'And don't keep calling him me dad! He's not! He's just Jimmy.' Suddenly desperate to escape her mother, she made to dart across the road, straight into the path of an oncoming car. The driver was forced to slam on the brakes and swerve sharply to avoid knocking her over. She gasped and clutched double-handed at the shiny coachwork to steady herself, eyes closed tight and wincing at the driver's angry holler. It was a moment before she opened her eyes and recognised the fellow who was in the process of leaping out of the vehicle, his expression thunderous.

Edie had seen Robert Wild too and she was just in the mood to bring something to his attention. It had been eating away at her for a good while, but she'd not seen him to air her grievance since the day they'd moved into Campbell Road.

'So it's you,' she started, seeming oblivious to the fact that her daughter had narrowly avoided being hurt. 'You smashed my crockery and I don't doubt you did it on purpose. The mood you was in that day when you found out we was moving in, you'd have destroyed everything we had, wouldn't you, you spiteful sod.'

'Are you all right?' Rob asked Faye, ignoring Edie's rant. 'You nearly got yourself killed, rushing into the road like that, you stupid little fool.'

Faye nodded mutely, accepting the blame, but stayed where she was, leaning against the car and trying to steady her erratic breathing. She'd gone ashen, but more from the shock of what her mother was saying than from having narrowly escaped physical injury.

'I'm fine,' she finally gasped out. 'Sorry...' She caught at her mother's arm to try to pull her away.

Edie was having none of it. Freeing her elbow from her daughter's grip, she confronted Rob with her hands on her bony hips. 'I ain't told Jimmy 'cos I don't want no trouble. But if yer father finds out you've smashed me best china he'll be after you. He ain't scared of you 'cos you done all right fer yerself...'

'You've got your china. I bought some for you,' Faye muttered and again jerked on her mother's arm to drag her away.

'And it was good of you to lay out yer own money for it, love,' Edie said with a significant nod. 'But that's just tat; what he broke on purpose were your gran's bone china wot she had when she got married to yer granddad, God rest 'em. I remember she told me it came out of Bourne & Hollingsworth,' Edie lied. 'I remember she said it were worth quite a lot, that set.'

'How much was it worth?' Robert asked drily, his shrewd eyes focused on Faye's evasive gaze.

A wave of heat rose up from her throat and Faye knew she was blushing guiltily. She flicked back her blonde head and boldly stared at him, chin up, inviting him to do his worst and expose her as a cheat and a liar.

'Wouldn't get no change out of a guinea,' Edie stated shamelessly. In fact the set had been one of her own wedding gifts when she'd married Faye's father. When her sister-in-law gave it to them she'd complained to her new husband that it was nothing more than Petticoat Lane crap, and secondhand crap at that, with a chipped cup and tea-stains. It was worth no more than a bob or two, even back then.

'A guinea, eh?' Rob mockingly considered it. 'As much as that? I'd've said ten bob, if you're lucky.' He looked at Faye. 'What d'you reckon it was worth?'

'How should I know?' Faye shrilled. 'It was just a bloody tea-set.' She caught her mother glaring at her. 'Five pounds,' she said suddenly with deliberate defiance. 'That's what I reckon it was worth.'

Edie choked. 'Don't be daft, Faye,' she burbled. 'A guinea'll set us straight.' Her greedy eyes, then her fingers, darted immediately to the coins Rob had dug from a pocket and exposed on a palm. As though she feared he might grab them back, she set off at a trot along the road. 'Goin' to the shop...' was sent back over her shoulder. The next minute she'd disappeared from view in the direction of the off licence. If she couldn't get a meat pie, a few brown ales would soon cheer the miserable bugger up.

'Why didn't you tell her?'

'Why didn't you?'

'Why d'you give her more? You got money to throw about?'

'Seems I have...' he said, self-mockery tugging at a corner of his mouth.

'You think I'm a greedy cow, just out for meself,' Faye stated, her fierce gaze clashing on his watching eyes. 'Well, I'm not. I haven't spent a penny of that fiver. I bought her the tea-set out of me wages to replace the one you broke.'

'Going to give me it back, were you?' he taunted.

'No... Yes... I'll give it you back,' Faye choked. 'If I had it with me, you could take it now and good riddance. I never asked you for it.'

'I never said you did.'

Faye knew her cheeks were scarlet and she hated him knowing of her embarrassment. Despite her insolence she felt mean and greedy, and that made her insides squirm. What did she care what he thought of her? But then, it was because she had an inkling of what he thought of her that her stomach was churning.

Since she'd turned fourteen, and filled out, men looked at her all the time. People told her she was pretty. She knew she'd only got the job in the baker's because Mr Travis had taken a fancy to her. There hadn't been a day had gone by since she'd started her job when he'd not found an opportunity to squeeze past her at the counter and rub his groin against her hip. Or his hands would sit a little too long on her waist while he pretended to shift her out of the way so he could use the till drawer. She could guess why Jimmy's son was so generous to her. If the lecher had made her brother, Michael, drop his box of china he'd probably have given him a tube of glue.

He had a fancy for her. And him just married too! But then old Mr Travis was married with four kids. His wife often brought them all into the shop and Faye was always pleased to see them. The randy old sod usually let her off early on those occasions his family turned up.

Briefly she met his eyes and knew he'd read her thoughts. He didn't seem put out that she had him down as a womaniser; in fact, it looked as if he was about to smile. She started off quickly after her mother. His next words stopped her in her tracks.

'You saving up to get away from them and get a place of your own?'

Momentarily she hesitated, but why deny it? If anyone knew what hell it was being around Jimmy, he probably did. She nodded and took a glance at him. 'Yeah... I can't stand it any more,' she said quietly. 'But you'll still get your money back. I was going to give it to you anyhow.'

''Course...' he murmured in a tone of voice that let her know he reckoned she was lying.

'No need to be so bloody sarky,' she shouted and angrily lunged towards him as though she might lash out. She froze as the bakery door opened and Mr Travis came out.

'Hello, Robert,' her boss blurted in surprise before swallowing audibly. 'I've not seen you in a while.' Mr Travis jangled the keys in his hand and blinked over his shoulder at them. 'But I ... er ... I've been expecting to see you, of course,' he said in a quiet, nervous tone that was so unusual Faye stared at him. The Mr Travis she knew was an arrogant, confident individual. She'd heard him snap at customers who asked for credit. He didn't give way even when they were just a penny short of what they needed and promised to pop it in tomorrow. They had to suffer the shame of having bread or cakes unwrapped and returned to the rack. Now he'd come over all meek and mild, fiddling with the key in his hand and looking from one to the other of them. 'Do you want to come in or ... will you come back tomorrow?' He cleared his throat.

'I'm not here to see you,' Robert told him.

'Oh ... I see...' The relief in Mr Travis's voice was accentuated by his gasping chortle. He gave Faye a long look. 'I'll see you in the morning, Faye,' he said before striding away.

'You working in the baker's?'

Faye nodded. 'He thinks you're your brother – he called you Robert.'

'It's you thinks I'm my brother. Do you want a lift home?' He was already by his car and his half-smile told her he anticipated a rebuff even before he'd raised his eyes to see her shake her head. 'Suit yourself.' A moment later the car was on its way up the street.

'Any work going hereabouts, Til?'

Tilly halted in her march to the shop and swung about to find Jimmy lounging against a railing. She suspected he'd been loitering out of sight, waiting for her to pass by before emerging from the hallway of the house where he lived. It was a hot August afternoon and he was wearing a vest belted into his trousers. She remembered he'd liked to display his biceps when younger; now the muscles looked withered and the skin covering them crêpey. The sight of the cobra twisting on his left arm caused a stabbing tension in her guts. The faded tattoo aroused memories she'd believed she'd buried long ago with her sister.

'Why? What's it to you?' Matilda scoffed. 'You going to change the habit of a lifetime and get off yer arse for an honest day's pay?' She strode on without a backward glance. Ten minutes later she came back down the street with her twist of tea and bottle of milk to find he was in the same place, waiting for her.

'Don't need to be honest work, luv.' He resumed their conversation as though there'd been no break in it. 'That's why I'm asking you fer a tip-off. You always did know about ducking 'n' diving, Til, I'll give you that. Don't want no crap wages, mind.'

'Don't know of nuthin',' Tilly barked and carried on walking, her teeth clamped so tightly in an effort to bite back on saying anything else that her jaw ached.

'Was right sorry to hear about Jack,' Jimmy called out. 'One o' life's good 'uns was your Jack.'

Tilly flung herself around, her face boiling with rage. 'Don't you dare mention him,' she blasted out. 'You ain't fit to even speak his name.' With that she let fly with the bottle of milk.

Jimmy ducked and it whistled past to shatter against the wall of the house. He'd intended to rile her, but hadn't expected such a violent reaction, and it stole the smirk from his face. With a shrug he turned and disappeared inside.

In the months that had passed since Jimmy had moved back into the street, though there had been many occasions when she was sorely tempted, Tilly had resisted the urge to set about her erstwhile brother-in-law. Her daughters had pleaded with her not to cause a rumpus, but it was someone else whose advice had persuaded her to leave well alone.

Reg Donovan was a pikey, a term she used to his face, as did others. A tinker by trade, Reg had lived for a number of years in Queensland Road with his parents and had gone more or less unnoticed by Matilda. But a chance encounter outside Beattie's, when Reg was mending her neighbour's pots, had brought them together. Tilly – with a broken pan and a nose for a discount – had sauntered over to slip hers in on Beattie's deal and had got chatting to him. That had been many months ago and Tilly had known straight away that Reg had taken a liking to her. After that, he often found excuses to come into The Bunk and loiter about near her place. A couple of times she'd found herself looking out of the window for him. She was well aware that she was acting like a soppy schoolgirl with a crush, yet, for the first time in many years, she'd felt light-hearted.

After her beloved Jack had perished in the Great War, Tilly had been certain no other man would ever stir her interest or affection. But the passing of the years had rubbed the rough edges off her grief and something about Reg's Irish charm appealed to her. Besides, Tilly was a realist and had scraped by in The Bunk on her own for long enough. It was sensible for two people to pull together rather than try to battle on against the odds solo. Lucy, her youngest child, had been the last to leave home. She'd gone to work in service with Sophy, her eldest, near Southend. Her daughters all had their own lives now. The eldest three were married. When Reg had popped the question to her a few weeks ago, she'd said yes straight away. As soon as they'd put by the cash to pay for the service – and a little knees-up at the Duke afterwards, of course – they'd do the deed. But neither of them were in any rush.

Tilly had ceased raging about what damages she'd like to inflict on Jimmy after recognising wisdom in her fiancé's blunt advice on the matter: 'If ye let on he can rile ye like that, then he'll stick around for ever. He's pulling strings 'n' yer dancing for him, Tilly.' So Tilly had been careful not to let Jimmy know that his presence in Campbell Road bothered her, although at times it almost killed her to hold her tongue when she sauntered past his doorway. Now she was kicking herself for having let him see that her indifference to him was just a sham.

Jimmy peeped round the brickwork and watched Matilda through narrowed vision until she'd disappeared. Then he turned his attention to his stepdaughter, who was on her way down the road towards him. His eyes immediately fell to the bag in Faye's hand.

'Brought yer dad a few nice bits for his tea?' The question sounded casual enough, but there was an undertone of menace that demanded the right answer.

'I've told you, I'm not filching stuff any more.' Faye tried to pass, but Jimmy blocked her way.

'Well, aren't you Miss Prim 'n' Proper,' he sneered. 'You'll learn when you live round here that's how we go on. Nobody gives yer nuthin', so you take wot yer need.'

'If you want to think so, think so. My dad taught me thieving's wrong and...'

Jimmy pinched her chin in a playful grip that tightened painfully. 'But yer dad ain't here now, is he?' he purred. 'He's pushin' up daisies, thinkin' himself lucky 'n' all, and it's fallen to me to do his job for him.'

Faye ripped her face free from his fingers. 'Thinking himself *lucky?'* she echoed, appalled by his callousness. 'That's a wicked thing to say about a man ... *a gentleman,'* she added damningly, 'who perished on the Somme. Where were you hiding when it was all going on over there?' she hissed. Faye knew that Jimmy hadn't gone to fight. Somehow or other he'd managed to escape doing his duty, and that didn't surprise her. In the time she'd known him, he'd never shown himself to be anything other than selfish and cowardly. Her beloved dad, and all the other honourable men who'd shipped out to fight the Hun, had paid the ultimate price for their bravery. The likes of Jimmy Wild would never rob her of her cherished memories of her heroic father, no matter what spiteful stuff he might come out with.

Jimmy stared at her for so long that Faye thought he was about to give her an answer, but suddenly his sly eyes veered away and he croaked one of his laughs. They were as false as everything else about him and Faye shook her head contemptuously and made to push past.

Jimmy gripped her elbow and yanked her back. 'I'm looking out for you 'cos I'm yer stepdad, and don't you forget it. So tomorrer make sure you fetch me in something…'

'I'm looking out for myself,' she interrupted him. 'So I'm not losing me job thieving. As for the others … getting yourself work might help you look out for them.' Faye realised he wasn't listening any more but squinting over her shoulder. She turned her head and saw what had caught his eye. His son, Stephen, had emerged from a house close to the bottom of the road. Faye had seen him coming out of the property before. Usually he walked up and entered a couple of other places as well. She'd assumed he was collecting his brother's rents.

The two brothers were similar in height and in their dark good looks. She could understand why, seeing him at a distance, her mother had mistaken Robert for his brother on the day they moved into The Bunk. Unfortunately for Faye, the embarrassment of confusing the two of them still had the power to make her blush. She'd thought Robert Wild a newly married man with a roving eye. Now she knew that the pretty dark-haired young woman who'd been sitting beside him in his car, and whom she'd taken for his wife, was one of Matilda Keiver's daughters, and a cousin of his.

Since that day Faye had seen Alice go into Matilda's house on several occasions; sometimes she had a little girl with her who looked about five years old. Faye supposed the fair-haired man who occasionally accompanied them was her husband. She'd not wanted to question Jimmy over his dead wife's relatives, but she'd got snippets of information from her mother. Slowly Edie was coming to know the local families and their gossip. Her mother had warned her to avoid the Keivers because they were out to cause trouble. Faye reckoned that if anything the family were keen to avoid *them*. Anyway, she'd needed no such telling. She'd no desire to get to know anyone. As soon as she could, she'd be leaving.

FOUR

'How you doing, son?'

Jimmy's voice startled Faye from her reflection. Quickly she made to go inside, but Jimmy casually placed a hand on both railings, keeping her where she was.

'Stay 'n' say hello to him, you rude li'l cow,' he breathed close to her face.

Jimmy had hailed Stephen on previous occasions but had been ignored. He hadn't exchanged a word with his youngest son since the evening of the wedding reception, several months ago. 'Business booming?' Jimmy remarked in a jolly tone once he'd gained Stephen's attention. He could guess why his son was staring and tightened his grip on the railings in case his stepdaughter tried again to get past him.

Stephen slowed down and stuck his hands in his pockets. Robert constantly warned him to ignore Jimmy if he tried to cosy up to him when he was in Campbell Road. Stephen hated his father yet, illogically, a worming curiosity was urging him to walk over and find out a few things. He longed to know what Jimmy had been doing, and where he'd been in the missing years.

Despite painful memories of the beatings his father had dealt out, Stevie had retained a spark of optimism that there might be some reason to be proud of the man who'd sired him. Back when he was a lot younger, he'd convinced himself that Jimmy Wild, like the unknown warrior and the men who'd lived in the neighbourhood, such as his uncle Jack Keiver and Geoff Lovat, had perished nobly on foreign soil for king and country. Later, when no official notification ever arrived about Jimmy Wild being missing, presumed dead, Stevie's hopes had taken a different turn. His father might have returned, dreadfully wounded and suffering from amnesia. He had heard of fellows – seen them, too – who'd been shell-shocked, or had their minds destroyed by the terrible things they'd witnessed in the trenches. Then he'd wondered whether he might have been one of those unlucky civilians caught up in the London bombings, which had left many corpses too horribly mutilated for identification. Obstinately Stephen had clung to the fantasy that something other than callous self-interest might have prevented his father coming back home.

Now he inwardly mocked himself for having

wallowed in such sentimental guff. Yet he remained where he was; the old man was standing with his stepdaughter, and she had a face that'd draw any bloke in for a closer look. A couple of times he'd seen her walking down the road, but she'd crossed over and ignored him. He'd learned from Robert that their father had taken on a stepfamily when he'd got involved with Edie Greaves. He knew one of Edie's kids was a girl aged about eighteen, called Faye. An odd note in his brother's voice when he'd mentioned her had alerted Stephen to the fact that Rob had an interest there. But he'd not questioned him over it. Robert could be aggravatingly uncommunicative when it came to personal matters, especially where women or money were concerned.

Curiosity was creeping over Faye too, so she ceased straining against the cruel grip Jimmy had placed on her arm. She'd only previously seen Stephen Wild at a distance. Now, as he slowly approached, she noticed that his hair was styled short, probably to tame its curls, and had a coarse appearance. Neither was the colour as dark brown as Robert's sleek, straight mane. Stephen also looked to be a few inches shorter in height than his brother, although they shared a similar spare build. His eyes appeared lighter, too; more the colour of caramel than chocolate, and he had a slightly softer set to his lips. On the couple of occasions Faye had been with Robert she'd noticed the slant to his mouth that made him look constantly on the verge of being sarcastic. Possibly, when he'd been in his twenties, their father might have resembled his handsome sons. Now

Jimmy was a bloated, grizzled wreck of a man; only a few dark threads in his lank grey hair hinted at his lost youth.

'Still here then?' Stephen greeted his father sourly as he approached and stopped close to the kerb. He cocked his head, looking them up and down.

''Course we're still here. We ain't goin' nowhere,' was Jimmy's blunt reply. 'Next time I leave The Bunk, it'll be in a pine box.'

'They all right with that?' Stephen nodded at Faye as his eyes swept over her, a crooked smile on his lips. Now he was close to her, he could see it wasn't only her face that was lovely; she had a sweet figure on her too. 'Don't know of any nice young lady who'd be grateful to be dragged here to live permanently.'

'Faye's a good gel; she'll do as her dad tells her.' Jimmy slung a possessive arm about her narrow shoulders.

Faye shrugged him off immediately in a way that taught Stephen a lot about their relationship, and her obedience.

'Yeah ... can see she's devoted to her new dad,' he scoffed, watching her slender back as she disappeared, unhindered by Jimmy, into the house.

'Don't matter about her,' Jimmy said, lip curling. 'It's me boys – me *own* boys, that is – who I care about.'

Stephen hooted an acid laugh. 'Yeah, we noticed how much you cared about us when we was growin' up.' He started on his way, but halted on hearing his father's next comment.

'Always thought it'd be you, y'know, who'd

make summat of himself.' Jimmy smiled, having regained Stephen's attention. 'You was always the brightest of the two of yers.'

'How d'you work that out? Weren't me wot done any good at school; Rob did.'

'Don't need no schoolin' to be shrewd.' Jimmy nodded at him. 'You was the one learned the right lessons.'

'Wot ... like not to wet the bed 'cos I'd get the belt?' Stephen took a step forward and put his lips close to his father's unshaven cheek. 'Yeah, I learned that lesson all right,' emerged in a hiss.

'And it were a lesson you needed to learn, son,' Jimmy said in his weary, gentle way. 'Did you want all the kids round here teasing the life outta yer 'n' callin you names like "piss-pants"?' Before Stephen could recover from the shock of hearing his father finally acknowledge his brutality, Jimmy continued, 'You knew early on that you gotta be ambitious and make some money.' A paternal hand patted his son's shoulder. 'When you was just a nipper, you was the one always wanted to earn himself coppers when the gambling school was up 'n' running on a Sunday dinnertime; always acting doggerout for us, wasn't you. Your brother was too fond of sparring down the boys' club with pals, or kicking a football about, as I remember.'

'Yeah ... 'n' I soon learned he was wiser, 'cos doin' little jobs for Solly fer nuthin' paid off eventually in a fuckin' big way. Anyhow, whatever I earned, you or Mum 'ud have it straight off me.'

Jimmy shrugged, all affable. 'Don't want to start no arguments with you, son, nor hear you speak bad about yer mum, God rest her. She did her best...'

'I'll never speak bad about *her* ... only *you!'* Stephen exploded. 'Don't you try to twist me words, you crafty bastard.'

'Right ... right ... calm down,' Jimmy crooned soothingly. 'All I'm saying, Stevie, is I'm surprised you're the sidekick and Bobbie's in charge. That's all I'm sayin'...'

'Yeah ... well, tell someone else,' Stephen spat and strode off. His hands were thrust casually in his pockets, but his face was flushed and his mouth compressed in a thin line.

Faye moved back from the doorway as she glimpsed Stephen crossing the road. She wouldn't usually eavesdrop on other's conversations, but she'd stopped, out of sight, just behind the doorjamb because she'd had an inkling her stepfather might try to stir up trouble. But the trouble he seemed to want to cause wasn't the sort she'd anticipated. She'd thought he'd wind Stephen up and point him in the direction of the Keivers. She knew Jimmy was itching to start a war with Tilly Keiver; she'd seen the way he stared obsessively at the woman when she passed by, nose in the air, or occasionally two fingers in the air, when he tried to accost her and she couldn't be bothered to tell him to piss off. But, instead, it seemed Jimmy's intention was to drive a wedge between his sons. Silently, Faye hurried up the stairs in case he came in and saw her and guessed she'd been loitering and listening.

Jimmy stayed where he was and watched, slit-eyed against the afternoon sun, as Stephen went about his business. When his son disappeared into a hallway opposite he turned and shuffled back inside, looking smug.

The moment Faye entered the room, Adam immediately put out his arms to be picked up. She settled him against her hip then felt the dampness from his bottom seep into her skirt. She sighed and touched his posterior.

'He wet?' Edie demanded as she noticed her daughter's actions.

Faye nodded.

'Get him in the back room and clean him up 'fore yer dad finds out,' Edie garbled. 'Y'know he reckons it's high time Adam was trained.'

'He's only two and a bit,' Faye protested. 'He's bound to have an accident now 'n' again.'

'You 'n' Michael was dry by then,' Edie said querulously, shooting an anxious look at the door as she saw the handle turning.

Faye did as she'd been told and immediately took the boy to change him. The exchange she'd just overheard between Stephen and his father had confirmed her worst suspicions about Jimmy Wild. He was a brutal man, and if he felt disgruntled enough he wouldn't hold back on disciplining Adam for wetting himself any more than he had with his own flesh and blood. She touched the soft cheek of the child lying on the bed then bent to plant a kiss where her fingers had stroked. Adam had been only six months old when Jimmy Wild walked into their lives. Faye felt bitterly upset that the little boy might soon, with her mother's blessing, start to call the vile man daddy.

That awful thought made her determined to get away for an hour or so, and take Adam with her. Though it was late afternoon, it was warm and would stay light for some hours yet. Carefully she withdrew the rolled-up five-pound note from its hiding place. She'd secreted it in the channel of fabric where string was threaded to hold up a rag that served as a curtain at the window. Having loosened her clothes, and slipped the money into her cleavage, she dried off Adam then went back into the other room, leading him by the hand.

'Going off out for a while. I'll take Adam with me for a bit of air.'

'Where you off to?' her mother demanded.

'Just out,' Faye said in exasperation. 'Can't stay cooped up in this dump all the time.'

'You only just finished work,' Edie pointed out

'So?' Faye made an impatient gesture. 'If you must know, I said I'd meet Marge and we'd take a stroll just for something to do,' she lied. Marge, the young widow who helped out at the bakery on Wednesdays and Saturdays, was about ten years older than she was, and had lost her husband in the Great War, but they'd struck up a bit of a friendship. After all, they had something in common in that they'd both had enough of Mr Travis's sweaty hands on them.

Adam started to grizzle and immediately drew Jimmy's surly attention. 'Gawd's sake, let her take him off out. The kid never stops whining.'

Once down the stairs Faye set Adam on the ground and his mood seemed improved by the sunshine. She glanced down at the house where Matilda Keiver lived and drew in a deep breath, plucking up the courage to go and find her.

She'd moved no more than a yard or two when she realised she might not need to approach Matilda to get the information she needed. Her daughter, Alice, was just coming out of her house and was starting up the road towards her, leading a little girl by the hand.

Faye took a quick look up at her window. She didn't want her mother or Jimmy seeing her talking to any of the Keivers; she'd be interrogated for days over what had been said. She set off briskly round the corner into Paddington Street and loitered there, feeling nervous. As Alice drew level she made her way towards her.

'Sorry to bother you, I'm just wondering if you could tell me where your cousin Robert lives.'

Alice looked at Faye and then at the blond child who was sucking his thumb. A moment later her daughter Lilian took one of his hands and began to swing it, making him laugh.

'Why do you want him?' Alice replied, trying not to sound suspicious. She knew this pretty young woman was Jimmy's stepdaughter, and she knew her uncle wasn't above sending somebody else out to do his dirty work.

'It's nothing to do with Jimmy, or my mum,' Faye said sharply, guessing what was running through her mind. 'It's just...' She moistened her lips. She knew nothing about Alice, but instinctively, from the first moment she'd spotted her laughing in Robert's car, she'd decided that she looked the sort of person you'd want as a friend.

'Your cousin gave me a bit of money ... a loan. I want to give it back.'

Alice could tell from her uneasiness that it had taken courage for Faye Greaves to stop her and ask how to find Robert. Her cousin was popular with the girls; all the family were aware of that. By anybody's standards, Rob had done all right for himself, and ambitious women shamelessly chased him because of it.

Faye could tell Alice assumed she was after her wealthy cousin to wheedle for more not pay anything back. Swallowing the lump of indignation that closed her throat, she pulled the banknote out of her blouse and thrust it at Alice.

'Give him this, will you.'

'Give it to him yourself,' Alice returned, but not unkindly. She smiled at the little boy who was skipping on and off the pavement with her daughter. 'What's his name?'

'Adam.'

'How old?'

'Two 'n' a bit.' Another brusque answer.

'Do you want me to write the address down?'

'I can remember it, thanks,' Faye said gruffly. Having achieved what she'd set out to do, she scooped Adam up, soothing him as he tried to wriggle free to continue his game with Lilian. Having mumbled a goodbye, Faye carried on down Paddington Street, Adam squirming in her arms.

It was a good walk to Tufnell Park. Faye didn't yet know this North London territory well and twice had to stop and ask for directions after taking a wrong turning. Little Adam was flagging before they'd made halfway. But she urged him on, lifting him when necessary. Finally she was glad to see a Street name high up on a wall that told her she'd arrived at her destination. She stared along the neat row of houses in wonderment. She had no doubt that she was in a good area. A similar neighbourhood to this existed in Dartford. It had been some distance from the decaying turning that she and her family had inhabited, just as this place was a safe distance from Campbell Road.

Her thoughts were interrupted by a smartly dressed couple who descended the steps of one of the villas and sedately sauntered by, arm in arm. Adam was whimpering again so Faye swung him once more into her arms and walked to the end of the street. She looked up at a large house set on its own. Her mouth felt arid and for two pins she'd have turned right around and gone back the way she'd come. Robert Wild lived in the best house in the road. She realised he wouldn't believe, any more than had his cousin Alice, that she really wanted to return his money. Hadn't she already learned from his sarcasm that he doubted she'd willingly give up her treasure? The driveway at the side of the house was empty. He was out in his car. She knew it was cowardly to be glad she'd missed him, nevertheless she was feeling relieved.

Adam had wriggled his hand free of hers and darted forward to chase a cat that had been languidly stretching against warm stone. It rose and stalked off towards a green iron gate, then slipped beneath, thwarting the toddler's attempt to grab its tail and drag it back.

Faye scooped him up, but he stiffened in temper. Soon he was howling loud enough to make a curtain next door twitch, so she dropped him back on his feet and quickly sped up the steps with the intention of posting the five-pound note through the letterbox. He'd know where it had come from. She'd reached the top and her hand was reaching towards a brass letter plate when the sound of a car approaching made her turn. As the vehicle headed towards her, she met his eyes through the windscreen. There was no way she'd make it to the bottom step, let alone escape before he got out.

'I've brought you this,' Faye blurted, descending a step. She hurried down the rest, one hand outstretched. When he simply looked at her offering, she put it down on the warm bonnet of the car.

'Decided to stay put with Jimmy, have you?' he asked in that acerbic way he had. His eyes slew to the child as Adam clung to her legs and mewed.

'He's tired. It was a long walk.'

'Have you given up your plan to get away from them?'

Faye vigorously shook her head in answer. 'I shouldn't have brought him. It wasn't fair, expecting him to walk so far.'

'You'll need that then.' Robert picked up the cash and held it out.

Adam snatched it, scrunching it in his little fist.

'Smart kid,' Robert observed with a soundless laugh. His eyes narrowed on her as he noticed she looked to be on the point of crying. 'Are you going to come in for a minute?'

She shook her head, stroking Adam's face to soothe his whimpering while simultaneously trying to prise open his fingers to rescue the money before it got torn.

'Do you want a drink?'

'No thanks.'

'Tea? Coffee?'

'Milk.'

They both looked at Adam.

'Drink of milk,' he piped up again, then turned shy and dropped his chin. 'Please,' he whispered and peeped up at Robert from beneath long baby lashes.

'Well mannered, too,' Rob said. 'He didn't get that from Jimmy.'

'He got it from me,' Faye stated tartly.

'Yeah ... I can believe that.' He took her arm and steered her up the steps.

'Do you live here alone?'

'Mostly,' he said, watching for her reaction as he stuck the key in the lock.

'It's a big house ... a family house.'

'Yeah ... there's plenty of room.'

Faye's eyes slipped to his and then swerved away. She regretted her comment. He thought she was hinting there was enough room for her. 'I'm going back to Kent to live,' she blurted. 'Soon as I can, I'm moving out of The Bunk, and going right far away from here.'

'I grew up chanting that phrase.' He ushered her into the hallway, taking her elbow to propel her forward when she seemed reluctant to move across the threshold.

'It's nice,' Faye said, looking about. It was an absurd understatement, considering what she'd been used to. The hallway was spacious and uncluttered. The air smelled vaguely of lavender polish and, having registered the scent, her eyes darted to the gleaming mahogany furniture set back against the walls. 'You've got a char?'

'No. I keep it clean.' He gave a slightly diffident smile. 'Comes from growing up in a shithole, I expect... Sorry,' he muttered, noting her frown at his language and look at the child.

'Milk...' Adam said, struggling to break free. The new environment seemed to keep him amused and he toddled from place to place before settling on his knees on the patterned rug that stretched the length of the passageway.

'Are you going to sit down for a moment, or d'you intend to stand there making the place look untidy?'

Faye gave a tiny laugh. 'Thanks very much.' Her amusement faded. 'Can't stop long; it's almost time Adam was in bed and it's a bit of a trek.'

'I'll take you back,' Rob said, lightly amused. 'Did you think I'd let you walk?'

'I didn't think about it. Anyway, why would you want to go out when you've just this minute got home?'

'Because I've got manners too, just don't always remember to use them,' he ruefully admitted as he walked off towards the back of the house. 'I'll get a cup of milk for him.'

'His name's Adam. You might as well remember that. He is your stepbrother, after all.'

'And who d'you think you are? My sister?' he sent over a shoulder.

He returned with a cup of milk and gave it to the boy, who gulped greedily at it. Faye quickly went to him, worried Adam might spill some on the beautiful rug. Surreptitiously she felt his bottom in case he'd wet himself. He had and she lifted him quickly on to his feet and took the cup from him. A dark ring remained where his bottom had been.

'Thanks ... we've got to go now.' She looked about for somewhere to deposit the beaker and gingerly placed it on a glass-like wooden surface. Her eyes returned to the stain on the rug and she looked up to find Rob watching her. He knew and was waiting to see if she'd got manners and would own up. 'Sorry ... Adam's had a little accident.' She moistened her lips. 'It's not much. I shouldn't have let him have a drink. It's my fault.'

'Don't worry, it happens,' he said. 'D'you think of me as a brother?'

'Have you got a cloth? I'll just mop it up. It won't stain if we're quick,' she said, turning about on the spot as though she'd willingly fetch a rag herself if he pointed her in the right direction.

'Fuck the rug!' Robert exploded beneath his breath. 'Do you think of me as your brother?'

'I think you ought to wash your mouth out with soap,' she snapped, glaring at him. Taking Adam by the hand, she turned deliberately away from him.

'That's just the sort of thing a bloody sister would say.'

'It's just the sort of thing a *bloody mother* would

say,' Faye rounded on him. A moment later she'd turned her back on him again.

'Well, you were obviously luckier in your mother than I was in mine,' he said through his teeth. He wrenched open the front door. 'Come on then ... let's go.'

FIVE

'Would you stop in Seven Sisters Road?'

'Yeah ... I was going to anyway.'

'Thanks,' Faye mumbled.

It was almost dusk and she was glad of the cover of twilight. Sometimes, in the early evenings, Jimmy would hang about with a pal outside, chatting by the railings, or drinking beer. If he were brassic and feeling particularly in need of a friend, he'd share his bottle with a passer-by to get himself a conversation. Faye didn't want her stepfather seeing her getting out of his son's car. He'd want to know all the ins and outs, especially her reason for seeking Robert out. But the area looked unusually quiet, probably because a light drizzle had started. Just a few people, dressed lightly for summer, were hurrying into Campbell Road with their heads down as if to avoid getting wet. She watched the windscreen wipers arc across the glass before Robert turned off the engine and they sat for a moment in silence with the rain pattering on the car roof. It was a somnolent sound and Faye drew a breath, settled back, and sighed.

She felt warm, strangely serene, cocooned against the dismal reality of what awaited outside. Soon a pulse in the atmosphere was spoiling her contentment and she remembered the hostility between them.

'Thanks for the lift.' Her fingers fumbled for the door handle and she shifted Adam on her lap. When they'd started out, the boy had been fractious and Robert had said, not unkindly considering the grim expression that had accompanied the statement, he would take a roundabout route to get him off to sleep. It had worked. The rocking motion of the car had soon had his little lids fluttering. She'd smiled inwardly as they'd sped along and almost felt inclined to ask how he knew that handy trick, but the memory of their cross words had made her keep her thoughts to herself.

'Take it. I want you to have it.'

Faye turned her head to see him thrusting the five-pound note at her.

'Go on, take it. My contribution to your escape fund.' He folded the note and stuck it into the breast pocket of her jacket, withdrawing his fingers quickly. 'I know what it's like to want to scarper from this slum. If you need any more, ask.'

'Thanks,' Faye said hoarsely. She felt guilty now that she'd too readily snapped at him for swearing. She'd felt embarrassed over Adam soiling the carpet, and had forgotten to warn him that Jimmy was trying to stir things up for him with Stephen.

'I didn't just come to give you back your money,' she admitted. 'You did me a favour over the tea-set. Even though it was your fault it got broken, you could've made things awkward for me by telling Mum you'd paid for it straight away.' She looked up, an odd mixture of gratitude and aggression in her eyes. 'I know you protected me, even though I never asked you to. So I wanted to do you a favour back.' She frowned, wondering if she'd been too sensitive over it all. Would he think a conversation between his father and brother was none of her business and she'd no right to stick her nose in? 'Stephen was in the road earlier today. I overheard Jimmy and him talking,' she blurted, then paused to gauge his reaction. She saw that his eyes had narrowed in interest.

'Go on,' he encouraged.

'I think Jimmy'll cause trouble for you two, if he can. I've not known him that long: about a year and a half he's been with my mum. But God knows it's been long enough and I know he's a malicious bugger. From what he was saying, I reckon he intends to try and play you off one against the other.'

'Yeah, he'll do that, all right,' Robert muttered grimly. 'Thanks for letting me know.'

She gave a little nod of acknowledgement.

'What did he say exactly?' he asked, stopping her again as she reached to open the car door.

'Oh, just that he's surprised that Stevie isn't the guvnor as he's always been smarter than you.'

Robert smiled, a proper smile that made her breath catch in her throat as it transformed to a husky chuckle.

'Don't you mind that he's going to try to put a

spoke in things for you?'

'Nah ... not really,' Rob said, his eyes focused on his hand as he flexed his fingers. 'Done me a favour, in a way. A showdown's been brewing a while; things've got worse since Steve got married.' He abruptly got out of the car and a moment later he'd opened her door and was taking Adam from her so she could get out.

'Mind you don't get wet,' she said as the boy's damp rump settled on his dark suit sleeve.

He looked at her stained skirt and as their eyes met they simultaneously grimaced.

'Thanks for the lift,' Faye said quietly, taking Adam back.

'Yeah ... you told me.'

'And for your contribution.'

'Yeah ... you said that too. My pleasure ... no, really. Sooner you're on your way back to Kent the better. Let me know if you need more.'

''Course I bloody need more,' she choked, unaccountably miffed by his attitude. It was insultingly clear that he'd be glad to see the back of her. He might as well have told her right out to piss off. 'Won't get me far, will it? A fucking fiver?'

'Well, you know where I live now. Come and see me.' He strolled back round the vehicle. 'All right for you to swear in front of the kid, is it?' he muttered sarcastically as he got in and slammed the door.

Faye watched the car pull off along Seven Sisters Road, anger and indignation burning in her chest. She stuck up two fingers and hoped he'd see her defiant gesture in his rear-view mirror, for she was sure he'd use it to look back at her. Then she felt silly and ashamed for having done it. The rain became steadily stronger and started Adam to a grizzling wakefulness. Pulling her jacket over him to shield him a bit she put her head down and hurried towards home.

He stopped the car under the gas lamp so she'd see him. Drawing out his cigarettes, he lit one and leaned back against the leather seat. Ten minutes later, right on time,and just as he was fishing in the pack of Players again, Gloria finished her shift and came out of the side door of the Duke. She saw him waiting and with a delighted grin hurried over.

'Why didn't you come in and have a drink?' she asked as she settled into the passenger seat.

'Didn't want one.' He held out the pack of cigarettes and she slid one out then waited for him to light it for her. They sat smoking, Rob sending a grey haze drifting through the open window at his side, Gloria blowing upwards and scrutinising him as he glared into the deserted night.

'That Vicky Watson been giving you a hard time?'

She got no response. Not even a flicker of an eyelid betrayed that he'd heard her sly probing. Taking a final drag, Gloria leaned across him and flicked her dog-end into the darkness. Her fingers trailed suggestively across his thighs as she moved back to snuggle into her seat.

'We gonna sit here all night doing nuthin', or are you gonna take me home with you so we can do something?'

'Yeah ... ready?' he asked, as though just

startled from a dream.

She leaned across and kissed him full on the lips; an immediate sexy one that entangled their tobacco-tangy tongues. Her fingers went to his shirt and she opened a few buttons and slipped her hands inside. Her flat palms smoothed on his chest before she lowered her head to his groin and undid buttons there too.

'Chrissake, Rob!' she gurgled a laugh. 'You been carrying this around all day? You should've come to see me sooner. I went home on me dinner break; you could've come too.' Her small hand curved halfway about solid buoyant muscle and she teased it with her fingers before her lips took over.

'Drop you home?' he said ten minutes later when she was buttoning him up again.

'Home? I thought we was going to yours.'

Robert started the ignition. He wanted to tell her he no longer needed her to come to his, but he knew that if he did he'd be acting like his bastard of a father, who'd force his mother to the bed, order him and Stephen out of the house, then minutes later breeze out into the street to head off, whistling, towards the pub. So, despite the fact that he didn't particularly want to spend another minute with Gloria, let alone the night, he asked politely, 'D'you want to stop and get a bite to eat?'

She settled back into the car's upholstery. 'Yeah ... be nice. Could murder a steak dinner. Tight-fisted git only let me take a few biscuits for me tea, 'n' there was pies goin' stale 'n' all.'

Her reference to the legendary parsimony of

the Duke's landlord drew from him a skewed smile. 'Right,' he said as he let off the brake, 'I'll head up west.'

'Well, I reckon your father's got a point, and I'm glad he said what he did.' Pam Wild got up gingerly from her armchair, a hand supporting the small of her back. Her pregnant belly got a massage from her other fingers. She was now six months gone and already huge. 'I've been saying for a while you'd be as good as he is running the show if you was given half a chance. You don't get out of this business what you should.'

'Yeah, and I've told you it's not *this* business ... it's *his* business.' Stephen continued rolling tobacco then licked an edge of paper and stuck the smoke between his lips.

'Still, he should've let you in as his partner ages ago.'

'He would've done,' Stephen mumbled past the obstacle in his lips. 'But I've never had the money to put in, have I?' A look passed between them. 'Even when he's given me the soddin' money to put in, I've messed up.'

'He could've lent you more.'

'He ain't that stupid,' Stephen barked harshly and raked impatient fingers through his short, wiry hair. 'You think he's going to shell out again so you can run through the bleedin' lot?' His tone had become edgy.

'Well, he could've give you another hundred, as a loan,' she retorted sullenly. 'Not as if he ain't had it to give, is it? I reckon–'

'Fuck's sake, shut up, will you,' Stephen snarled

past the drooping cigarette and slung himself back in an armchair that faced the one Pam had just vacated. He twiddled half-heartedly at the knobs on the radiogram by his side, producing a whining medley of varying volume.

Pamela watched him from beneath her lashes, looking as though she might be on the point of adding something. She mouthed something obscene at his profile then shuffled to the table and started to pour tea from the pot. Once the cups were filled she waddled to the sideboard and got the biscuit box.

'What's to eat?' Stephen snapped meaningfully as he stared at the oblong tin she was about to offer him. His eyes shifted to the open doorway that led into the small kitchenette. 'Forgotten we've got a nice new cooker out there, have yer?'

She pulled a face. 'I'm not hungry; feelin' a bit sick, actually. If you're *that* hungry can't you go to the fish shop and get yourself something?'

'I've been to the chippy every bleeding night this week, you lazy mare. You said you wanted a new cooker and I got a sub off Rob to buy you one. But you can't be bothered to do a bit o' grub for me when I get in from work, can you?'

'I'm pregnant, in case you ain't noticed,' Pamela sniped back, swiping a hand over her bloated belly.

'I've noticed, don't you worry about that,' Stephen sent back acidly as he jerked forward in the chair and started rolling down his sleeves. He whipped a resentful glance at her fat figure as he snatched up his jacket from the chair back then headed for the door with his wife's indignant stare following him.

When he got back with newspaper wrapped around his hot fish supper, Pam had got the plates out. Stephen noticed there were two of them.

'Not feeling so sick now?' he jibed.

'Oh, have it all yerself then,' she said tremulously. 'I was only trying to be a bit of company for you. I was only trying to give you a bit of advice over what your father said, 'n' all. Can't do nuthin' right though, can I? And it ain't fair, you takin' it out on me cos your brother keeps you under his thumb. I'm going to bed.'

Stephen sighed and went and put his hands on her shoulders before she could storm off along the passageway towards the bedroom. 'Can't keep arguing all the time like this, Pam.' He drew her back into the sitting room. 'Kid'll be with us soon.' Inwardly he wished to God it wouldn't be. His petite, chatty wife had in a matter of months transformed into a hefty whiner. But what riled him more than anything was the knowledge that, if he'd taken his brother's advice and been sensible with that hundred pounds, investing it where Rob had told him to, he could have been a partner in the business, taking profits instead of a wage each week. It was all right her moaning now, but she'd wanted the day out with her family at the dog track, and she'd been the one wanted to show off in front of them all, betting big money on outsiders.

In addition to paying for their wedding, Rob had given him some cash as a wedding gift. He'd said he could invest it as he saw fit: to buy a stake in the company, or to start his own enterprise if he preferred to go it alone. Stephen wished he'd never told Pam about it. When he'd hared home with the wad, she'd still been revelling in big-day excitement. They'd only recently returned from their Brighton honeymoon – a week's holiday reluctantly paid for by his father-in-law, who had become aware that his failure to contribute to his daughter's wedding was the subject of gossip. Pam had counted the wedding cash out and announced she wanted a few more little honeymoon treats before they got back to normal. So they'd gone for a night at the dogs with a big party of family and friends, and come out of the stadium with not a lot more than their cab fare home.

That had been months ago now, but it was still causing arguments between them. In a way, Stephen wished his brother had never given him the money at all, for it had planted a seed of ambition in him that previously he'd failed to acknowledge, or nurture.

Robert had said nothing when he'd found out that Stephen had squandered his wedding present. He hadn't needed to: the look he'd given him had been witheringly explicit.

'I don't want to be rowing with you all the time neither,' Pam mumbled. 'I know I look a fright. Sorry I can't be more ... y'know ... attractive for you. I know you miss doing what we used to do...'

'Yeah...' Stephen sighed. He turned her fully towards him so he could insert a finger down her cleavage. 'Got this advantage though...' Before she'd got pregnant she'd been quite flat-chested; now she had a round heavy bosom and Stephen couldn't get enough of it. He put down the fish supper and growled a laugh. He roughly yanked open buttons and lowered his head to her warm swollen flesh. While he was occupied, Pam shuffled sideways and, one-handed, began removing the newspaper wrapping so she could get stuck into the chips before they got cold.

'You spoke to Jimmy last week.'

'Who told you that?'

'Don't matter who told me. I thought we agreed to give him a wide berth because he's trouble.'

'He's me father and if I want to speak to him, I will,' Stephen retorted. 'You pay me wages, you don't rule me life. Got them keys?'

It was five o'clock on a misty October morning and they were standing in the hallway of Rob's house. It had been arranged the previous week that Stephen would call by early and collect the keys to the warehouse next door to Rob's office, just off the Holloway Road. The place was stacked floor to ceiling with market-stall stock and Stephen's job today was to load stuff on to one of the vans and distribute it around London to be stashed away in smaller stores close to their various pitches.

Robert pulled several sets of keys out of his pockets and sorted through them before putting one on the table.

'Perhaps one day I'll get me own set, will I?' Stephen suggested sarcastically.

'Yeah ... it'll be the day you put your money where your mouth is,' Robert said quietly. 'Got anything else you want to say to me before you get off?'

Stephen shuffled uneasily before meeting his brother's dark stare. He could tell from that steady challenge that Rob had been told, or had guessed, what Jimmy and him had been talking about. He wouldn't put it past his father to have told Robert himself. Jimmy was itching to start trouble. He was also angling to get involved in the business and grab a share of the money. Stephen knew his father wasn't above getting him the sack so he could take his job if he thought Rob would wear it. Fortunately for Stephen, he knew Robert hated their father so much he wouldn't even slow down to piss on him if he was on fire.

'Yeah, I've got somethin' to say,' he suddenly blurted out. 'I want a rise. We got a baby due soon and I got things to buy. Pam's seen a pram she wants in Gamages...'

'And you're expecting me to pay for it? You got her pregnant.'

'I know I fucking got her pregnant!' Stephen snarled.

Previously, Robert hadn't been certain that his brother regretted getting himself tied down, he'd simply sensed it from his moodiness. Now he knew for sure, but curbed his urge to tell Stephen that it was his own stupid fault he'd got stuck with a woman who was greedy and selfish and would be a burden for life. He simply shook his head, dropping it back so he could scowl at the ceiling.

'You know you're already earning good money, don't you? You're getting more than any of the others.'

'Fuck me, is that a hardship for you?' Stephen shouted. 'I'm family, ain't I? Don't I deserve a bit of special treatment?'

'Yeah, and I deserve a bit of loyalty and extra effort. But you're no better at doing your job than Dave and Gil, are you? In fact, if anyone's going to slope off early, it's generally you.'

Stephen coloured. Pam had told him to have it out with Rob about getting a rise and a stake in the company, but now he wished he'd kept his mouth shut. 'So what are you saying?'

'I'm saying that, if you weren't my brother, you'd be out on your ear. That's what I'm saying. I'm also saying that if you'd put that money I give you to good use, you'd have made yourself a nice amount and could have been a junior partner. Then you'd have your own set of keys to the warehouse. Those radios and cameras made a good profit. Four hundred and fifty quid, and it was yours for the taking.' Rob came closer to him. 'But what I'm really saying is I wish you'd used the cash to piss off and set up on your own, 'cos I'm sick of you whining and sulking every fucking day. Ain't my fault you got forced into a marriage you don't want.'

'Well, give us the money again. A loan this time. I'll pay you back – and interest too,' Stephen hissed. 'Just give us another fuckin' chance and I'll be off quick as yer like.'

The brothers locked eyes, then Robert said, 'Right. Come back this evening and you can have a hundred as a loan, and your cards.'

Stephen swallowed and licked his lips, then he swiped the keys from the table and marched out.

SIX

'You're a sight for sore eyes, gel.'

Nellie Tucker swung round and looked the fellow up and down. He was standing in the gutter and Nellie thought that was where he deserved to be. She couldn't blame all her rotten luck on him, but neither had he ever been good for her. If she hadn't already heard on the grapevine that Jimmy Wild was back, she'd have struggled to recognise him, despite the fact they'd lived together on and off for over three years. Her eyes lingered on his craggy, caved-in cheek.

'You look a bit worse fer wear,' she remarked spitefully before walking on.

Jimmy's mouth narrowed as she blatantly cold-shouldered him. Though he hadn't seen her in over a decade, he'd been confident of soft-soaping Nellie just like he'd always done in the past. He needed to get some information from the cow, so couldn't let her slip away just yet. It had taken him several months to find her; she kept moving around London and was liable to turn up anywhere she could hook up with a ponce who'd put a roof over her head. By lucky chance he'd spotted her emerging from a tobacconist's in her old stamping ground near Finsbury Park.

He slouched behind her, hands in his pockets and a roll-up dangling from his mouth. A jaundiced eye assessed her plump rump and thick waist. She was dressed in cheap clothes and shoes that accentuated the fact she'd lost her shapely legs and her figure. Once she'd been a stunning blonde who'd pulled in a good few bob per punter, keeping them both in good times. Now she looked to be a brassy old bag who'd be lucky to get a couple of clients at chucking-out time.

'Piss off, Jimmy. Ain't got nuthin' to say to you no more,' she threw over her shoulder, aware he was following her. She lit a cigarette from the pack she'd just bought and sent the smoke from her first drag back at him too.

'Just thought you'd like to have a drink with me fer old time's sake,' Jimmy suggested softly. 'We was good together, you 'n' me. Thought about you a lot, y'know, gel, while we been apart.'

Nellie swung about and cocked her head so coarse blonde curls dangled over a stout shoulder. She had known handsome, strong fellows who had gone to war and come back looking as though they'd aged twenty years. Jimmy Wild had been handsome – his dark good looks had been what attracted her to him. He'd been strong too – there had been many occasions when she'd experienced first-hand the power behind one of his punches. Now he looked spindly of limb and bloated of belly, and she wouldn't have bet on him being able to battle his way out of a paper bag. As far as she knew, his physical disintegration had nothing to do with fighting for king and country. But she was curious to find out where he'd gone after his sudden disappearance and what he'd got up to.

After all, she'd been threatened with a prison sentence for aiding and abetting in his murder. 'Gonna take me fer a drink, are you?' she jeered. 'Who's paying? Me?' She started to cross the road, but at a leisurely pace that lured him to follow.

'You think I got no money?' Jimmy asked softly, walking by her side now. 'You don't know about my eldest boy then.' With deliberate nonchalance he pulled from his pocket a couple of bank notes he'd been putting by for the rent. He was a month in arrears, and old man Keane was already cutting up rough about it. Edie had refused to lay out any more for rent from her wages as a char. Faye was more inclined to buy her brothers stuff than bother keeping a roof over their heads. Last week the selfish little cow had bought Michael a pair of boots off Billy the totter and a few vests for the little 'un.

Nellie slanted a look at the pound notes and gave him a sly smile. Like most people who'd spent time in Campbell Bunk, she took an interest in those who'd risen above the squalor and disadvantage of their background and made something of themselves. She knew Rob Wild was getting rich. She also knew he hated his father – and her. She'd caused trouble between Jimmy and his late wife, but had shrugged off the guilt. Jimmy Wild would be a wrong 'un wherever he was and whoever he was with. But ... she turned her head away to conceal the calculating glint in her eyes ... she was between pimps, in need of some money, and definitely in need of a drink.

'So how's life been treating you, gel?' Jimmy took a swallow from his glass of ale and set the tankard back on the table.

'Better'n you, by the looks of things,' Nellie returned drily before emptying her glass of gin and orange in a couple of gulps.

Jimmy bit back a scathing response to her insult. She obviously didn't have a mirror about the place where she kipped. 'You always was a fine looker, Nel,' he said gamely. 'Had some good times 'cos of it, as I recall.'

'Gonna fill this up for me?' Nellie twirled her empty glass by its stem.

'Got a thirst on you then?'

'Yeah,' she said. 'Got a thirst most of the time these days.'

A few minutes later Jimmy was back and sliding on to the stool opposite her.

'Where you living now?' he asked abruptly.

'Where you living?' she countered, sipping slowly this time. She fished out the slice of lemon and sucked it before discarding it on the table.

'Back in The Bunk.'

'Shacked up?'

'Yeah. Edie's her name. She's all right, I suppose. Got stepkids too.'

'Christ! Didn't you get a bellyful of that first time round?'

'You not got no kids, Nellie?'

'Nah. Made sure of it three times, an' after that it never happened again, thank Gawd.'

'Any of 'em mine?' he asked blithely.

She shook her head, setting her bleached frizz jigging about her face.

‘Saul Bateman?’ Jimmy suggested, finally mentioning the fellow he had a burning need to know about.

‘What about him?’ Nellie snapped suspiciously, setting down her glass with a thump.

‘Just wondered if he’d made you get rid of one of his kids. You was seeing him for a while…’ He cast a resentful look on her from beneath his grey eyebrows. ‘Sleeping with him fer a good while before I caught you at it, weren’t you?’

‘Yeah,’ Nellie said, unrepentant. She glanced idly about the smoky environment, chuckling to herself at the memory. She was a working girl, for Christ’s sake, what the hell had Jimmy expected her to do when a bloke showed an interest in her? Have him round for tea?

‘Don’t suppose that flash bastard would have been too pleased to have a prossie’s brat cramping his style.’

‘Time I was off. Thanks fer the drink.’ Nellie pushed back her stool, ready to leave.

Jimmy caught her wrist. ‘Don’t go yet. Bleedin’ hell, we only just started. If two gins is yer limit you ain’t the gel I knew.’

‘I ain’t the gel you knew, but I’ll have another if you’re still in the chair.’ The temptation of free drink was already subduing Nellie’s suspicion he was after information about Bateman, and her indignation at being called a prossie. She might inwardly acknowledge what she was, but she resented anyone else pointing the finger. Especially some money-grabbing ponce like Jimmy Wild, she thought viciously as she watched him slope off towards the bar.

Jimmy's smile was slipping with every shuffling step he took. He hoped it wouldn't take more than a few gins before Nellie opened up enough to tell him what he needed to know. If he spent too much of his cash he'd be left with only a piddling amount to hand over to Keane's rent collector. The last thing he wanted was his landlord sending the boys round to turf them all out on the street.

'Where was you hidin' all them years then?' Nellie slurred halfway through her third drink. 'Weren't in France, was yer?'

'Me?' he drawled. 'You know me, Nel ... I was here there ... everywhere...' Jimmy smiled wonkily and stroked his fingertips on her slack hand, watching her closely. He was glad now he'd shelled out for a double and saved himself another trip to the bar.

'Fuckin' Scarlet Pimpernel was yer?' she giggled. She stuck an elbow on the table and leaned her chins on a cupped palm. 'Where was yer, Jim?'

'In hospital for a while,' he said carefully. 'Got injured and went to hospital; then after that moved about Kent. Got a job as a hospital porter...' His eyes closed to slits. 'Met Edie... Never mind that, though. Who've you been knocking about with, Nel?'

'You got injured?' Nellie's inquisitiveness wasn't to be put off. She'd got nothing new to tell him about herself; the past ten years had all been more or less the same, because she was more or less the same. She'd trust a man to treat her right because that's what he promised he'd do, only for him to go and do the dirty on her, same as her stepfather had done, back when she was just a kid and didn't know any better. 'What ... so you *did* fight in the war?' Nellie settled her jaw more firmly on her palm and waited for an answer. And waited. Just as she was about to repeat the question he gave her an answer.

'Was going to do me bit and enlist,' he lied. 'But got set about, so I couldn't.'

Nellie blinked bloodshot eyes at him. Somewhere in her befuddled brain remained a grain of caution, but curiosity got the better of her. 'Was it Saul done it to you?' she whispered, agog. 'I know you had a fight over me, but you was well enough to run off, as I recall. Weren't on yer last legs by no means – was you?'

Jimmy swigged from his glass. He could've done without being reminded of the night Saul Bateman had given him a good hiding and sent him running off like a whipped cur. It had been the knowledge that his cash cow had been stolen away, and the humiliation of being thrashed in front of Nellie, that had spawned the carnage that followed.

'I got questioned, you know,' Nellie hissed, breaking into Jimmy's brooding. 'D'you remember that copper, Ralph Franks, wot used to do the beat around The Bunk? Well, he come by wanting to know what happened between you and Saul that night. Didn't tell him nuthin'. Didn't want to get dragged into it.' She leaned across the table to whisper, 'But I heard a rumour that they was investigating a headless body that'd got dragged out o' the river. The dead bloke must've resembled you in some way, Jim, and after you disappeared, the police must've got information about the two of yers being in a bad scrap and thought Saul had murdered you.' Nellie slouched back in her chair. 'That's what I reckon, anyhow. 'Course Saul knew he hadn't done it but when he got wind they was after him, he scarpered to France. Bleeding hell, he's gonna cuss you when he finds out you ain't dead after all.' She widened her eyes at Jimmy before burying her nose in her glass and tipping back her head to drain it.

'He's still about then, is he?' Jimmy pounced. 'Where's he living?'

'Got injured terrible, he did.' Nellie shuddered at the memory. 'Couldn't believe what I was seeing when I clapped eyes on him for the first time after he got back,' she added. One of her wrists rotated weakly. 'Got all this side of his face scarred and puckered up, and lost sight in an eye too. Burns, it were.' She wiped away a tear; in her inebriated state she felt quite emotional about the fate of her handsome blond pimp who'd avoided arrest by escaping to France, only to return horribly disfigured.

Jimmy seemed unmoved by the gruesome fate of his erstwhile rival for Nellie's earnings, or to know that he'd once been written off as a headless corpse. 'So he's off the scene and tame now, I take it,' he suggested with a relieved beam.

'No, he ain't!' Nellie spluttered, eyes popping. 'He's worse'n ever he was. Bitter as hell about losing his looks, he is. He's one o' the lucky ones, though. Most poor sods that come back in his condition can't get work for love nor money.

Saul's done all right for himself. He got in with a fellow up west, name of Johnny Blake, who runs all the drinking clubs.' She twiddled the stem of her empty glass. 'This Blake geezer must've took pity on him when he got back and give him a job. Now Saul's his right-hand man. I hear Saul's right vicious; takes it out on other people, I suppose, 'cos he's so ugly.' Nellie shook her shaggy head. 'Not had no more to do with him, and don't want to neither,' she muttered.

Jimmy sat staring silently at her for a moment as though confounded. 'Shit!' was then ejected through his teeth.

'He ain't gonna be too happy, knowing you're back around,' Nellie repeated her warning. 'But fer believing you was murdered, he wouldn't have gone to France at all. He was right narked over it. I remember him ranting 'n' raving something chronic when he was getting ready to ship out. He thought he was safe; wouldn't be conscripted, what with him having a couple of kids ... though he never saw much of 'em, it's true.' She frowned at the pitted pub table then lifted her bleary eyes to Jimmy's. 'Bit like you. You never saw much of your'n, did you, Jim? Not if you could help it, any rate. Your eldest boy going to see you all right, is he?' she asked craftily. 'He's got a nice car, ain't he? Seen him in it, I have.'

Jimmy wasn't listening. Having got what he came for, he was already on his feet. The alarming information was churning his guts; he'd hoped that Saul Bateman had died in France. But he was back. And whereas in the old days he was just a second-rate hoodlum who could land the odd lucky punch, he'd got properly vicious and involved with the big boys.

''Ere!' Nellie wobbled her empty glass at him. 'What about this?'

Jimmy slung her a contemptuous look then, ignoring Nellie's raucous oath, barged through the dinnertime imbibers towards the door.

He walked swiftly along Holloway Road, head down and collar up, as though he feared Saul Bateman might even now be on the prowl. Sooner or later – perhaps six months from now, perhaps a year – Saul would hear on the grapevine that he was alive. Then he'd be after him, and Jimmy knew he'd not be as lucky next time. Not that Saul had been responsible for the beating and stabbing that had brought him so close to death. No ... he'd fallen foul of people far closer to home, and they'd pay eventually, he'd make sure of that. He snapped his head up as he caught a glimpse of someone he recognised. He crossed the road and tapped Stephen on the shoulder. 'All right, son?'

'I was, till I saw you.' Stephen swung away and continued assisting a fellow who was carrying some shabby chairs out of a house. Together they were loading them on to a handcart that already held a battered wardrobe and chest of drawers.

'What you doing?'

'What's it look like I'm fuckin' doin'?' Stephen snarled, not bothering to turn around.

'Didn't think Bobbie got involved in this sort of house clearance. Thought he dealt more in good stuff, like antiques. Bit beneath him, ain't it?' Jimmy cast a disdainful eye over the furniture.

'He won't get much fer that pile o' shit.'

'I've set up on me own. It's my pile o' shit,' Stephen forced out through his teeth. 'Now, if you don't mind, I'm busy.'

Jimmy blinked in surprise, took a step back, a shuttered expression on his face as he ruminated on that news. When he'd calculated the best way forward, he approached Stephen again. 'If you're starting up, son – and I'm glad you are, 'cos as I said to you once before, you've got a good head on your shoulders – then you could do with keeping all your profits in yer pocket and not payin' out wages.'

Sid Withers, the old fellow who'd been lashing the chairs to the cart, sent him a venomous look on hearing that.

'Ain't Bobbie had the decency to lend you one of his vans to shift this little lot?'

'Yeah, 'course he has, but I thought I'd use a handcart instead,' Stephen snapped sarcastically. 'Need the bleedin' exercise, don't I?'

Jimmy could tell that Stephen had been in a foul mood long before he stopped to talk to him. Obviously his youngest son was already regretting striking out on his own and giving up his regular pay. 'Selfish bleeder, your brother,' Jimmy muttered. 'You know why that is, don't you, Stevie? He knows you could be a serious rival once you get up 'n' running. Don't you let him hold you back; you just carry on workin' as hard as you can.' Aware his advice was being ignored, Jimmy tapped his son's shoulder again to get his attention.

Irritably Stephen swung about.

'Tell you what, Stevie,' Jimmy said, all help and sympathy. 'If you need a bit of a hand to get you going, just say the word and I'll give it yer.' A meek look followed his generous offer. 'I know I wasn't the best dad in the world...' He shuffled a bit. 'Didn't have a lot of patience when you was kids. I know I could've done things better – there, I admit it. So if you need a free pair of hands for a while to help move you on to better things, just come by and let me know and I'll do me best to make it up to yer.' He jerked his head at the old fellow who'd gone to fetch a box of pots and pans that had been dumped inside the doorway of the house. 'What you paying him? Whatever it is, you can put it in yer own pocket if you take me on.' As the fellow came closer, squinting suspiciously at Jimmy, Jimmy gave him an affable nod.

'What you got in there, mate? Old woman's after a decent saucepan. Clumsy cow's had the handle off'n ours.'

Stephen impatiently pulled a pot from the top of the box and thrust it at his father. 'Go on, shove off, will you, I've got work to do.'

'I can see that, son, so I'll leave yers be.' He took a step away then stopped and nodded disdain at a wormy table. 'Gotta start at the bottom, I suppose, if Bobbie won't give you no help. But you don't want to be doing this too long, do yer?' He patted a paternal hand on Stephen's shoulder. 'Good luck, son,' he sighed, and strolled on, saucepan swinging in his hand. Momentarily he'd forgotten about Saul Bateman, and Nellie, and the danger that might lie ahead. He was engrossed now in how he might turn the rift between his sons to his own advantage.

He knew he'd get nothing out of Bobbie; but Stevie was a different matter. His youngest had always been soft as shit and easy to manipulate. Stephen had his own concern up and running now, and Jimmy knew that he'd eventually manage to muscle in on it. It hadn't, after all, been a waste of time upping sticks in Kent and coming here.

Jimmy was whistling cheerily as he crossed the road, heading towards The Bunk; even without turning about to check, he knew he'd given Stevie food for thought, and he would be watching him.

SEVEN

'Got the rent?'

'It's been paid.' Edie had only opened the door an inch or two because she'd guessed the identity of the person hammering on it.

Despite his bulk, Podge Peters struck swift as a snake, wedging a large black boot on the threshold, preventing her slamming the door in his face.

'You owe six weeks and Mr Keane said to tell you he ain't waitin' no longer.'

'Me husband's paid it, you lying git.' Edie pulled open the door and thrust her head close to the shiny, moon face of the rent collector. 'You tryin' it on with me?' she blasted. ''Cos if you are,

I'll tell your Mr Keane that you're a thievin' toerag. What you done with me rent? Spent it on grub, you fat bastard?'

Podge propped a hefty fist on the doorjamb and raised his eyebrows, unmoved by her insults and accusations. He had heard it all before; residents in The Bunk had a repertoire of excuses as to why they couldn't pay, or how they already had paid. He continued his slack-mouthed chewing, staring at her. When she stuck up her chin and glared back he shoved away from his support to withdraw a black book from an inside pocket. He tapped the cover with a pencil drawn from behind a pink ear. 'If you'd paid it, luv, it'd be down in the book. Ain't down in the book. You ain't paid.'

A slight movement behind him caught Edie's eye, making her spring on to tiptoe. Over his shoulder she saw Jimmy at the top of the flight of stairs, stepping on to the landing. She also saw his expression change as he digested the scene in front of him. With no thought for her predicament, he silently retraced his steps and disappeared again.

Edie blinked and swallowed. She needed no explanation for her husband's furtiveness. The selfish, rotten spendthrift had again proved he couldn't be trusted with the rent money. When they'd lived in Kent he'd constantly blown the kitty. Though he'd swear on the kids' lives that he'd had his pocket picked down the market, or some such rubbish, she'd guessed he'd squandered the money drinking and backing losers. She'd backed a loser too, she understood that all right, and she bitterly rued the day she'd seen him pushing a broom in that hospital and brought herself to his notice by stopping and speaking to him.

She fished in her pinafore pocket and thrust some coins towards Podge. 'Here ... take that; it's all I got fer now. I'll settle up next week.'

Podge looked mournfully at the two half-crowns. 'That ain't gonna do it, luv.' He pocketed them anyhow.

'Mark it down in the book,' Edie screamed and whacked the notebook. 'See what I mean? You took me money, but ain't made a note. How do I know you ain't took it off me 'usband already and not ticked it off?'

''Cos I told you he ain't give it to me, that's how you know,' Podge threatened wearily. 'Now Jimmy Wild's been livin' around these parts on 'n' off for as long as I can remember, so he knows how it goes. But you're new, so I've been making exceptions for you – up to now. I reckon it's high time you toed the line. From now on you pay yer rent when it's due and you don't go round accusing yer landlord's agent, that's me, of telling lies, not if you don't want no trouble, that is.'

'What's the matter?'

The commotion had drawn Faye out of the back room to join her mother at the door.

'He says we ain't paid the rent for six weeks. Yer dad's paid it, I know he has,' Edie lied desperately, although a flicker of guilt in her eyes betrayed her.

'How much is it?' Faye asked quickly, her eyes on the sinister-looking black book in Podge's hand. She suppressed a feeling of nausea at the sweat marks from his fingers staining the edges.

Podge dragged his eyes away from Faye's stunning appearance and consulted his book, flipping pages this way and that. 'Nine shillin' a week by six weeks makes...'

'Two pounds fourteen shillings,' Faye said and looked in alarm at her mother.

'Yeah...' Podge agreed. 'That's what it makes, and if you lot want to be kipping here tomorrow you'd better pay up.'

Faye stared at her mother's profile until finally Edie turned and glanced sheepishly up at her.

'I've given him all I've got,' Edie quavered and jabbed a finger at his book. 'You can take that five bob off, 'n' all.'

'Two pounds nine shillin' then,' Podge said sourly before returning his attention to Faye.

'Well, darlin', you got anything to contribute?'

Faye turned an icy glare on him. It wasn't the first time she'd felt him mentally undressing her. Those tiny black eyes of his, set far back in folds of flushed, sweaty flesh, always made her skin crawl as they wandered over her body. She avoided opening the door to him on rent-collection day, but a couple of times she had seen him cocking his head to peer inside and catch a glimpse of her. Once he'd caught her eye he'd wink and twitch his head, indicating he wanted her to come over. Adam had once made a dash for the landing while the door was open and she'd had to squeeze past the obstruction of Podge's gross body to catch him. The feel of his blubbery flesh moulding about her had been repulsive, as had his fingers pinching her buttocks, forcing her against him.

‘Got any little bit extra, Faye, to help out?’ Edie hoarsely wheedled. ‘Reckon he means what he says; bailiffs’ll be round in the morning.’

‘Yeah, I mean wot I say,’ Podge stressed softly. His tongue slithered on his lips, wetting them as he waited.

‘Got anything…?’ Edie wheedled again.

‘Yes! All right! I heard you!’ Faye snapped beneath her breath at her mother, anger overtaking her anxiety. She’d already put in her share of the rent, and more, but if they were to stay put and keep a roof over their heads, she knew she must forfeit her precious five-pound note. ‘I’ll take a look and see what I can spare.’

‘I’ll just pop out ’n’ see if yer dad’s knocking about outside and can chip in.’ Edie was already heading along the landing. Her face was set in grim lines as she rushed down the rickety stairs. Ignoring Faye’s loud objection, she determinedly sped into the street. She swung her head, squinting into the fading light for a sight of him, then set off at a jog towards Seven Sisters Road. She was going to catch up with Jimmy if it killed her and then she’d give him what for.

‘So, what you got to offer me?’ Podge looked Faye up and down in a way that made her feel bilious. She knew exactly what he was after, and if she agreed she’d still have her money when he signed off the debt.

Colin Peters, better known as Podge to Bunk inhabitants, had been Mr Keane’s rent collector for almost a decade. In that time he’d been offered all sorts of inducements to fiddle the books and help desperate people stay housed a bit longer. Just a few days ago he'd been invited by a local brass to come in and take what he liked. To tempt him to agree, Connie Whitton had dropped her skirt by the open door then turned and sauntered off towards the dirty bed in her underwear. She was a pretty, full-bosomed blonde, and Podge knew he was fat and ugly. Women scoffed at him and his clumsy attempts to chat them up. Any chance offers of sex were welcomed, even though clearing their arrears that way invariably cost him more than ten minutes with a tart down Finsbury Park. But not all of the women were on the game, or even doing half-and-half. Nervous wives with nothing else to offer as payment would reluctantly allow him over the threshold then, when on their backs, try to peer over his shoulder, urging him to hurry up in case their old man turned up unexpectedly.

Now, as Podge stared at the luminous beauty of Faye Greaves, he felt blood pounding through his skull, making him feel dizzy with heat. Connie Whitton, attractive as she was, was a rough old sort compared to this girl. 'Can write all of it off, whole bleedin' lot y'know,' he whispered, winking. 'All you got to do, sweet'eart, is be nice to me just for a little while. Won't take long, promise. Be done before yer ma gets back.' He winked again, pulled out the two half-crowns that Edie had given him. Opening his palm, he offered them to her. 'Take them back 'n' all, if yer want. Go on,' he urged and stuck his damp, quivering palm closer to her face.

Faye took the coins, rubbing the moisture off

them on to her skirt with a grimace of disgust. 'Wait there.' She shut the door in his face, oblivious to his mounting excitement. A few minutes later she was back and offering him a five-pound note.

Podge stared at it, incredulity and disappointment crumpling his expression. 'Where'd you get that?'

'None of your business. Have you got change?'

''Course I've got bleedin' change,' he muttered as he delved into his money pouch and brought out a handful of silver and a couple of pound notes. Having counted out the right amount, he tipped the cash into her upturned palm and sulkily turned to go.

'Haven't you forgotten something?'

Optimism lifted his drooping jowls as he bounded back.

'Write it down in the book and I'll sign it.' Faye nodded at the place where he'd pocketed the little ledger.

Meekly he did as he was told and Faye signed next to the amount.

'Seen Jim about, have yer?'

Beattie Evans shook her head and turned to watch her visibly irate neighbour pound on up the road. 'Could be in the Duke,' Beattie yelled after Edie. 'You should kick him into touch now, luv, if you've got any sense,' Beattie muttered beneath her breath as she headed on home with the bread and jam for her tea clutched to her chest.

She'd known Jimmy for decades; she'd seen his

first wife and his fancy pieces sporting the bruises he'd given to them. Sooner or later this one too would have enough of his womanising and gambling, and get his dander up by telling him so. So far, Beattie hadn't noticed any damage on Edie Greaves, or any of her kids. She wondered if she should hang about outside a while and see if today might be the day Edie got a taste of Jimmy's vicious streak. The woman looked as though she was at the end of her tether and out for a fight. Beattie shook her head to herself. She'd seen Jimmy's stepchildren about the place and thought them lovely kids. They were all polite, and such good lookers with their blue eyes and fair hair. Not like the rough tykes she was used to living amongst. That little Adam reminded her of an angel with his blond curls and chubby, rosy cheeks. Beattie inwardly shuddered at the thought of such innocence at the mercy of Jimmy Wild on a rampage. She stopped by her door and looked up the street. There was no sign of Edie or Jimmy and, as her stomach grumbled, she gave up on the idea of loitering in the hope of a bit of drama and gossip and went in to have her tea.

Edie spotted Tilly Keiver at the same time as Tilly noticed her puffing along the pavement. They had been living in close proximity for many months now and, although they'd never had a proper conversation, early hostilities had thawed enough for them to exchange a curt nod and a grunted greeting when they passed in the Street. As for Jimmy, Tilly religiously ignored him whenever he tried to put himself in her way.

'Somethin' up?' Tilly barked out as Edie came level with her in Fonthill Road. Tilly could tell that Edie was on a mission and itching to spar with someone. It didn't take much thought to come up with who that person might be.

Edie came to a halt and massaged her aching ribs. She had a stitch from racing along without stopping, but she was determined to find Jimmy while her anger was still red-hot. She'd had enough and was going to tell him so. She was sick of his lies and his threats. She'd call his bluff, chuck him out, and see if he'd really tell Faye and Michael all about when he'd been a porter in that hospital in Kent. But even as Edie thought it, tears blurred her vision at them finding out the awful truth and her courage ebbed away. She turned her head from Matilda to scrub at her watery eyes and try to calm herself down. They might be living together as man and wife, she reminded herself, but at least she'd never taken the trip to the Town Hall with Jimmy to make it formal. There'd come a time when she'd offload him, she vowed to herself, but for now getting the rent out of him was her priority. After that she'd nag him till he found regular employment.

Apart from a day here and there helping out on market stalls, or doing a bit of sweeping up down the railway yard, he'd done nothing in the way of work since the day they moved into Campbell Road back in June. He was living off her and Faye, and she was sick of defending him when her daughter told her he was a useless parasite. What few bob he did pull in, he kept to himself for his booze and snout. Well, she was done with that! It was high time he made a proper contribution.

'After Jimmy,' Edie panted when she'd sufficient breath to do so. 'Seen him?'

'Yeah, I seen him,' Matilda said.

'Where is he?'

'You sure you want to go after him, in that temper?'

'What's it to you?' Edie snapped.

Matilda shrugged and made to walk on, then hesitated. 'Just doin' you a favour, that's all. If you'd seen the state of me sister every time she had it out with him when he were boozed-up and she were irate, you'd turn about now and head back home to yer kids.' Tilly cocked her head. 'You've got a little 'un to think about.' Matilda gave a sage nod. 'Wait till the nasty bastard's sobered up, or he might just let his fists fly in all directions.'

'They ain't his kids. He wouldn't touch the kids.'

'You'd better hope not. But I reckon he's whacked you in the past,' Tilly said in a knowing tone.

Edie coloured spontaneously on hearing that. But she didn't lie or defend him. 'He wouldn't dare smack me kids,' was all she muttered.

'Hope you're right,' Tilly said, and set off down the Street.

After a moment Edie sprinted after her and caught at her arm. 'It was a mistake getting in with him, I know that now. I'm just waiting fer the right time to kick him out. Or if he won't go, I'll be leaving.' She dropped her chin to hide the shine in her eyes. 'Seen him go in a pub, have you? Is that how you know he's likely to be pissed?'

Matilda gave a single nod.

'Might've guessed that's where the rent money's gone. He'd keep it safe, he said. Should never have let him get me into a stupid routine of handin' over most o' me wages to him every week, 'cos–'

''Cos now he won't let you stop,' Matilda finished for her. 'He were the same with me sister Fran. He wouldn't never let the poor cow keep a penny for herself.'

'Now we owe six weeks and the rent collector says we're gonna be evicted.' Edie ran a finger swiftly under her weeping nose. 'I've left me daughter trying to sweet-talk Podge Peters while I find Jimmy and try 'n' get some money off him, if he ain't already run through the lot, that is.'

'He ain't never going to change, you know that, don't yer?' Tilly's mouth skewed into a travesty of a smile. 'Waiting for the right time to kick him out, are you? Heard the same thing so many times off me sister, God rest her – that's when she could get a few words out through her thick lips, of course. Right time's now, Edie...' Matilda noticed that Edie's gaze was fixed over her shoulder.

'Here he is,' Edie spat. 'I'm gonna have 'im.'

Jimmy's eyes narrowed. Through tightening lips he muttered a curse, but he sauntered on as though unperturbed by the scene that met his eyes. Matilda bloody Keiver was trouble, as far as he was concerned. She loathed him, and with good reason, he had to give her that. But the last thing he wanted was for her to be dripping poison in his missus's ear. He speeded up towards them, a winning smile stretching his mouth. As he saw Edie striding towards him, snarling, he drew from his pocket the money he'd just blagged. He'd had a feeling for a while now that Edie was ready to pack his bags for him and tell him to do his worst. Just now it suited him to stick around, so he knew he'd need to keep her sweet and that meant keeping his lip buttoned.

'There y'are, luv,' he said in a martyred tone. 'Got the rent money. I saw you was havin' a hard time of it with Podge, so did what I had to do to get the cash back. Stevie ain't happy, but you and the family come first and that's that.' He folded her fingers over the three pound notes he'd just placed on her palm, then patted them.

Edie's jaw clacked shut and she gawped at her hand. While she was still too dazed to resist, Jimmy steered her about and urged her to walk on with him. Arm in arm, they approached Tilly Keiver.

Tilly recognised the crowing triumph on his face as he got closer. But the way his lips had flattened on clenched teeth let her know he wasn't as cocksure as he'd like to make out.

She'd seen him when she was coming off her shift, charring for a client in Holloway Road, heading into the Nag's Head pub with Nellie Tucker. It had come as no surprise to see them looking cosy; Nellie was going downhill and needed a pimp, and Jimmy was always on the lookout for a free ride. She reckoned it was inevitable that sooner or later they'd be drawn back together. He hadn't noticed her watching, but it didn't seem like he cared if anyone spotted him. But then Jimmy Wild always had been one to shit on his own doorstep.

'What d'you mean, Stephen had it? What you goin' on about?' Edie finally blurted out, waving the notes beneath Jimmy's nose but making sure to keep a tight hold on the money. 'What you doing, givin' our rent to yer son, anyhow?'

Jimmy patted her fingers, which were gripping his arm. 'Was investing it, Edie. Got some good news for you.' He glanced up as Tilly swung about with a harsh laugh and strode on.

'Good news?' Edie snorted, but managed a wry twitch of the lips. 'That'll be a first. Let's have it.'

'Yeah,' Jimmy said, more relaxed now his nemesis was putting distance between them. 'Unusual, ain't it, for us to be lucky?' he continued chirpily. 'Stevie's setting up on his own. And I reckon we're gonna profit from it too. He's got his own business going. In competition with Bobbie, he is – and you know how well *he's* done for 'imself.'

'Yeah?' Edie sounded dubious. 'And how does any of it help us? And how does it explain you giving him our rent money?'

'Well, if you'd shut up for a minute, I'd tell you.' Her questions were starting to irritate him. He was making it up as he went along and needed a minute or two to get things straight in his mind. 'Stevie's given me a job. Might get to be a partner in the firm pretty soon.'

Edie gawped up at Jimmy's profile. An incipient smile withered away. 'So ... if he's set up, and giving you a job, how come you had to give him our rent money?' she asked suspiciously.

'Bit of a cash-flow problem, that's all,' Jimmy fluently lied. 'He just needed a few quid to pay for some stock he'd bought and couldn't get home to get the money in time. Now I got like a proper interest in him making good profits, I lent him the money. I knew he'd give it back with a bit of interest, see.' He gave her fingers a playful tickle. He could tell that he was winning her over and pressed home his advantage: 'I come back earlier to share the good news with you, didn't I? Then I saw Podge standing there, so took meself off quick 'cos I knew what he'd be after. Didn't want you getting a hard time. Don't deserve it, gel, do you? So I just whipped back to Stephen and got me cash back.'

'How d'you do that, if he'd got his stock then?' Edie interrogated. 'Didn't he do the deal after all?'

'All the stuff were on the cart by then anyhow, so the fellow would've had a fight on his hands getting his furniture took back inside.' Jimmy was done with telling his tale. He was getting properly narked now, and if Edie asked one more stupid question he'd make her regret it. 'Look, I told you what I done. You keep goin' on about me getting work, so now I got work lined up with me son. And still yer nagging me all the bleedin' time.' He withdrew his arm from hers and roughly pushed her away. 'I'm goin' off down the Duke for a bit o' peace 'n' quiet.'

'Jim...' Edie called apologetically, trotting after him to thread her arm through his again. 'Didn't mean to nag, y'know, it's just that ... well, that slimy Podge said we'd be evicted tomorrow if we didn't pay up. Left poor old Faye with him, I did, and you know how the dirty bleeder is around the girls.'

'Did yer now?' Jimmy said with a sly look. 'Don't suppose he complained about that.' His top lip curled. 'Fat git's probably still there then, coppin' an eyeful while he waits for his money.'

EIGHT

'What's that? You after paying the next six weeks up front?'

'What you on about?' Edie whipped back the three banknotes she'd been holding out.

Jimmy had been hanging about in the background, hands in pockets, dog-end dangling from his lips, leaving Edie to do the necessary with Podge. The rent collector had just been emerging from a house in Campbell Road when they'd crossed paths. The sight of him wobbling towards them had made Jimmy again cuss under his breath. He'd been hoping that Podge might have given up trying to get into his prim step-daughter's knickers and instead gone off for a feed. Now that hope was dashed. He'd been counting on returning the three pounds he'd borrowed by Friday dinnertime. If he was late, he knew Lenny would be round like a shot to collect the money.

'You trying to be funny?' Edie accused Podge. 'Pay up front, indeed! Just mark off what we owe in the book and don't forget neither that I give you five bob earlier.'

'Yer daughter's paid up,' Podge muttered, shoving past her on his way to the next doorway.

Jimmy's feigned nonchalance collapsed; he exchanged a startled look with Edie. Shock and revulsion deepened the lines in Edie's face; Jimmy looked decidedly thoughtful.

'What d'you mean, me daughter's paid up?' Edie charged after Podge. 'You wanted two pound nine shillin'. She never had all of that, I know.'

'She had a five-pound note,' Podge informed. He swung about to taunt nastily, 'Wanna see it?' He dragged a note out of his leather pouch and waved it, then nodded at the cash in Edie's hand: 'You can still give me that on account 'n' all, if you like.' He was still feeling narked at failing to bed her daughter. Nobody around these parts – especially not young women living with family – had that sort of cash to hand. After she'd sent him packing, he'd stomped down the stairs wondering where the little scrubber might have got it.

Edie gawped at the notes gripped in her fingers; slowly it dawned on her she had three pounds going spare. The miracle was soon whipped away. Jimmy, having silently come up beside her, snatched the cash and was loping up the street with it before she could react.

Now that the money was back in his hands, Jimmy was determined to put it to the use for which it had been intended without further ado. He'd borrowed off Len so he could set Nellie up. He hadn't told his pal the truth of the matter, of course. Neither had he got around to telling Nellie he was going to be looking after her again. But he knew she'd agree without much persuading. She looked to be close to rock bottom, living hand to mouth and in need of a bit of geeing up.

Jimmy planned to rent a cheap room for her down Finsbury Park way. If he could keep her off the gin and smarten her up a bit, perhaps get her to lose a bit of flab, he reckoned she'd manage to pull in a decent bit of money for both of them. She wasn't that old – early forties, he guessed – but she looked a decade more because she'd let herself go.

At the back of his mind niggled a thought and he tucked it away for later consideration. His stepdaughter had hidden away a five-pound note and he wanted to know how she'd managed to get that sort of cash in the first place.

Edie was pondering the same thing as she went up the stairs.

'Where d'you get five pounds from?' she barked at Faye before she was properly in the front room.

'Saved it.'

'Saved five pound from your wages?' Edie sounded incredulous. 'Only one way I know gels get that sort of money, 'n' it's off men with one thing on their minds.'

'I saved it.' Faye kept her eyes on the newspaper on the table. She turned over a page. Her mother might have hit the nail on the head. She had got the money off a man with one thing on his mind. What her mother didn't know, and neither did she, was whether at some time he'd turn as callous as his father and call in the debt.

'Well, you can give over the change.'

'Why should I? It's mine.'

''Cos if you had that sort of money you should've kept it, not given it to Podge.'

'And done what?' Faye asked quietly. 'Did you think I'd invite that creep in to settle the rent and stop us getting evicted?'

'Well, it wouldn't be the first time you've dropped your drawers, would it, miss?' Edie hissed. 'Least this time it'd be for a bleedin' good reason. And now you've got five-pound notes to give away, I ain't sure it was the only time, neither, that you've misbehaved.' Edie pressed her lips together. She regretted letting loose her tongue. Had she not been seething mad at allowing Jimmy to escape with the money, she probably wouldn't have been so spiteful. The toerag had no doubt taken the money back to his son to pay for old furniture, leaving them with nothing for their tea. Even the drop of milk left in the bottle had gone sour.

Faye blinked at her mother in shock. She hadn't been expecting *that* to be thrown at her when she'd just done them all a favour by paying off the rent arrears. Of course, she'd known her mother would demand an explanation for how she came to manage it. She'd prayed that Podge might be gone from the road when Edie returned. Then her mother would just think she'd scraped together the two pounds nine shillings. But even having that sum would have taken some explaining.

She'd been sitting with Adam, waiting for Edie to return so they could get tea ready. Now she closed the paper and stood up. Grabbing her jacket from where it had been hooked on the back of the door, she shoved her arms into it.

'Don't want tea,' she muttered. 'I'm going out.'

'Wouldn't get no tea, anyhow,' Edie shouted. 'Ain't nuthin' to have, is there, unless you get to the shop 'n' buy us all a bit of bread 'n' marge. You've got enough change outta that flyer, I take it?' she added sarcastically.

Faye stopped in the doorway, her face flushing angrily. 'And I take it you didn't find Jimmy?' she stormed. 'Or if you did, he's sent you packing with nothing, as usual. What a surprise!'

'Don't you use that tone with me! He wouldn't ever have got his foot in me door at all if it hadn't been fer you!' Edie bawled. 'If we'd stuck where we was in Erith instead of going to Dartford, we wouldn't never have come into contact with Jimmy Wild.'

'You've had plenty of time since to chuck him out!' Faye raged back.

Adam started to grizzle and suck his thumb. He was young enough to still be sensitive to angry voices. Michael was used to his mother and sister rowing about Jimmy and the lack of food and cash, but since they'd arrived in London their arguments had got much worse. He came in from the back room, where he'd been lounging on the bed waiting for something to eat, and asked wearily, 'We getting any tea, or not?'

'Not unless your sister buys us something from the shop. I give over all wot I had to Podge Peters, she knows that. She saw me give him me last two half-crowns.'

Michael stared at Faye. 'I'll run up the shop, if you like,' he offered hopefully. He was hungry. He'd eaten nothing since his free school dinner, and that hadn't been much: just thin soup and a wedge of bread.

Faye felt in her pocket for the few coins she'd put there earlier. The notes she'd got in change had gone straight back in their hiding place in the curtain. But now her mother knew about her nest egg, and Jimmy was sure to find out too, sooner or later, they'd never leave off till she'd put it all in the kitty. In fact, her mother would probably start searching for it the moment Faye went out the door. And if it were discovered, Jimmy would bully Edie until he had charge of it. Then he'd be the only one to benefit from what remained of his son's generosity. She'd sooner return the money than let Jimmy get his filthy fingers on it.

'I borrowed it,' Faye told her mother as she buttoned her coat. 'If you must know, I borrowed the money 'cos I'm sick of living in this dump with that lazy pig you're too weak to stand up to. I'm going to get enough together to get me own place.' She sighed. 'To save you the bother of searching for the notes I got in change, I can tell you now I've got them in me pocket and I'm giving them right back where I got them from. I'd sooner that than let Jimmy have the money.'

'We getting any tea or not?' Michael sounded increasingly pessimistic.

Faye pulled two silver shillings from her pocket and handed them to her brother. Then she went and picked up Adam and rocked him to and fro on her hip until he stopped crying.

'Don't give it back, dear,' Edie wheedled. Her eyelashes batted rapidly; she was tearfully aware that her daughter might indeed be het up enough to return what she'd borrowed. 'Sorry about what I said ... it's just ... you know how things are...'

'Yeah, I know all right,' Faye said bitterly. She dropped a kiss on Adam's silky curls then followed Michael towards the door.

'You got more'n enough there to get four stale loaves and marge and jam and milk and tea,' Edie instructed Michael, pointing a finger at him. 'And don't you let that old Smithie give you no brown loaves, neither, or you'll be takin' 'em straight back. If he's got any broken biscuits going, we'll have a bag or two of them 'n' all. Then bring us back all the change.'

Faye turned in the opposite direction to Michael. Although there were several shops dotted along Campbell Road, Michael had gone, as usual to Smithie's, the closest. She walked aimlessly towards Lennox Road, instinctively starting for her place of work even though the bakery was shut and dusk had long since fallen. She'd sooner be out in Campbell Road at night when the decrepit tenements that flanked the pavements were just shadows. But even though the extent of the street's decay was less evident after dark, the stench of it wasn't; after months of living in this slum, the mingling of damp and ordure still made Faye wrinkle her nose in disgust whenever she passed a particularly foul overflowing privy. 'How d'you find Campbell Road from Kent, dear?' one of Mr Travis's customers had asked her not long after she'd arrived. 'Just follow your nose,' had been Mr Travis's sour response.

Campbell Road was slashed in half by Paddington Street and on one corner stood a kip-house. Two fellows were lounging against the wall outside, and Faye could see the glow of their cigarettes and hear a rumble of conversation. They turned to boldly eye her up and down as she drew level, so she crossed the road and speeded up her pace to make it seem she had somewhere to go and wasn't aimlessly strolling. She dug her hands into her pockets and wondered whether to pop in the shop and buy Adam and Michael some liquorice before going home again. But the thought of returning was too depressing. She nodded at Beattie Evans, who'd just come out of the shop with a bag swinging in one hand. They both jumped as a man roared, but on turning in the direction of the noise they realised neither of them had started him off. Behind a grimy sheet that served as a curtain at the window of a nearby house, two silhouetted figures, one male, one female, were rigidly inclining towards one another. The woman suddenly tottered out of sight, having taken a blow. Beattie shook her head and raised her eyebrows at Faye before hurrying off towards home. Faye proceeded quickly in the opposite direction.

Little illumination came from the interiors of the houses, even though many windows had no covering strung across them at all. Most people who needed to inhabit a room here were reluctant to shell out for lamp fuel or an endless supply of candles. Instead they passed dreary evenings in muted light. Faye understood why so many of the inhabitants, unable to endure the grim boredom a moment longer, preferred to spend their evenings lingering over a cup of tea in a cafe, or supping a half of stout in one of the local pubs. The stark reality of life in The Bunk, now she was part of it, had softened her opinion of such people. Most, like her own unlucky family, were not wastrels and didn't deserve their fate. Jimmy Wild, on the other hand, was a wastrel. The knowledge that they were involved with such a man burned like acid in her guts.

She felt the lump in her throat thickening until a sob burst through it. She hadn't felt as low as this since the day they'd turned up in this dump. The five-pound note that Robert Wild had given her had symbolised her hope and determination and her future. She'd been sure that, so long as she kept it whole, safely and secretly tucked away, she'd manage to add to it and build her better life.

Having turned the corner into Lennox Road she walked on towards Stroud Green. She had taken a circuitous route to Travis's Bakery in Blackstock Road. In the mornings she'd take the quickest way, but she'd been anxious to avoid following her brother towards Seven Sisters Road, fearing his questions about how she'd managed to come by a five-pound note.

A couple of young fellows whistled and shouted at her from the opposite pavement. She recognised one of them as a youth Michael had been hanging around with, but she ignored them. It was inevitable that a lone woman out after dark would arouse unwanted attention, and she knew she ought to turn around but instead she put her head down and strode on, aware of hunger gnawing her belly. Bread and marge and broken biscuits didn't amount to much of a tea but it was better than nothing. She'd not eaten since midday, when Mr Travis had let her have a hot sausage roll, just out of the oven. She'd had to gobble it up quickly too, burning her mouth in the process, and with just a tepid cup of tea to wash it down because he'd cut her break to a few minutes this week.

For the last few weeks her boss had been busy baking for a wedding. Today he had been putting the final touches to a beautiful two-tier cake. He certainly knew how to do fancy icing and had let her try her hand at it. He'd not been pleased with her few stars and had impatiently scraped them away, clucking his tongue, before sending her back to supervise the shop. She'd been run off her feet serving alone for most of the day. Her friend Marge had called in sick earlier in the week and Faye reckoned she was about to jack it in. Marge had said she was tempted to go and work in the laundry. The old miser paid her so little Marge reckoned she might be quids in up to her armpits in dirty washing. The thought that dirty washing might one day be her fate made the lump in Faye's chest tighten and her eyes sting.

She'd had hopes of getting a good job. She'd dreamed of training as a clerk or secretary and working in an office in the City. She was bright; the teachers at her old school in Kent had told her that. But she'd missed a lot of schooling, looking after Michael when he was little so her widowed mother could work and keep them. When her mother remarried she'd been ten but, nice as he was, her stepfather had never had much money because he got little work due to his ill health. He'd been gassed in the war and suffered something awful from shortness of breath. As soon as she was old enough to leave school, Faye had been forced to get the first job offered to her: scullery maid in a big house. It had been the worst mistake of her life. Though her mother blamed her for what had followed, it had been Edie who'd forced her to take up the position...

The familiar clatter of the bell on the bakery door interrupted her thoughts. She jerked up her head, frowning and squinting into the dusk. Mr Travis was never usually this late going home; sometimes he followed her out of the door at six o'clock. She watched as the gas lamp burning at the kerb illuminated his dumpy figure emerging into the street, followed by another man whom she also recognised. The sight of his lean profile made a bittersweet ache clutch at her stomach.

Faye's step faltered as she recalled a time, months ago now, when she'd overheard a brief conversation between Mr Travis and Robert Wild. She never had found out what that was all about.

Robert had seen her and, dismissing her boss with a nod and brief handshake, he approached her at a leisurely pace. Mr Travis looked flustered, but he raised his hat to her before striding off in the opposite direction.

'Where you headed?'

'Nowhere. What were you doing in there with him at this time of night?' As soon as the words were out, Faye realised how impertinent she'd been. Whatever business her boss had with Robert Wild was between them and nothing to do with her. 'Sorry,' she mumbled. 'I shouldn't have asked ... it's nothing to do with me.'

''S'all right,' Robert said, pulling out a packet of Weights. He lit one and took a drag, careful to send smoke from the corner of his mouth, away from her. 'Travis took a loan from me, that's all. He'd sooner we did business when the shop's shut.'

Faye transferred her gaze to the disappearing figure of her boss. 'You're a moneylender?'

'Amongst other things.' His tone sounded sour as usual. He shot her a look. 'It wasn't a loan I gave you, don't worry.'

'I'm not,' Faye said, and gave a mirthless little laugh. 'Too late if you want it back now, anyhow.' It was a wistful mutter to the night and she hoped he'd not heard it. 'Perhaps you shouldn't have told me about your business with me boss. It's confidential, between the two of you, isn't it,' she blurted, hoping to distract him. He looked thoughtful, as though he'd guessed what had happened at home to make her aimlessly trudge the streets after dark.

'Yeah, it's confidential,' he finally said. 'But I trust you not to blab my business about. Would you?'

She shook her head quickly and to avoid his eye looked at the packet of cigarettes in his hand. 'Aren't you going to offer me one?'

'You don't smoke.'

'How d'you know whether I do or don't?' she returned sharply.

'Brothers just know these things about their sisters,' he intoned drily.

'Don't be ridiculous,' she mumbled.

'What's ridiculous about it?'

She made a bored huffing sound and made to step away, but he caught her arm, pulled her back, and crowded her against the shop window, barring her escape with an arm planted each side of her. 'Why's it ridiculous, Faye?'

She gazed up into his fierce, black eyes, the funny feeling in her guts increasing. 'Because if I really considered Jimmy Wild to be my father ... even my stepfather ... I'd run in front of your car again and hope you'd knock me down this time, that's why. My mum and your dad aren't married. I'm not your sister, or anything else. I'm nothing to do with any of you Wilds, thank God! I don't want to know any of you.'

'Yet you don't mind your brothers being my stepbrothers.'

She yanked at one of the arms imprisoning her. He flexed muscle, keeping her where she was. 'So

I'm good enough to know them, but not to know you. Why's that?'

Faye flung herself back against the glass and glared at him. 'Because if they end up living round here ... perhaps never getting away from this horrible dump ... they'll need looking after,' she burst out. 'I can't get enough together to take them with me straight away. They'll have to stay, and you'll have to see they're all right until I've got enough for all of us, 'cos if it's left to my mum, God knows what'll happen to them. She can't even get a farthing out of Jimmy. All she gets out of him is lies and punches to shut her up.'

Tears of exasperation glittered in her eyes and she tossed her head in temper. She hadn't wanted to let him know that her mother was a shameful, weak woman who'd let his parasite of a father get the better of her. A couple of times Faye had tried to intervene when Jimmy had been looming over her cowed, crying mother. But Edie had rounded on her, bawling at her to mind her own business. And so that was what Faye had done. She'd seen the panic in her mother's eyes and suspected that, in her own way, she was trying to protect them all. But she blamed her mother for letting the vile bully live with them in the first place, so her sympathy was thin. It was wearing thinner still with every day that passed.

The thought of going away and leaving Adam behind had been eating at her insides for months. She knew that she'd have to go alone at first. It was an impossible fantasy to suppose she'd be able to get the boys through school and keep the three of them housed and fed on her wages. If she were lucky enough to be taken on in an office where they'd train her, she'd earn very little to start with.

Rob had watched the searing emotions tautening and shaping her profile. Now he dropped his arms to his sides and flicked his cigarette butt to the ground. 'They're nothing to me,' he said, and strolled off to where he'd parked his car at the kerb.

He got in but didn't drive off and she saw the red dot of another cigarette lit in the dark interior. Faye started back the way she'd come. Before she'd made a few yards her steps were faltering. She went back and glared at the car, trying to subdue her pride and go over and get in. She knew that was what he was waiting there for. He was expecting her to back down. She shuffled agitatedly on the spot, hating him for what he was doing, making her humble herself and plead with him to look after the two people she cared most about. But there was nobody else to ask, except him. Finally she sped over and yanked open the door.

'Satisfied?' she snapped as she tumbled into the seat.

He looked at her and smiled slowly; it turned into a hoarse, scathing laugh. 'Yeah ... 'course. Everything's all right now.' He crashed the car into gear and it lurched forward.

'Where we going?'

'Fuck knows!' He swerved his head aside. 'Yeah, I know, filthy mouth.'

'At least you could apologise.'
'Sorry.'
'As though you meant it.'
'Don't push your luck.'
Faye swung her face and stared into the night. There'd been no humour in his tone, although she'd tried to ease the tension between them by teasingly reprimanding him. 'I want you to look out for Michael in particular. I think he's been getting into trouble with some local boys. My mum doesn't know about this, but the other day he came in with cigarettes in his pocket. He must have stolen them, 'cos he's not got the money to buy any. He hid them behind the wardrobe. He probably thought I hadn't seen them...' Her breathless voice tailed away and she frowned at his reflection in the glass. He continued smoking and steering as though he'd not even heard her. Frustration and anxiety bubbled in her chest until finally she could stand it no longer.
'You said you'd help me get away from here!' she burst out, and in exasperation her small fist punched his hand as it rested idle on the gear stick. 'You said, last time we spoke, that you'd give me more money if I wanted. You can keep your money – just help them. That's all I want.'
He whipped into a side street and came to such an abrupt stop she nearly shot off her seat.
'What about what I want?'
Faye flicked her chin from fingers that had just jerked it towards him.
'What else did I say?' he asked, staring straight ahead.
'I don't know,' Faye lied. 'Can't remember

every little thing, can I, just the important bits.'

'Yeah ... that's what I remember: the important bits. I said now you know where I live, come and see me.'

She felt her face heating and was glad of the darkness hiding her flushed complexion. She'd never been back to his house. She knew quite well what had prompted his invitation and the idea of it frightened her. 'Well, I've been busy. I'm seeing you now, aren't I?'

'I reckon it's time for cards on the table,' Robert said quietly, drumming the pack of Weights on the steering wheel.

'I've put mine on the table from the start,' Faye passionately insisted. 'I let you know straight away I hated it here ... hated your father. I didn't ask you to help me, you offered. It's you being awkward, not me. If you've said things you don't mean, offered me money you don't want me to have, you've only to say. I'm not bothered if we never see each other again.'

'Yeah, I know, that's the problem, because I definitely want to see a lot more of you. But you already know that, don't you.'

'I'm not going to sleep with you.'

It was as if her words had exploded the tension that had been building between them from the first day they'd met. There was a long moment of silence before Rob spoke again.

'Why not?'

'Because I'm not getting married ... not for a long time.'

'Well, that's a relief, neither am I. I don't want you to marry me, just to sleep with me.'

'I know that.'

'Now you've lost me.'

Faye swung her face to his, her eyes large and bright in her white complexion. 'And what about children?'

'I don't want any yet.'

'Neither did I ... yet,' Faye whispered.

Despite the shadows striping his features she could tell he was frowning, though she was unable to read his eyes. Then when he reached for her, dragged up her chin, she didn't need to look at him to realise he knew. A moment later he'd let her go and was searching again with shaking hands for his cigarettes.

He'd hoped, at first, she wasn't a virgin. They were bloody hard work and not usually worth the effort. From the start, something in her defiance and knowing ways had encouraged him to think she might have had a sweetheart in Kent who'd broken her in. She'd understood immediately why he was interested in her, but the longer she held back the more frustrated he'd become. He knew he wasn't bad looking and he kept himself trim and well groomed. Women around here always gave him the come-on. He never paid for sex; not openly, anyhow. In a roundabout way it cost him, but he'd no objection to shelling out for clothes, or dinners, or unpaid rent for women he'd fancied. He'd never let any of them move in with him, despite having implied to Faye that he had. Yet he'd have moved her in a long while ago, if she'd have come. Now he felt cheated; but he wasn't sure why. Then a nauseating possibility occurred to him and drove every other thought from his mind.

'Jimmy?'

Faye blinked in confusion; inwardly she was shocked to the core that she'd told him – a virtual stranger and Jimmy Wild's son – her precious secret. The significance behind his barked demand suddenly hit home, making bile rise in her throat. 'No! He's never touched me. God, no!'

'Someone back in Kent?' He extended the hand holding the cigarettes. 'Go on, take one. I bet you smoke, too, don't you.'

Hurt by his callous amusement, she knocked away his hand, scattering the contents of the pack on the floor. 'I don't smoke.'

'Who was it?'

Her lips clamped together and for a moment she remained undecided whether to reveal anything else; then it seemed pointless not to. 'My boss's son. I worked as a maid in a house ... it was my first job. I'd only been there a short while when he told me he'd fallen in love with me and wanted to marry me when I was old enough.' Her fingers, held in her lap, clenched tighter. 'I was fourteen, and he didn't, of course ... love me or want to marry me.' She snapped back her head. 'He was a bit like you, only younger and fair. But he was arrogant and had money and was nice and charming – till he couldn't get his own way.'

'Did he rape you?'

'Don't think so...' She turned her head and looked out into blackness. 'He said I'd led him on, saying I loved him and letting him kiss me... He probably thought I knew what he was doing to me...'

'You mean you didn't know?'

'I'm not talking about it any more,' Faye said shrilly. 'Don't ask...'

'Does Jimmy know about Adam?'

It was the first time he'd used her son's name and hearing it shattered her determination to tell him nothing else. Words started to spill out of her as though a dam inside her had broken. 'My mum promised me she'd never tell him. I made her promise not to tell anyone. Your father thinks Adam is Edie's. Everyone thinks that, even Michael. Anyhow, even if I hadn't asked her to keep quiet, she wouldn't ever say anything different 'cos she's too ashamed ... more ashamed than I am.' Again she entwined her stiff fingers in her lap. 'My stepdad .... my proper stepdad, a nice man he was,' she added wistfully, 'he'd got gassed in the war so wasn't ever very well and they weren't married long. But at least he came back from France ... not like my real dad. My dad didn't even come home.' She bit her lip to stop it trembling. 'My stepdad passed away six months before Adam was born. He never knew I was pregnant. Nor did my mum, at the time. I didn't show till almost the end.' Her voice tailed off, then sprang into life again. 'I thought she'd kill me the day I told her. She packed everything up and moved us to a different part of Kent, just so the old gossips in our neighbourhood couldn't start talking about us. By the time we arrived in Dartford, Mum had just been widowed again and she pretended the new baby was hers. Nobody thought any different. But she was so ashamed of me. She kept reminding me I was lucky she hadn't chucked me out on the streets. I know I was lucky too. Our neighbours in Kent disowned their daughter when she fell pregnant. She was their only child...' Pulling herself together, she finished on a defiant note: 'That's it, and I don't want anyone to know.'

In the heavy silence that followed, she sensed he was demanding an explanation as to why she'd told him in that case.

'I wish I hadn't told you.' She stared through the car window. 'But ... perhaps in a way I trust you, I don't know why. I suppose it's because I know you sometimes trust me and that's why you told me about lending my boss money. It's the same thing, isn't it?'

'It's nothing like it.' His eyes slammed on hers and when he next spoke his voice sounded flat. 'Believe me, you'll know what's happening to you this time. And if you fall again, I'll see you all right. You don't need to worry that I'd leave you in the lurch.'

'I've said I'm not getting married for a long while.'

'And I've said neither am I. There's ways and means of preventing it happening. I'll do my bit. But if you're unlucky and don't want to keep the kid this time, then there's an answer to that too.'

Their eyes held for a long moment.

'Like what?'

'Like doctors who don't mind doing a bit of moonlighting on the side. I'm not some tight-fisted git who'll send you to a backstreet abortionist, if that's what's worrying you.'

Spontaneously Faye let fly with a small hand. Although he ducked, her blow made contact and was hefty enough to send his head sideways. The sound of her strike seemed to reverberate for a long while, longer than it took for him to jerk his head around. She shrank back from that slit-eyed stare, tensing and wondering whether he would hit her back. She'd yet to find out just how much like his father he was. When he seemed about to move, she struck out again, before his hand had travelled an inch, battering against his arm to keep him at bay. Finally, exhausted, she forced out an answer: 'Abortionists don't worry me 'cos I won't ever need one. But thanks anyway,' she added in a voice of shaky sarcasm. She scrambled out of the car, leaving the door open, and raced away, not looking back.

NINE

'Mum's told us congratulations are in order for the new father.'

Alice and Bethany had been strolling towards Campbell Road to visit Matilda when they'd spotted Stephen loading some furniture into the back of a battered old van. They'd immediately crossed the road to speak to him; having heard earlier in the week that Pam had had the baby, they were eager to pass on their good wishes to Stevie on the birth of his son.

'Yeah ... thanks.' Stephen gave a faint smile before turning his attention back to a worm-eaten table.

'Got a name yet?' Bethany asked brightly, hiding her surprise at Stephen's lack of enthusiasm for the new arrival.

'Don't think Pam's made up her mind yet.' Stephen shrugged and blew into his cupped hands to warm them. It was mid December and very cold, despite a pale sun splintering through the clouds.

'Plenty of time to choose,' Alice said. She too had noticed something odd in her cousin's attitude. Most men would be delighted to talk about their first-born child, and perhaps have ready a few names of their own to suggest.

'See you're blooming,' Stephen turned the focus of the conversation on to Alice, making her blush.

She glanced down at her little bump beneath her winter coat. 'Got a long way to go yet,' she said, giving it a pat. 'Not due till about May.'

Bethany rocked the pram that held her daughter. 'Don't look at me, Stephen Wild. I've no news like that. I've got me hands full with Sally, thanks very much.'

'How old is she now?' Stephen asked chattily.

'Coming up to eleven months and starting to get on her feet. Now I need eyes in me backside to keep up with her.'

'How is Pam?'

'Pam all right?'

The sisters simultaneously chorused enquiries after Stephen's wife.

'Yeah, she's doin' all right; she's at her mum's. Had the kid there so her mum could help with the necessary. She's staying put for a few more days for a rest.' He rubbed at the bridge of his nose in a self-conscious way as uncharitable thoughts about his new family crept back into his mind. He wouldn't mind if Pam stayed there for a month or more. When he'd visited her yesterday after work, she'd done nothing but blub, and the boy had been screaming non-stop alongside her. His mother-in-law had looked at her wits end and asked him to take them both home. Luckily Stephen had walked rather than driven to Highgate. The old van he'd bought was a temperamental bugger and he hadn't managed to get it started at all yesterday. He'd said he'd call back for them later in the evening, but he hadn't. And he knew he'd avoid going there today, too.

'Best thing for her to get a good rest.' Bethany nodded sagely and looked about as though searching for an alternative topic of conversation.

'Coming over ours Christmas Day?' Alice came to everybody's rescue and changed the subject. For the past few years she'd been hosting a Christmas Day party for family at her little council house in Wood Green. Now that it was under two weeks away, she was checking up on numbers. Those people who couldn't make it for a roast-turkey dinner could come later for a supper of turkey sandwiches and pickles. There was always a host of sweet and savoury treats and a large, home-baked Christmas cake would take pride of place on the table. Everybody chipped in to help out with the work and the cost, especially for a bit of necessary Christmas spirit, sipped around the piano; the merry evening singsong invariably went on till the early hours of Boxing Day.

'Not sure yet,' Stephen answered evasively. 'Pam might have made arrangements with her people. But you know I'll come if I can. I haven't forgotten the good time we had last year.' He grinned, looking genuinely happy at last. 'Your Josh's brother can be a right card. Matthew's his name, isn't it?'

Alice nodded. 'Well, it'd be nice to see you, but don't worry if you can't make it...' Her voice faded as she saw who was ambling out of the house carrying a piano stool.

'Nice to see you two young ladies,' Jimmy called to his nieces. 'What's this about a Christmas knees-up?'

Alice turned away and, taking her sister's arm, immediately urged her to walk on.

''Bye, Stevie,' she called. 'If he thinks he's invited, he can think again.' Alice spoke to Bethany but loudly enough that her uncle would hear. 'He's never ever setting foot in a house of mine.'

'Don't know why Stevie's got involved with him,' Bethany commented quietly, peeking over her shoulder. 'He's only going to cause trouble.'

'I reckon he already *has* caused trouble and that's why Rob and Steve aren't getting on.' Alice sorrowfully shook her head. 'Those brothers have come through a lot together. Rob did his best to look after Stephen when Aunt Fran died, even though he wasn't much more than a kid himself at the time. If Jimmy hadn't turned up, I bet they'd still be rubbing along all right.' She flicked a frown back at father and son. 'Rob's done Stephen a lot of good turns. You've only to think back to the wedding he gave him to know that.'

'Mum reckons Pam's got a lot to do with them falling out 'cos she's lazy, and she wants what Stevie can't afford to buy her.'

Alice had also heard it said that Pam was too idle and greedy for her own good. 'They've not been married long,' Alice replied. 'It takes a while to get a nice home around you.'

'Not sure it's a nice home Pam's after,' Beth retorted. 'Last time I was round there on a visit with Mum the place looked a real mess. She'd got a flash handbag on the table but didn't have a drop of milk about the place to offer us a cup of tea. Stephen didn't look happy, I can tell you, when he turned up on his dinner break. She couldn't even scrape together a sandwich for him.'

'Well, I'm not sure they'd be married at all if Pam had managed to keep her knickers on.'

Beth gave her sister a scandalously amused smile. 'Shhh...' She put a finger to her lips. 'But I reckon you're right,' she whispered. 'We can all count, and unless that baby's premature he shouldn't be with us yet. Couldn't bring meself to ask Stevie how much he weighed.'

'Bet your life he was a porker. Even if he were a honeymoon baby, he'd not be due till the New Year,' Alice chuckled. A moment later her smile withered. 'But it's not right, Jimmy making things worse. He'll never change. He'll not let go of Stevie now he's got the chance to get a bit of money out of him for booze and bacca and a fancy woman.'

'Fancy woman? *Him?*' Beth wrinkled her nose

in disgust. 'He might have been a good-looking bloke when we were kids, but he ain't up to much any more.'

'Neither is Nellie Tucker ... *any more...'* Alice followed that up with a significant nod.

'No!' Beth breathed, shooting her sister a wide-eyed look.

'Mum saw them looking cosy together in Holloway Road.'

'Well, she don't learn then,' Beth announced pithily. 'I remember how he used to bash her up. They deserve each other!' she finished emphatically.

'I feel sorry for his new family,' Alice sighed. 'Edie Greaves must be kicking herself for getting hooked up with him. Her daughter, Faye, seems decent enough, and she's really pretty too. I've spoken to her a couple of times in the street.' Alice didn't disclose that on the first occasion they'd had a conversation Faye had offered her a five-pound note and asked her to return it to Rob. She recognised the courage it had taken for Faye to approach her that day and, although she trusted Bethany not to gossip about it, Alice knew she would be breaking an unspoken pact by telling anyone about the incident. 'And the little boy, Adam, is a real sweetie,' Alice resumed giving her opinion of the Greaves family. 'Lilian's taken a real shine to him and keeps asking to come over to see her nan so she can play with him again.'

Alice helped Beth get the pram over the threshold and into the dank hallway of their mother's house. Carefully Beth lifted her chunky-limbed daughter from her warm cocoon of shawls and sheets and they started up the stairs together.

'Jimmy is their dad, though, when all's said and done,' Beth carried on their conversation. 'I expect Stevie's given him a job out of loyalty.'

'He didn't exactly look as if he was setting the world alight, did he?' Alice mocked, recalling the sight of Jimmy shuffling along with a featherweight piece of furniture. 'Looked to me as though Stevie was the one doing all the real work.'

'Well, I suppose Jimmy is getting on a bit.'

'He's no older than Mum!' Alice remonstrated. 'I know he looks ancient, but I reckon he's about forty-four. Anyhow, he's never been any different. Dad always used to say that Jimmy Wild didn't have a good day's work in him. And he would've known. He used to take him painting and decorating with him all the time, just to keep Aunt Fran happy and get her a bit of money.'

The sisters had reached their mother's room and Alice tapped on the door, calling, 'Hope you've got that kettle on in there!'

'Where d'you get that?'

Michael spun about looking guilty, but he held on to the two pound notes scrunched in his fist.

Faye came further into the room and closed the door behind her before repeating her question in a very quiet voice.

Michael's eyes flicked involuntarily to the curtain and she knew immediately that he'd found her little nest egg ... or what had been left of it since she'd paid the rent arrears. She'd been sure her hidey-hole would remain undiscovered when she'd realised Edie and Jimmy had given up searching for it. For weeks after that incident with Podge she'd come home from work to find the mattress skew-whiff on the bed where somebody had shifted it. The wardrobe had been moved as well and carelessly shoved back at an angle to the wall. When no chaos ensued about Michael's hidden cigarettes, Faye realised her brother must have been cunning enough to read the signs and quickly move his treasure elsewhere. He'd also been smart enough to watch and wait and eventually locate her money. Faye extended a palm towards her brother. 'Give it here at once,' she ordered.

Her brother shook his head, looking defiant. 'Need it. Owe out more than this.' He deliberately stuck the money in his trouser pocket.

Suddenly Faye realised that her younger brother had got bigger and taller without her noticing. He was a youth now, and quite a strapping one for his eleven years. She knew, too, if she tried to take back her pound notes Michael would stop her in any way he could.

'Those are mine, Michael, you know they are,' she reasoned calmly, firmly. 'Give them back and I won't say anything about you stealing from me.'

'You ain't gonna say nuthin' anyhow,' he replied nastily. He jerked his head towards the connecting room. 'If they find out you've still got a stash, they'll have it off yer.' He backed away from her, looking belligerent. 'Mum might be daft enough to believe you'd give it back where it come from, but I knew you'd never do it.'

'You've been searching for it for a while, have you?' Faye asked tightly.

'Yeah ... I have. I'm sick of havin' no grub when you got money put by,' he ejected in a sullen hiss. 'Anyhow, I ain't lyin'; I owe somebody some money.'

'Give it back to me, you thief!' Faye shouted, her temper rising.

'You keep hollerin', they'll be in here,' Michael warned. 'If he finds out the money's been hid all this time, he'll have it. And I reckon you'll get a clump just for making him wait for it. He's been in here searching loads of times when you've been out at work, but he's never found it. *I* found it,' Michael added proudly, 'So, you might just as well let me have it as lose it to Jimmy.'

Faye lunged forward in a blind rage. The two pound notes were all that remained of her glimmering hope for a decent future and she knew their loss would be hard to bear. 'Give it here!' Her hands tore at his pocket, trying to delve into it, but he roughly shoved her away and darted past.

'Got to pay up or I'll get thumped.' It was all the apology she got for his thievery before he slipped out of the door.

Faye clutched at the wall to steady herself. He'd winded her, but when she'd regained her breath and balance she whipped out after him.

'You been arguing with Michael?' Edie demanded, seeing her daughter's flushed face and heaving chest. 'He's gawn tearing off out without sayin' a word.'

Jimmy looked up from the table and gave Faye

a malicious look. He'd still not forgiven her for being stupid enough to return the money she'd borrowed. In fact he wasn't sure the little cow had given it back. But she never went out on the town, or dressed herself up, so Jimmy was hard pressed to decide what his stepdaughter could have done with a couple of quid. Yet he was sure it had gone. He'd turned the back room inside out several times, even prising up the floorboards, without finding so much as a farthing.

Faye grabbed her coat and rushed towards the door with a jumbled explanation about going to the shop for something.

'What?' Her mother gawped at her disappearing figure.

On the corner of Paddington Street she saw Michael standing with a few other lads. When they saw her striding purposefully towards them they stopped talking and ambled further into the shadows cast by the kip-house, then stood watching her approach. Faye recognised two of the boys. They were both about Michael's age and usually walked with him to school in the mornings. One was Beattie Evans's nephew, Roderick. The other boy lived next door to Beattie and she believed the family were called Cummins. It was the tallest of Michael's friends who made her feel apprehensive. She didn't recognise him from around here and he looked old enough to be real trouble. But she didn't slow down and she kept her features grimly set into an expression she hoped would let them all know she meant business. She was determined to get her money back.

As she got closer, the big boy sauntered towards her, ready to confront her. A gas lamp illuminated a shadow of stubble on his jaw and she realised he was probably as old as she was. In his fist he had her pound notes. She held his stare steadily, suddenly realising he'd been one of the fellows who'd whistled at her in Blackstock Road on the evening she'd handed over to Podge Peters her precious five-pound note. It had been just before she'd seen Robert Wild emerge from the bakery with her boss. But any further memory of that traumatic meeting with Rob was pushed from her mind as the youth spoke to her.

'What d'you want, darlin'?' he asked cockily.

'My money.'

He pretended to look confused. 'How's that? What ... you looking to *me* to give *you* money? You'd need to come across first, luv.' He stretched out a hand and boldly stroked her breasts before sending a chortle back at his young friends.

Michael glared furiously at Faye. She could tell he was embarrassed, and now unsure whether to side with her or his pals.

'That's my money. Michael took it; now give it here.'

'Ain't your money, darlin''. It's mine.'

'Shut up,' Michael hissed at her. He rushed forward and shoved against her shoulder. 'Go home, go on. Leave us alone.'

'I think *you'd* better go home,' Faye returned, trying not to show that he'd hurt her. Her arm throbbed where his hand had landed.

'Give me that back or I'll have the police on you.' It was an impetuous threat and Faye regretted at once having used it. Nobody in this neighbourhood involved the coppers in their disputes, no matter how serious they might be.

'Get the law on me, would yer?' the youth muttered threateningly. 'It'd be the last thing you ever did, I can promise yer that.'

He gripped a handful of her thick, fair hair and twisted it so hard that Faye shrieked and instinctively swung out with a fist. It caught him on the cheek, making him grunt and reflexively punch her back. Faye was sent reeling back against the wall of the kip-house, where she collapsed clutching the side of her face.

'You'd better have a word with yer sister, Greavesie, 'n' tell her not to cause no more trouble, or you'll get trouble.' Having delivered his warning, the thug turned and loped off in the direction of Seven Sisters Road.

Through watery vision, Faye watched the other two boys jog across the street towards their homes leaving her alone with Michael. She pressed her cheekbone and moaned whilst wiping tears of pain and frustration from her eyes.

'See what you done?' Michael blasted at her in frustration. He crouched by her and gazed, shocked, at her blood-streaked face. 'Now you've landed us both in it, you stupid cow.'

He yanked at her arm to help her to her feet, but Faye, despite her injury, was still too furious with him to allow him near her. She staggered against brickwork, fumbling in her pocket for a handkerchief to mop the warm stickiness from her cheek.

Michael paced to and fro in agitation, peering

towards Seven Sisters as though expecting the lout to return and start on them both.

'What's his name?' Faye croaked then sniffed. 'The one who hit me ... what's his name?'

'Why d'you want to know that?' Michael immediately demanded, rushing back towards her. He stuck a threatening finger under her nose. 'Don't you go tellin' the police on him. It's yer own fault, anyhow. You hit him first, I saw you, and I'll say that 'n' all.' As though his conscience had overtaken his panic, he croaked, 'You all right?' He thumped a hand on his thigh in despair. 'Bleedin' hell, you look a fright. What we gonna say?' He gazed back at their house. 'Mum'll go spare, and Jimmy won't stop till he's had all the ins and outs.' He came and rested back against the wall with her, peering intently sideways at her damaged cheek. 'You could've fallen over. You could've been chasing me up the road and come off the kerb.'

'Did you steal my money to pay him for the cigarettes?'

'What?' Michael adopted a look of innocence, but a furtive glance to left and right betrayed him.

'I know you had cigarettes hidden in the back room. They were behind the wardrobe, so don't bother lying.' Feeling a little steadier, Faye took a couple of tentative steps. 'I thought you'd stolen them, but you've been getting him to buy them for you, haven't you?'

'You been spying on me?' Michael spat, irate. But he dropped his eyes to shield his thoughts from his sister's astute gaze. 'So what if I have had a crafty puff? Everyone has a smoke.'

'Not when they're eleven, they don't. And everyone doesn't steal money from their sister to get their fags,' Faye hissed back before beginning to gingerly walk home.

She'd already decided it would be better to pass her injury off as an accident than let her mother and Jimmy know what had gone on. She knew she was unlikely to get any sympathy if she told the truth. Firstly, they'd have been furious that she'd managed to keep her cash hidden from them, and secondly, the motto everybody round here lived by was that you never went looking for trouble 'cos it'd find you soon enough. She'd gone looking, and in her heart she knew she'd been an idiot. She'd set about recovering her money in an insanely reckless way. She'd had less chance of wrestling two pound notes off that bully than of starting a well-paid office job tomorrow.

TEN

'Goodness gracious!'

Mr Travis gawped at Faye's bruised face. Finally he burst out, 'What on earth has happened to you, my dear?'

'I tripped over, Mr Travis,' Faye lied, hoping this time she sounded convincing. So far she'd been obliged to fib to several people and all had avoided her eye whilst mumbling their sympathy for her *accident*.

Mr Travis shifted his gaze away too. He knew that she lived in Campbell Road amongst the dregs of North London society. It wasn't unusual to see people who lived in The Bunk coming into the shop sporting black eyes or other signs of violence on their person. But Faye Greaves had seemed different: a beauty with nice manners, and, as a new arrival to the area, he had given her the benefit of the doubt. His customers had appreciated being served by her, but now it seemed she might be showing her true colours ... or that of her family. She'd always been quite reticent about where she lived, and who lived there with her, but Mr Travis had been curious enough, having seen her talking with Rob Wild, to make a few enquiries. The last thing he'd wanted was one of his employees coming to hear of his mounting debts.

Mr Travis had thought their relationship might be romantic; Faye was such a pretty lass and Robert was known to be popular with the girls. But he'd discovered that Jimmy Wild was Faye's stepfather, so the young couple were, in a roundabout way, related. He'd felt more at ease then, knowing it unlikely that Robert would discuss his business with his stepsister.

Jimmy Wild's abusive nature was no secret to Mr Travis. He'd worked as his father's assistant in the bakery before taking over the business on the old man's death. In those days, the Wilds and their kin, the Keivers, were renowned as a bunch of ruffians best avoided. But of course he'd serve them as customers, selling them the stale loaves or misshapen buns that he'd discounted to shift.

He could recall seeing Wild's first wife, and his two sons, coming into the bakery bearing bruises, courtesy of Jimmy. Along with most people in the area, he'd been glad to hear of Jimmy's demise. But it seemed the old bully was not an easy man to put down.

The shop bell clattered, cutting into Mr Travis's musing. 'Gawd luv us!' he heard Mrs Dexter exclaim. 'What's happened to your lovely face, Faye?'

'I fell off the kerb when I was running along and bashed my cheek. Stupid of me,' Faye politely recited for the umpteenth time whilst buttoning her overall and keeping her bruises averted.

'Go out the back and see if the delivery boy's turned up yet,' Mr Travis snapped at her.

She did as she was told, knowing that the very thing she'd feared might happen when her boss saw the state of her, was about to happen. Mr Travis was going to send her home because she looked a fright and it was upsetting his customers. She hoped desperately that he wouldn't sack her. In a few days the worst of the swelling would subside, although she knew it might take a week or more before her complexion was properly back to normal. She couldn't afford to lose a week's money. She couldn't afford to lose a day's pay, for that matter – as her mother had pointed out when she'd got home with Michael yesterday evening.

They'd been expecting to be interrogated by Jimmy, but had found, to their relief, that he had gone out. They hadn't seen him this morning either. Wherever he'd gone, he hadn't returned by seven o'clock when she'd set off for work. It wasn't the first time he'd been out all night and Faye knew her mother was starting to get suspicious. Faye hoped and prayed he *had* got himself another woman. With luck, he might be preparing to move in with the stupid fool…

Edie had swallowed the tale that Faye had turned her ankle on the kerb and fallen over. Her mother knew that, since they'd arrived in The Bunk, she and her brother had been bickering, so it hadn't occurred to her to doubt that Faye had come a cropper while haring after Michael for giving her lip. Having applied a wet flannel to her daughter's cheek, and called her a clumsy so-and-so, Edie's first concern was what Mr Travis would make of it and how they would manage if he sent her packing as a result.

'You should go off home, my dear,' Mr Travis said, proving Faye's anxieties, and her mother's, well founded. He'd come in behind her, closing the door that led from the shop.

'I'm fine, really, Mr Travis,' Faye stammered, trying to smile in a way that was painless.

'No, you're not. And you can't serve in the shop looking like that!' he exclaimed. 'I'm sorry, Faye, but you'll have to go home. And if I can't persuade Marge to do your shifts until that's properly healed,' he jabbed his forehead at her purple profile, 'I'll need to advertise for someone new.' The sound of the shop bell made him start, and he reached for the door handle. Before disappearing back into the shop, he hissed at her, 'Go on, take yourself off home – and go out the back way.'

Faye put on her coat. She stood outside the

shop in the yard and cried silently. Even when the delivery boy turned up she couldn't stop the tears from streaming down her cheeks, stinging the cut on her face. She ignored his slack-jawed gawping and sank down on to her haunches. Turning her face against gritty brickwork she inwardly railed at the injustice of it.

'Saw that Greaves gel this morning,' Beattie Evans announced to Matilda by way of greeting. 'Should've seen the poor cow, Til. And there was me thinkin' that Jimmy might've changed his ways. Don't look like the brute has. Cor, Faye didn't half look a state.'

Matilda stopped in her tracks. 'Jimmy's whacked her?'

'Well, *she* says she bashed her face on the kerb when she fell over.' Beattie slid Matilda a significant look. 'I remember your Fran using *that* one...'

Matilda's eyes narrowed, but she resumed her brisk pace towards the bus stop. 'Ain't nuthin' to do with me no more, thank Gawd.'

'Bet you're glad o' that 'n' all,' Beattie responded.

'Never been gladder of anythin' in me life.' Matilda veered off to the left towards the bus queue.

'Wonder what his sons'll think when they find out he's bashing up his new family?' Beattie called after her.

Matilda had been wondering the same thing. She also knew that Alice had taken a bit of a shine to Edie's daughter and would be upset to hear this news. From the sound of it, this Faye was no pushover. And Jimmy didn't like women who answered back.

The people at the bus stop were stamping their feet and clapping gloved palms in an effort to keep warm on this frosty December morning. Tilly got on the end of the queue, so sunk in thought that she didn't hear the car horn tooting. It wasn't until her nephew wound down the window and offered her a lift that she was startled from her brooding. Tilly sauntered proudly forward and got into Rob's shiny Tourer.

'Where you off to, Aunt Til?'

'Got a new client over Marylebone way. Been charring there fer a few weeks. Not sure I'll keep it up. Bit of a trek, and the bus fare's a cost I could do without. Running late this morning, so I'm glad to see you.'

She gave him a sideways look, wondering whether to share what Beattie had just told her or to mind her own business. She decided to get it off her chest. Years ago when they were motherless teenagers, her sister's boys had been treated like her own sons. They were decent young fellows, even if Stephen had let himself down a bit by getting hooked up to a lazy slut. Matilda hadn't been happy to learn that he'd fallen out with Rob, or that he'd given his father work. Considering that, out of the two brothers, it had been Stephen who'd borne the brunt of Jimmy's beatings, Tilly was amazed he would even give his father the time of day. In her opinion, no good would come of them cosying up. Wherever Jimmy went, trouble was sure to follow – and Tilly reckoned Stevie had enough of that on his plate already, with that wife of his.

'Just heard from Beattie that Edie Greaves's daughter's going around with a black eye.'

Rob shot her a stare then manoeuvred crazily to the side of the road, ignoring the blasts from car horns as he found the kerb and pulled up.

'Jimmy's hit her?' Rob's savage black eyes were fixed on his aunt's face as he waited for her answer.

'Can't say for sure,' Matilda said fairly. 'According to Beattie, Faye reckons she fell over. She run into the poor cow this morning. And knowing what a miserable old git Travis is, he'll have something to say about it.'

Rob put the car back into gear and set off at such speed that his aunt was forced to cling to her seat and holler, ''Ere, steady on, Rob. I'd like to get to me lady in one piece, yer know.'

'What on earth's happened to you?'

Faye's teeth ground together. If she heard that question one more time today... She turned to see Alice Chaplin closing the door of a house she'd just walked past in Moray Road. She liked Alice and gave a small welcoming smile as the young woman hurried forward. Alice peered closely at her damaged face, and then her eyes squeezed shut in disbelief. Faye knew she was blaming Jimmy Wild for her injury, as had everybody else who'd stared at her that morning.

For hours she'd been walking slowly through the back streets huddled into her coat with the collar turned up to hide her blemished cheek, but now she was heading back towards Campbell Road. She hadn't wanted to go home and find Jimmy there. Once he saw her, he might guess people were pinning the blame on him and, with good reason, be properly narked. Faye began to trot out the usual excuse, then stopped and sighed. For some reason she didn't want to lie to Alice. She'd already told her a secret and she believed that confidence had never been betrayed. They might not yet be proper friends, but Faye trusted her nevertheless. 'Someone hit me,' she said quietly. 'It wasn't your uncle, so don't go blaming him.'

'Who was it?' Alice asked. She touched aside Faye's collar to get a better look at the injury. There followed a genuine hiss of shock and dismay.

'My brother Michael's in with a bad crowd,' Faye finally said.

'Your brother didn't do it?' Alice sounded angry.

Faye shook her head. 'It was somebody Michael's been hanging around with. He's about eighteen, I'd say. He certainly looks too old to be friendly with a bunch of school kids. I don't know his name. I'm sure he doesn't live in The Bunk. He was with Beattie Evans's nephew and one of the Cummins boys. I think all the younger ones have been messing around with cigarettes and this thug has taken advantage of them somehow. Michael's stolen my money to pay him off. I went after him and...' Faye shrugged, knowing it was unnecessary to explain further.

'I think I know who you mean,' Alice burst out. 'I've seen him a couple of times when I've been visiting Mum.' She widened her eyes expressively. 'His name's Donald Bateman. They're a rough lot, the Batemans. I don't know why he's hanging around here. I thought the lot of them had cleared off to South London years ago.'

'Well, I wish he'd take himself off back there,' Faye returned vehemently. 'I think I've lost me job over it,' she added gruffly. 'Old Mr Travis nearly had a fit when he saw the state of me. He's sent me home and told me not to come back till it's better. If Marge can't cover my shifts, he's getting somebody new in.'

'Never rains but it pours,' Alice commiserated softly. 'I'll walk a ways with you,' she added kindly, and slipped her hand through Faye's arm. 'Just been in to see me sister, Beth,' she continued conversationally. 'She's got a top room with her husband and little girl.' Alice jerked her head back to indicate the house from which she'd just emerged. 'Beth doesn't seem to mind sticking around here; I couldn't wait to get away.'

'That's what I want ... to get away. Cost's though, doesn't it?'

'Oh, yeah ... it certainly do,' Alice said ruefully. She cast a sideways look at Faye. 'But you'll do it, same as I did. I know you will.'

They stood quietly for a moment close to the turning into Campbell Road.

'Got to get the bus home to fetch Lilian from school. Too late to walk it.'

Faye nodded and faintly smiled farewell.

'If you want to talk ... you know, about things...' Faye nodded again. 'Yeah ... thanks,' she said, turning and walking slowly towards The Bunk.

A moment later Alice had caught up with her again.

'I'm having a bit of a party on Christmas afternoon. I'd like it if you came along, and your little brother too. Lilian talks about him a lot. She'd love to see him. 'Course I couldn't have Jimmy ... not him ... not after what's gone on, so it's not an invitation for everyone, you see...'

'He was dreadful to your aunt, wasn't he?' Faye said gently. 'It's all right, you don't have to say. I know what a brute he is. He's thumped my mum, so I know...'

Alice dropped her gaze to the pavement. 'You make sure you get away from him,' she said huskily, 'soon as you can.' She looked up with a smile. 'So I'd like it if you and Adam could come along for tea.'

'Well ... I ... umm...' Faye mumbled. She wanted desperately to accept, but, caught unawares, she wasn't sure how to respond until she'd spoken to her mother. Nothing much would take place in theirs over the Christmas holiday. If they managed to put a boiled bacon dinner on the table it would be a treat. But she felt guilty that her mother and Michael might feel left out if she went to a party. She just knew that at the Chaplins there would be good things to eat, and good company to enjoy, and she felt selfish and ashamed for longing to be part of it.

'No need to tell me yes or no,' Alice said. 'Just turn up. Mum'll let you have the address, or Rob will.'

ELEVEN

'He ain't here, I tell you.' Edie planted her fists on her hipbones and stuck up her chin. He might be a good-looking fellow with plenty of money; he might also be Jimmy's son, but he wasn't going to ride roughshod over her. She told him so. 'Don't think you can come round here throwing yer weight around, Robert Wild. I don't care who you think you are, you ain't bullyin' me.'

'That Jimmy's job, is it?' Rob remarked scathingly.

Edie coloured as that hit home. 'Come in and see, if you don't believe me. He ain't here. Ain't seen him since yesterday.'

'Count yerself lucky then, can't you,' Rob muttered, striding past her into the room. The little boy, Adam, was sitting up at the table, a cup of milky tea in front of him. He grinned as though he remembered him, and Robert's lips involuntarily twitched in response.

'See, he ain't here. I'm just waiting for me son ... me other son...' she corrected herself, 'to get back from school so's he can watch out fer the little 'un this afternoon. I've got me job to get to.'

Rob opened the door to the back room and looked into a space that was empty but for decrepit furniture. He'd spent twenty years of his life in just such a room. As he turned back, the door opened and Faye walked in. On seeing him she stopped dead with a stricken expression.

Edie gawped at her daughter. 'Early, ain't you? What you doing back?' Her face dropped. 'Oh ... don't tell me the bleeder's sent you home 'cos of how you look.' The lack of response told Edie she'd hit the nail right on the head. In her agitation she barely noticed that her daughter seemed to be staring at the wall in an effort to conceal her ugly injury from Rob Wild. 'Well, I'd better get meself off to work then,' Edie snapped. 'One of us needs to pull somethin' in, or we'll be getting turfed out by the bailiffs.' With that she stomped to the door and ripped her coat off the peg.

'What happened to you?'

'What are you doing here?'

The moment the door closed behind Edie they blurted out their questions simultaneously, voices rising in volume.

Rob strode towards her and angled his head to see her damaged profile as she tried to turn it from him. 'I said, what happened to you?'

'I fell over.'

He laughed, a vicious sound that sent a shiver through her. ''Course you did,' he agreed, softly. 'My mum used to fall over a lot. She'd trip down the stairs too, or crack her head on the wardrobe. Thing is, it was usually when she hadn't been drinking. Anyhow, it was all her own fault – clumsy cow.'

Faye felt her heart beating furiously. She was vain enough not to want him, of all people, to see her looking like this. Much as she despised

Jimmy Wild, she couldn't back a rumour that he was the one who'd set about her. But that hadn't stopped people who knew his reputation from jumping to that conclusion. She'd seen it in Beattie Evans's eyes, and Alice's.

'It wasn't your father ... he's not laid a finger on me.'

'Yeah ... I remember you told me that before.' His eyes veered to the boy, who was trying to get down from the table. Adam slid off the chair, bumping his chin in the process, and started to grizzle.

Faye picked up her son and his crying made her composure crumble. Tears welled in her eyes again, wetting her lashes before being blinked back. It had been hours since Mr Travis had sent her home. She'd been aimlessly tramping the cold streets before bumping into Alice Chaplin. Anything rather than come back here to face her mother's whining about what the loss of her earnings would mean.

'Oh, just piss off, will you,' Faye choked. 'It's not your father's fault, so you can go away with a clear conscience.' She looked up at him through bleary vision. 'You're itching for a reason to have a fight with him, aren't you?' She turned about, hugging Adam to her, burying her throbbing face in his silky hair. 'Well, I'm not going to give it to you, so go away.'

'Has Travis sacked you?'

'Don't know.' She choked a little laugh. 'Probably.'

'Do you still want the job?'

'Of course I do.'

She let him take Adam from her and set him down on the floor. As he took her arm and drew her closer, she dragged back. But he persisted, tugging her forward until she rested against him, trembling. One of his hands rose and tenderly cupped the damaged side of her face. 'If I find out you're lying, and someone did this to you, there'll be murders.'

'I'm not ... honest,' Faye mumbled and rested her weary forehead on his shoulder. His warmth and comfort were soon whipped away as Adam started to grizzle again and determinedly wedged himself between them.

Then Michael came in and swung a look between her and Rob. He swallowed and licked his lips nervously. He seemed about to turn and go out again but with a gruff mutter he rushed on through into the back room.

Faye recognised Rob's thoughtful look pinned to the closed door. She pivoted away from him before that penetrating gaze could be transferred to her. She'd sooner lie and say Jimmy was to blame for her injuries than embroil her brother in trouble that might be much more serious than she'd first thought.

'Bleedin' hell! What you done to yerself?' Jimmy was gawping at Faye from the threshold.

'I fell over and bashed meself on the pavement,' Faye muttered and, picking up Adam, she plonked him back at the table then took the chair next to him.

Any lingering suspicion of his father's guilt withered away as Rob saw genuine shock and amazement drop Jimmy's jaw.

'How's she come by them marks?' Jimmy turned his attention to his eldest son. Having inflicted similar damage on women over the years, he squinted judiciously at Rob's knuckles for scraped skin.

'That's what I'm here to find out,' Rob answered levelly. He'd immediately recognised the unsubtle accusation and the underlying hint of masculine pride. His father was pleased to think one of his boys might have taken after him and given a mouthy woman a smack to keep her in line.

'Yeah ... 'course, yer only here to see her.' Jimmy swung a leer between the young couple. 'Didn't think you'd be here visiting me, son.' He shrugged off his jacket. 'So, none the wiser then how she's come by that black eye?'

'You both deaf?' Faye cried. 'I just said: I tripped over in the street and bashed me cheek on the kerb.' She shoved back her chair and, swinging Adam into her arms, disappeared into the back room, slamming the door after her.

'Touchy, ain't she?' Jimmy stared at the closed door then settled a sidling look on his son. 'Got anything to say about yer interest in that direction, considering I'm her dad?'

'Yeah, I've got something to say: you're not her dad, and if I see one mark on her, or any of 'em, I'm gonna assume it was you. If the little 'un gets a grazed knee, I'm gonna think it's your fault and be back to lay you out. So you'd best make sure you take real good care of them.' He grunted a harsh laugh. 'Not easy for you, I know, but let's pretend you're capable of it ... eh?' He pushed past him towards the door, but before exiting the room he asked acidly, 'How's that old tart Nellie doing?'

Rob was gone before Jimmy could think of an answer to that one. His son had guessed what'd kept him away overnight, and he knew it wouldn't be long before Edie cottoned on too. So far she'd been none the wiser when he'd said that he was kipping at his pal's house because a gambling school was going on till late. She'd had a bit of a grumble, but shut up smartish when he'd pulled out a couple of half-crowns and said they were his winnings, and she could have them for the rent. It had been almost all of his commission from Nellie's earnings that night and he'd resented giving it up just to keep Edie sweet. He wasn't certain yet that he and Nellie were on an even keel and, until he was, he wasn't about to slacken his hold on Edie. Not when she might still come in useful. Jimmy thought it best to hedge his bets for the time being.

Nellie wasn't the Nellie of old. For a start, she was refusing to hand over the thick end of her pay to him, as she once had, for looking out for her. Last night she'd turned up less than a quid strolling the streets around Finsbury Park for a bit of business to take back to the room he'd rented for her. In desperation, Jimmy had swallowed the cost of a cab to get her up west in time for the theatres chucking out. She'd done a bit better with the gents around the side streets near Shaftesbury Avenue. Already he was losing patience with her lazy ways and itching to slap some sense into her. But he knew that, just as she was no longer the shivering slip of a girl she'd once been, he wasn't as fit and energetic these days. If he landed her one it was likely she'd hit him back. She was built like a shot-putter now and scraping the barrel for punters over the years had toughened her up. She'd not stopped drinking, or lost any weight, and he'd had to shell out for cosmetics and fancy clothes to try to disguise the fact she was nothing but a fat old bag.

Added to that irritation, and constantly at the back of his mind, was the threat that Saul Bateman presented. Nellie had clammed up on the subject and wouldn't tell him any more. Jimmy knew that she was frightened of Bateman and his associates; it only took a mention of his name to make her wince and whiten. As a result, Jimmy was becoming increasingly uneasy. He was desperate to know exactly where in London Bateman was operating so he could give him a wide berth. In the meantime it was tempting fate, venturing into London's heartland with Nellie, but that was where the money was. Even with stiff competition from the fresh young birds parading about Soho, a rough old boiler like Nellie could soon pull in enough to make the trip worthwhile. He cast a look at the back room. Considering the three kids were behind the door it seemed unusually quiet. He sat down at the table and gave the teapot a feel and a shake. It was lukewarm and virtually empty causing him to scowl. He rolled a smoke instead, frowning, as he turned his mind back to his stepdaughter's bruise. Something was going on but he'd let Edie sort that one out. He'd got enough on his plate.

Faye heard the door shut after Rob and quelled an urge to run after him and beg him to take her and Adam with him, whatever that might cost her.

Michael had heard the sound too and, knowing the coast was clear, he gave up his pretence of dozing on the mattress on the floor. He reared up on an elbow and demanded hoarsely, 'You told Jimmy's flash son about what went on?'

Faye shook her head.

'You better not've done 'n' all,' Michael growled, but relief was apparent in his voice. 'Goin' out ... hungry,' he mumbled. In a second he'd scrambled to his feet and slipped from the room.

Faye knew her brother was feeling guilty over what had happened, but Michael had yet to apologise, or even acknowledge that he was to blame. It was clear he was worried about any further repercussions that might ensue. Everybody hereabouts knew that you didn't upset a powerful man like Rob Wild. Faye had heard hints and whispers – mostly from Marge, who admitted to having a bit of a *pash* for him – that in the past Rob had seen off rivals who tried to encroach on his territory. Faye had deduced that he was the local heartthrob, and that he could be brutal if need be; she'd kept close-lipped about the fact that she wasn't immune to his charms. She didn't want to admit that to anyone ... even herself.

With a sigh she sat down on the bed with Adam on her lap. Her son turned to her and frowned at her face for a few moments before pinching the damage on her cheek as though he was curious about the colourful mark.

'Poor-poor,' she explained, flinching from his careless touch. When he'd started walking he'd taken tumbles and learned that, when something hurt, it was called being poorly. When he took a tumble, he'd display the sore part to her and insist he was poor-poor while holding out his arms to be comforted and picked up. For a moment he studied her with a serious expression on his face, then he leant forward and planted a moist, sweet-breathed mouth to her bruised cheek, mimicking the way she would kiss away his pain.

Faye hugged him tightly to her, racked with silent sobs, and only let go when he squealed angrily and fought to escape from her hungry grip. She lay down on the groaning bed and he settled beside her, oddly subdued, as though he'd adopted her melancholy mood.

Peeling plasterwork on the ceiling held her eyes as she thought back over the events that had brought her to this sorry state, and of how it all might end.

She realised she would probably need to find another job, and that wouldn't be easy with the dole queues growing every day. But even that grave concern couldn't chase away something else that had been niggling at her since her conversation with Alice Chaplin. She knew now the name of the youth who'd hit her, and that the Batemans were a rough handful. She realised with a pang that it wasn't just her brother she wanted to protect from their malice. If Rob went looking for revenge, Donald might not be the only Bateman he had to deal with.

Faye's impression of Donald was that he might be a thug, but he wasn't a very good one. The note of genuine alarm in Alice's voice when she'd spoken about the Batemans suggested that the clan included far more experienced villains in its number. The Keivers were known as people who could look after themselves; but for all that Rob was considered a fellow you didn't mess with, he wasn't a hardened criminal. Faye knew she'd never forgive herself if she stirred up trouble for Rob with people who might prove to be relentless, vicious enemies.

TWELVE

'You're welcome to come along with us tomorrow to Wood Green. It'll be me 'n' me fiancé going. Reg is his name. Me daughter Beth and her husband are setting off early for a turkey dinner, so there's plenty of room in the car for some more.' Matilda jammed her cold hands into her coat pockets. It was the first time she'd had a proper conversation with Faye Greaves. Usually they'd just nod or grunt as they passed in the street. But today Matilda had made a point of keeping a lookout for her. Alice had asked her to try to persuade Faye to come to her Christmas Day party.

'Thanks, that's nice of you,' Faye said, 'but I'm not sure what we're going to be up to yet...'

'It's Christmas Eve,' Tilly reminded her bluntly. 'Ain't got long now to make up yer mind, have you?' She gave her a half-smile. 'Can't believe anyone 'ud want to hang around Jimmy Wild on Christmas afternoon.'

'Me mum's got to.'

'Her choice, though, ain't he,' Matilda pointed out flatly. 'Anyhow, the little lad'll have a playmate in Lilian. She talks about him a lot, y'know.'

'He remembers her too,' Faye replied.

'Well, that's settled, then,' Matilda stated. 'After all, Christmas is for the kids, ain't it? And don't go fretting how to get back home. We won't be stopping past midnight; you'll get a lift back with us. So walk down to ours about four o'clock tomorrer. We'll be raring to go by then.'

'But...'

Matilda was already striding away into the late afternoon mist and just raised a hand in farewell.

Faye smiled. Deep down, she was pleased that the decision about the party had been made for her. She would love to go, and it would be such a treat for Adam to have fun with a friend. Midnight was late for her son to still be up ... but it was Christmas! She could perhaps get him to have a nap after his Christmas dinner if she laid down with him and cuddled him till he fell asleep.

It was to be a fair meal after all for them at home, not the miserable bacon knuckle she'd anticipated. She and Edie had clubbed together – even Jimmy had contributed a few bob without too much complaining – to buy a Christmas feast of chicken and sausage-meat stuffing and a little plum pudding for afters. Earlier that day Michael had lugged the coal pail, filled to the brim, from the merchants so that they'd be able to stoke up the temperamental cooking range first thing in the morning. The boys' stockings had been hidden away for months and she and Edie had been slowly filling them with sweets. That morning they'd secretly whipped them out and topped them up with some fruit and mixed nuts. As they'd worked together for a few minutes, chatting, a little bit of Christmas magic had warmed Faye, reminding her of days long ago when her dad had been alive. Michael had been a baby then and, if money had not been plentiful, she certainly didn't remember it being in such dreadfully short supply as now. But much had happened in the intervening years to set their family back. And she couldn't just blame fate, or her mother, for worsening their lot: she'd acted selfishly and stupidly too.

The best – and the worst – Christmas had been when her father had had leave from the war in France. She'd been excited for weeks at the prospect of seeing him and had rushed home each day after school to help her mum get everything perfect, ready to welcome him home. Each little preparation, whether decorating the house with holly or stirring the plum pudding, had been a thrilling treat. She could remember, too, sobbing her little heart out as she waved him goodbye at the railway station on that bitter January morning. As he walked away with his kitbag over a shoulder, she'd left her mum cradling Michael in her arms and run after him, skidding and sliding on the icy platform, and clung to his legs till he'd lifted her up and hugged her again. It had been the last time she'd ever seen him. Now all she and Michael had left was a photo of him in his uniform. Since they'd arrived in The Bunk, Michael frequently took it out of the drawer to stare at his father's face.

Faye shook off her sadness and turned to walk home. All she had to do now was break the news to her mother that after they'd eaten Christmas dinner she and Adam were off out and wouldn't be back till very late.

'You getting in or standing there all day?'

Faye had been stamping her feet to warm them, and rocking Adam to and fro in her arms to warm him, when a very familiar sleek car had turned the corner and drawn to a halt at the kerb. The passenger door had just been flung open from inside and she'd had that shouted at her instead of a proper greeting.

Faye put Adam on his feet then dipped down her head and gazed through the dusk at the driver. 'I thought ... that is, your aunt said we could go with her and her fiancé to Alice's.'

'You are going with them,' Rob said. 'Her 'n' Reg are getting a lift off me as well. Matilda told me she'd arranged for you to come with them at four o'clock. Sorry I'm a few minutes late. There's room in the car for everyone, so get in. They can have the back seat.'

Faye swallowed in embarrassment as she realised Matilda had dumped her and Adam on him at very short notice. 'Sorry ... I didn't know it'd be you... I thought her fiancé was to drive...' Her voice tailed away. 'Do you mind?' It was a stilted question.

'Yeah ... 'course...' he muttered drily. 'You know I can't stand the sight of you.'

His sarcasm thrust into Faye's mind a recurring anxiety. Once the drama of her getting injured had receded from her thoughts, she'd immediately started to fret about something else. She stared at the pavement, trying to come up with a way to ask him whether he'd betrayed her that didn't sound insulting. But since she'd rejected him – and in a manner that had definitely stung – he might have been careless about keeping her secret. She'd sooner go back home than turn up at the Chaplins and see people whispering behind their hands about her being Adam's mother.

Rob leaned back against the leather upholstery and watched her, an unyielding slant to his mouth. He wasn't about to make anything easy for her. If she'd something to say she could come right out and say it.

The stand-off was abruptly brought to an end. Wriggling his fingers free of hers, Adam, dressed in a smart sailor suit, climbed on to the passenger seat and sat there, little legs sticking straight out in front of him. A moment later Matilda and a companion could be seen ambling arm in arm and, judging by their flushed faces and boisterous manner, already full of Christmas cheer.

'Looks like those two have been having afters at the Duke,' Rob remarked, and his features softened into a smile.

Faye quickly slid on to the seat and manoeuvred Adam on to her lap, trying not to squash the little box of chocolates she'd bought the Chaplins as a thank you gift for inviting them. 'That's for Alice,' she mumbled as she let Rob take the box from her and slide it on to the dashboard out of harm's way.

She could feel his eyes on her profile, examining it. It was the first time they'd seen one another since she'd been hit a couple of weeks ago. She'd used a bit of face powder to camouflage her sallow cheek but knew, even in fading light, it wouldn't escape his eagle eyes.

'You look nice. Smell nice too.' His low-lidded eyes slipped over her, making her blush.

She'd put on her best coat and beneath it wore a pale blue velvet shift dress that late yesterday afternoon she'd haggled hard to get from a secondhand stall on Chapel Street market. After her talk with Tilly, she'd decided she'd treat herself to something pretty to wear to Alice's. It had been a wonderfully exciting last-minute shopping trip. It was the first new dress she'd had in ages. She'd bought Adam's little sailor suit from the same trader and reckoned she'd managed to get a bargain at seven and six for the two. The scent she wore had been a Christmas present from her boss. She'd sooner have received a small cash bonus than a gift, but was surprised and grateful to have got anything at all. The battered carton the scent came in had given away the fact it wasn't new, or bought for her. It had probably lain for some while, unwanted, in Mrs Travis's dressing-table drawer. But Rob's mention of her perfume had jogged her memory about something. Her eyes slipped sideways at him; she should say her piece quickly while they still had a little privacy. His aunt was almost on them.

'I know you helped me keep me job. I was going to come and see you and say thanks for putting in a word for me with Mr Travis. I didn't lose even a day's pay.'

He shrugged. 'Nothing to do with me.'

'Don't lie!' Her reprimand held a smile.

'I'll stop when you do.' His dark eyes darted back to her cheek, and he made a show of studying the fading bruise before challengingly meeting her gaze. 'Were you really going to come and see me?' Her silence tugged up a corner of his mouth. 'Right ... let's try this instead... Who hit you? Was it anything to do with your brother, Michael or his mates? You told me he's been stealing cigarettes. Anything to do with that?' He didn't get an answer, and he wasn't fooled by her bolshie look. Her nervousness only increased his suspicion that her brother was involved in some way.

Rob had been making a few discreet enquiries and had discovered that Michael Greaves and some friends had been making a nuisance of themselves outside the off licence, larking about and pestering people, trying to cadge cigarettes. Rob recalled doing much the same at that age – and worse – so hadn't felt a need to approach him and frighten him off too soon. If Michael was up to something more serious – and he'd looked guilty as hell when he'd seen him that day – he'd do better to find out exactly what had been going on before he weighed in and tore a strip off him.

Rob saw his aunt Matilda several times a week and always questioned her about what was happening with Jimmy and his family. If he'd heard about any of the kids going around with bruises he would have been round there like a shot. He knew Matilda had guessed he'd fallen for Faye, but she was keeping her thoughts to herself on the subject. Still, the constant worry over Faye's welfare – and he had to admit that the little kid was getting under his skin too – was making him irritable. 'You going to answer me?' he asked brusquely. 'And for Christ's sake don't tell me you fell over.'

Faye jerked up her head about to tell him to mind his own business when Adam suddenly pulled out of his pocket the toy engine she'd bought him as a present. Her son shoved the small wooden train under Rob's nose to show him, making him lean back to focus on it.

'That's nice. Who got you that then?'

'Mum,' he said, making Rob stab a look at Faye.

'We all got it for you, didn't we?' Faye burbled. 'Mum 'n' me 'n' Michael, 'cos it's Christmas Day and you've been a good boy, haven't you.' She was thankful that Adam had caused a distraction at that precise moment and prevented them bickering. She'd been preparing for another interrogation from Rob over her injury and had decided to stick with her original story. Michael had been as nice as pie to her once he'd been satisfied she'd not grassed him up. She desperately didn't want to get him into trouble now things had settled down a bit. She suspected he might be in enough of that already.

Adam slowly nodded his head. 'Been good...' he mumbled, wheeling the train back and forth on his knee.

'Been good, have you?' Rob dug in his pocket and found a pound note and handed it over to him. 'I didn't know what to get him,' he lied. He'd known all right. He'd done his Christmas shopping in Gamages and bought his newborn nephew a present of a large teddy bear to be delivered on Christmas Eve. He'd strolled up and down, looking at the splendid toys, knowing how thrilled he'd have been to have received a shiny spinning top or a set of colourful tin soldiers when he was Adam's age. But he'd bought nothing, knowing that even a kid's Christmas present wouldn't be safe from Jimmy when he needed a few bob for a drink or a smoke. He'd pawn it, or sell it off, without a second thought about breaking the boy's heart. Perhaps Edie too would stoop so low as to be able to hand over some cash on rent-collection day because the parasite she'd shacked up with was whoring or drinking away everything he had.

Adam automatically dropped the pound note on Faye's lap. Even when he received coins from kindly neighbours for sweets he knew now to offer them up. Edie was pleased that his angelic blond looks caused women to coo over him and press farthings into his hand. She'd relieve him of their generosity as soon as they were indoors.

'Buy him something ... sweets or something...'

'He doesn't need a pound's worth of sweets,' Faye returned huskily. 'A few pennies will do.'

'Well, get him clothes ... boots ... anything ... I don't know...'

'Have you told anyone about...?' The words that had been rotating in her brain began to tumble out, but the gist of her suspicion went unuttered. Matilda had yanked open the car door and bounced on to the back seat. She wriggled further in to let Reg sit beside her.

It was a long second later that Faye tore her eyes away from Rob's steady, flinty stare. He'd known what she was about to accuse him of and she could tell that he wasn't pleased she'd decided he couldn't be trusted after all.

'A happy Christmas to yers all,' Matilda boomed into the heavy atmosphere. With boozy bonhomie she leaned forward and ruffled Adam's blond curls, making him grin.

'That's a handsome little lad, so he is,' Reg announced in his Irish burr and settled back.

Alcoholic fumes bathed the car interior.

'No need to ask if you two have been having a good one,' Rob commented drily as he put the car in gear and pulled away.

THIRTEEN

'Did your mum mind about you coming here this afternoon?'

Faye cradled her glass between her palms. 'I was expecting her to, but she surprised me,' she told Alice. 'Her and Jimmy had already made other plans.' She took a tiny sip of sherry. 'One of your uncle's friends – Lenny, I think he's called – had asked them over for a bit of a drink after dinner. We weren't invited in any case. Mum said Lenny and his wife don't have any kids and Jimmy reckoned it'd be best if us lot stayed put at home.'

'That's nice!' Alice exclaimed. 'So you and your brothers would have been left stuck indoors.'

'Wouldn't have minded; it's a relief when he's not about.'

'I know what you mean,' Alice said gruffly. 'Once I was old enough to know the real Jimmy, I'd avoid him like the plague.' She brightened up. 'Shame your other brother is on his own though. You could have brought him along. I wouldn't have minded him coming, honest.'

'No; it's all right, really it is.' Faye circled a finger on the rim of her glass. 'He looked happy when he knew he was getting the place to himself. I wouldn't be surprised if he gets together with a few friends; or if he picks the chicken carcass clean.' She smiled. 'We had a good dinner. Anyhow, Michael and me are not exactly best pals at the moment.'

'Enough said on that score.'

Faye gave her hostess a grateful look. She knew it was Alice's way of reassuring her that she'd not broken her confidence.

'It's healed well. Can't see the mark at all,' Alice whispered kindly. 'And you look lovely in that dress. Where did you get it?'

'Chapel Street market ... secondhand.'

'I used to get all my stuff down there...' Alice paused, her thoughts already turned from pretty clothes. 'Have you told Rob the truth about what went on that day?' she asked in an undertone. She had a feeling that Rob might not be looking so carefree if he knew Faye's fading bruise was the result of a thug's punch. She gave her handsome cousin a smile, despite being aware she wasn't the one drawing his frequent glances. Rob was standing with a group of men, Stevie included, and Alice was glad the brothers seemed relaxed together, if not quite as chatty as they once would have been.

Faye shook her head. 'Don't want any trouble stirring up, just want to forget about it.'

'Rob likes you, y'know.' Seeing Faye's frown, Alice gave a reassuring chuckle. 'Oh, don't worry: he's not said a word to me. But I've got eyes in me head.'

'I think your cousin Rob likes quite a few girls.' Faye gave a rather wistful smile and reached down to Adam, playing on the floor in front of her. She and Alice were sitting on a small sofa in a crowded front room that was filled with savoury aromas and jovial people.

Lilian had a doll and a golliwog perched on a toy chair just in front of the sofa and her and Adam had been taking it in turns to bring them little biscuits or cakes from the delicious spread laid out in the dining room next door. Having offered up the food to the close-lipped toys, they would then giggle and gobble it themselves.

'I think Adam's had enough,' Faye said ruefully as she watched her son chewing icing lined with marzipan. He'd discarded the dark fruity cake on the plate. She took out her handkerchief and wiped clean his sticky fingers and mouth, making him squirm and mew. He was flushed, and felt hot, and she knew he might soon start to grizzle. 'I'll take Adam to the bathroom and give him a wash, if that's all right. He needs to cool down or he'll be a ratty so and so.'

At that moment a pretty, dark-haired teenager came and perched on the arm of the sofa close to Alice. Alice affectionately took hold of her youngest sister's fingers and gave them a squeeze. 'All right there, Little Luce?'

'I am, Al,' Lucy answered on a satiated sigh. 'I'm stuffed to the gills. Me 'n' Beth were just saying, we like your dress,' she told Faye. 'Right nice colour blue, that is.'

'Secondhand, down Chapel Street market,' Faye again explained.

'No...' Luce murmured in disbelief. 'Well, I reckon it came out of Bond Street first time round. It's a beauty, ain't it, Al?'

'I got a right bargain, I know.' Faye settled back,

smiling. She knew that the few sherries she'd downed had probably contributed to her feeling of contentment; but so had the company. Everybody had been kind and friendly and had fussed over Adam. Bethany and Lucy had treated her as though they'd known her for years and Alice's husband, Josh, had been attentive and made sure they had drinks and anything else they wanted. He came over now and placed a loving hand on his wife's head of dark hair.

'Matt's going to have a bash on the piano in a minute. And George,' he tilted his head towards Beth's husband, 'is going to borrow the banjo and have a go accompanying him.'

Alice got up, announcing briskly, 'Better get some turkey sandwiches made. A good singsong always gets everyone peckish. Fetch the pickles out of the pantry, will you, Josh, and make room for them on the table?'

'Can I help you with the sandwiches?' Faye asked, half-rising.

'No! You stay right there and finish your drink and enjoy yourself.' Alice turned back to add, 'The bathroom is right at the top of the stairs, first door you come to. And if little Adam wants a nap, just put him down on our bed next door.'

'Your little brother is a real cutie.' Lucy ruffled Adam's soft curls.

'He is most of the time,' Faye agreed wryly, 'But he looks as if he's brewing up a bit of a tantrum 'cos he's too hot.' She rose and lifted him on to his feet. 'I'm going to take him upstairs and give him a wash to cool him down. I suppose the time must be getting on.' She'd have liked to stay forever in this cosy house, but, at some point, she knew she'd have to ask Rob to take them back to Campbell Road.

'Oh, you can't go yet,' Lucy exclaimed. She had liked Faye as soon as they'd been introduced a few hours ago and didn't want her to leave early. 'Party's just getting started. Alice won't mind at all if you put him on her bed for a little kip. Just move all our coats out of the way.'

Faye negotiated a path through obliging people who jostled this way and that to help her get to the foot of the stairs.

Moments later, heads turned in the sitting room at the sound of a shrill, angry voice. 'Oh, for Chrissake – take him off me for a while, will you?' said Pam, bundling her son into her husband's arms. Little Christopher had been fretful since they'd arrived and hadn't quietened after she'd impatiently offered him his bottle. She'd just got back from trundling up and down the cul-de-sac in an effort to rock him back to sleep. That had seemed to work, but as soon as she'd parked the pram and started off in search of a drink, he'd woken and let out a yell, making her return to curse at him.

'Where you off to then?' Stevie scowled at his wife.

'Get something to eat,' Pam snapped.

'Reckon you've had enough,' he muttered under his breath, flicking a scornful glance at her plump rump.

She swung back, having heard his sarcasm. 'Yeah, 'n' I've seen how many light ales you've been tuckin' away 'n' all.'

'Been counting, have yer? Well, I've seen you necking sherry like it's the last bottle.'

Josh had been on the alert for signs of domestic strife, Alice having warned him that Stevie and his wife had decided to come after all, but would probably be sniping at one another. The whole family now knew things there definitely weren't right. Josh had noticed the unhappy couple drinking steadily and knew there was a danger things could turn rowdy. He bowled over with a plate of turkey sandwiches. 'Any takers?' he asked brightly.

'Thanks, Josh,' Pam slurred with a smile before her lips thinned in her husband's direction. She jerked up the sandwich at him. It could just as easily have been two fingers.

Their son squirmed and whimpered before letting out a shriek. Stevie shot out of his chair and began rocking the boy in his arms, looking harassed. The violent bouncing simply made Christopher's wails become louder.

'What's up with him?'

Stevie glanced sullenly at his brother, who'd come to stand in front of him. 'Fuck knows,' he muttered. 'He never stops crying. Don't think she feeds him properly.'

'Let's have a go then.' Rob could see that his brother was two parts pissed and hindering rather than helping with the child. Stevie gratefully relinquished his son and Rob took Christopher towards the window. His little face was scrunched up and ruby red. Despite it being December, a window had been opened to let a breath of air stir the close atmosphere. Rob wasn't sure if cooling him down had done the trick or whether the drop of beer he'd spilled on his hands earlier was keeping the little mite quiet. When he'd used a knuckle to stroke the boy's cheek, Christopher had pounced on it and was sucking insistently.

'Looks like you're a natural. Shame you're not his dad instead.'

Rob turned a long, expressionless look on Pam until the bold, flirtatious look in her eyes died.

'Me 'n' kids don't mix. Not for more'n a few minutes, anyhow.' He handed the quietened boy to his mother and would have moved away but she caught at his arm.

'Wanted a word with you, Rob,' Pam hissed, glancing here and there to locate her husband. She spotted him leaving the room – probably in search of another beer, she realised sourly. As soon as he'd disappeared, she resumed in a tipsy whisper, 'Any chance of Stevie getting his job back?'

Rob leaned back against the wall and shoved his hands in his trouser pockets. 'Didn't know he wanted his job back.'

'He's getting nowhere on his own.' She hoisted her son to a shoulder and swayed her empty glass in a gesture of contempt. 'He just ain't got the right attitude to make a success of it like you. He's still shifting old furniture, and paying Jimmy's wages ain't helping, 'specially as the lying git promised he'd work for nothing but now he won't.' Pam bit her lip. Too late she'd remembered that Stevie had told her not to mention Jimmy in Rob's hearing because he hated their father. 'I warned him he'd regret it if he packed it in with you,' she lied, wide-eyed. 'You was good to him. I reckon he knows it 'n' all, only he's too proud to admit he was wrong.'

'Yeah? Well, I'll be blowed. There was me thinking you might have had a hand in stirring things up.'

Rob's sarcasm penetrated Pam's inebriation and she self-consciously nibbled the inside of her cheek and swayed to and fro to keep Christopher quiet.

'Well, if Stevie wants to have a word, I'll be about tomorrow, at home.'

'We're going to me mum 'n' dad's Boxing Day.'

'Well ... whenever then,' Rob said breezily, and pushed away from the wall.

Pam grabbed at his arm again and waggled her empty glass at him. 'Get us another one, Rob, be a dear. I'll let you have a kiss under the mistletoe, if you do.' Her coy glance flitted to the little bit of greenery dangling from the centre light.

'Tell you what, Pam, I'll get the baby's bottle instead, shall I?' He nodded at Christopher's puckering face turning restlessly on her shoulder. 'I reckon that poor little sod's thirstier than you are.'

It had been a long time since Stevie had seen such a sweet arse on a woman. Especially on a woman lying with her back to him on a bed. The only view he got of his wife nowadays when they lay down was her back, and it'd been that way for months. Quietly he advanced into the room and stared hungrily at the peachy shape straining velvet.

The hair on her nape prickled and Faye jerked

over on to her elbows.

'Getting the little 'un off to sleep, are you?' Stevie whispered hoarsely.

'Yeah...' Faye sat bolt upright then shimmied to the edge of the bed and got up. She clumsily forced her feet into her shoes. 'He likes being stroked to get him off...'

'Know how he feels,' Stevie growled on a guttural laugh and again moved forward.

'Well ... better get back downstairs; be making tracks home soon. We're going back with Matilda in Rob's car...' Faye rattled off, feeling uneasy. Although it was dark – just a crack of light was leaking into Alice's bedroom from the landing – she'd noticed a dangerous gleam in Stephen's half-closed eyes. But it seemed Stephen had no intention of moving out of the way. He'd deliberately stationed himself between her and the door so she'd need to brush past him, or remain where she was.

'Are you after your coats ... your wife's coat?' Faye blurted and fumbled through the garments on the bed, hoping to distract him by mentioning his wife. The tension in the room was unbearable.

Stephen had come closer and leaned over her shoulder as though he too was searching for his coat. A hand settled on her shoulder, moved past to twitch fur then tweed before it again withdrew to touch her neck. She could feel his boozy breath stirring her hair.

'You look good enough to eat, y'know that?' he mouthed against her cheek.

The stubble on his jaw was abrading her skin,

then hot hard fingers moved over her velvet back, lingered on her hip...

'Don't take after yer mum, do you, that's fer sure. Yer old man must've been the looker. And the little 'un's the spit of you, y'know that?'

Faye tensed rigid as his hand settled on her bottom, cupping a cheek, but it was his sly comment that had stolen her breath and caused her heart to thunder beneath her ribs. She was frightened he was hinting he knew she was Adam's mother. But she was angry too and determined that he wouldn't spoil what had so far been a very good day. She shoved past him, breathing rapidly at the same time as the light in the room increased then quickly dimmed as the door was again closed.

'Pam's looking for you.'

'Just getting our things,' Stevie mumbled, whilst pulling two coats out of the heap on the bed. 'We're off home.'

'Yeah ... be best,' Rob agreed in a soft, sinister way. As his brother came towards him he opened the door to let him out then followed him and yanked the door closed behind him. In an instant his free hand was at Stevie's throat, squeezing. 'Don't even think about it, y'hear?' He pushed his brother away so forcefully Stevie tottered perilously close to the top of the stairs.

'Keeping her for yourself, are yer?' Stephen sneered, rubbing at the red mark on his neck. 'Would've thought Gloria was enough to keep even you satisfied, way she's stacked.' He grunted a laugh. 'But then you always did want bleedin' everything, didn't yer? Tell you what – you get first pick ... like always,' he rasped. 'Just let me know which of 'em you don't want, and I'll have yer leftovers, like always...'

'Piss off home and sober up,' Rob snarled, then turned and went back inside the room.

'You all right?'

Faye nodded vigorously.

'He's drunk.'

Again she quickly nodded agreement.

Rob's eyes were drawn to the sleeping child.

'He said...' she swallowed before blurting with a hint of accusation, 'that Adam looks like me.'

'He doesn't know anything. Nobody knows, not from me anyhow. He does look like you.'

Again she nodded acceptance of what he'd said, while her chest heaved and she battled to bring order to her spinning thoughts. She didn't imagine Stephen would have attempted to do anything other than kiss or touch her. Not here ... not at such a lovely party with all his family downstairs having a good time. But then someone else had once forced her down on a bed for a few minutes, when his family were close by, and Adam had been the result.

'Do you want to go home?'

Faye shook her head. 'No; I'm having a smashing time,' she said huskily. 'He hasn't spoiled it.'

She hadn't needed to overhear the exchange between the two brothers to know about Gloria. She knew about Vicky Watson too. Marge had months ago confirmed what she'd already guessed about Rob Wild: he was a womaniser. Marge made a point of knowing all the local gossip. She had said Gloria, a barmaid at the Duke, and another girl called Vicky, were scratching it out to be Rob

Wild's number one fancy. Apparently Vicky had been bridesmaid at Stephen's wedding and was now putting it about she'd soon be getting Rob up the aisle.

It didn't matter to Faye; she liked Rob, thought him handsome, and when he wasn't being sarcastic he could be good company. He had treated her generously, but she wasn't fooled. He was still Jimmy's son and, at some time, as his brother had just proved possible, bad blood might turn him nasty.

Besides, she knew if she wasn't pretty he wouldn't give her the time of day. There was only one thing about her Rob was interested in, and she wasn't sure she'd ever let a man do that to her again. She'd learned the very hard way a man's sweet talk was just a load of lies to get into a girl's knickers. Then, rather than face the consequences of his deceit, he'd more than likely blame you and side with his parents in calling you a scrubber.

Rob had said he'd get her a proper abortionist if she fell pregnant by him, which was more help than Simon had offered her when she'd told him she was having his baby. He'd just hidden behind his mother's skirts and watched her suffer.

And Rob hadn't even pretended to be in love with her. He'd been honest in saying he wanted to sleep with her, not marry her. She just wanted to keep him as a friend. She wanted his help. And if that was selfish and mercenary of her, so be it. The one thing that horrible time before Adam was born had taught her was to toughen up and take instead of give.

After a protracted silence while he intently

studied her expression, Rob's lips skewed into a cynical smile. Inwardly he cursed his brother and his big mouth to damnation. Politely he asked, 'You sure you don't want to go home?'

'No. I can't remember when I last enjoyed myself this much.' It was an understatement. The clean, lavender-scented house was a joy to be in. The bathroom – the like of which she'd never seen before, with its shiny white sanitary ware and gleaming taps – had held her spellbound. She could have just sat in there on the toilet seat looking and longing for such a wonderful place to be hers. It had been depressing, knowing soon she would be traipsing out to the filthy brick outhouse in Campbell Road. She drew a breath and smiled. 'I'm not going to let your drunken brother ruin my Christmas Day.' A burst of music from below seemed to shake the floor-boards on which they stood. She glanced quickly at Adam to see if it had disturbed him. 'Shall we go down and join the others for a singsong? He'll nap for at least half an hour if the noise doesn't worry him. Then, I suppose we'd better go.'

This time she readily approached the man guarding the door and when he raised a hand, smoothed the backs of his fingers over her cheek in an odd, apologetic way, she didn't object at all to his touch.

FOURTEEN

Faye tilted her head to take a look at the upstairs window of the house. It was in darkness. 'Either they're all asleep or they're not yet back from Jimmy's pal's place.'

'I'll come up with you,' Rob said.

'No need...' Faye rebuffed him with a smile. 'You never know, Jimmy might be in there, drunk as a skunk and argumentative.'

'All the more reason to come up with you.'

Faye shook her head. 'If he's home, he'll not get a cross word out of me whatever he comes out with. I'm straight to bed. Thanks for bringing us back.'

Matilda hadn't after all wanted to return at midnight to Campbell Road. She and Reg had been belting out carols at the tops of their voices and having too much fun to call it a night. But during a lull as someone else took over from Josh's brother at the piano, and before Faye had got a chance to mention it was time she took Adam home, Rob had said he was ready to leave.

He had carried Adam, still soundly sleeping, down the stairs and laid him on the back seat of his car. They'd then driven the miles home in awkward silence. Faye had attempted to make conversation, but she'd sensed him withdraw after each brief reply. She'd asked him where he'd eaten his Christmas dinner, thinking his brother might have asked him over, or perhaps Alice had invited him to eat with them. She could tell that Alice and Rob were fond of one another. But he'd told her he'd stayed home and hadn't felt hungry enough to cook. He'd not seemed bothered by it, but she'd felt sad for him and had been on the point of saying he should have come to theirs for chicken and stuffing and plum pudding. The words had withered away when she'd realised he'd sooner have been alone in his beautiful house eating a sandwich than sharing a meal with his father.

'I've had a good time,' she said simply. 'One of the best days I can remember.'

'Good.'

'So I won't let Jimmy rile me and spoil it, no matter how cantankerous he is.'

She got no response to that and flicked a glance at his profile. His mouth was set aslant and she knew he was brooding on what had happened in Alice's bedroom. She sensed he wasn't just angry because his brother had made a pass at her. He'd guessed she'd overheard the conversation between him and Stephen. She wanted to tell him she hadn't eavesdropped on purpose and wasn't bothered how many women he knocked about with ... as long as he continued being good to her. She wondered whether to just lean over and kiss his cheek and prove it to him that way. She wouldn't mind if he then kissed her properly. In fact, she sensed she'd like it. When he'd held her after Donald Bateman had hit her, she'd felt comforted by his warmth and strength. But he'd never made any attempt to kiss or cuddle her before or since when they'd been alone together. She glanced up at the starry sky and unconsciously snuggled back into the leather upholstery, wanting to drain every drop of pleasure from what remained of Christmas. The sherries had coated her insides with warmth and, despite his moodiness, she remained cosy and content.

'Do you want a goodnight kiss?' It had rolled off her tongue as easily as a sigh, but her eyes sprang open as though someone else had spoken and startled her.

'No.'

Faye blinked and slid forward, feeling a wretched fool. 'Well, thanks for bringing us home...' she breathed and fumbled clumsily with the door handle.

He leaned across and opened it and just for a moment their faces almost touched before he jerked back into his seat. 'You sure you don't want me to come up? He's still asleep. You're not going to drop him halfway up the stairs are you?'

'No, I'm not!' Faye returned indignantly. 'I've carried him up the stairs before.'

'Not after sinking half a dozen sherries you haven't.'

'Why're you being so bloody miserable?' she hissed in frustration, unable this time to ignore his acid tone. Abruptly she swallowed a lump that had sprung to her throat. 'It's been a lovely day, why'd you have to ruin it? If you wanted to stay longer at Alice's with the others, you didn't have to bring us back yet you know...'

He suddenly shot a hand in her direction, making her reflexively flinch away, but he dragged her against him despite her struggles.

'All right, you're tipsy and I'm past goodnight kisses. But what the fuck ... it's Christmas. Let's act like kids.'

When his mouth plunged on hers, Faye lashed out. When he caught the fist racing towards him again she jerked her mouth free of his and buried her face against his shoulder. 'You're no different to them, are you? You're just a nasty selfish lecher like your father and your brother and...' Abruptly she bit her lip before she named Simon. He didn't know him, neither would he care to hear her complaints about the man who'd taken her virginity and given her Adam. 'I must be bloody mad to ever have thought you might be decent.' Her punishing fingers tightened on his arms, spearing nails through his sleeves.

Rob thrust a hand behind him to open the car door and plunged out, leaving her to clutch at air then his empty seat for support.

He opened the back door and lifted Adam and was into the dingy hallway of the house and half-way up the stairs with her son before she'd slammed the car door.

Faye followed him wearily up the rickety treads then found him waiting on the landing for her. She unlocked the door and peered into the room's interior. The bed was empty. Her mother and Jimmy were still out.

'Get a light going,' Rob said tonelessly.

She struck a match with an unsteady hand and lit the oil lamp on the table. 'Michael's in the back room, I expect.'

A slight jolting made Adam stir and stretch as

Rob tipped him into her arms. He was back at the door and had it half open when he forced through his teeth, 'Call me any name you like, but don't ever again say I'm like my father.' He seemed to remember something and took a step back into the room, pulling a small box from his pocket. It was tossed carelessly on to the table. 'It doesn't mean anything. Just something you can sell to help you get out of here. Didn't think you'd want me to give you money. Do us both a favour and get going.' His next words were as bitter as his laughter. 'Happy Christmas.'

Faye listened to the clatter of his feet swiftly descending the stairs. A moment later she heard the car engine roar into life.

'When I see terrible injuries like that I'm glad that my Wally never made it back from France.' Marge was ducking and bobbing in order to peer through the shop window while at the same time trying to keep out of sight.

Faye gave up stacking loaves on to a shelf, wiped her floury hands on her overall, and came round the counter to join Marge. Her curiosity transformed to pity as she focused on the fellow who was loitering outside. One side of his face was visibly scarred despite his effort to shield the damage with the brim of his hat.

'I couldn't have coped with Wally if he'd come back in that state. He had a head wound too, but he died on the train taking him to the field hospital.' Marge shook her head and sighed heavily. 'I know I shouldn't say it, 'cos life's life, ain't it? But what sort of life's he got, poor sod?

And what sort of life's his wife got, I wonder? I know I couldn't have been lying all the while and telling Wally it didn't matter that he looked a fright.'

Unfortunately, it wasn't unusual to see living proof of the carnage of the Great War. Men who'd been blinded or crippled could be seen leaning on sticks on street corners, desperately trying to scrape a living by hawking odds and ends. Those who were able-bodied enough might be seen singing or dancing to entertain the theatre crowds and earn themselves a few bob for their trouble. The land fit for heroes that the politicians had promised the returning troops had never materialised. For some wretched war casualties a meagre pension was all they'd had to look forward to for a decade. And there was no prospect of things improving now, not when even fit and healthy employees were being laid off.

A melancholy feeling settled on Faye as she wondered how her mother would have coped had her dad returned to them crippled or mutilated. There wasn't a day passed she didn't think of him and want him, and their happy family life, back. Yet what Marge had said in her blunt way was true: the reality of dealing with somebody so dreadfully maimed, and no doubt angry and bitter to boot, must surely test even the strongest soul's love and dedication. And she now knew, thanks to Jimmy Wild, that her mother could be awfully weak.

Oddly, the fellow outside the shop seemed well-to-do, and jovial. His attitude suggested that Marge might have been a bit hasty in her opinion that he had had no life. He was smartly dressed in a double-breasted suit, and the hat, jauntily set to shadow his puckered profile, looked to be expensive. A moment later Faye was startled from her reflection and alarm, not sympathy, was shaping her features.

Donald Bateman had strolled into view and joined the man they'd been watching. She instinctively retreated a few steps, hoping the two of them weren't about to enter the bakery.

'You'd think he'd go for one of them copper masks for blokes who've been burned, wouldn't you?' Marge was still craning her neck, a look of fascinated disgust contorting her features.

They fell silent as Mrs Smith bustled into the shop, muttering beneath her breath. She closed the door with a hefty shove, making the bell clatter madly, then slid a glance over her shoulder at the two men now dragging on cigarettes. 'Hope he don't hang about there too long; he'll frighten off your customers.'

'Morning, Mrs Smith.' Mr Travis had emerged with a tray of warm currant buns. He put them on the counter and cocked his head to see the man who had prompted her comment. His face whitened and he almost jumped back in shock.

'Horrible, ain't it?' Marge said to her boss, noticing his stricken expression. 'Just saying ... glad my Wally never come back from France looking like that. He'd sooner've copped it there, I know he would, God rest him.'

'It's Saul Bateman,' Mr Travis blurted. 'A nasty piece of work – although of course it's a tragedy what's happened to him. They say the Lord pays debts without money...' No sooner had he mumbled that last remark than he quickly retreated to the back room, leaving the door half-open so he could still spy on the shop.

Mr Travis knew all about Saul Bateman. The fellow had been no good before he went off to fight in France, and he'd not changed on his return, despite his gruesome injuries. From what he'd heard, Bateman had fallen straight back into his old ways. If anything, it sounded as though his resentment and bitterness had made him even more vicious. It was unnerving to see him hanging around these parts; the Bateman family had all upped sticks and moved south of the river some years ago – much to Mr Travis's relief.

There had been a time, before the war, when Mr Travis's love of a flutter on the geegees had left him owing Saul a substantial amount of money. He'd soon learned to rue the day he'd got himself involved with the nasty bastard and his illegal gambling ring. Saul's henchmen had given him quite a pasting when he'd not managed to pay his dues on time. Now, as he peered through the aperture between door and frame, he hoped that Bateman and his son – he'd guessed that was who the swaggering youth must be, because he looked the image of Saul when young – would take themselves off without entering his premises. At the clatter of the shop bell, he hastily pushed the door closed.

Faye, too, cringed at the sound. She'd seen Donald Bateman catch sight of her through the window and noticed a gleam of recognition narrow his eyes. Immediately her mind was racing back to the last time she'd seen Donald, on the evening he'd hit her. In the months that had followed, as the bruising faded and disappeared, she'd gradually started to forget about the horrible incident. Now it was again thrust to the forefront of her mind.

Michael had been quite subdued ever since and Faye had not found any more cigarettes hidden behind the wardrobe. But if her brother were still up to his tricks he'd be crafty enough to cover his tracks more carefully this time. She knew that Jimmy was still ferreting about in their room when they were out, looking and hoping...

'I'd better be off,' Mrs Smith swiftly tipped her coins down on the wooden counter and grabbed her bread. She charged for the door, head down, sending one peek back over her shoulder before hurrying outside.

'Two of your steak 'n' ale pies please, luv. The big 'uns.'

Nobody moved. Faye slid a glance at Marge, who was desperately trying to keep her eyes averted from the shiny scarlet skin on the profile presented to her. Suddenly her friend pivoted about and started whizzing the buns from the tray on to an empty shelf, leaving Faye, alone, facing the two men.

Faye got a paper bag and stuffed two meat pies into it.

'You're Greavesie's sister, ain't you?'

Faye nodded whilst giving Donald a hard stare that told him she'd not forgotten him either. Her challenge simply made him chuckle.

'Yeah ... I remember you, all right,' he said

softly, slowly nodding. 'Shame we never got to know one another a bit better that night.'

'Ask her to walk out with you, then you'll get to know her. Pretty girl like that's probably got a lot of fellows after her though.' Saul Bateman grinned at her, stretching the drooping side of his mouth into a weird shape. 'Me son's not as shy as he seems, I'll promise you that, miss.'

Faye tore her eyes from his veined straining cheek and faintly smiled. 'Eight pence, please.'

'Cheap at half the price,' he quipped. 'Don't worry, you can look at me face, miss,' he told her. 'I don't get offended no more. Not a pretty sight, is it? Got it courtesy of Fritz.' He dug into his pocket and searched through the silver and copper coins on his palm.

'I'm very sorry,' Faye said. And she was. She might loathe his son, she might recall Alice's description of the family as a rough lot, still she felt compelled to voice her sympathy for his injury. He courteously accepted her commiseration by doffing his hat, displaying an angry-looking bald patch on his scalp.

Saul rested an elbow on the counter and turned to his son. 'Go on then, ask the young lady out to the flicks before we go. If you don't, some other fellow will. She's polite as well as pretty, and she'll attract the boys like bees to a honeypot.'

'I can't ... sorry ... I've got a sweetheart,' Faye rattled off the lie and quickly slid towards her the coins he'd put down.

Saul stopped lounging. 'See ... it's yer own fault, Donnie. Got to act straight away or you lose out with the best girls.' He turned back to

Faye. 'Bet you come from good family too, don't you?' He winked at her with his white, blind eye. 'You're a peach, I reckon. So you be lucky, sweetheart.' A moment later they were gone from the shop and Donald was leering at her over a shoulder as he walked away.

'So who is she?'

'One of me pal's sisters. Only we ain't really pally now. Michael Greaves is his name and he's a right little ponce.' Donald stuck a hand in the paper bag and pulled out a pie. He bit off a mouthful and spluttered through pastry, 'Been getting him fags 'n' booze on the cheap off ol' man Foster who works down the docks.' He chewed and swallowed. 'Been waiting for me money off him for months, the little shit. Even waited up the school gate to catch him out.'

Saul had listened with a thoughtful expression crinkling his good side. 'How old is he?'

'Just a kid – about twelve.' Donald stuck the pie in his mouth again.

'Kid or not, it'll get round if you let people take the piss out of yer, son. What've I told you about that? Now it's good you're doing a bit of duckin' 'n' divin' to earn yerself a few bob instead of always being on my ear'ole. But what're you doing hanging about with school kids? Ain't you got no pals yer own age roundabouts?'

'Can I come back home 'n' live with you?' Donald whined at his father, ignoring his question.

'No, you bleedin' can't. You upset Sandra every time you open your mouth. You stay put in

Islington with yer mother. Time you got your own place anyhow, ain't it?' He looked his strapping son up and down with one dull blue eye. 'You're nineteen soon, by my reckoning. Get yerself hooked up with a nice gel – Greavesie's sister, if she'll have you – and I'll find a month's rent on a room till you get the kitty sorted out between the two of yers.' He chuckled. 'You never know, if you did manage to pull that sweet little thing she might get out of her brother what the toerag owes you.'

'She won't have me. She don't like me.' Donald didn't add that he'd clumped her. His father might be a violent criminal, but he didn't hold with hitting women. Not any more, anyhow. Now he looked grotesque, his father was glad of any female company he could get, and pandered to any old slag to keep her sweet. Donald knew too that his father had lied when he'd told Faye Greaves that he wasn't offended if people stared at him. His father was bitter and twisted about the loss of his looks. Donald had seen him snarl and shake his fist at people who gawped at him; he'd looked on as his father cut up into little pieces all the photos showing him as he'd once been, before he'd got burned in the war.

Even though Saul now had a top job with Johnny Blake, and liked to flash his cash about, still a lot of women couldn't stomach him. Donald knew his father's latest fancy piece stayed with him because it was better than returning to her husband and getting knocked about. Personally, Donald reckoned Sandra's old man had a point; he'd often felt like whacking her himself. It was one of the reasons he'd had to move in with his mother rather than stay with his father south of the river. Sandra didn't like him, and Donald hated her. She'd had too much to say for herself from the start, in Donald's opinion. For the last ten years he'd been hanging on to the hope that his mother would get over the fact that her handsome husband now looked like a freak and move back in with him.

FIFTEEN

Nellie had just seated herself in a corner of the Nag's Head in Holloway Road, and begun to ease off her shoes under the table, when a booming male voice addressed her.

'Nellie Tucker ... well, well, well. Long time no see, eh, gel?'

Nellie twisted about on her chair and choked on her gin. She gulped, thumped her chest and shot to her feet, nearly tipping over the table as her stout thighs caught it. Despite being scared witless, she was aware that people in the pub were staring. And she understood why: on odd occasions over the years, and at a distance, she'd caught a glimpse of Saul and had thought his face looked horrible; close to, he was monstrously ugly.

'Yeah, long time, all right... What you doin' around here?' she hoarsely croaked. 'Ain't spoken to you in ages. Crikey! You give me such a fright ...

no ... not yer face,' she garbled, 'You snuck up on me a bit quick like.' Nellie gave up trying to be tactful and spluttered out, 'Fuckin' hell, Saul, do it still hurt?' Her eyes remained fixed on the florid, distorted features looming over her. Her jaw continued sagging towards her chest.

'Nah ... bit of a twinge now 'n' then, that's all.'

Having placed his pint pot next to Nellie's glass, Saul pulled out a chair and sat down. Nellie plopped back into her seat opposite him.

'Look dreadful you do, mate,' she whispered.

'So do you, Nellie,' Saul replied insouciantly. 'What's happened to yer? At least I got a bleedin' good reason for lookin' a state. What's yours?'

Nellie swallowed and licked her lips. She'd thought she was past being offended at being called a scabby old tart. And she knew that was what Saul was thinking, even if he hadn't said it in so many words.

But hearing it from him hurt because Saul had been special. There had been a time when she'd thought she really loved him. Just over a decade ago he'd been blond and handsome and good to her. He was hung like a donkey and he'd certainly known how to move. She wondered forlornly if he'd got any damage there that might have ruined his best attribute. He was the only man she'd ever fucked who, money aside, had made it worth her while. Although he'd taken a good amount of her earnings, he'd always left her enough, and that was more than Jimmy Wild ever did. In fact, Jimmy never had been up to much as a pimp or a lover, even ten years ago when in his prime. But he'd been a handsome man with a toned body he'd been proud of. Now he was bloated, and had ugly scars on his face and body, and wasn't much use to her in any respect. Some days he couldn't turn up a punter or a stiffy.

Reminiscing had made tears well up. She sniffed, stuck knuckles against a watering eye. But her answer came in a jaunty tone. 'Usual thing for an old prossie, ain't it, Saul ... too much booze ... too many rotten bastards...'

The first rotten bastard had been her stepfather. On the night her mother had been in labour with her sixth child at Aunt Wilhemina's, he'd got into bed with Nellie and her younger sister, Vera, in the room they shared in Campbell Road. Vera had clambered over Nellie, shaking like a leaf. When her sister had discovered there was no way out because he'd locked the door, she'd scuttled under the iron bedstead to escape him. To prevent her stepfather carrying out his threat to drag her eleven-year-old sister back to bed, Nellie had stopped fighting the brute off, even though by then she'd managed to give him a few hefty whacks. He'd made sure he hurt her back that night, and many other nights. Months later, when finally she'd plucked up the courage to defy him and tell her mother what he'd been doing, her mother had let fly with a punch too and called her a lying tyke. At the age of thirteen she'd been kicked out with nothing but a bag of old clothes that had been chucked out of a window to land on the step beside her. She'd returned at intervals to live with her mother, usually when she'd heard on the grapevine that her stepfather had been kicked out. But he'd always wheedled her mother into letting him move back in. When that happened, Nellie packed her bags herself, and willingly walked out of the door.

Nellie raked her fingers through her coarse hair and gamely smiled. She tipped up her chin and pointed to a thick ridge of scar tissue that ran across her throat, courtesy of a more recent rotten bastard. The mark was usually hidden in flab. 'Tried a new patch around Wapping a few years back. Got that off some foreigner came in on a boat.' She pulled aside her frizzy white fringe to display another blemish close to her hairline. 'Would yer believe it! Very same night, some bitch smacked me with her shoe 'cos she reckoned I'd poached her patch.' She gave him a wonky smile. 'It wouldn't have happened when you was looking after me; I done all right then. You'd've made the foreign sod pay up. I couldn't. I just got paid.'

'You got nobody lookin' out for you now?'

Nellie blinked and stared at her gin. She shook her shaggy head and sunk her face further in her glass. She was well on the way to being drunk but, nevertheless, realised it'd be wise to button it. Jimmy would kill her if she mentioned his name to this man. That was if Saul didn't get wind that Jimmy was alive and got to him first. 'Anyhow, what you doing round here, Saul? You never said,' she burst out.

'Me youngest son's come back this way to live. Since me eldest boy moved up North to work in his father-in-law's business, I only got one of 'em poncing off me. Wish I'd never got a telephone line put on; he's always ringing me up, moaning fer money. I come over today to see Donnie and weigh him out, take a look around the old place while I was at it.' He took a swig of beer and wiped the back of a hand across what remained of his lips. 'Just dropped him at his mum's place, down Hornsey Road. Thought I'd come and have one for the road before I set off home.' He took another gulp from his glass before continuing. 'Donnie wants to come back and live with me; wants me to get him in working for Johnny Blake in the clubs up west, but I ain't having none of it.'

'Why's that?' Nellie felt it was safe to look up, certain, at last, that the conversation had turned.

'Tosspot, he is,' Saul declared flatly. 'He'd be an embarrassment. Might be me son, but it's got to be said.' He shrugged. 'Trouble is, these kids today don't know how lucky they've got it. What most of 'em need is a few weeks in a stinkin' French trench, then they'd know how bleedin' well off they are.' Having drained his tankard, he banged it down. 'He can't even find himself a decent gel to settle down with. Speakin' of which, me lady friend don't like him, so that's that as far as me and him living together.'

'Lady friend? No wife now?' Nellie asked carefully.

'Linda scarpered back in 1918, soon as she got a look at me. Didn't even wait till I got out of hospital before she packed her bags...'

Having elbowed a path through the crowded saloon bar, Jimmy slowed down on seeing Nellie sitting with a stranger. He'd had a feeling he'd catch the cow out boozing, or pulling punters behind his back. He puffed out his chest and was just about to bowl over and act belligerent when the fellow turned his way.

Saul swooped an eye over fellow drinkers. Nobody now seemed much interested in gawping at him; only some fat bloke with grey hair who looked like he needed a bath. He turned back to Nellie to see she'd gone pale beneath her boozy blush and was scraping back her chair to get up.

'Gotta be off. Take care o' yerself, Saul,' she muttered, grabbing her handbag.

'Want another?' he offered cheerily. 'Come on ... have another gin, fer old times sake,' he cajoled. 'Then I'll give you a ride home in me car, Nel.'

She waggled her head and fled towards the exit. Saul watched her as she weaved through people and tottered after the fat grey-haired bloke, who was already at the door.

'Was that who I think it was?' Jimmy had hauled her savagely around the side of the pub, out of sight, before blasting her in a strangled voice.

Nellie's head trembled an affirmative along with the rest of her. 'Didn't know he was about, honest, Jim. Couldn't avoid him, honest, I couldn't. He sort of crept up on me.'

Jimmy's pop-eyed stare swung left and right, then he tugged her further up an alleyway. 'What you told him about me? What you said?'

'Nuthin''. He never mentioned you. If he had, I honest to God don't know what I'd've done. Passed out, I reckon.'

Jimmy was still darting looks here and there like

a hunted animal. Nellie started chewing nervously on a thumbnail.

'He's off home south of the water tonight,' Nellie blurted helpfully. 'Only come over this way to see his son. His youngest's back living with his mother in Hornsey Road. Saul and her split up after he got back from France and she clocked him looking like Frankenstein.'

'Got his life history, have you?' Jimmy sneered viciously. His heartbeat was steadying now he'd got his shock and fear under control. He knew that the only reason Saul hadn't come running out after them was because he hadn't recognised him.

In his prime, Jimmy had been a very vain individual, but he wasn't now. He was well aware that he'd lost his looks, and his virility, and he blamed it all on the fight with Geoff Lovat that had nearly killed him, conveniently overlooking the sapping effects of his degrading lifestyle before and after the episode. In the months it had taken to recuperate, his hair had turned grey, and his muscles had turned to flab, and he couldn't even summon up the energy to womanise. His prowess had never fully returned, and a few of his conquests had felt his fists for jeering because of it. That's why, on the whole, Edie suited him; she made no demands on him, apart from whining for rent money. And when he felt the urge, she was usually willing to put up with it for a quiet life. Of course, there'd been times when the worm had looked ready to turn and he'd had to remind her of a few things to keep her tame.

Suddenly Jimmy felt very thankful he no longer

resembled that swarthy, muscled Casanova who'd once scrapped with Saul Bateman over Nellie Tucker's immoral earnings.

'Don't hurt to keep a bit friendly with Saul, do it? Why rile him?' Nellie ventured. 'I feel a bit sorry for him, actually.'

'Yeah, maybe you're right. If he comes back this way, you keep on the right side of him. Good job I don't look like I did. Anyhow, he thinks I croaked years back.'

'Yeah,' Nellie agreed with a tentative smile. She was relieved Jimmy seemed calmer; when he was frightened and anxious he was liable to turn brutal. Just for good measure, she added soothingly, 'All that business between you 'n' Saul's long forgot, Jim, ain't it?'

'What's the matter?'

'Nothing.'

Faye raised herself on an elbow on the bed and peered down at Michael. He was lying on his side on the mattress on the floor, facing away from her.

'Why're you crying?' she whispered, keeping her voice low and level so as not to wake Adam, sleeping soundly beside her on the bed.

'Ain't crying; just sniffing.' Michael got the threadbare old blanket by an edge and tugged it over him as though to hide himself from view. The abrupt movement made him again stifle a sob.

Faye got swiftly out of bed and lit the small oil lamp that perched on a chair in the corner. Picking it up, she hurried towards him. 'You might as well tell me what's up, 'cos if you don't I'll get Mum in here and you can explain to her instead.'

That threat had Michael lunging upright and the effort made him muffle a moan with a fist.

Faye dropped to her knees beside him and the sudden movement almost extinguished the lamp's flame. 'What's up?' she urgently hissed. 'Have you got the bellyache?' Faye knew that the disgusting state of the privies out the back had given diarrhoea to people living on the floor above. She always made Adam go on his potty rather than risk taking him out to use the filthy toilet. It annoyed her that Edie didn't always take the same care with him.

Faye recalled that Michael hadn't seemed queasy earlier, or off his food when they'd had their teas. What she did remember was that he'd reeked of tobacco. She knew that her brother was still getting hold of cigarettes. There had been a number of occasions recently when he'd come home with his clothes and breath stinking of smoke. She was sure she'd caught a whiff of alcohol about him too. But if their mother had guessed about her son's habits she kept it to herself. Faye suspected Edie had no energy to spare to discipline Michael. She seemed exhausted from her constant battle to extract a measly amount of money from Jimmy to keep a roof over their heads and a bit of food on the table.

They all knew Jimmy had been getting a regular wage from Stephen for many months, yet still he pleaded poverty and stuck to his story that he was doing favours for his son. The more he stayed away overnight, the less inclined he was to part with a penny. Faye knew now for sure that he had a fancy piece. She'd spotted him huddled with a chubby blonde woman when she'd walked home from work a few weeks ago. She reckoned her mother knew what was going on and was in two minds whether to confront him and finally kick him out. She also reckoned it was the loss of his paltry contribution to the housekeeping that had been keeping Edie quiet, not the idea of losing the lying, cheating pig to another woman.

Faye squinted at Michael's face, searching for signs of fever. He looked white, but there seemed to be nothing else wrong with him. In a fit of affection she reached out and gave him a hug to comfort him because he looked so terribly sad.

The pressure of her arms on his body drew a groan from him and he struggled free. Putting the lamp on the floor, she grabbed an edge of his shirt and, slapping away his defensive hands, tugged it up. The sight that met her eyes made her fall backwards on to her bottom and sit there gawping at him, hugging her knees to her chin. His torso was mottled with dark skin and she didn't need to examine the blemishes to identify them as huge bruises.

'Did Donald Bateman do that to you?' she eventually breathed.

'Who told you his name?' Michael demanded, sounding agitated.

'He came into the baker's with his father,' Faye replied hoarsely. 'Mr Travis knows the family. I was bound to find out sooner or later, wasn't I?' she reasoned, glad she'd answered honestly yet had kept back the fact that it was Alice who'd first told her the thug's identity.

Michael turned his head but she could hear him snuffling against his shoulder.

Yanking aside her nightdress to keep it from tearing, she skittered forward on bare boards, wincing as splinters nipped at her knees. 'You'd better tell me, Michael.' Grabbing her brother's chin, she forced him to look at her. '*Was* it that bully who beat you up?'

Michael sucked in a painful breath. 'If I tell you who did it, you ain't gonna tell Mum or Jimmy are you, and start trouble?'

'I'd never tell anything to Jimmy. And I didn't say anything to Mum the last time, did I?'

'I owe Bateman again for fags and a few bottles of drink. So he bashed me up. Said he'd do me a favour and leave me face alone so Mum 'n' Jimmy wouldn't know unless I showed 'em. Said if anyone got the law on him, I'd get some more.'

'Oh, Michael...' Faye blinked her burning eyes and sank her teeth into her quivering lower lip. A volcano of emotions seemed to simmer within, but her exasperation had soon suppressed her sympathy. 'You know what a bully he is,' she snapped. 'Why can't you just stay away from him, you idiot?'

''Cos he gets me a few smokes and beers,' Michael hissed. 'I can't buy them for meself and I need something to put up with living in this dump.' He hiccoughed, swiping his knuckles under his nose. 'He come by the school and give me a hidin' in front of me mates. Made me look a right fool, he did.'

'Didn't any of your friends stick up for you?'

'Tony Cummins jumped on his back and tried to get him off me, but that was it. The others didn't want to get involved. They all know he's a nutter and he'll turn on them next. He's mental, just like his old man.'

Faye felt her insides clench as she remembered what Alice had told her about the Bateman clan's violent reputation.

'His father's a gangster up the West End,' Michael continued in a low tone. 'Donald boasts about him all the time and all the flash stuff he's got. He reckons his dad's motor cost more than a thousand quid.'

Faye could believe it to be true. Mr Bateman, despite his ugly disfigurement, had appeared affluent and brash. 'How much do you owe Donald this time?'

'He says it's nearly two quid, but I know he's lyin',' Michael spat defensively. 'He's putting on interest wot I never agreed to pay.'

'Perhaps I should have a word with him for you. I won't get out of me pram or take a swipe at him, promise.'

'No!' Michael shot on to his knees then clutched at his chest as his bruises throbbed. 'Don't! That's what he wants.' He sagged back on to his heels. 'He's after you. He told me he fancies you. I reckon that's why he's makin' out I owe him more'n I do. He wants me to tell you, so's you'll go looking for him and be nice to him.' Her brother shook his head and added earnestly, 'You can't get hooked up with him. He's a wrong 'un, all right.'

Faye huffed a hollow laugh. 'Yeah, he is!' she spat sarcastically. 'So why've you got involved with him, you bloody little fool?' Her scathing tone made her brother hang his head. 'Donald Bateman can think again if he reckons I'll have anything to do with him,' she announced. 'I'm not frightened of him, the vile bully.'

'Say you won't go!' Michael grabbed at her and squeezed her arm in a painful, demanding grip. 'Say it,' he keened.

'All right,' she soothed. 'I won't; but in return you've got to promise to stay away from him.'

He nodded and sank back gingerly on the mattress. Faye climbed into bed, suddenly conscious how chilled she was. She cuddled up to Adam and pulled the thin cover up to her chin. She stared down at her brother but, sensing her eyes on him, he stiffly rolled over to avoid her searching gaze. 'I've only got about five shillings I can let you have, Michael,' she breathed out quietly. It was all the money she'd managed to save from her wages since the loss of her five-pound note. But she still had something else…

Instinctively her fingers slipped to her throat and she touched the gold that nestled warmly against her skin, hidden beneath the collar of her nightdress. She never took off her Christmas present from Rob and she prayed nobody had ever caught a glimpse of it. But she'd pawn it if need be, just as she'd surrendered his five-pound note to protect her family. Besides, Robert Wild didn't seem to give a monkey's what she did with the valuable things he gave her. The beautiful gold rope had been lobbed her way as though it were of little consequence whether she liked it or not. It was just something to sell to see her on her way, he'd carelessly said, and urged her to get going, as though he wanted to see the back of her.

But she knew he'd lied; just as she lied to herself every day that she didn't give a damn he'd made no attempt to stop and speak to her in the months that had passed since then. She'd seen him on a couple of occasions as he'd driven past in his car, sometimes alone, sometimes with a woman. On one occasion Faye had recognised his sister-in-law sitting beside him with her baby on her lap. The other woman she'd never seen before and, as she'd marched on by, never hesitating or glancing his way, Faye had wondered whether it was the barmaid or the bridesmaid sitting there beside him.

With a sigh that seemed to well from deep within, Faye blew out the lamp.

SIXTEEN

'You've been to see him again, ain't you?'

'What?' Pam's smiling expression feigned puzzlement. She continued turning the pages of the magazine open on her lap.

'You've been to see Bobbie again, don't try denying it.' Stephen paced back and forth in the sitting room, then abruptly sat in the chair opposite hers.

‘What makes you say that?’ Pam immediately leapt from her seat and went to pick up her son from his pram. She wedged Christopher in a corner of the small sofa.

‘Always know when you’ve been to see him; you walk round with a smile on your face for a change,’ Stephen accused. ‘Well, you’re still wasting yer time. I’m never asking Bobbie for me old job back and that’s that.’

‘Why not?’ Pam screeched, making the baby jump and start wailing. ‘You ain’t bringing in enough on yer own, are you? If he starts charging us rent on this place, we’re done for. He only let us have it in the first place as a favour.’

‘He let us have it ’cos I’m his brother, and he knows he owes me from way back.’

‘For what?’ Pam demanded, and smiled thinly when Stephen seemed stuck for an answer. ‘He don’t owe you nuthin’! We was doing all right till you started shooting yer mouth off and lost a good job.’

‘Yeah ... and who was it nagged me to shoot me mouth off?’ Stephen jibed.

Pam’s lips knotted into a pout. ‘You’re just a selfish git!’ she sideswiped at him. ‘All you think about’s yer pride, never mind about me ’n’ little Christopher going without. What if your brother turns nasty and chucks us out?’

Stephen jumped to his feet and swung his screaming son up into his arms. ‘If he was going to do that, I reckon he’d have shown us the door months ago when I first jacked it in.’ Stephen put the baby to a shoulder, shushing him. ‘Anyhow, I don’t give a toss if he does chuck us out. I’ll get us another place.'

'Not like this one, you won't; not on the sort of money you make.'

'I make enough!' Stephen roared, his wiry body tense as a spring. 'Trouble is, you don't know how to keep house. You couldn't keep a rabbit hutch, you! Never a bit of grub about the place...' He stormed over to the pram, stationed under the window, and started pulling the blanket to and fro. 'What shopping d'you get when you was out? I give you a few bob this morning. What you bought? If you say nuthin', you can give us it back.' He stuck out a palm, waiting.

'Got the bus, didn't I,' Pam yelled, nervously straightening the covers in the pram. 'Costs, don't it? D'you expect me to walk all the way to Rob's office?'

'No! I expect you to stop chasing after my brother. And I reckon he wants the same.' Stephen brought his face close to his wife's. Fighting for control, he snapped bluish lips over bared teeth and spun away from her.

Having laid his son back down on the sofa, he strode through into the kitchen. Pam could hear the cupboard doors being opened and crashed shut. A moment later Stephen came back into the living room.

'Not a sodding thing to eat, just as I thought.'

'Well, if you'd just go and speak to Rob and get yer job back...'

Stephen made a bound for the chair she'd vacated and snatched up the magazine on the seat. A moment later he'd ripped it in half and flung fluttering pages towards the cold, empty grate. 'Bring in enough fer you to buy this crap, don't I?' he said through clenched teeth. 'If I find out you've been to see Robert behind me back one more time, you can stay there with him, you listening?' He sneered a smile. 'That's if he'll have you, of course. And you know what? I don't reckon he would. He didn't want you before and he won't have you now, not even if you offered it to him on a plate like the rest of 'em do. So you better think about what I've said.'

Casting one last look at his sobbing son, he swiped up his jacket and slammed out of the door.

Pam grabbed the child, stuck him back in his pram and rocked it energetically. Stephen had hit a raw nerve, taunting her like that. A few times now she'd tried to flirt with her brother-in-law and got nowhere. She'd felt humiliated this afternoon when Rob had told her he was too busy to talk for long. He'd virtually chucked her out of his office, yet still she knew she'd be going to see him again. And it wasn't simply the genuine fear that he might evict them that'd taken her there.

When she and her friend Vicky had first met the Wild brothers at a friend's wedding, it had been Bobbie she'd set out to hook, not Stevie. She'd fancied him ever since and had been jealous when Vicky had been the one he'd invited to the New Year dance. Grudgingly she'd agreed to partner Stevie; after that, they'd fallen into walking out together once or twice a week. It hadn't taken Stevie long to cotton on he was her second choice and to become resentful. Pam had sensed he'd been on the point of throwing her over when she discovered she was pregnant and forced a proposal from him.

She'd never got over wanting Bobbie, or the lifestyle she might have had. And the more her brother-in-law acted cool towards her, the more Pam's pride demanded she make him want her right back. She didn't even care that her friend considered herself his sweetheart. Vicky thought that if she clung on long enough, he'd marry her. He never would. Everyone knew that he was tired of her. He never took her out any more. So Pam reckoned Bobbie was still fair game, and she hadn't been put off at Christmas when he'd been paying attention to Jimmy's stepdaughter. Faye Greaves, pretty as she was, had no more chance of getting a ring on her finger than did Vicky, or the tart behind the bar at the Duke. Robert Wild was just a user where women were concerned and he'd never settle down while he could play the field.

The baby's screaming set her teeth on edge and she thrust a hand under the pillow that supported her son's fretful head and drew out a small brown bottle. It hadn't only been bus fare and magazines that had used up the few shillings Stevie had given her. She'd stopped at a place where she knew she could get something to quieten Christopher. Her mother's friend, who was a mad old biddy, had been getting a little soother to settle her nerves on the sly as she didn't want her husband to know she was taking laudanum. Pam knew if Stevie found out what she was doing he'd probably kill her. But then it was all right for him; as soon as he'd had enough of the hellish noise, he'd just piss off, like always. So she'd hung about till the bloke had appeared and bought something to shut the brat up for a while because she couldn't stand his racket any more.

After about ten minutes the laudanum seemed to have worked and sent him off to sleep, but she continued rocking the pram, gently now, while glancing about. It wasn't a large home, but they had all they needed: a little sitting room with a kitchenette off, and a couple of bedrooms. The people who rented upstairs from Bobbie were easy enough to live with. The money Stephen was making would barely cover a room in Campbell Road for them all. She'd sooner go back and live with her parents than move round the corner to the worst street in North London. But if she did go back home she'd have to admit they'd been right all along: Stephen Wild was a loser and a chip off his father's block.

'Me old man in there?'

Faye shook her head. She'd just quit the house and was on her way to work when Stephen had come up behind her firing a question at her back and making her spin around by the railings.

Although she'd spotted him in the vicinity several times, she'd not spoken to him since Christmas Day. She'd put his randy behaviour down to him being too far under the festive influence and bore no grudges over it. The Keiver clan liked to have a merry time and Faye hoped she wasn't a killjoy or a prude. She could tell from Stephen's uncomfortable stance that, drunk or not that evening, he could remember the incident and was feeling awkward. He seemed to be in two minds whether to apologise or let sleeping dogs lie. To signal all was forgiven and forgotten, she gave him a bright smile.

'Not seen Jimmy for a couple of days. And to be honest, that suits me fine.'

Encouraged by her relaxed attitude, Stephen fell in step beside her as she headed briskly for Seven Sisters Road. 'Y'know what he's getting up to, I s'pose, when he stops away?'

'Yeah, I know,' Faye admitted drily. 'I reckon my mum knows too.'

'Him and Nellie Tucker used to be thick as thieves years ago,' he added conversationally. 'He'd moved out to live with her quite a while before he went missing. Best time of our lives as kids that were, not having him around.'

Faye had previously thought Stephen rather a surly character, but today he'd surprised her by his willingness to chat.

'He'd turn up, out of the blue, on odd weekends and take us boating down Finsbury Park,' Stephen continued. 'Knowing him, he probably thought rowing a boat made up for us being hungry and running about with our arses hanging out of our trousers. He kept our mum short all the time.' Stephen snorted a laugh. 'Rows they used to have over him handing over a bit of his wages.'

'He's not changed then,' Faye observed wryly. 'He brought in a bag of liquorice for Adam last week, all smarmy smiles, but wouldn't give Edie a shilling for the rent.'

It was a crisp spring morning in late March and

Faye had started out at a fast pace to keep warm. She settled into a sedate stroll with Stephen as they carried on talking.

'Yeah, that's Jimmy all right. Me 'n' Bobbie just let our mum sort it out with him. And did they sort it out! Feel bad about it now; should have backed her up more. At the time, we didn't give a monkey's who he was with, s'long as it wasn't us.'

That harsh statement drew a solemn glance from Faye. She'd heard gossip about how badly Jimmy had treated his first wife, and his sons. He was still a cruel man, but she suspected the passing years had softened his brutality whether he'd wanted it to or not.

'Don't suppose you were old enough to stand up to him,' she said kindly.

'When he went off with Nellie, Bobbie was coming up eleven and big for his age.' Stephen's remark held a hint of complaint. 'I was always in his shadow and a bit of a runt. Not much changes,' he muttered in an aside.

Faye ignored his self-pity and concentrated on thinking that Stephen was blaming Robert unfairly. Her brother Michael was a good size for his eleven years, yet she wouldn't expect him to take Jimmy on, fat and unfit as Jimmy was. 'Why does this Nellie put up with him then?'

'Nellie's an old brass; 'spect she's got used to taking a punch in the gob. My mum never did. Aunt Til made sure of it.'

'Good for them,' Faye stated emphatically. Inwardly she prayed her mother continued to have enough gumption to challenge Jimmy rather than meekly take whatever he dished out.

After a few quiet minutes when Stephen seemed content to amble beside her, she asked pointedly, 'Is your father late for work? Is that why you're round here looking for him this morning?'

'Sort of... Not that it matters now. I've got to put him off.'

Faye halted and twisted towards him with a shocked expression. 'You're sacking him?'

'Yeah, got to. Work's tight.' Faye's abrupt halt had meant that Stephen was a yard or two in front. He retraced his steps so they were again close. 'Struggling to keep meself in wages, let alone him.' He stuck his hands in his pockets while protecting his face from the cold breeze with hunched-up shoulders. He knew he should have found the backbone to get rid of Jimmy months ago, when he'd started demanding a bigger cut of the profits. But, despite his grizzled appearance, his father had a way of looking at him, back teeth set and chin jutting, that could make him recall the sting of his old man's fists and turn his guts to water. 'You seen Bobbie lately?'

Still mulling over how to break the news to her mother that Jimmy was again unemployed, Faye was taken aback by the question. 'No ... I haven't seen him lately,' she mumbled.

'Oh ... right. Thought you 'n' him were sort of ... getting friendly, like.'

'I think we're still friends,' Faye said carefully, hoping it was true. 'Just not seen him around here much.' She started walking again. She wanted to see Robert ... hoped every day he'd stop so she could speak to him and say thank you for the Christmas present he'd given her. She wanted to say sorry, too, that she'd called him names and said he was like Jimmy. He was nothing like Jimmy; if he were, he wouldn't bother keeping a watchful eye on her, and she was sure that he was.

She'd seen his car parked outside his Aunt Matilda's house on several occasions, and she knew that he kept up to date with what went on with her family because Matilda had told her that he always asked after her. On one occasion, when she'd got back from work and had noticed his car there, she'd hung about by the railings outside, hoping to catch him when he came out of his aunt's. He'd seen her, but had simply raised a hand to acknowledge her wave before driving off.

'Know what? I reckon he's a fool if he's not been around here for a while...' Stephen was looking her over with sleepy eyes. 'At Christmas he seemed as if he wanted to get to know you better.' He angled his head towards her, scanning her features. ''Course you don't look stupid, so I reckon you've twigged he likes to get to know lots of girls better. How old are you, anyhow?' he whispered huskily.

'Eighteen,' Faye said, turning her head quickly away from his hovering lips. She was relieved to spot Marge on the opposite pavement, making her way towards the bakery. 'Got to go. Me friend's expecting me to walk into work with her. Nice to see you.' With that, she trotted across the road and, catching up with Marge, linked arms with her.

'See your admirer's up and about early this morning,' was Marge's amused greeting.

Faye's frown lifted when she realised it wasn't Stephen Wild who'd prompted her friend's sly comment but another fellow. Marge indicated a young man on the opposite pavement by tilting her head at him. Faye raised a hand and returned Timothy Lovat's salute.

The Lovats were a nice family and friends of the Keivers. They lived close to the better end of Campbell Road, although she'd learned from Alice, when she'd been telling her a bit about her time in the street, that the Keivers and the Lovats used to be next-door neighbours. Some Campbell Bunk families, when they could afford it, apparently chose to get better rooms in a house situated close to the junction with Lennox Road. From Alice's rolling-eyed expression, Faye had concluded that she thought if they had any sense they'd simply scarper elsewhere as fast as their legs would carry them.

Timothy was the eldest of the brood still living at home. Faye guessed he was about nineteen and, on the few occasions they'd had a chat, she'd thought him rather sweet. She'd also discovered that, like her, he was saving to escape but had been hampered by his mother's eagerness to keep him right where he was so he could help fill the family kitty.

But Tim had recently had some news that had made him optimistic about moving on. His brother, Danny, worked in service in Essex and had let Tim know that a position at the house might soon become available. He'd told Tim he'd put in a good word with his boss.

'I reckon that young man's been getting out early so he can bump into you. I reckon if you was on your own, he'd be over here quick as a rat up a drainpipe,' Marge said archly.

'Don't be daft.' Privately, Faye agreed with her friend. She'd had an inkling for a while that Timothy liked her and, with a little encouragement, would ask her to walk out with him. It was true that he had a tendency to materialise alongside her when she was on her way to work. He had a job in the outfitter's shop where his brother Geoff used to work, before he'd perished in the Great War. Old Mr Milligan remembered Geoff Lovat with fondness, as did a lot of people, and had gladly allowed his brother to take a job with him as soon as he'd turned fourteen.

'Alice Chaplin's sister is married to one of the Lovats,' Faye told Marge, hoping to wipe away her knowing smirk. 'Sophy and Danny Lovat weren't at Alice's Christmas party, though. I didn't meet them 'cos they had to stay and take charge of all the festivities in the big house in Essex where they work.'

'Lucky them,' Marge muttered on a sigh. 'Wish I had a job in service and got all me grub and a place to kip rent free.'

'I met Alice's youngest sister, Lucy,' Faye carried on reminiscing about her lovely time that day. 'She works in service with them in Essex but she got allowed time off. She said Sophy managed to swing that one for her 'cos she's got influence. Their employers rely on her and Danny so much, they sort of run the place. Lucy was really nice...'

'Well, perhaps it might turn out you'll end up with a Lovat as your husband 'n' all,' Marge interrupted with a crafty laugh and an elbow digging into Faye's ribs.

'Give over,' Faye said impatiently and, disentangling her arm from Marge's, she pushed open the bakery shop door.

'Has Michael been getting into fights, d'yer know?'

Faye had been cutting Adam's bread and jam into fingers when her mother barged in with a shopping bag and shot that question at her. It was a moment before she carefully answered, 'What makes you say that?'

'I just caught sight of him doing his sweeping down the railway yard and he looked like he's got a bruise coming up on his cheek. I didn't go charging in and question him 'cos I noticed his guvnor were prowling about. Michael went out of here this morning looking all right, I'm sure of it,' Edie added with a worried frown.

'Well ... you know how boys are,' Faye replied lightly, 'they do like a rough and tumble in the playground.'

'I can see a right big barney with him on the horizon.' Edie dumped her bag on the table and pulled out some groceries. 'I reckon he's been getting hold of cigarettes, and when I find out how he's getting hold of them, there'll be trouble. His shirt stank of smoke when I washed it. I can't hardly get a penny out of him lately, and no wonder, if that's what he's been up to.' She stabbed a look at Faye, who seemed to be concentrating on feeding Adam his bread and jam. 'I know Michael's only doing a few weekend and evening shifts to earn a bit, but he's old enough to put some in the pot. And he was too, no trouble, a while back. Now it's like I'm askin' fer the world if I want a couple of coppers off him.'

Since they'd arrived in Campbell Road almost a year ago, Michael had been doing any little jobs he could find after school and at weekends. Apart from sweeping up, or carrying bags, down at Finsbury Park station, he'd been running errands for Mr Smith, who had the corner shop, whenever his regular boy was off. At first Michael had handed over most of his earnings to his mother to help out. But he was reluctant to give up anything now and Faye was certain she knew the reason why, even if Edie didn't. Her brother was handing all of it over to Donald Bateman for his comforts, as he called his booze and fags. She'd given up her five shillings of savings to help him clear the debt, but it had all been in vain: he'd gone straight back on his word to stay away from Bateman. After spotting Michael on a number of occasions huddled together with Donald and a group of other boys, she'd come to the depressing conclusion that her brother liked what he was doing too much to ever stop.

Now Jimmy had been sacked, and had turned to sulking and snarling more than usual because of it, Edie was scraping about for every penny she could get hold of to keep the household going. Faye had been giving up all but half a crown of her wages to her mother. She knew it was ridiculous to hold on to her gold necklace when things were so tight. Twice she had taken it off and put it in a pocket with every intention of pawning it. But, when loitering outside the shop, she couldn't, on either occasion, bring herself to go inside and part with it. Once gone, it would stay gone; she knew she'd never find the means to get it back. It was the most beautiful thing she had ever owned and she knew she'd only once in her life have anything as precious.

The news that Michael was sporting a shiner could mean only one thing: he was getting in deeper trouble with Bateman. A feeling of trepidation was writhing in Faye's guts, for she knew the situation couldn't be allowed to continue. Michael was only a kid, but if the debt was mounting up Mr Bateman senior might eventually get involved, and the consequences of that didn't bear thinking about.

SEVENTEEN

'Oi, Greavesie, over 'ere.'

Michael ignored Donald Bateman and his two pals, who had been watching him working, and catcalling from a few yards away. He continued sweeping up along the station concourse, his eyes lowered to the ground.

'Oi, Greavesie ... missed a bit ... over 'ere...'

Deliberately Donald tossed an empty cigarette packet on the cobbles, then kicked it. He took the cigarette from his lips, flicked ash and hooted a laugh.

Michael coloured in mortification but carried on working, aware that his supervisor was watching what was going on from the little hut close by. Mr Forbes was craning his neck and Michael could tell from his expression that he was angry. He rapidly started pushing the broom in Donald's direction and when close enough hissed, 'Piss off or I'll lose me job, then you'll not get a soddin' penny off what I owe you, will yer, numbskull.'

Whitening in rage, Donald snaked a hand to Michael's throat. He'd been showing off to his new pals, doling out free cigarettes and brown ales because he was feeling flush. His father had dropped by and shelled out earlier in the week. 'Who you callin' a numbskull?'

'Di'n't mean it,' Michael gasped, wriggling to free his neck from the pain. 'Just if I ain't got no work, ain't got no money.'

'Greaves! Come here!'

The bawled command from his boss made Michael jerk back his head, causing Bateman's nails to deeply score his skin.

As Mr Forbes strode up, Donald and his pals turned and sauntered away.

'Wouldn't mind a bit of time in the back row of the flicks with her,' one of Donald's friends muttered lewdly.

After she'd found out from her mother that Michael had again been beaten, Faye had set out as soon as she could for Finsbury Park station. She felt a bit guilty, keeping the truth from Edie.

But she'd promised Michael she wouldn't betray him. She wouldn't break her word before she'd privately warned him that their mother was on to him and the game was up. She'd been hurrying along, head down, deep in thought. Now as she raised her eyes and saw who was heading towards her, she groaned a curse beneath her breath. But she kept going and sent Donald a filthy look that made him snigger and step in front of her, blocking her way.

He caught her arm, jerking her around as she again tried to sweep past. 'Me mate was just saying he wouldn't mind a trip to the flicks with you. I reckon you'd sooner go with me, wouldn't yer, luv?'

'Get lost.' Faye attempted to fling off his fingers.

'That ain't nice,' he said, all mock injury. 'Ask you to come out with me 'n' get insulted fer me trouble.'

'Playing hard to get, ain't she…' one of Donald's pals chipped in, eyeing her lustfully.

'That right? You playing hard to get?' Donald forced her hand against his groin and moved it around. 'I'll give you hard, darlin'…'

'You got trouble there, Faye?'

Donald let her go and spun about. 'What's it to you, mate?' He belligerently sized up Timothy Lovat.

'She's me friend. What you doing to her?' Faye's white face caused him to frown. 'They been hurting you?' He came quickly closer. He'd just got off the train, having delivered a new waterproof to an elderly client, and was now on his way home to Campbell Road.

Gulping in a steadying breath, Faye hurried towards him to stop him approaching Bateman. 'No ... it's nothing, really.' She glanced back and could tell from Donald's expression, and the way his friends were watching expectantly, that they were intent on starting a fight. A few more disembarked passengers were coming along the road, slipping suspicious looks their way, adding to a mounting atmosphere. Faye grabbed her friend's arm, trying to drag him on with her towards the safety of the station, but Bateman's bawled challenge made Timothy turn back.

'Come on, mate ... let's be 'avin' yer. You want to act the big man? Not running off scared, are yer?' Donald swaggered up to Timothy and gave his shoulder a shove. He looked at his mates for approval, then transferred his gaze to a few dawdling commuters who seemed interested in the outcome of this confrontation.

Timothy, also conscious of spectators, felt obliged to push him back, and that was it. Donald swung a punch at his head and Timothy, recovering from the blow, returned a jab that sent his opponent tottering back with a surprised grunt. Bateman's two pals then happily considered it their duty to pitch in and, by the time two guards from the station sprinted out to see what the commotion was about, Timothy was sprawled on the floor, semi-conscious, and Bateman and his friends had scattered.

'You still here? Thought you'd be long gone, back to Kent.'

'No you didn't,' Faye challenged immediately.

'You drove past me in Blackstock Road earlier in the week.' His sarcastic welcome, after they hadn't spoken to one another for so long, had needled her, so, despite her intention to play it cool and casual with him, she added for good measure, 'I know you saw me that day.'

Rob swivelled slowly to and fro on the chair behind the desk and held her gaze, his expression unreadable. Abruptly he stood up and she thought for a moment he was going to come over to her. But he stayed where he was, behind the desk, and leaned back against the wall with his hands plunged in his pockets.

'Well, let's put it another way then ... why are you still here? The gold I gave you should have fetched enough to get you going.'

'I told you, I won't leave them behind.' She raised accusing eyes to his face. 'And as you made it clear you won't look out for the boys if I go away...' She was determined not to be provoked into an argument with him. It had taken a lot to muster the courage to come here. 'Anyway, things have changed since then.'

'In what way?'

The door of his office opened and the abrupt interruption made her start. A fellow in overalls walked in, carrying a fistful of papers. He stopped short on seeing his boss had a visitor. 'Need some monikers,' he explained, slanting a curious glance at Faye.

Rob beckoned him in and stooped to impatiently scrawl on dockets littering his desk. A jerk of his head saw the fellow on his way. 'What's changed?' he repeated his question once the door had closed.

Faye shrugged, unable yet to recount to him her family's troubles. First she needed a sign that he was amenable to listening to them.

'So ... how have you been?' he asked.

She nodded vigorously in response, glad of some idle chit-chat, and that he seemed to be thawing at last. 'You?' she asked politely.

He spread his hands in a gesture that asked her to judge for herself. He looked as he always did: smart, confident ... unpredictable.

'Not spoken to you in ages,' Faye said brightly. 'I… I know we sort of parted on a frosty note Christmas Day but I'd like it if we were still friends. And by the way, thank you for the necklace.'

'Took you a while to remember your manners.'

She shot him a sharp look, aware he was intentionally goading her, but she was determined not to rise to it. 'As I said, unfortunately we parted on bad terms.' She'd repeated it so civilly his mouth slanted in amusement, making her squirm. 'It seemed best to let things settle for a while,' she added through set teeth. 'Are we still friends?'

He smiled at the table where his cigarette pack was and picked it up. 'What do you think?'

'I don't bloody know, do I!' Faye stormed, unable to hold her temper longer. 'That's why I've got off work early to come here and ask.'

'Docked yer pay, has he, for getting off early?'

'Most likely,' she retorted.

'Should've come after work and seen me at home. You remember where that is, do you?'

The intentional sultriness in his voice reminded

her of the bittersweet unfinished business between them.

'What do you want, Faye?' He lit a cigarette and drew deeply on it before tossing the pack back on the desk. 'I'm busy. Say your bit and go.'

Mortified by his bored tone, she marched back to the door. She stood with her fingers clenched on the handle while thoughts and emotions raged within. If she went away now, it would have all been a squandered effort. For days she'd kept a lookout for Matilda to ask for his work address so she could humble herself and come here. But, shoving aside her pride, there was a far greater reason to stay and do what she'd set out to do. She knew she couldn't deal on her own with the mess Michael had made. She also knew that her mother was even less up to the job of unravelling it than she was.

Tim Lovat had been lucky to escape with cuts and bruises after the beating he'd taken earlier in the week, and her brother had lost his job at the railway station and was nursing fresh injuries. Worst of all, Jimmy now knew about it and had begun adding to the problem rather than helping solve it. When Edie had reluctantly told him Michael was being bullied, he'd been incensed – but not on Michael's behalf. He'd taken Michael's beating as a personal insult. He'd called Michael a nancy boy who couldn't stand up for himself, and had proceeded to train him with spiteful slaps and jabs until Faye had yanked her humiliated brother out of harm's way into the back room.

Even before Jimmy had turned up and stuck his oar in, the Greaves household had been in uproar.

Once Edie had got the full story about her son's debts and habits, she'd thrown a fit. She would have belted Michael herself, had she managed to pounce before he fled her rampaging and sped off up the road. But on one matter Edie and her kids were united: it was best to keep from Jimmy who the culprit was, because he would just make things ten times worse if he went looking for Donald Bateman, spouting his mouth off.

'You're bloody rude, d'you know that?' Faye finally turned from the door to face Rob. 'Never in my life met anyone so bloody arrogant and rude...' She glared at him, willing him to say something instead of lazily dragging on a cigarette and staring through smoke. 'And *just like your father.*'

This time the insult was deliberately meant to provoke and wound him, but it seemed to have lost its potency. He pushed off the wall and approached her. 'That was stupid. Only reason you're here is because you want something. Then you come out with something like that.'

'Yeah ... well, as I told you before, I am stupid.' Her fingers were clenching and unclenching, her guts writhing in frustration. 'I'm stupid to have wasted my time! You're not going to help, are you? You'd made your mind up on that as soon as I walked in the door.' She yanked on the handle but a fist whacked over her head slamming wood back into the frame before it had moved a few inches.

'Michael still in trouble, is he? Gonna tell me the truth about it this time, are you?'

After a tense moment she nodded her head.

'Who hit you?'

'Michael,' she lied.

'Your brother hit you?'

Again she nodded and quickly slipped sideways away from his overpowering proximity. She'd hoped she'd feel a bit indifferent to him after they'd been apart for a while, but the urge to throw her arms about him, and beg him to sort it all out, was an unbearable temptation. She put more distance between them. She wasn't falling for the likes of Rob Wild. The next time she gave away her heart, she wanted someone else's in return.

'He packs quite a punch for a kid.'

'We'd been arguing for a while.' Faye ignored his blatant scepticism. 'It all started with the five-pound note you gave me,' she doggedly carried on whilst pacing aimlessly to and fro. 'I had to break into it to pay our rent arrears, 'cos Podge Peters said we'd be evicted.' She glanced up at him. The incident seemed such a long time ago and she'd forgotten he'd never known about it. 'Once they realised I still had a couple of pounds in change, they were all looking for it.' She approached his desk, fiddled with a pen, pulling and pushing the top on and off. 'I told them I'd borrowed the fiver to help me get out of that dump and had given back what was left. Jimmy didn't believe me, of course. Well, none of them did. Jimmy turned the back room upside down looking for the cash, and I think Edie had been having a nose about too.' A forlorn smile skewed her lips. 'But I didn't twig that Michael had been quietly keeping an eye on things. He found the notes where I'd hidden them in the curtain, and wouldn't give me them back. He wanted the money to pay for cigarettes and ... well, you can guess the rest.'

'Not quite ... who was he going to pay for the cigarettes?'

Faye blinked at the desk, hoping her shrug looked passably casual. 'No idea...'

'Really? I've got an idea. Perhaps it was Donald Bateman. What d'you think?'

'Who?'

Rob's gruff laugh called her bluff better than any words could have done. But he explained briefly, 'Bateman junior's a wide boy who deals in this and that, and he's been hanging around with your brother.'

'How do you know that?' Faye blurted. 'Have you been keeping an eye on Michael?'

'I've seen them together,' he replied shortly. 'How much did you make on the necklace?'

His abrupt demand startled her into opening the top buttons on her coat and giving him a glimpse of gold. She wished she hadn't when it drew him closer. He touched a long finger to the warm gold circlet before raising his eyes to hers.

'Why d'you keep it? It's worth twenty quid at least, secondhand.'

'For a rainy day,' she answered huskily. 'I guessed there'd be worse to come.' She had too. Every time she'd thought she could stand no more of The Bunk and would chase her dream of moving away and training to be a secretary on Rob Wild's generosity, she'd look at her mother's careworn face and realise she'd never cope alone. If she went, the boys would suffer. Her sympathy was wearing thin where Michael was concerned, but Adam was a different matter. Each evening, when she got back from work, her sweet son would run up to cuddle her knees and make her feel wretchedly selfish for ever having dreamt of leaving him behind.

'We're in a worse mess at home,' she began quietly. 'You probably know that your brother's put Jimmy off 'cos there's not enough work to go round–'

'If you're going to ask me to take him on you'll be wasting your breath,' Rob harshly interrupted.

'No ... not him...' She paused, struck by an idea. 'But Michael could do with a job. He needs some work for after school and weekends.' She glanced about the small, tidy office. It was spartanly furnished with just a big wooden desk and several filing cabinets. When she'd arrived, she'd noticed the warehouse adjacent to this building. The doors had been wide open and inside it was packed floor to ceiling with boxes. A couple of men had been loading stuff on to vans and had looked very busy. In fact, they'd looked in need of another pair of hands. 'He wouldn't want much in wages, and he could help out here, sweeping up or doing odd jobs. He needs to be occupied but, most of all, he needs an older brother to keep him in line and tell him how stupid he's acting. He won't listen to me ... and God help him if he listens to someone like Jimmy.' Even before she saw his smile she realised she'd given him ammunition to fire back at her.

'Me? Now, how can I help?' Rob savagely mocked. 'A moment ago you told me I am "someone like Jimmy".'

'I didn't mean it ... you know I didn't,' she

mumbled, blushing.

'What I know is, you'll say it again.'

'I won't. I'm sorry I said it ... it's just ... you make me so annoyed sometimes.'

'Yeah, likewise...' He snatched up the pack of Players and flicked his lighter at another cigarette. 'If your brother's copped a few right-handers off Bateman, it's probably 'cos he deserved them for taking stuff he can't afford.' He'd spoken while getting alight the cigarette, then exhaled smoke and squinted at her through a grey mist. 'If at some time I find out it's true he's hit you, I'll clump him as well, and you won't like that, will you? So, I'm not giving him a job, or making things easy for him 'cos the only way for him to learn is the hard way. It'd be best for everyone if I stay out of it. It's nothing to do with me.'

'Of course it's to do with you!' Faye cried, indignant that he'd so quickly refused to help, and carelessly let her know he suspected she'd lied to him. She had; but the only reason she'd blamed Michael for hitting her was to protect Rob from getting involved in a feud with a vicious mob like the Batemans. But it seemed worrying about him had backfired on her. 'I know Michael's been acting like a fool, but you owe us some loyalty. We've all suffered having to live with your father.'

'Come home, has he? Thought Jimmy was shacked up with Nellie Tucker again.'

'He is, most of the time, but he crawls back when he's after something or other ... a handout usually.' She made a contemptuous gesture but wasn't to be distracted from the task in hand by talking about Jimmy Wild. 'If you'd done the decent thing and been a brother to Michael sooner, when I first asked, perhaps he might not be in such trouble. He hates it in Campbell Road as much as I do.' She paused for his reaction. When none came, she burst out, 'If my mother hadn't got involved with your father we wouldn't have been dragged here in the first place. And Michael says he needs to smoke and drink to put up with how depressed he feels.'

'Tough life, ain't it?'

Faye's temper exploded and she impetuously yanked off her necklace to hurl it savagely at him. 'Yeah, it's a fucking tough life, all right, so have that back and I'll make it the same way Michael does, on my own, and without your help.'

She was out of his office and halfway towards the junction with Holloway Road when the car came to a halt beside her. She crossed over and speeded up, trying to keep her tear-streaked face averted from him.

'Chrissake! Get in, will you? I'm not chasing you down the road.'

'Good! Fuck off!' she choked out at him over a shoulder.

This time when the car screeched beside her it bumped up the kerb and angled in front of her, trapping her against a wall. Tears of anger and frustration glittered in her eyes but she glared through them. Twice she slapped away the long fingers that approached her.

Impatiently he used two hands and jerked her against him, pinning her arms down at her sides. 'Get in the car, please,' he requested, solemn and polite.

She turned her head away from him, aware that her eyes and nose were dripping. Wriggling free a hand she swiped it across her face to clear the mess. 'Got a hanky?' she gurgled.

He let her go, dug in a pocket and handed over a cloth. She mopped her face as she got in the car.

EIGHTEEN

'Why d'you still lie to me all the time?'

'I don't.'

'Did Michael hit you?'

The silence that followed proved his point.

Rob had taken some back turnings and parked in a deserted street by a piece of bomb-damaged wasteland. It had been a gloomy day and heavy cloud was making it prematurely dark. As Faye gazed out over a landscape of mutilated concrete she was glad that her tear-stained complexion was in shadow.

'I thought you might be lenient if you believed it was Michael,' she owned up. 'I didn't want you going after Donald Bateman and getting involved with that lot. Your cousin Alice told me they're a vicious bunch.'

'Yeah ... they are,' he agreed. 'Saul Bateman works for Johnny Blake and he runs an outfit way out of my league.' He gave her a diffident smile that demolished his brittle image and allowed Faye a glimpse of a vulnerable boy. 'Were you worried about me?'

'I'd be worried about anybody who got on the wrong side of people like that. It didn't seem fair to drag you too deeply into it. I just want you to look out for Michael. It's not too much to want, is it?'

'And what about what I want? Is that too much?'

He looked steadily at her until she swerved aside her eyes, unsettled by tension gripping her belly that felt like excitement. 'S'pose not. It doesn't matter anyway. I've done it before. As my mother would say, at least this time I'd be dropping me drawers for a bleedin' good reason.'

He twisted a smile at her that strengthened into a cutting laugh. 'Right ... well, thanks all the same, but I already got a few girls who'll do that for me.' He turned the ignition. 'And with a lot more enthusiasm and talent than I reckon you'll show.'

Faye got out of the car in Seven Sisters Road. He'd brought her directly home, the drive taking only a few minutes and passing in complete silence. Humiliation was still shrouding her like an icy blanket as she hurried along in the gloom towards Campbell Road. Yet, numb as she was, she couldn't shake off a feeling she might just have lost something more precious than her gold necklace.

'You look much better.' Faye smiled at Tim, scanning his features. He was a pleasant-looking fellow of medium build and height with neat, regular features and a mop of wavy brown hair. It would have been a rotten shame if Bateman's beating had left him with any permanent blemish. Thankfully, just a yellow patch on a cheek and a graze on the bridge of his nose showed he'd recently been in a fight. 'See you're nearly all healed up, thank goodness.' When he'd hailed her from the opposite pavement, then sprinted across Campbell Road, Faye had immediately hurried to meet him.

Self-consciously Tim touched his sallow skin. He'd wanted to prove himself man enough to protect Faye on the day he'd squared up to Bateman, yet had ended up sprawled at her feet, groaning. 'Wasn't nothing really,' he mumbled, rubbing his scabbed nose. 'If Bateman had been on his own...'

'Yeah, I know,' Faye said gently, aware of his embarrassment. 'Trouble is, with bullies like him, they make sure they never are alone when they're out to start something.' She paused before gravely adding, 'Make sure you keep well away from him, Tim. He's from a bad lot. His father's a headcase, so I've heard.'

'He's got his comeuppance, in any case,' Tim told her, grinning. 'I saw him the other day and he's the one with a couple of black eyes now.'

'Who did that to him?' Faye demanded, agog. Her amusement faded away as she realised the answer might be Rob Wild.

'No idea. I asked around a bit and nobody knows,' Tim allayed her fears. 'Bateman has been telling everyone he got jumped by a gang. I reckon he's lying. In a straight fight, anybody could wipe the floor with him.' He bit his lip, regretting having brought the subject back to his drubbing. 'D'you fancy coming out to the flicks later in the week?' he blurted.

Faye could tell it had taken courage for Tim to finally ask her out. She could also tell he was now unsure whether to try to persuade her, or make a joke of his offer before she rejected him. She liked Tim; he was just the sort of decent, hard-working young fellow she'd always imagined she would meet and eventually settle down with. From the time she'd turned thirteen and had started to notice boys – who always had noticed her back – she had fantasised about one day having a sweetheart and falling in love. They'd pull together and save for a cosy future and raise a family in a neat house like Alice's that had a little garden with plots of flowers and vegetables. Then, before she'd even had her fifteenth birthday, fate had intervened and withered her dreams to ashes. If Tim knew what Rob Wild knew about her past, would he still ask her to go out with him?

Faye thrust all thought of Rob from her mind. She knew she'd acted childishly with him but was nonetheless still smarting from their last encounter, when he'd flung in her face that he had his pick of experienced lovers. Well, they were all welcome to him!

'Be nice, that would,' she brightly told Tim. 'Not been to the flicks for ages.'

'Fancy a bite to eat?'

Faye nodded, and didn't object when Tim put an arm lightly about her shoulders to escort her across the road towards Kenny's café. They'd come out of the picture house where a Buster Keaton had been showing and enjoyed a pleasant stroll, chatting and chuckling at the memory of the actor's antics, as they'd headed back, taking the long way round, to The Bunk.

'D'you want a pie, or fish, or something else with chips 'n' peas?'

Faye shook her head. 'A cup of tea and a bun will do me fine, thanks.' She did feel a bit peckish, but she knew Tim probably couldn't afford to treat her to a dinner. She knew he gave up most of his wages to his mother, just as she did.

Tim went to the counter to fetch their suppers, and Faye picked her way towards the window and pulled out a chair. The cafe was quite crowded, but these chairs had just been vacated and the remnants of a meal remained on the table. A listless-looking waitress appeared and stacked the used crockery on a tray, then gave the tabletop a cursory wipe before shuffling off.

'Had some good news the other day...' Tim took the seat opposite her and set their cups and plates down. He was obliquely aware that he was getting envious looks from other fellows who were eyeing his pretty companion, and he felt proud because of it.

Faye took a tentative sip of steaming tea and raised her eyebrows at him enquiringly.

'Got a letter yesterday from me brother, Danny, who works in Essex.'

'Oh, I've heard you talk about him,' Faye said conversationally, putting down her cup. 'He's married to Alice's sister, isn't he?'

Tim nodded. 'Sophy's got a job 'n' all, working as a housekeeper at Lockley Grange. They've done all right, the two of 'em, since they started there. Mind you, they've been there a good few years. I was just a school kid when they went off to Essex.' He swallowed some tea before continuing: 'Lucy Keiver's there, too. She's training up as a lady's maid...' Tim took a bite of bun and chewed. 'Danny wrote to tell me there's definitely a job going spare in a few months' time. One of his assistants is jacking it in and going off to Devon, 'cos he's inherited a bit of money off his granddad. At first this fellow wasn't sure whether he was upping sticks ... but now he is.' Tim's grey eyes were steady on her face as he added, 'Got an interview coming up at the weekend. I think I'll take the job, if it's offered. Not that me mum 'n' dad are goin' to like it. Biffie's gone 'n' joined the army, so that'll leave just Janet and Katie to help them fill the kitty. But I'd be a fool to pass it up. I'm in with a real chance, too, 'cos Danny's already put in a good word. I've been on at him fer ages to get me a foot in the door. He knows I'm going mad round here.'

'You 'n' me both...' Faye sighed.

'That's the thing...' Tim's voice had taken on a quiet significance, bringing Faye's eyes swerving to his. 'When this fellow leaves, he's taking his fiancée with him, so there's a maid's job coming up too.'

Faye stared at him and her cup hovered in front of her lips before being suddenly plonked back on its saucer.

'Just thought I'd mention it, 'cos I know you're keen to get away from round here,' Tim said, looking embarrassed. He'd guessed from Faye's reaction that she wasn't interested in the position, or anything else he might offer. Quickly he took another mouthful of bun.

'Well ... er ... thanks for ... for letting me know,' Faye stuttered. 'But I'm really set on training up to be an office typist. That's what I want.'

'Yeah ... 'course ... just thought I'd mention it,' Tim interrupted her. He gave her a smile in the hope she'd think he wasn't bothered. 'Even if I don't get the job, it'll be a break from this dump, just going to Essex for the interview. The Grange is quite close to the coast. Can't remember the last time I saw the sea...' Having rattled that off, and in doing so successfully dispersing the bit of remaining tension, he fell quiet.

'Adam's never seen the sea,' Faye said wistfully.

'Why don't you come along for the ride and bring your little brother?' The offer was genuine, but he shrugged to indicate it was no big deal to him whether she accepted or rejected it. 'Danny planned the interview especially for this weekend as he knew I could get a lift and save me train fare. Matilda arranged to visit them in Essex a few weeks ago, 'cos she reckons it's high time Sophy was introduced to Reg, seeing as he's gonna be her stepdad.'

'But they might not want more passengers...'

'Be pleased as punch, they will. The more the merrier is always Tilly's motto.'

Faye nibbled the inside of her cheek as she considered the invitation, but a small smile was soon tugging at one side of her full lips. The idea of a day at the seaside with Adam was hugely tempting. 'He would love it...' she breathed.

'That's settled then,' Tim said quickly, before she could change her mind. 'Don't worry; I'll sort it. You just get yer bucket and spade ready.'

'You'd better not be late back for work, miss, come Monday morning.'

'I said, it's just a day-trip. We'll be back Saturday evening, so there's no chance of that happening.'

'You don't know what problems you might hit,' Edie pointed out grumpily. 'The car might break down on the road, or something else unexpected...'

Faye put her arm around her mother's bony shoulders and gave her a squeeze. She knew Edie was moody due to being a little bit jealous that she wasn't able to escape her grim surroundings and have a holiday by the sea too. When her dad had been alive they'd often take day-trips to Margate or Broadstairs during the summer months. Faye could remember how much her mother had loved it. Edie would toil for days beforehand preparing food to take for their picnic.

Matilda had called by yesterday and personally invited her and Adam to join them for the day in Essex. During the conversation, Edie had discovered that Tim Lovat was also going to be a passenger as he was attending a job interview. Faye had felt her mother's shrewd eyes whip to her face, but if Edie'd had any thoughts on the subject, she'd kept them to herself.

'Be a bit of a squash, won't it, all of you in the car together? Adam'll get ratty and it won't please the others if he starts hollering or pees his pants.'

'Adam can wear a nappy for the journey and sit on my lap,' Faye had returned immediately. She wasn't about to let her mother dampen her enthusiasm for the outing. 'He'll be fine. It'll be a real treat for him to play on a beach. I hope it doesn't rain,' Faye finished, indignant that anything so mundane might spoil the treat.

'Last time I went on a charabanc, I was sick...' had been Edie's pessimistic parting shot as she'd got her coat and stomped towards the door.

'Bring you back a stick of rock, if you like,' Faye had called, smiling at her mother's back.

But her mother had been right about one thing, Faye realised as she sat now, staring out at sparkling water: Adam hadn't taken well to a long car journey. They had set out early that morning at seven o'clock, and it was just as well they had, or Tim might have missed the appointed time for his interview.

Several times on the journey Reg had offered to stop when the toddler started to grizzle. Reg's car had been borrowed from his friend for the day. It was a small, modest vehicle, with a rather battered, musty interior, and was nothing like Rob's sleek Tourer. They'd all been grateful to have a few breaks en route, and had scrambled out of the car to stretch their legs.

Reg had seemed well acquainted with the tavern forecourts the small car had chugged on to. 'That little lad can smell a pint, so he can,' Reg had joyfully announced when they'd taken a final rest, just outside Southend. He and Matilda had then happily set off, arm in arm, in the direction of the saloon bar. Once Faye had taken

Adam to the privy, she and Tim had kept her son amused by playing ball with him on a little bit of green at the back of the pub.

Faye lay back on the tartan rug spread on sand and shielded her eyes from the sun's glare. She let her lids fall, revelling in the warmth on her face and the soft breeze stirring her hair. It was a gloriously mild April day; not a rain cloud in sight. Despite the sunshine, there were not many other people on the beach.

'Crikey, he's worn me out,' a laughing voice exclaimed, making Faye again sit up.

Lucy dropped down next to her on the rug. 'Your little brother's a right livewire.'

Faye smiled and squinted at the toddler, who was darting here and there on the sand, squealing, as Reg pretended to chase him. Further on she could see Matilda, her skirts hoisted to her knees, paddling in foam on the shore. 'He was a miserable so and so on the way here, but I think he should sleep soundly all the way back to London.'

'It's so nice to see you again,' Lucy said warmly, spontaneously enclosing Faye in a hug. 'I got a surprise when you got out of the car, I can tell you. We were expecting to see Tim, of course...'

'I wonder if he's got the job,' Faye said musingly.

'His interview will be finished by now,' Lucy replied. 'So you'll know soon enough. The master was going off out at midday and I'd say it's gone that now. As soon as he's away, Sophy and Danny will get our picnic together and come and join us. They've been given a few hours off, same as me.

Tim'll be coming along with them, don't fret.' Lucy slid an arch, sideways look at Faye. 'Are you and Tim walking out?'

Faye blushed and shook her head. 'We've been out together, but we're friends, that's all.'

'Sorry, didn't mean to pry; just thought, if you were, you might be persuaded to take the maid's job that's on offer. It'd be smashing to have you working here with us.'

'I'd not work in service ever again.'

'Didn't know you had.'

'First job I took was working as a scullion in a big house in Kent.' It was a subdued response.

'Not all it's cracked up to be, is it?' Lucy said with a conspiratorial grimace. She'd detected the hint of regret in Faye's voice. 'I know there's plenty of worse jobs out there. But ... there's moments when I think it'd be nice to have a bit more privacy. I reckon it'd be a real treat to have me own little home, like Alice has.' She choked a laugh. 'A good man like Josh wouldn't go amiss either. Sophy went to a lot of trouble to get me out of The Bunk and into this job. Thought it were the best thing in the world at the time. Sound ungrateful, don't I?' she said ruefully.

'No ... you sound ... unsure about what you want in the future,' Faye said solemnly. 'That's how I feel.' She chuckled, lightening her mood. 'But I can tell you what you *don't* want, and that's Campbell Road. I wish we'd never gone there, and I certainly can't wait to leave. I'm saving to get out and get trained as a typist.'

'What's Rob say to that?'

'Who knows? Who cares? Don't see a lot of

him.' Faye gazed out to sea.

'Come on ... we could all see he was interested in you at Christmas. That's why I was surprised to see you with Tim today. Are you telling me Rob's not taken you out since then?'

'No ... he hasn't,' Faye replied truthfully and quickly changed the subject. 'Tim told me you've done well here and are now training to be a proper lady's maid.'

'I am,' Lucy said in a posh tone, feigning hauteur. 'Shame the new mistress ain't a proper lady,' she muttered pithily, then slapped a hand to her mouth to cover a giggle. 'Could get meself in right big trouble, saying that. But I know you wouldn't tell a soul.'

Faye was intrigued, and very much enjoying having a girly chat with Lucy. They'd fallen back into casual friendship as though it had been barely a week since last they'd spoken. 'Go on then,' Faye prodded Lucy to continue her scandalous tale. 'You can't whet my appetite then clam up.'

'She's the master's second wife.' Lucy leaned forward to whisper. 'He lost his first wife. It was a tragedy; she was only forty-five and got ill and died, just like that.' Lucy sighed and shook her head. 'She was a lovely woman ... kind and considerate, but the master got engaged a year later, and married not long after that. This new one's not much older than his daughter, Monica, and a bit too hoity-toity.' Lucy drew her knees up and rested her chin on them. 'I can see the mistress and Monica having a ding-dong soon. Then the master's gonna have to choose between his wife and his daughter.'

'My money would be on the wife winning,' Faye warned.

'Mine too.' Lucy agreed with a grimace. Faye suddenly looked past Lucy and waved. 'Here's Tim, and that must be your sister and brother-in-law with him.' A group of people had descended the steps that led to the beach and were approaching them. Tim was smartly dressed today in his interview suit; the man and woman with him were in sombre dark servants' garb. Lucy had told Faye she was going to change back into her uniform when she returned to the house. It was a treat to be in a pretty dress for a change, she'd said, twirling about with her floral skirt held out by its edges.

Having seen her sister lugging a box, Lucy sprang up and went to assist Sophy with the picnic food. Behind Sophy strode her husband, laden down with a bigger wicker basket. By Danny's side was his brother, Tim, his arms crammed with blankets for the ground.

Matilda had spotted her eldest daughter from the shoreline. Shaking the water off her toes, she bounded up the beach towards her. Having given over the picnic box to Lucy, Sophy ran to meet her mother halfway. The two women embraced warmly before walking back, arm in arm, towards the others.

'How did it go?' Faye immediately asked Tim as he dropped the rugs on the sand.

'Good,' he answered with a grin. 'Job's mine, if I want it. I said I'd have to speak to me mum 'n' dad; give them fair warning and so on, before I said fer definite I'd take it. I explained how me dad's got a gammy leg and doesn't get a lot of decent work come his way. Me new boss was understanding and said I could have time to consider. He said if I was anything like Danny, I'd be worth waiting for.'

Faye listened, smiling, whilst hoping that the tiny part of her that regretted hearing Tim's news didn't show. Soon she'd lose Tim's friendship, and it was only recently that it had blossomed. She felt mean and selfish in hoping he might not take up this wonderful opportunity to escape from The Bunk. She pinned a wider smile to her lips and told him she was genuinely pleased for him. 'Got to fetch Adam,' she said, jumping to her feet. 'I'll take him to have a paddle, and cool him off, before he has his sandwiches.'

Faye took Adam's hand and led him to the water's edge. She crouched down beside him and gently bathed his hands and flushed face with the cool brine. He stood breathing heavily, laughing silently at the horizon. Her eyes adored him as he pointed out to sea where a boat bobbed at anchor.

'Big boat,' she said, and planted a kiss on his moist forehead. 'Hungry?'

He nodded and put out his hand, impatient for her to take him back to the others. He was happy, Faye realised; happier than she'd seen him in a long while. Her eyes skimmed past to the group of jovial people who were settling billowing blankets on the beach and emptying the wicker baskets of all the good things to eat and drink.

It would be a fine thing to be part of such a

family. If she and Tim were sweethearts, and she moved to Essex to work with him, she would be part of it, she realised. She'd have the Keivers and Lovats as kith and kin. She knew Tim was already halfway in love with her, and were she the sort to exploit a fellow's feelings, she could easily do so. But she'd not willingly work again in service. It wasn't that she was scared of letting another rich, powerful man take advantage of her, as Simon had. If she were still naïve and weak, she'd have succumbed to Rob Wild months ago.

She'd not abandon her family to better her prospects, or make worse the tangle of lies that surrounded Adam's parentage by becoming the sweetheart of a man who thought her son was her brother. At some time soon, before he grew much older, she wanted Adam to call her Mum. Besides, at the back of her mind, something else, other than her conscience, was stopping her from doing wrong, and she suspected it had everything to do with Robert Wild and the violent emotions he caused her to feel. Faye got to her feet, feeling melancholy that even on such a carefree day as this she'd allowed him to intrude on her thoughts. With a sigh, she led her son back to the picnic.

NINETEEN

'Got any more o' them nice crisp fivers knockin' about have you, luv?' Podge Peters, just emerging from a doorway, called after her.

Faye didn't slow down. 'Yeah, stacks of 'em. Right comedian, aren't you...' she sent back witheringly.

'You won't be laughin' soon, sweet'eart,' he gloated softly. 'Your old lady don't come across soon with what she owes, you'll all be out on yer ear, no messin'.'

It was a sunny Saturday afternoon in early May and Faye had been on her way to meet Marge. They'd arranged to go together to the local public baths in Hornsey Road, and then on to Chapel Street to look at the summer clothes just appearing in the market now the weather had turned warmer. But she stopped and turned around with a frown. As far as she was aware, the rent was paid up to date.

Podge smiled smugly as slowly she retraced her steps. He leaned his bulk against the railings, chewing rhythmically, as he got out his little black book. 'Here we are then ... four weeks since I last got any rent out yer ma.'

Impulsively Faye snatched at the book to stare at a page that showed the last entry was dated at the beginning of April. Having shoved the ledger back at him, she turned and marched home.

'Could probably do you a deal darlin',' he cooed craftily after her. 'No fivers, no problem – not where you're concerned.'

'Just saw Podge in the road,' Faye burst out before she was halfway through the door. 'He says you've not paid any rent in four weeks.'

Edie whipped her head to one side and, ignoring her daughter, yelled at her son: 'Michael get outta there and get going, will you? Adam's driving me round the bend, whining. Take him up the shop with you.'

'You going to answer me?' Faye demanded. 'Is that fat creep having me on, or are we a month in arrears?'

''Course we are,' Edie hissed beneath her breath. 'D'you think I've got a money tree growing out the back and I just pick what I want off it?'

'I've been giving you nearly everything I earn to keep this poxy roof over our heads,' Faye shouted. She was feeling irate not only because of the depressing news of the debt but because she'd been looking forward to browsing the market stalls in the spring sunshine. She'd no money or enthusiasm for a shopping trip now. 'What've you done with the cash I've handed over?'

'Michael get out here and get up the shop, and take this list with you,' Edie shouted, waving a bit of paper that had a few words scrawled on it.

Faye grabbed hold of her mother's outstretched arm and shook it, trying to make her turn to meet her eyes. Her rough touch caused Edie to spring up and slap her daughter hard across the face.

Michael had come out of the back room just in time to witness his sister stumbling back clutching a cheek. Swinging an apprehensive glance between the two women, he snatched the paper, grabbed Adam's hand, and hauled him towards the door. Having seen the blow, the little boy's quivering lips were parted in a wail before they'd reached the landing.

'Sorry,' Edie mumbled. 'Sorry...' She sank back into her chair by the table. A moment later her head dropped into her cupped palms and soundless sobs made her shoulders quake.

'What is it?' Faye crouched by Edie, still massaging her stinging cheek. Her voice was hoarse with shock. Rarely had her mother raised a hand to her. The last time she'd taken a blow was when she'd admitted to Edie she was pregnant.

At first Edie shook her head as though she couldn't, or wouldn't, say. Then suddenly words tumbled from her that made Faye sink to the floor, stunned.

'I'm in the family way. I've got to get rid of it. And that costs.'

'What?' Faye breathed, her heart drumming madly.

'I'm expecting. I've got to get rid of it. Don't you tell no one, you hear? Don't breathe a word to a soul. I've been keeping back the rent money to save up to pay for it.'

After a silent moment, Faye garbled, 'Is it Jimmy's?'

''Course it is,' her mother snapped. 'What d'you think I am?'

'No ... didn't mean ... it's just ... he's not been

here much...'

'Been here once too bleedin' often, though, hasn't he,' her mother rasped bitterly.

'Does he know? Have you told him?'

Edie shook her head. 'Don't want him to know neither. Getting it dealt with before anybody knows.' Her forehead sank again into her hands. 'Oh, why in God's name did this happen? At my age?'

Faye placed an unsteady hand on her mother's bowed head. She looked far too old to be still having babies, but Faye realised Edie wouldn't turn forty-two till the end of the year.

'I wish we'd never come here,' Faye raggedly exclaimed.

'Well, we wouldn't have done, miss, would we, if you'd managed to keep your legs closed,' Edie snarled through her teeth. 'Got you a good job in a good house, didn't I, and two months later you're ruined. It's all your fault I had to get involved with a pig like Jimmy Wild and we all ended up with him in this dump.'

'That's not fair,' Faye protested quietly, but she hung her head as tears stung her eyes. In her heart, and much as she hated acknowledging such an awful truth, she'd always known that bolting from their employment, and her shame, to another part of Kent, had put pressure on her mother to find a man ... any man ... to share the burden of keeping them all. She realised too that there had been times since Adam had been born when her mother had been torn between telling her to get out and get herself wed, and take her son with her, and pleading with her to promise to always stay and keep helping out.

But Adam's birth was some way in the past and Faye couldn't understand why Edie still put up with Jimmy.

He was neither use nor ornament; he'd never improve, he'd only get worse. And a baby would definitely make him worse; she understood her mother's unspoken fears on that score. She had regular work at the bakery, and reasonable wages, and her mother had several ladies she charred for. Even Michael was bringing in a little bit. It would be tough for them to manage till Michael was out and earning full time, but they'd be better off without that parasite Jimmy Wild on their backs. He always took out of the pot more than he put in.

Faye's misty eyes passed over her mother's bony body. 'How far gone are you?'

'Few months, I reckon,' Edie answered bleakly. 'I've been praying it weren't true and no regular monthlies meant the curse was lifted and I didn't need to be careful no more. Just ain't my luck though, is it?'

'Couldn't you keep it?' Faye suggested huskily. The idea of a tiny sister or brother being dug out of her mother and thrown away made bile block her throat. 'We'll manage; just us. We'll move and leave Jimmy behind. You let me keep Adam...'

'Yeah ... well ... things have gone downhill fast since then,' Edie muttered. Abruptly she stood up and shook the kettle to see if it had water in it. 'Thought that'd be it, as far as me 'n' bringin' up babies was concerned. And it is.' With that she trudged towards the door to go and fill the kettle from the tap on the landing. Before she quit the room, she threatened dully, 'It's just between us, you hear? With any luck I'll be sorted out by the end of next week.'

Faye followed her mother on to the landing. Her mind was in turmoil, but she knew this was a fateful moment and she must somehow persuade Edie to ditch Jimmy. She also needed to know exactly what her mother intended to do about getting rid of the baby. 'You'll need enough money for a proper doctor, not...' She couldn't bring herself to utter the word abortionist. Rob had promised to provide her with a doctor so she wouldn't be at the mercy of a backstreet butcher if she were unlucky and fell with his baby. The memory of his cold logic still stung. The fact that his father had managed to do to her mother what she wouldn't allow him to do to her made her seethe with impotent fury, and words exploded from her: 'It's a life! One of us! Let's get shot of Jimmy and think carefully about it all rather than be hasty. He's always been bloody useless. We don't need him! Why've you let him cling on all this time? You've got to think about us now, not him.'

'I've been thinking about you all this time! That's why I've let him cling on,' Edie suddenly shrieked. 'D'you think I'd put up with the pig otherwise? 'S'only to protect you 'n' Michael I've done it.' Edie suddenly clamped together her quivering lips and her pale complexion took on a greyish tinge. She looked equally as stunned as Faye following her unguarded rant.

'What d'you mean?' Faye whispered. 'What've

you done to protect me ’n’ Michael?’ An icy chill was creeping over her. She’d sensed for a long while that her mother might be keeping something from her. Now, as she reflected on those suspicions, it suddenly occurred to her that reminiscing about her dad had often brought that haunted look to Edie’s eyes. When her mother had snapped at her to give over talking about him, Faye had naturally imagined the memory of her loss was still too raw to bear, but now she wondered if something sinister had been to blame. ‘Is it something to do with when Dad died?’ she croaked.

Edie stared at her with huge, unblinking eyes, then her head moved in slow nods. Her shoulders slumped as though a huge weight had been lifted from them.

‘Tell me...’ Faye pleaded huskily and, although she felt numb with foreboding, she raised a shaking hand to touch her mother’s arm and comfort her.

‘Didn’t die in France ... died in Kent, in hospital.’ The swift, jerky explanation seemed to have been torn from her mother’s guts.

Faye licked her lips and blinked. The silence seemed interminable; finally she whispered, ‘Dad came back alive?’

‘Weren’t alive ... not really...’ Her mother covered her face with her hands to muffle the sobs. ‘Were a poor, demented thing, with his body and mind blown to bits.’ Edie abruptly dropped her hands and whipped up her pinafore to dry her face. She kept behind the linen cover for some moments before letting it fall. ‘Didn’t want you and Michael to know how terrible a state he were in. I was told he'd died in France, so that's what I told you; I didn't tell you lies. They said that's what they'd expected that in days he'd die there in a field hospital, so that's what we were told. But he didn't, he hung on, so they shipped him back, even though there was no hope...' Edie's voice cracked. She raised bleary eyes to the ceiling, blinking and swallowing before continuing, 'God knows how the poor soul survived that journey. When I said I was going to visit yer uncle Fred, I was, so that weren't a lie neither. We both used to go and see yer dad in hospital.' Edie's mouth worked silently for a moment. 'He didn't know who I was, or who his brother was. He didn't know who *he* was...' She snorted back a sob. 'He passed away five months later, and it were a blessing... God knows it were a blessing.' Edie's eyes screwed shut and a sigh shuddered through her puckered lips. 'Jimmy worked there as a porter, so he knew all about yer dad. When we bolted to Dartford, all those years later, after losing yer stepdad and getting Adam, Jimmy recognised me. 'S'how we got together in the first place. He seemed all sympathy – you know how he is, the weasel. I trusted him; told him how you and Michael had idolised yer dad. I told him I didn't ever want you both to know how dreadful it had been for him in those months before he got release...'

'You were frightened he'd tell us out of spite if you kicked him out...'

Edie nodded. 'He calls it his parting gift; waves it in me face every time we have a serious set-to.

He wouldn't think twice about doing it.' Edie looked about at their decrepit surroundings. 'When he first talked about coming to London I thought it'd be good to have a fresh start, away from unhappy memories in Kent. The liar told me we'd be in clover coming here, leaving all those debts behind. Said his rich son would see us all right in Islington.' Her mouth twisted bitterly. 'Rob wouldn't even give him the time of day. Then when I realised what sort of dump he'd brought us to I told him I was heading back and taking you kids with me.' Edie gave a despairing shake of the head. 'So out he come again with his threats to have a little word with you and Michael.'

Faye hadn't realised she'd been silently crying whilst listening to her mother. She put up the heel of a hand to smear away the tears. 'He can go to hell! I'll tell Michael before he can!' she gurgled and opened her arms as her mother rushed at her. For a moment they clung together, sobbing, tormented by images of a gentle-natured man enduring agonies even an evil wretch shouldn't face. Finally the new life growing in Edie again infiltrated their minds and quietened their grief.

'So we get away from Jimmy now...?' Faye whispered against her mother's lank hair. 'Gonna help you as much as I can, I swear.'

Edie nodded. 'Get this baby sorted out then we'll start afresh.' She pulled out of her daughter's arms and gave a businesslike sniff. 'Don't you tell me to keep it, right, 'cos I can't. Don't want it. I'm too old and tired for any of that. 'Sides, it's his, and I don't want any reminders when we go.

So, I just need to get the money together and get it all sorted out.'

For a moment Faye was on the point of arguing with her mother about keeping the baby, but she realised she had no right to do so. She turned her attention elsewhere. 'It's his fault you're pregnant. He should help out, not get away scot-free.' Faye was surfacing from the horror of her mother's ghastly news ... all of it ... and realised the practicalities must be dealt with. She could later, in private, turn her thoughts again to her beloved dad.

'It's more my fault than his,' Edie admitted dully. 'Told Jimmy a while ago we didn't need to worry about being so careful no more. He's not much of a man in that way either, if you know what I mean, so it's not as if we was doing it often.' She hesitated, on the point of cutting short a conversation that should have made her feel awkward. But Edie realised she felt only relief at having her daughter to confide in. 'He only got the urge once in a while,' she continued in a mumble. 'But, God knows, I wish I'd never let him that night, even though it were easier just to let him get done and get going.'

'He's equally responsible, Mum,' Faye gently argued. 'Don't let him put it all on you...'

'I said *I'll* deal with it!' Edie hissed.

Faye paced to and fro on the landing, twisting together her palsied fingers and thinking. 'Where will you go?' she quietly demanded. 'Has someone recommended a doctor?' A hand instinctively sprang to her throat as it always had when she was fretting over money. But she'd forgotten she'd allowed her temper to get the better of her; there was no longer a reassuring bump beneath her collar. Her fingers curled and came away. She'd have sold the necklace today to keep her mother in safe hands. 'You can take everything I've got,' Faye offered hoarsely. 'It's not much, about six bob I've saved, but you can have it all.'

'Thanks,' Edie muttered.

'How much have you got? Is it enough? If it's short and you don't want to see Jimmy, I'll go after him. Promise you won't go to some backstreet abor–'

'Shut up!' Edie screeched at her, then swung a glance that encompassed the landing they were on and the dark halls above and below. 'Just shut up,' she croaked miserably, her eyes filling with tears. 'Do you think I don't know all of that?' She pushed past her daughter with the heavy kettle and went back in the room.

Faye took a few steps after her mother, then halted. Her wheeling thoughts had suddenly stopped on the mundane fact that Marge would be waiting for her, wondering where she'd got to. Scrubbing her eyes, she took a deep, calming breath and headed towards the top of the stairs.

Jimmy waited until Faye had disappeared into the street before emerging from the shadows beneath the staircase. He looked up at the dingy doors ranged above. He'd been hoping to wheedle a few bob out of Edie this afternoon because Nellie, curse her, was laid up and unable to take punters for a few days. After what he'd just overheard, his only plan was to avoid Edie like the plague and go on the missing list for a while. He hoped by the time he got back Edie would have done what she'd said she'd do and sorted things out without bothering him for a farthing.

Now that Faye had been put in the picture over her dad, Jimmy knew his days were numbered where Edie was concerned. She was a lost cause, so he wasn't putting money down the drain even if she was knocked up with his kid. He pulled up the collar of his coat and hunched his shoulders to his ears as though the paltry disguise might help him pass through Campbell Road unrecognised. On the threshold of the house he glanced to and fro, hoping to spot which direction Faye had set off in. So busy was he scouring the street that he didn't hear the click of the back door that led to the yard where the privy was.

Silently Michael took up position where Jimmy had concealed himself, beneath the stairs. As Adam started to babble, he put a hand over the toddler's mouth, and smiled as though they were playing a game. Having spotted Faye's fair head in the distance, Jimmy quickly stepped out and set off in the opposite direction. Michael moved too. Clutching his few groceries in one hand, and Adam's wrist in the other, he started to climb the stairs.

TWENTY

'How you doin', darlin'?' Donald Bateman strolled out from the alleyway in which he'd been loitering and started walking by Faye's side.

'I told you yesterday to stay away from me.'

'Didn't mean it, though, did you?' he slung an arm about her shoulders. 'Don't mind you playing hard to get. I like it that you ain't easy like some of 'em.'

He'd sounded so condescending that Faye felt inclined to laugh. But her mood was too sombre for humour. 'Get lost, will you, I'm on my way to work.' She undulated her shoulders to get him off her.

'I know you're off to work. What you doing on yer dinner break?' He angled his face closer to hers to read her expression. 'Take you to Kenny's cafe, if you like.'

Faye noticed the shadow of a bruise on his face. Despite being disgusted by his proximity, she examined it closely because she needed to know.

'See you've been fighting again.'

He snapped his head back. 'Ain't been fighting,' he declared cockily. 'If I'd been fighting, luv, it'd be the other geezer with the bashed-in face. Got jumped, di'n't I, down an alley.'

'Did he rob you?' Faye pursued.

'Nah; didn't take nuthin'. Just a nutcase, weren't he, out to cause trouble.'

'Like you, you mean,' Faye muttered, wondering if he was too dense to realise he fitted his own description. She turned her head to look in shop windows. She believed what he'd said, and knew that if it had been Rob who'd arranged for him to get a beating, he'd thankfully been sensible enough to do it on the sly.

Faye had a way to go yet before she reached the Travis Bakery and she didn't relish the idea of walking the route with this toad by her side. She suddenly stopped and nipped across the road in an effort to shake him off.

Donald Bateman had been lying in wait for her yesterday morning too. That had been the first time she'd clapped eyes on him since the day he'd beaten up her brother and Tim Lovat, a couple of weeks ago. But he hadn't approached her yesterday; he'd just watched her from the opposite pavement.

She'd been hoping that the shock of what had occurred had finally brought Michael to his senses, and it seemed to have done so. Her brother now seemed ashamed that his stupidity was becoming common knowledge, and that a neighbour's son had been hurt in a fracas because of him. He had hardly gone out since, except to do errands to earn a few coppers. But it seemed Bateman hadn't been similarly affected by his conscience. Faye now knew he had no intention of leaving them alone.

After a moment's indecision, Donald sprinted after her, dodging vehicles, his expression registering his displeasure at having had to exert himself. He caught at her arm, spinning her about.

'You know something, luv? It'd do you and yer brother a favour if you was a bit nice to me, 'stead of pissing me off all the time.' He peered at her profile. 'What's up?' he sneered. 'You sweet on Tim Lovat? If you are, I'd better make sure I smash his face in a bit better next time.'

'No, I'm not sweet on him,' Faye retorted. 'He's just a friend. So leave him alone.' She ripped her arm free and speeded up. 'If me stepfather finds out you're pestering me, he'll have you.' It had been a desperate threat to prevent him brooding on Tim, but a moment later it occurred to her that, if Jimmy got a bashing off Donald Bateman, it wouldn't bother her one bit. It was no more than he deserved.

Bateman's scoffing hoot of laughter was understandable. Jimmy Wild didn't look capable of fighting a fellow his own age, let alone a thug who'd probably not yet turned twenty. In Faye's estimation all the swine was able to do was lie and cheat and blackmail. Unfortunately, the inadequate was still man enough to get a woman pregnant.

'Just leave me alone!' Faye blasted out as Donald again tried to pull her close to him.

'Don't think you really want me to do that. I've left your brother alone 'cos I like you,' Donald whispered sinisterly in her ear. 'But he still owes me a lot of money.'

'That's your fault,' Faye snapped. 'Don't give him stuff when you know he can't pay for it.'

'That's not how it works, darlin'.' He smirked. 'I sell it to mugs and they've *got* to pay for it, one way or another. Either they pay or get paid, if you get my meaning.'

'Yeah, I do...' Faye lilted sarcastically.

'But in your brother's case, I'm willing to make an exception, see. All you gotta do is say you'll come out with me and I'll tell him he don't owe me nuthin' no more.'

She'd shrugged him off again, so Donald stuck his hands in his pockets and sauntered beside her. He fancied her, but there was more to it than that. A couple of times his father had asked how he was getting on with chatting up Greavesie's sister. Donald knew it'd please his dad if he could say they were going out together. Then he could tell him he needed money to get his own place so she'd move in with him. Donald wasn't bothered whether Faye stuck around after that. Once he was set up in a room of his own, he reckoned he'd manage to wangle a regular allowance out of his father. Saul would do anything, he realised bitterly, to keep him from going back to live with him. And he knew that, once he was out, his mother would rent his room and never let him back in with her either.

Faye pushed open the shop door and nipped in quickly without glancing Donald's way. Her heart was hammering and not simply because of the pace at which she'd been marching along. Bateman's persistence was starting to alarm her. So were his threats of violence towards Michael and Tim. If for one moment she'd believed that Donald was sincere in saying he'd write off Michael's debts, she'd go out with him. But she knew he was a liar as well as everything else. It wouldn't end there. If she refused to sleep with him he'd probably double Michael's debt and beat up him and Tim as well.

Her mother's imminent abortion was constantly on her mind and Faye resented Bateman putting an added burden on her. She didn't want anything else presently cluttering her thoughts. Edie was avoiding answering any of her questions. Faye still had no idea what arrangements her mother had made, or whether she had enough money to pay for a proper doctor in a few days' time. But she knew from her own experience that it wasn't a false alarm. Her mother had been sick a few times in the morning, although she'd tried to hide it. She was looking more pale and exhausted than usual too. But Edie's body showed no obvious signs of pregnancy. In fact, she looked scrawnier. Faye was hoping against hope that perhaps nature would be kind to her mother and do the deed soon so they could dispense with the doctor.

'What's this?'

Pam flicked over a page before looking up at Stevie. Quickly she closed the magazine and jumped to her feet.

'Where d'you get that?'

'Out of Christopher's pram when you went down the shop. Wanna tell me why you've been hiding it there?'

'Give it here.' Pam darted forward and tried to snatch the laudanum away.

Stevie held the small bottle out of her reach. 'Now I'm gonna ask you again. What's it doing in his pram?'

'I've been taking a little bit, if you must know,'

she sullenly lied. 'Helps me with me nerves.' She flung him an agitated look. 'Need something, don't I, living round here. I didn't say nuthin' 'cos I knew it'd only start you off.'

'You? Nerves?' Stevie snorted cynically. 'You ain't got any feelings.' He suddenly gripped a handful of her hair. 'I'll tell you what I think, shall I? He dragged her with him to where the pram stood by the window and shoved her face close to the still form of their son. 'I reckon you've been pouring it down his throat and that's why he's gone so quiet and never wants no feeds. That's what I reckon.'

Pam started to cry; her scalp was throbbing madly but it was the shame and fear of having been caught drugging their son that really started her wailing. ''S'all right fer you to criticise. Don't tell me you hadn't had enough of him screamin' all the time. But you'd just piss off out soon as he started. Weren't getting on your nerves all the time like he was mine, was he?'

'Well, here y'are. Have some of this to calm you down.' He got the top off the bottle with his teeth and, yanking back her head, tried to jam the liquid through her lips.

Pam dribbled and screamed as glass ground against her teeth.

'Don't want it?' he rasped. *'Don't want it?* Neither does Christopher, you selfish, useless bitch!' He finally let her go, shoving her away from him so forcefully that she sprawled on the floor. 'Get yer coat,' he spat out, his face white with wrath. He picked up the thin little boy who barely stirred when disturbed.

'What you doing?' Pam garbled.

'Get yer coat!' Stevie roared.

Quickly she stumbled to her feet and pulled on her coat.

'Now get outside to the van.'

'Where we going?'

'Just do it,' Stevie said dully, as though the rage in him had burned out. 'Do it before I do something that I'll regret all me life.' He gently wrapped his floppy-limbed son in a blanket and followed his wife out of the door.

'What's this? What's going on?'

Having spluttered out his indignation, Mr Plummer stuck his pipe back between his teeth and sucked energetically on it as he stood craning his neck to peer around the plump figure of his wife blocking his view in the narrow passageway. They'd been listening to the wireless, enjoying a cup of tea with a few ginger biscuits, when a loud hammering on the front door had startled them to their feet.

Stephen barged past them both, cradling his son in one arm and propelling his wife in front of him with the other. Grim-faced, he headed straight for the front room and waited for his dazed in-laws to catch up with him.

'D'you want to tell them, or shall I?' Stevie barked at his dishevelled wife.

Pam yanked her arm out of his grip and fled to stand with her slack-jawed parents, who'd just hurried back into the room. Her father immediately turned down the volume on the wireless and whipped a glance between the couple.

'You can have back that evil cow of a daughter of yours. You can have me son, too, till he's better. And you make sure he do get better 'n' all. If he needs to go to hospital, you take him. Then when he's back to normal and eating properly, I'll be back for him every weekend to take him home.'

'What? What's going on?' a bewildered Mrs Plummer asked her daughter. She transferred her myopic gaze to her grandson. 'What's up with Christopher?' she asked, squinting at him but not daring to get closer to her enraged son-in-law.

'She ain't going to say, and if she does tell you a tale it won't be the truth.' Stevie gently put his son's listless body down on the sofa and pulled the laudanum out of his pocket. 'She's been dosing him with this to keep him quiet so she can sit on her fat arse reading magazines and drinking tea all day. Took me a while to realise why he's been sleeping all the time without hardly waking up for a feed.'

'What is it?' Mr and Mrs Plummer chorused fearfully, gazing at Stephen's raised hand.

'Laudanum.'

Pam's parents sent aghast looks their daughter's way.

'He's exaggerating everything,' she screamed. 'You know what he's like ... what his scummy family's like. You was right about him all along. Should never have got married.'

'Fucking right on that score!' Stevie choked a bitter laugh. 'And while we're at it, if you think my family's scum, what sort of parents brings up a daughter to be as wicked as you?'

'At least me father don't knock about with

whores down Finsbury Park,' she bawled through spittle-flecked lips.

'Yeah ... and at least my brother's got more sense than to be interested in you flashing yer knickers at him. Fuckin' shame I didn't follow his lead.'

In the pulsing silence that followed, Mrs Plummer finally asked weakly, 'Have you given Christopher some of that, Pam?'

'Only a drop ... he exaggerates everything...' She flicked a wrist dismissively.

'Yeah, 'course I do,' Stephen said, but there was a quiet satisfaction in his voice because he could tell from Mr and Mrs Plummer's distraught expressions that, much as they didn't want to, they believed him, not her. On the threshold of the room he turned to look at them all, his face a mask of contempt. 'If I knew what to do with him, I'd keep him. But I can't feed a baby or make him well and earn a living at the same time. I'm warning you though, I'll be back for him when I've sorted something out, 'cos he's not stayin' with her. She ain't got it in her to be a mother ... or a wife, if it comes to it. If you try and stop me, I'll have the law on the lot of yers and tell 'em what's gone on.' A moment later he was out in the hallway and, ignoring the pandemonium he'd left behind in the sitting room, he slammed out of the front door.

'Where you rushing off to?'

Matilda, having spotted Faye in Hornsey Road, hurried to catch up with her.

'Oh, just delivered a birthday cake and now on

me way back to the shop,' Faye said. 'How's Alice doing? Must be due about now, isn't she?' The thought of babies was constantly in her mind and seeing Matilda had reminded her that Alice's time was near.

Matilda had a sort of blunt wisdom that Faye could sorely use right now. She was tempted to pour out her heart to the woman, but knew she mustn't because she'd promised her mother she wouldn't tell a soul about it.

'She's got a bonny little lad,' Matilda replied with a grin. 'I saw him yesterday for the first time.'

'Bet she's pleased it's all over.'

'She is. Rob came on a visit too; bought little Bennie an enormous teddy bear, he did. That's what Alice has called the little lad: Benjamin.'

'That's nice...'

'So how's all your lot?' Matilda could tell that something was wrong. Despite Faye's attempt to present a cheery exterior, it seemed the young woman had cares weighing heavily on her.

'So-so...' Faye said quietly. 'You know how it is, living round here. Must be off; Mr Travis'll be wondering where I've got to.'

Matilda put a hand on her arm, halting her. 'Not seen your mum about much. Last time I saw her, she looked green about the gills and hurried inside. Jimmy's not been using his fists has he?' she asked, concerned.

'No, nothing like that ... it's ... nothing.' Faye managed a weak smile and walked on. It was Friday, the end of the week, and still she didn't know whether her mother had made arrangements to have an abortion today. That morning she'd given Edie all the money she had saved – seven shillings – and offered to stay home from work and go with her. Edie had taken the money, but she'd refused Faye's offer to accompany her and had insisted she must get herself off to work as usual. Then, while Faye was pulling on her coat, Edie had mumbled that she'd not yet decided what to do, and didn't need an inquisition all the time.

Matilda watched Faye thoughtfully for a moment before she proceeded on her way. She hadn't seen Jimmy about for a while either, and her agile mind began to wonder why that might be. She knew, of course, that he was living on and off with Nellie, but he could usually be seen beetling up and down the road at least a couple of times a week.

On reaching Campbell Road, Matilda spotted Edie in the distance, coming out of Smithie's shop with a bag in her hand. She also noticed Beattie Evans was out the front bashing her rug against the railings. Matilda went over to chat to Beattie, keeping leeside of the woman to avoid a cloud of dust, whilst waiting for Edie to draw closer so she could casually bump into her. When Edie had got to a convenient spot Matilda strolled across the road.

'How you doing?'

A twitch of a smile was Edie's response.

'Not seen Jimmy about lately.'

Edie speared her a look. 'Well, I expect you know same as I do that he's got a tart on the side.' She'd sounded testy but now regretted snapping. She could use some information from Matilda. 'Speakin' of which, I think it's about time I made a stand, and things got sorted out one way or another between us. Up to here with it all, I am.' The backs of her fingers tapped the underside of her chin. 'D'you know where this old bag lives – the one that he knocks about with?'

'Yeah, I do know,' Matilda said.

'Good,' Edie declared, with a satisfied nod.

TWENTY-ONE

'Can I have me job back?'

Rob hadn't got the door open far when he heard his brother's voice firing that at him. He jerked the door fully open and saw Stephen standing on his step. Rob gestured him into the hallway.

When they were inside the sitting room, Rob went straight to the cabinet and picked up a bottle of brandy. He proffered it in wordless invitation.

Stephen shook his head. 'Can I have me job back?' he insisted in a resigned voice.

'Pam sent you here?' Rob asked neutrally.

'I've kicked her out. I'm getting a divorce.'

Rob put the bottle back and rubbed a hand over his mouth. His amazement at what he'd heard was limited to a whistling exhalation of breath unsealing his lips. 'Right ... well ... job's yours, if you want it. It always was. You only had to ask.'

'Yeah,' Stephen said acidly. 'Well, you've got your way. I've come cap in hand and asked, ain't I. Feel better?' He spun on a heel and headed for the door. 'Be in tomorrow then, same time as usual?'

'What's gone on?' Rob caught up with him before he quit the room.

The hostility between the brothers hadn't completely disintegrated, but neither had the bond forged between them in childhood. Even before their mother had died, they'd clung to one another for comfort and support because neither of their parents could be relied on to provide much for them. From a very young age they'd realised they only had each other to trust and confide in.

Instinctively Rob knew that if Stephen was going to tell anybody the truth of what had gone on between him and his wife, it would be him. He put a lightly restraining hand on Stephen's shoulder to make him turn around. 'It's a bit sudden, ain't it? You caught Pam out?'

'Yeah ... you could say that. But don't worry, it weren't nuthin' to do with her throwing herself at you.' He looked away from Rob's unflinching dark gaze. If he'd hoped to disconcert his brother, or make him feel guilty, by coming out with that it hadn't worked. 'I knew you never wanted her. Come to think of it, I'm not sure I ever wanted her either.' Stephen fished a packet of cigarettes from his pocket and lit one with an unsteady hand. 'She's been dosing Christopher up with laudanum to shut him up so she can laze about doing nuthin' all day. He's not an easy kid, I know. He cries a lot, but to do something like that till the poor little soul looks like a bag o' bones...' He hung his head before shaking it in despair. 'Found the bottle hidden in his pram.' The words were ejected in a breathless gasp and he stood staring at his shoes then suddenly pressed closed his eyes with thumb and finger. 'I come home early and found him on his own ... just lying there, still as a statue, in his pram. She'd gone off to the shop to get herself fags and a magazine. When I couldn't wake him up I thought he was dead...'

Rob reached out a comforting hand, but he shook it off and took a pace back. He snorted back a sob, made an effort to control himself, then continued: 'So, I've kicked her out. Took her back to her parents and told 'em they can have the bitch back. It'd suit me if I never clapped eyes on her again.' He took a long drag on his cigarette. 'Had to take Christopher there 'n' all, 'cos I can't look after him and work at the same time. 'Specially can't be running things meself or I'll never get a minute spare to see him. So, that's the end of me business.' He slanted a self-mocking smile. 'Weren't never any good at it, anyhow. Pam weren't right about much, but she was right about that. I just ain't got the nous to make a profit. Paid Jimmy more'n I paid meself, most weeks.'

He took a final suck on his cigarette and glanced about for somewhere to dump the stub. When he couldn't spot an ashtray, he cupped a palm under smouldering ash. At home he'd have dropped it on the filthy floor and put his foot on it.

Rob didn't smoke in the house because he hated the reek that hung about for days. He usually didn't allow anybody else to smoke indoors either. Without an ashtray to hand he collected a porcelain dish and put it on the polished surface of a table beside his brother. Carefully Stephen ground out the butt on Coalport roses. 'So that's why I need me job back, if that's all right. Got to have regular days and wages. Can't be doing all the hours God sends, or I'll never see nuthin' of Christopher. I've told them I'm having him with me every weekend. And that's what I'm doing.'

Edie knew she was no oil painting, but next to that old dog she reckoned she was Greta Garbo.

She'd recognised Nellie Tucker as soon as she turned the corner and spotted her on the opposite pavement. It hadn't just been Matilda's fair description of a fat, brassy blonde who looked like she'd seen better days that had helped her identify her husband's lover; a while back Edie had spotted Jimmy going into a pub in Holloway Road with Nellie and had had a smirk to herself.

Since Edie had told her daughter about her condition she'd been considering Faye's response: Why should Jimmy Wild get away scot-free with everything? She was wondering if he had somehow guessed she was knocked up and that was the reason she'd not seen him. He usually came round at least a couple of times a week to try to keep her sweet with ludicrous lies about why he could only spare a little bit of cash. But while he kept giving – paltry amount though it was – Edie was determined to keep taking. As far as she was concerned, a contribution towards the rent was the least the bastard owed her until this was sorted out and she got rid of him for good.

Out of five pregnancies, Edie had only two surviving children. She'd hoped that, given her age and frailty, she'd lose another. When she'd seen a bit of blood the previous week, her spirits had soared. She'd been so optimistic that a miscarriage was imminent she'd reluctantly surrendered some of her abortion savings to Podge Peters. He'd caught her by the railings, blocking her way into the house until she'd handed over something. She'd given him two weeks' rent and a barrage of abuse.

When no more shows of blood had arrived, Edie had decided to help things along a bit. She'd taken a bottle of gin, hidden in her bag, to the public baths and stayed for half an hour swigging from it while immersed in water that she'd normally have found too hot to bear. But endure it she did, and she'd come out tottering and looking red as a lobster.

But she obviously wasn't in luck. This week she'd felt a little fluttering in her guts and it had made her crumple to the floor and weep. She knew she couldn't wait any longer; she also knew she needed to replace the money she'd lost to Podge, and she was determined one way or another she'd get it out of Jimmy.

The sound of an argument started her from her reflection. A weasel-faced little fellow had accosted Nellie as she loitered on the corner and, for some reason or other, she'd sent him on his way with a bawled curse and a two-fingered salute.

Edie nipped across the road before her courage failed. She'd sooner catch the woman here than have to go to the address Matilda had given her. 'Believe you're Nellie Tucker,' Edie announced with her head tilted at an aggressive angle.

'Yeah ... what's it to you?' Nellie snapped. She was in a foul mood, having just been propositioned by a pervert. She was also – in common with Edie, although she didn't yet know it – fed up to the back teeth with Jimmy Wild. He'd gone missing owing her money and without paying the rent on her room. Despite being May it was a vile, damp night and she was bedraggled, tired and hungry. She'd been standing around for over an hour without making even enough for a day's rent and a decent drink.

'Me name's Edie Greaves and I believe you're messin' about with me husband.'

Nellie gawped at her then moistened her lips nervously. She slipped a glance right and left. Edie Greaves was a skinny, shrunken little thing in her estimation, but even so Nellie could tell she was no pushover. 'Take it up with Jimmy,' she retorted and showed Edie her back.

Edie grabbed a chunky arm and yanked her around. 'Yeah, I will, when I find him. Fer now I'm taking it up with you. Where is he? Ain't seen him and I need to speak to him urgent.'

Nellie shook Edie's bony fingers off her arm but studied her rival more thoughtfully. She reckoned that Edie Greaves had known for a good many months about Jimmy and her. If she'd come this evening to find him, something urgent had brought her out after dark. 'Dunno where he is,' Nellie replied flatly. 'Truth is, I need to speak to him urgent 'n' all. But then he always do manage to disappear when he owes me a good amount.'

'Yeah, don't he just,' Edie sourly agreed. She knew Nellie was telling the truth. She'd recognised the self-loathing and disillusionment in the woman's expression. She saw that look every day, staring back at her from the dirty mirror in her room.

'You after money off him 'n' all?' Nellie ventured.

Edie gave a nod.

'When ... if ... he surfaces, I'll tell him it's urgent,' Nellie said with a softening in her voice.

'It might not wait till he surfaces,' Edie muttered bleakly and unconsciously a hand touched her stirring belly.

Nellie had managed to avoid motherhood but she'd been pregnant several times and recognised the tell-tale sign. She gawped disbelievingly at Edie's old, weathered face and flat, shapeless body. 'Not that, surely?'

Edie stuck up her chin, annoyed she'd unwittingly betrayed herself. 'None o' yer business.'

'Bleedin' hell,' Nellie breathed. 'Didn't think he had it in him. Bet he didn't neither! No wonder he's done a runner.'

'He don't know. Never told him,' Edie blurted. It was a moment before she realised she'd confirmed Nellie's suspicions. With a shrug she added, 'He might've guessed but don't reckon he could've. It don't show and he don't take no notice of anybody anyhow. He's always too wrapped up in himself.'

'Ain't that the truth,' Nellie scathingly endorsed. 'If you want him back, you can have him. When he turns up I'm telling the git I've had enough of him. Wish I'd never in me life got involved with him.'

'Yeah...' Edie's one bitter word spoke volumes.

As Edie walked away, Nellie went after her. 'What you gonna do?'

'Get a knitting needle. It's all I can do 'cos I ain't got enough for any sort of job. Maggie Phipps wants two quid,' she said. For several years Maggie had run a thriving business aborting unwanted babies in Campbell Road. Despite her reputation as a drunken slut, and the fact that the only 'qualification' she could lay claim to was that her late mother had been a nurse, desperate women still flocked to her. Realising that Nellie still had hold of her, Edie liberated her arm with a wrench.

'Don't you go to her,' Nellie warned, renewing her clutch on Edie's elbow. 'Catch her at the wrong time, when she's had a few sherbets, and she won't know which end of you to start on. You'd be safer with yer knitting needle and save yerself two quid.'

'Ain't ready to go anywhere yet, anyhow,' Edie wearily confided.

'You got anything put by to pay for it?' Nellie gently enquired.

'Some ... not enough...' Edie admitted. 'Had rent money saved, but that bastard Podge caught me a few days ago and took most of it...' Her voice tailed away.

'If I had a bit, I'd let you have it, swear,' Nellie croaked. 'Been stood here bleedin' ages and got...' She dug in a pocket and pulled out a florin and a couple of sixpences. 'There ... take 'em and welcome, if it'll help.'

'Don't matter,' Edie said sharply, dragging her eyes from the coins glinting on Nellie's palm. 'Ain't your fault or your problem.' And with that she set off home.

'Still here then, luv?'

'Piss off.'

'Got seven bob fer yer. Come on ... you'll be lucky to get yourself a thrupenny bit on a night like this.' The rat-faced man looked up at the dark sky as a few fat raindrops hit his hat. He sidled up closer and grabbed a handful of Nellie's ample backside, kneading it. 'Never know, you might like it. Old girl like you should be used to it, 'cos I reckon you've slackened off a bit on the regular route, ain't yer.'

'Yeah, specially where a little runt like you's concerned,' Nellie jeered, sizing up his puny frame. Her gaze veered off and she stared into space for a moment, then stuck out a palm. 'Give us ten bob or nuthin' doin'.'

He gave her a poisonous smile and dug in a pocket. About to hand it over, he pulled it back teasingly out of her reach. 'If I didn't think it was gonna piss down any minute, I'd go up West 'n' get me money's worth off a sweet young dolly. You're a rough old sort to be driving an 'ard bargain of ten bob. So don't try 'n' short change me, 'cos I'm already browned off and might easily let you have it.'

Nellie snatched the bank note and stuck it down her bodice before stomping off down the alley with the miserly little runt in tow.

'What you doin' here?' Edie snarled and sprang outside the door, drawing it closed behind her. She glanced back as though worried one of her kids might hear her and come and investigate.

'Got yer this,' Nellie whispered. 'Ain't much, but it'll help get you a job done. Here's an address.' She shoved the ten shilling note and a scrap of paper with something scrawled on it at Edie. 'Don't worry about repaying it neither; I'll just put it on what Jimmy owes me.' Nellie winced, took a couple of tentative steps back. The bastard had really let her have it, despite her not having shortchanged him. He'd ridden her hard and long, savagely and deliberately knocking her head into the flint wall at the end of the alley until she couldn't take any more and had bucked and fought to tip him off her. The gash on her forehead was concealed beneath her fringe, her skinned, bloodied knees were covered by her coat.

'Where'd you get it?' Edie gawped at the cash. She hadn't been in long before Nellie came knocking on her door.

'Don't matter. Just don't do it with a knitting

needle,' Nellie pleaded softly, still pacing backwards away from Edie. 'Good friend of mine did that. I stayed with her ... told her not to ... tried to help afterwards, but I couldn't. In agony, she were – till she died a couple of days later.' She nodded at the paper. 'He'll sort you out fer about two guineas or so. Did it for me once, a few years back.' With that she turned and went carefully down the stairs.

'I'm doing it today.'

Faye glanced up, frowning, at her mother. She'd been in the process of shoving her sleeves into her coat. Almost two weeks had passed since the day she'd discovered Edie was pregnant. When her mother stopped being sick and her body stayed the same, Faye began to hope against hope that she'd miscarried. She'd asked her mother once, when they were alone, what was going on and had received a rare smile and the wonderful news that things looked to be sorting themselves out. Relief had swamped Faye when she'd heard that and, for the first time in a long while, she'd gone off to work with a spring in her step.

'But ... no... I thought ... you said... I hoped it would all come right,' Faye shrilly insisted.

'So did I,' Edie replied dully. 'But told you, didn't I, it just ain't my luck.'

Faye scrambled out of her coat. 'I'll come with you.'

'No!' Edie stuck a thin finger under her daughter's nose. 'You get to work. Last thing we need is any more missed shifts. We're up to our ears owing as it is. Time I've paid fer this, we'll be even worse off.'

'Where're you going?' Faye demanded. 'Tell me where you're going. You're not going to Maggie up the road, are you? Have you got enough? Is it a proper...'

'Got a recommendation. Someone down King's Cross. Got the money,' Edie rattled off. 'That's all you need to know.'

'I'll stay and look after Adam.' Faye glanced at her son, seated at the table, licking his sticky fingers in between gnawing on a hunk of bread and jam.

'You get yourself to work!' Edie hissed. 'I've told Michael he's off school today. He's gone up the shop for milk. Soon as he gets back, I'm off. He can keep an eye on Adam till I get back. I'll be home before you are, I expect, and resting up in bed. After a day or two I'll have to be back to work. But we'll do what we said and start afresh without Jimmy, I promise.' Edie turned away from her daughter. 'Get yourself off or you'll be late. I'll see you later.' As Faye rushed to her and hugged her, Edie just for a moment relented and tilted her head against her daughter's shoulder before elbowing her away.

TWENTY-TWO

'What is up with you?' Mr Travis snapped at Faye. 'First you give Mrs Hardy the wrong change, now Mrs Dexter's just been back in with her bread. You gave her brown not white and overcharged her.'

'Sorry, Mr Travis,' Faye murmured. 'I've got things on my mind.' She'd been sent to the back room to check whether the boy had returned to take out his next delivery when Mr Travis had burst in from the shop to complain about her work.

'Please see if you can focus on the job you're paid for, will you?' he muttered grumpily before the shop bell drew him, smiling, back through the door.

Faye closed her eyes against the heat of tears. She knew she'd been in a dither all morning. She couldn't concentrate on a thing because she couldn't for a second put the thought of her mother's ordeal out of her head. She was looking and listening with scant attention because she was keeping an eye constantly on the clock. Time and again she'd stared at the lazy brass hands travelling on its face, willing them to speed up, wondering whether her mother was yet on her way home. She was waiting to hear the little chime for one o'clock so she could sprint back to Campbell Road on her short dinner break and see if Edie had returned. But if Edie was still out, she knew she mustn't make Michael anxious by alerting him that something might be wrong.

She'd said nothing yet to her brother about their father's death in a hospital in Kent. But she would. As soon as their mother was well enough, and they'd planned their escape from The Bunk, she'd tell Michael the truth before Jimmy got to him.

'Faye!'

The barked summons startled Faye from her brooding and drew her quickly into the shop. Mr Travis gave her a forced smile.

'Mrs Cardew would like a steak-and-kidney pie.' He'd spoken whilst zealously swinging a paper bag to seal within two currant buns. 'Perhaps you'd do that while I finish serving this customer.'

When the shop was again empty Mr Travis turned to her, sighing in exasperation. 'If there's something up, my dear, perhaps you should have a few days off and sort it out,' he suggested. 'I can't do everything myself. If you like, I'll ask Marge if she can cover for you till...'

'No!' Faye quickly interrupted. 'I'm very sorry, Mr Travis. It won't happen again.'

He passed a critical eye over her. He'd heard on the grapevine that her younger brother had been in trouble, and was in with a bad lot. But if you lived with someone like Jimmy Wild, it was inevitable that sooner or later you'd be infected by his bad habits. Mr Travis was beginning to regret having allowed Faye to keep her job after she came in with a black eye. He'd never believed her tale about falling over. He thought it far more likely that she'd given Jimmy lip and he'd felt entitled to discipline her. Mr Travis wouldn't have let her stay working at the bakery but for Rob Wild's latent threat of consequences in the event that she lost her job. He was in deep with him and, having fallen behind in his payments, now was not the time to upset him.

A movement by the shop window drew his attention. A moment later his mouth compressed in annoyance as he recognised Saul Bateman's son. He had been hanging around outside quite a lot recently and, much as Mr Travis wanted trade, he didn't want his. Thankfully, he'd seen nothing of Saul Bateman since the day he'd come in for meat pies, and that was months ago. He was fearful that if Donald hung around in the vicinity it might draw his father back too.

Of course Mr Travis knew what the attraction was for that particular youth and it was another reason he'd been considering letting the girl go. Faye was a good hard worker, but thanks to her unsavoury connections, there would always be a disturbance of some sort in her life. From her vexed expression, he deduced she too had spotted Donald Bateman. It was clear that she didn't encourage him to keep ambushing her; Mr Travis had heard and observed her remonstrating with him. But if the son took after the father, the youth would be too arrogant to let her disgust put him off.

'I see your admirer is waiting for you,' Mr Travis pointed out. 'Will you please ask him not to obscure the window display all the time.'

'I don't like him pestering me any more than

you do!' Faye had let her anxiety make her snappy and soon regretted it. Her boss looked shocked by her impertinence. 'I'm sorry. Can I take an early dinner break, please?' she asked huskily. 'I'll tell him again to clear off, I promise.'

Rob slowed down when he caught sight of his father's wife. He didn't know Edie well, but he was pretty sure she wasn't a drunk or he'd surely have heard about it. Faye wouldn't have kept something as serious as that to herself. He braked again and watched her as she clutched at a wall for support before stumbling on.

He'd been driving through King's Cross, just coming back from doing a deal on a load of tinned fruit destined for his market stalls, when he'd spotted the woman staggering along. He'd grown up seeing his Aunt Matilda – his mother, too, on occasion – too rat-arsed to stand up. But it was an unusual sight for this time of day, and an odd feeling of alarm was stirring in his guts. He weaved through traffic to the kerb and stopped. As he got out and strode over to her, it occurred to him that, even if she had been out on an early bender, it was odd that she'd bother travelling this far to drink.

'Want a lift home?' he offered, touching her arm to make her turn towards him.

Edie had been propped against brickwork. Now she stiffly straightened and swung a chalk-white face at him. When she saw who'd spoken, her mouth worked soundlessly. 'I'm all right ... all right,' she finally ejected. Despite the incessant pain in her abdomen she was conscious of feeling terrible shame and embarrassment that Rob Wild had seen her like this. She could sense hot stickiness trickling between her thighs and punched her skirt, desperately trying to mop the flow by wedging material against it.

The old fellow who'd done the abortion had given her pads to use before taking his money and leaving her alone on the bed to sort herself out. She'd expected it to hurt but the dull dragging ache that had started as she'd stood up had very quickly turned into a raging torture as she'd set off along the street towards home. She'd quickly realised that the wadding in her drawers wasn't staunching the steady bleeding.

'What is it?' Rob bent to peer at her sickly complexion. 'You ill?' He could tell that she wasn't drunk. There was no reek of alcohol about her, although she did look on the point of collapse. 'Get in the car. I'll take you back to The Bunk.'

A ripping pain drew an involuntary groan from Edie and, as a wave of giddiness made her sway, she instinctively sank down close to the ground.

'Fuck's sake…' Rob muttered, alarmed. 'What's wrong?'

He was aware that people were now staring at them. A woman retraced her steps. 'What's up with her?' she asked, stooping to peer into Edie's contorted features. 'She having an 'eart attack, d'you reckon?'

'I'm all right!' Edie had found the voice and the energy to bawl that out, sending the woman scuttling backwards. But the next moment she had dropped forward on to her knees, panting. 'Take me home, would yer?' she pleaded with

Rob. But she felt too weak to get up and started to cry soundlessly when she realised that the skirt and coat she was wearing were already heavy and wet. 'Oh, Gawd help us...' she moaned.

Rob got hold of one of her elbows and tried to assist her to her feet. When she seemed incapable of moving, he grabbed her under the arms and hoisted her. It wasn't until he'd bundled her on to the back seat of his car that he realised he was covered in blood.

'So ... decided to show yer face again, have you?'

'Woss up, Nell?' Jimmy asked, a soppy smile spreading across his face. 'Missed me, have yer, gel?'

Nellie sat down on the sagging bed, still pulling a brush through her wiry hair. She was in her underclothes, having just had a wash in the bowl, and had been on the point of getting to bed for a couple of hours before she went out for business, when in he'd walked, bold as brass, as though he'd just nipped up the road for half an ounce of bacca.

'Where you been then?' she asked, a look sidling up at him from beneath her black, spiky lashes.

'With an old pal, if you must know,' he lied. He'd been very much on his own and had been dossing wherever he could for the past two weeks. Yesterday he'd calculated it would be safe to make tracks home with a tale to tell. Even he understood that an abortion was simpler, and less risky, done early rather than late. He'd also deduced it'd be cheaper if the job was done as soon as possible and had relied on Edie getting her skates on for that reason if no other.

'Sorry about goin' off like that, Nel, without giving you fair warning.' He could see Nellie was riled, and knew he'd need to crawl a bit to keep her sweet. 'But I met one of me old pals from down Kent way and he asked me to go back 'n' stay with him to give him a hand with a bit of business. Been working on his market stall 'cos his mate done the dirty on him.' He gestured his disgust. 'Some mate he turned out to be! Run off with a whole week's takings and left him in the lurch. Couldn't turn me pal down when he's had that kind o' luck, 'specially not as he did me a good turn when I didn't have a pot ter piss in a few years back.'

'So ... you've been doing favours fer a bloke, have you?' Nellie teased her fringe with the hairbrush.

'No harm in it, surely?'

Nellie could have laughed out loud. Jimmy Wild wouldn't even help out his own son, unless there was a payday in it. With him, favours were for getting, not giving. But she wasn't going to let her temper ruin her plan to get back at him.

His wife might not be sure whether Jimmy had guessed about the baby, but Nellie was convinced he had. And, like the selfish coward he was, he'd scarpered rather than face the consequences.

Over the years Nellie had been a bit on the side for many married men. In her prime, there'd been occasions when she'd been kept in style as a proper mistress. Those fellows' wives had never been rivals because Nellie had never had any illusions about her role in a punter's life. Years ago, before Jimmy had disappeared, he'd left his wife and young sons to live with her. At the time, her conscience had never been troubled by it. He'd been her pimp first and foremost, and any affection he'd shown her had been dependent on how well he did out of her. She'd always known he'd return to Fran like a shot if the money stopped rolling in. More than a decade later, nothing had changed apart from his wife's name.

In Nellie's profession it had always been a dog-eat-dog world. But something hard inside her had shrivelled since the moment she'd offered Edie her few silver coins. She'd watched the woman's eyes pounce on three shillings as though it was manna from heaven, yet Edie, desperate as she'd been, had found the pride and decency to let her keep it. Jimmy would have scooped up the coins then chivvied her to tell the pervert she'd changed her mind and he could have anything he liked for five bob.

'Yer wife's been after you.' Nellie dropped her brush on the bed and crossed her arms over her bosom. 'Poor cow's in the family way ... but perhaps you knew that, eh?'

Jimmy affected to look astonished. 'Nah ... not Edie she's too old for any o' that.'

'Seems she ain't,' Nellie begged to differ. She tilted her head and watched him. 'Come lookin' for you to give her some money to get herself sorted out.'

'Nah ... must be a mistake ... crafty cow's probably just spent the rent. She shouldn't go making things like that up fer a handout.' Jimmy shook his head and continued fiddling with a roll-up, his pinched features bent towards the tobacco tin. His guts were writhing in anger. He'd not believed Edie would find the gumption to come looking for him at Nellie's. He knew Edie had guessed a while back what kept him away so often, and he'd been pleased she seemed too mouse-like to challenge him over it. He struck a match at the wonky smoke he'd stuck between his lips. 'When I see her, I'll tear a strip off her,' he spluttered past the wagging cigarette. 'Cheek she's got, comin' here bothering you, luv.'

Nellie couldn't prevent a hoot of laughter at his false concern. 'Glad she did though, Jim, ain't I? Somehow it just showed me something about yer I've never properly seen before. Or perhaps I'd seen it but just kept ignoring it 'cos I ain't really that much better'n you, when all's said 'n' done. And knowing we're alike makes me feel sick to me stomach.'

'Woss up?' Jimmy spread his hands in appeal. 'You jealous 'cos I'm still pokin' her once in a while?' He crouched by her side and began stroking one of her flabby arms. 'Come on ... you've seen her ... she ain't a patch on you fer looks, Nel, is she?' He tilted his head so she'd get the benefit of his teasing grin. 'But I can't just dump her when she's got kids and's relying on me, can I?' He tipped closer to kiss Nellie's cheek, remembering just in time to remove the drooping roll-up from his lips. 'You 'n' me were made for one another, gel. That's why I love yer and always come back to yer.'

'Yeah...' Nellie muttered sourly, pulling back

the blanket on the mattress.

'Ain't getting to bed, are you?' Jimmy demanded, astonished. His sentimental expression had vanished and he quickly sat down beside her and slung an arm about her shoulders, keeping her upright. 'No time to kip, sweet'eart. Come on ... I'll take you up west, 'cos I'm back from Kent skint as yer like, and I bet you could do with a bit of help making a few bob.' He tightened his grip as she tried to shrug him off. 'There'll be a good Friday-night crowd Shaftesbury Avenue way. If you get in some earlies, we can get back home and have a nice fish supper and a couple o' bottles.' He nuzzled her cheek. 'After that I'll show yer just how much I missed yer.'

TWENTY-THREE

Faye had been walking fast enough to make her hot and breathless, and was almost home when she noticed Rob pull away from the kerb and drive towards her. It looked as though he'd been sitting in the car outside his aunt's, waiting for her to turn up. Her stomach lurched in a mixture of gladness and excitement that was in no way diminished by her constant worries about her mother. As he stopped by her, she came to a halt too with a hesitant smile for him. She knew she'd have to ask him to wait. She'd need to dash in for a few minutes first and make sure everything at home was all right before she got in his car and he took her somewhere so they could talk. She wouldn't be able to stay out long. Her mother would need some comfort and looking after this evening after what she'd been through. It would be up to her to sort the boys out with their teas, and in the morning get their breakfasts. Michael would be back to school tomorrow and, if her mother were well enough to be left on her own with Adam, she'd be off to work early in the hope that would pacify Mr Travis. She knew he was at the end of his tether and ready to sack her.

Rob was out of the car and coming towards her now, and her smile and her racing thoughts withered away. She frowned, trying to fathom out what was wrong with him and whether he was pale and grim-faced simply because he was still angry with her. She wanted to tell him straight off she was sorry for acting childishly last time they'd been together. She knew he'd been right when he'd said her brother needed to learn about life the hard way. She wanted to say too that she was sorry she'd made it sound as though sleeping with him would be an ordeal for her...

'Hello ... just got back from work. Bit late 'cos the miserable old so 'n' so made me wipe down all the counters before I could leave. Got to pop in and see me mum. She's not been well, but I'd like it if we could talk ... got something to say...'

'I've...' The word was barely audible and whatever else he'd been intending to add tailed away. He plunged his hands in his pockets then pulled one out again to massage his mouth. 'Come inside,' he said in a voice that filtered through his fingers and was again so hoarse she could hardly hear him.

Rob took her arm as though supporting her and propelled her into the dank hallway. 'Are the boys upstairs?'

Faye gazed up at him, searching his gaunt features with darting eyes. It occurred to her he looked strained and white enough to be ill. 'Yes ... I think so, and me mum too, I hope ... expect.' She glanced away. She didn't want to tell him yet about the abortion, but knew she would eventually. She realised there wasn't anyone she'd sooner trust with the secret. Then perhaps he'd understand why she was so fearful of letting him make love to her.

'Stay here.' It was an order before he took the stairs two at a time.

Faye peered upwards, blinking into the gloom as an uneasiness started to drip ice on her spine.

A moment later Rob was quickly descending, carrying Adam in his arms, and with Michael trailing moodily in his wake. He set Adam on the floor and immediately the little boy clasped Faye's legs and, thumb in mouth, peered up bashfully at Rob.

'Me aunt Matilda's gonna get your teas ready today,' he addressed Michael. 'Take your brother down there ... she's expecting you ... go on...'

Michael looked enquiringly at his sister, but Faye was gazing at Rob and a horrifying suspicion was starting to drain blood from her complexion.

'Where's Mum?' Michael demanded. When nobody spoke, he repeated it, alarm pitching his voice high.

'Get going,' Rob ordered and gave Michael's

back a little push.

Michael grabbed Adam's hand and started off, peering at intervals back over a shoulder until the two adults were just shadows in a murky corridor.

Faye felt as though her voice had become trapped in her throat while dreadful possibilities battered at her brain. Finally she pounced on one that caused her staring eyes to widen and speech to explode from her lips. 'Tell me,' she begged in a raw voice. 'What is it? What d'you know? Where's me mum?'

'Come upstairs,' Rob murmured gently. 'Let's go upstairs. Not here...'

Faye stuffed a fist to her mouth and swayed back against the rickety banister for support, her head making small shaking movements.

Rob bent his face close to hers and threaded fingers into her hair. 'Come upstairs...' he murmured against her cheek and, when she stood rigidly refusing to move, he put her on to the first step and forced her up two more. When her knees buckled he lifted her, crying, in his arms and carried her to her door.

'She wouldn't keep it. I wanted her to. But she wouldn't and she didn't want to let Jimmy know either. I said I'd go and tell him if she didn't want to. I said I'd get some money off him. She wouldn't let me...'

They were sitting on the bed, side by side. Rob had his elbows on his knees and his head in his cupped palms. Faye sat stiff and straight beside him, her eyes drying and her fractured mind now mended enough to allow her to pick over memories. She dissected each one then recounted it to him so he'd know what had led to her mother's death.

For an hour or more after he'd told her that, while she'd been at work, Edie had died this afternoon in hospital, she'd sobbed and shouted until exhaustion finally robbed her of voice and tears. Now she was uncontrollably quivering but calmer.

'She wouldn't let me stop home and go with her. I offered to, lots of times, but she wouldn't have it. Must work ... need the money...'

Rob straightened for a moment as though he might say something, but he remained silent then adopted the same pose as before, beside her on the mattress.

'I told her to get a proper doctor ... like the one you said you'd get for me. I was afraid she might go to Maggie Phipps up the road, just 'cos that's all she thought she should pay. But she said she'd got a recommendation and an address and the money. Where'd she get that?' She turned to look at the bowed dark head beside her.

Sensing her stare he said softly, 'Don't know, Faye ... don't know...'

'I said to her: you let me keep Adam, can't you keep it? But she said she was too old and tired and didn't want reminders of Jimmy. It would've been nice to have a brother or sister to share, wouldn't it?'

'Yeah...' Rob rushed a hand across the back of his neck before letting a heavy breath drift through pinching fingers.

'She said she was done with bringing up babies. Can't blame her ... another mouth to feed ... no decent man to help out...' Faye picked at her nails with palsied fingers. 'We were planning on getting away from Jimmy. Mum promised, when it was sorted out, we'd start afresh.'

Rob nodded, indicating he was pleased to hear it.

'She'd never have got mixed up with your father if it hadn't been for me. She told me that, and it's true,' Faye whimpered in anguish. 'When I got pregnant and lost me job, she lost hers too 'cos we had to move away so no one would know I was a disgrace.' She squeezed her eyes shut. 'We had nothing; me stepfather had died. All we had was another mouth to feed, so she tried to find a man to help out and ended up with Jimmy. It's my fault. If we hadn't got involved with him and come here she'd be alive...'

Rob took one of her hands in his, cradling it to comfort her, but in a moment she'd snatched it back.

'He was blackmailing her to stay with him, y'know. She knew him from years before, when he worked in a hospital down in Kent. She told me that the day I found out she was pregnant. She was protecting me 'n' Michael from knowing me dad died a horrible death in the hospital where Jimmy worked. He threatened he'd tell us if she kicked him out, that's why she stayed with him.' Her hands clutched her face and she rocked back and forth on the bed. 'We thought he'd got killed in the trenches. But he didn't, he suffered for months in hospital, and Jimmy was gonna tell us that if she ever left him. She put up with him 'cos she didn't want us upset; yet every day your father was around, he upset us. Knowing the truth about me dad's agony was horrible, but he's at rest now. Why couldn't she have seen that I'd sooner have known about it than have had to put up with Jimmy one day longer?'

Rob's thumb and finger tightened on his closed eyelids until the pain made him jerk upright. 'Don't know... I'm sorry...' he said hoarsely. He knew it was an inadequate response on learning this new aspect of Jimmy's wickedness. But Rob wanted to stay calm in the hope that it might be infectious and Faye wouldn't again be overcome by hysteria. He wanted to protect her, as Edie had tried to do, from the harmful influence of his father.

'And I was going to sell my necklace ... but I didn't have it.' A sudden fire behind Faye's lashes flickered but died for want of energy to get it alight. 'If I'd had that, it might have saved her. It would've paid for a proper job. First, I was too proud to come and ask you for it back. Then I thought I wouldn't need to in any case, 'cos Mum said things seemed to be naturally sorting themselves out. We thought she'd miscarry, you see. But it was stupid, chucking the necklace back at you like that. I was keeping it for a rainy day. Wasn't going to get worse'n that, was it? Stupid cow, I am. Stupid, stupid cow!' She burst out laughing. 'She'd be here now, if I hadn't done that. It's all my fault...'

Rob turned his head to look up at her. 'It's not. None of it's your fault, Faye–'

'It is! I could have got twenty pounds, you said, for that necklace. How much does a doctor charge for an abortion? You said you'd get one. How much?'

When he remained silent and his fingers clenched in his hair until his knuckles went white she suddenly screamed out, 'Tell me! You must know...'

He grabbed her in his arms and her racking sobs jolted her against his side and her streaming eyes and bubbling nose smeared his suit shoulder. 'I had more than enough, didn't I? Didn't I?' she sobbed, punching her fist down on his thigh.

He took her back on the mattress with him so they lay wrapped together until she fought free and twisted away from him. A moment later she needed his comfort and she rolled back and blinked, clearing her eyes so she could see his face. She drew her thighs up to her chest, so her knees touched him, and lowered her forehead so it rested against his.

'What'll I tell Michael?'

'We'll work that out tomorrow,' he answered gruffly.

'Need to think now,' she muttered. 'Shall I tell him the truth? He's old enough, I suppose. Adam ... Adam's different, of course. He won't understand, whatever we tell him.'

'We'll do it tomorrow. It's getting late now anyhow.'

'What time is it?' Faye sighed, allowing her gritty, hot eyes momentarily to close.

'Nine ... just after. Me aunt's gonna put them

to bed at hers. She said she would.'

'Must say thank you to her; s'pose everyone will know soon. Don't want to see them yet, or speak to them.' She tilted her chin, flicked up her lashes to see him watching her with velvet brown eyes. 'Who's gonna tell Jimmy?'

'Me...' Rob said. 'When I find him, I'll do it.'

'I don't want to be on my own...' She rubbed a finger under her nose and ground the side of her head against the mattress, digging in.

'I'll stay with you.'

She relaxed at once, nodding and sacrificing her curled position to shift her length against him. After a few minutes she cuddled up closer, hugging hungrily against his warm body as if it could absorb her trembling.

'Turn around.'

She did what he asked without questioning. When her back was to him he drew her against him with an arm about her middle then moulded his body to her curves. 'You warm enough?'

She nodded.

'If you can, go to sleep, Faye,' he urged softly. 'We'll sort things out in the morning.'

Rob elevated his face by shoving a fist under his cheek, trying to get the sour stench of the mattress out of his nostrils. It was an odour he recognised as his father's sweat. And his lust. He'd grown up with that reek in the air he breathed, in the musty old clothes that had been handed down to him. If he lived to be a hundred and ended up a millionaire, no amount of money or years would ever erase that stinking reminder of Jimmy Wild or his upbringing from his memory.

Three years ago he'd sworn on his mother's new marble headstone that, now he was out of The Bunk and doing all right, he'd stay out and never again spend a night under a Campbell Road roof. That was what he'd promised her. But she'd understand why he'd had to go back on his word.

Faye did sleep for a while, until the tormenting images again surfaced in her mind, robbing her of peace and jolting her to wakefulness. The oil had gone in the lamp and she howled in the darkness for her mother and no whispered words or tender touches could soothe her. She thrashed against him, forcing him away so she could shudder untouched in his obeying embrace.

'What do you know about it anyway?' she'd spat viciously at him. 'You with your flash car and fancy house? You'd have done it to me, if I'd let you.' And she'd shoved him hard, turning her rejection into an assault with beating fists that made him roll to the bed edge and get up. But he was there again beside her when dawn striped a light on the ceiling.

'D'you want a cup of tea?'

Faye looked up at him with blank eyes. 'I don't know.'

He was on his feet, brushing down his crumpled clothes and Faye watched him, realising that he'd slept in a suit that had probably cost more than six months' rent on their rooms. Her mouth felt dry and dirty and a throb in her temples was drumming persistently.

'I must see how the boys are...' She grabbed the

edge of the mattress and pulled herself towards it, feeling too weary still to sit upright. When she was on her feet, and searching for her shoes, he was putting the kettle on the hob. She watched him, feeling awkward in the presence of his kindness. She could remember ranting vilely at him just hours ago. She tried to comb her fingers through her matted hair before a glance down at her screwed-up clothes made her abandon any effort to tidy her appearance. 'Thanks,' she said quietly. 'Thanks for what you did for my mum. Thanks for taking her to hospital and staying with her. I'm glad she didn't suffer for long and wasn't on her own when she died. I couldn't bear that, the thought of her all alone...' Her gratitude ended in a gurgle and a little gesture that indicated she couldn't manage to express any more.

'Wasn't nothing... I love you. I'd do anything for you or for the people you love.' His expression was suddenly as diffident as hers. 'Do you want me to go and see how the boys are? Bring them back, shall I?' He paused. 'Ready for that, are you?'

She nodded, feeling her eyes welling at the awful prospect of having to deal with Michael's grief when not yet able to cope with her own. As he headed for the door, she suddenly slipped to intercept him before he left. She hugged him about the waist, as though to wordlessly impress on him all she wanted to tell him about her love and trust, but couldn't. She smiled as she felt his mouth brush her forehead in understanding. A moment later she'd turned away to search through blurry vision for the teapot.

'Seen Jimmy about?'

Nellie glanced over a shoulder to see that Rob Wild had pulled up by the kerb and spoken to her through his car window. She'd been about to get a little dinner-time snifter, but let the door to the Nag's Head swing closed and instead approached his car.

'Think he might've gone round yer brother's place. Ain't seen him since first thing, and I know he was after trying to get his job back with Stevie.' She stepped away again. She knew neither of Jimmy's sons liked her, and with good reason. Usually they ignored her if they met by accident. In fact, she was intrigued as to why Rob had stopped and summoned her. She realised he must want Jimmy very badly to have done so.

'Not seen him about for a while. Been away, has he?'

Nellie approached the car again and bent to stick her head in the open window. 'Yeah,' she confirmed. 'He's just got back off his travels, as it 'appens,' she added acidly. 'Wish he'd stayed away, the parasite.'

'Get in.'

Nellie's chins sagged in disbelief before a wondrous smile closed her mouth.

'Just get in,' Rob said drily. 'All I'm after is a chat about something.'

He waited until Nellie had settled her bulk beside him, then asked, 'Why'd he do a disappearing act?'

Nellie shrugged. 'Got me own ideas, but he reckons he was helping out an old pal on his market stall down Kent way.'

'Let's have your ideas then, and I'll let you know if they coincide with mine.' Rob opened a pack of Players, took one, then offered the pack to Nellie.

Once he'd lit her cigarette, Nellie took a long drag, all the time eyeing him calculatingly. 'Something serious, is it, what you need to speak to him about?'

'Yeah ... it's serious all right,' Rob said, letting smoke drift out of his window. He glanced about listlessly at the parade of Saturday shoppers in their summer clothes. 'So, let's have your theory.'

'I reckon he done a runner 'cos he found out his wife was knocked up and was gonna be after him fer money to get rid of it. He's come back 'cos he thinks it's safe 'n' all done 'n' dusted. Could be he's miscalculated on that one.' A smug smile tilted upwards the cigarette clamped in Nellie's lips.

'Did Jimmy tell you she was pregnant?'

Nellie shook her head. Normally she wouldn't have disclosed any of her own, or Jimmy's, private business. But she felt no loyalty to him any more and no guilt in possibly having grassed him up to his son. In fact, she reckoned Jimmy had guessed she'd had it with him and that was why he was making an effort to get his job back. But it was too late. She'd got set in her mind what she was going to do.

'How d'you find out then?' Rob asked.

'Off Edie; and that's how I know he might've crawled back too soon. Only saw her day before yesterday, and it'd be fast work to get it all arranged.' Nellie had been about to add that she'd given Edie the name of an abortionist, but she decided to keep that to herself. Instead she added, ''Course, Maggie Phipps would sort her out straight away. Do it pie-eyed at midnight, she would, for a coupla quid. I told Edie to stay away from her.' Nellie flicked her stub out of the window. 'Got another?'

Rob offered her the packet again. 'I didn't know you 'n' Edie were on good terms.'

'We ain't; she come looking for me, but only to find him. Felt sorry for the poor cow, I did. Gave her a ten-bob note 'cos she was talking about getting a knitting needle and doing it herself.' She frowned, unsure exactly what was making her feel uneasy. Her chubby fingers, gripping the cigarette, hovered in front of her mouth before dropping to her lap. 'Edie all right, is she? Is that why you've come looking for him?' When she got no immediate reply, she whispered fearfully, 'What's happened? Where is she?'

'In the morgue at the hospital,' Rob replied. The tone of his voice hadn't turned vindictive. He believed Nellie had told the truth and his loathing for Jimmy strengthened. An old whore had tried to help Edie because his father wouldn't.

'Oh, fuckin' hell!' Nellie groaned. 'No!'

''Fraid so,' Rob confirmed quietly. 'Abortionist in King's Cross messed her up. I need to find Jimmy and tell him.'

'Does yer brother know? Will Stevie tell him?' she burst out, knuckling her moist eyes.

Rob shook his head. 'She died late yesterday

afternoon. Only me aunt Matilda and Edie's children know about it so far.' He gave Nellie a twist of a smile. 'Thanks anyway, for trying to help her.' He dug in his pocket for some money to repay her the ten shillings.

Nellie quickly opened the car door to scramble out before she broke down. 'Don't you go givin' me nuthin'!' she croaked, and gazed fiercely at him with bloodshot eyes. 'I wanted to help her! I really did want to help her,' she whimpered. 'I thought she'd be all right...'

'Yeah, I know you did.' Rob put the cash away. He knew then for sure that Nellie had sent Edie to the abortionist. But it wasn't her fault that the old fellow hadn't been up to the job any more. The police had come back to the hospital just before he'd left and had told him they'd arrested someone who operated above a shop in King's Cross. He'd been a vet in his time and had done abortions on the sly. When his sight had started to fail a couple of years ago, he'd been sacked from his practice, leaving the animals safe. Instead he had turned all his attention to his illegal sideline. One of his other botched jobs had earned him a short prison sentence, but that patient had been luckier than Edie and had eventually recovered. And his conscience hadn't prevented him carrying on. The doctors at the hospital had told Rob that whoever butchered Edie might not even have realised they'd ruptured major blood vessels and caused her to bleed to death.

'You guessed yer father had disappeared to avoid having to give her anything, didn't you?'

Nellie's gravelly voice stopped Rob brooding on yesterday's tragic events.

'Grew up watching me mother in a terrible state 'cos he'd run off when she needed him for help or money.' Rob put the car in gear and let off the hand brake.

Nellie ducked down to peer tearfully at him, one final time, before he drove off. That last comment had wounded her, and she'd guessed he'd intended it should.

She remembered the day as though it were yesterday, although it had been perhaps as much as fourteen years ago now when Fran Wild had been in labour with her third child. Jimmy had refused to go back home to help out when told his wife was having the baby. He'd been with Nellie, banging her against a wall, when Matilda Keiver's husband, Jack, had eventually run him to ground to tell him that his wife had nearly died and his baby daughter was stillborn. The boys would have been old enough, she supposed, to have understood what had gone on.

Realising that Rob was waiting for her to move so he could go, she mumbled, 'I'm really sorry about it all, y'know.' A moment later she'd slammed the door shut and was walking away.

TWENTY-FOUR

'Well, this is nice; don't often see me boys together.' Jimmy swung a grin between his sons. 'Like old times, ain't it, all of us indoors like this, having a brew?' He saluted them with his mug.

His jolly remark drew a blank and he rose from the chair into which he'd plonked himself, uninvited by Stephen, and strolled to the pram. He bent to coo at his grandson in between taking gulps of tea. When Rob had arrived at Stevie's place a few minutes ago, he'd found Jimmy already there, looking very much at home.

'Don't wake him,' Stevie said shortly as he noticed his father tickling his son's cheek. 'Only got him off to sleep just before you turned up.'

'He's getting a bonny nipper,' Jimmy announced, peering at the puny infant.

'He's still underweight,' Stevie contradicted. 'Got to make sure he gets plenty of food and plenty of rest.'

Stephen hadn't been happy to see his father on his doorstep twenty minutes ago. He'd guessed what he was after, and had been relieved he could honestly say that he'd shut up shop and was back working for Rob. He'd hoped that news would send Jimmy on his way, but his father had seemed in no rush to go anywhere.

Minutes before his arrival, Stephen had made himself a pot of tea and, having tested the pot to see if it was still hot, Jimmy had helped himself to some. Under constant questioning about Pam's whereabouts, Stephen had eventually told his father his marriage was over, and had revealed the sordid background to their separation. Although he didn't relish Jimmy knowing his business, he didn't see the point in lying either. Jimmy would find out sooner or later what had gone on. The neighbours were already gossiping. Stephen hadn't bothered to correct anybody hinting Pam had run home to her mum because he'd battered her. He knew that their rows had been savage enough to raise the roof at times. Pam had been able to turn on the waterworks at full blast when things were going against her, so it was natural people would assume they'd come to blows, even though he'd never hit her. The memory of his mother, cowering in a corner with her hands fluttering around her face to ward off his father's fists, was an enduring, upsetting image in his mind. So, as far as Stephen was concerned, they could all sod off and think what they liked; his conscience was clear.

'Little Christopher'll be right as rain, once you feed him up.' Jimmy turned to Rob. 'Stevie's just been telling me about that maggot he married.' His mouth turned down, emphasising his disgust. 'Who'd've thought anybody could be so wicked as to do that? Well shot of her, he is.' He flicked another look at Rob, realising he had barely uttered a word since arriving, nor had his stony expression altered.

'What's up with you, Bobbie? Not said much; and what you got there?' As soon as his eldest son had walked in, Jimmy's eyes had pounced on the bag he was carrying. The smart emblem proclaimed it to be from a top tailor's shop and inside he guessed might be a very nice bit of clobber. If Bobbie had brought some of his cast-offs round for his younger brother, Jimmy was determined to have a gander, and first dabs on whatever was on offer. If it didn't fit – and it was unlikely it would, now he'd got a paunch – he knew he could always get a good few bob for quality secondhand gear.

'This?' Rob pulled a dark jacket then matching trousers out of the bag. 'It's your funeral suit.' He scrunched the garments in a fist and hurled them straight at his father. 'Make sure you wear it.'

'Eh? What?' Jimmy gawped at him then dropped to his knees to examine the fine mohair material. 'What you goin' on about?' Jimmy was interested enough in the value of the outfit to quickly inspect it. The stiffness in the cloth made him frown. 'It's all stained up. What yer done to it, Bobbie? What's that on it?' His disappointment coarsened his voice and expression.

'It's blood – Edie's blood. She died yesterday in hospital when her abortion went wrong.'

Jimmy was still half smiling at him. He shifted a glance between his sons as though waiting for someone to explain the sick joke to him.

Stephen licked his lips. 'What?' He stared in disbelief at Rob. 'What's happened ... what did you say?'

'I said Edie died yesterday because that bastard ran off and left her in the lurch with no money and no help. He knew she was pregnant, but instead of staying to face up to it, he went missing. She didn't know what to do, so got together what money she could and went to King's Cross. She got butchered by an old bloke who didn't have the eyesight to read, let alone carry out an operation.'

Stephen swung a horrified stare at his father. 'That true? I was wondering where you'd got to. Why didn't you let on Edie was in the family way?'

'What d'you mean, she's dead?' Having finally digested the awful news, Jimmy scrambled to his feet. 'She ... ain't ... dead...' he sang out. A moment later, he burst out desperately, 'She can't be...'

'She died yesterday afternoon in hospital. If I hadn't spotted her staggering along the street in agony, she'd've died right where she dropped. Doctors said she had no chance. Wouldn't have mattered how fast I got her to them, she'd've died anyhow.'

Jimmy fell back into the chair he'd vacated, his face ashen. 'Didn't know nuthin' about any of that...' he whined.

'You fuckin' liar!' Rob roared. 'You knew all right! Admit it! Why can't you once in yer miserable life own up to something? You'd worked out she was expecting and you scarpered! Like you always do! You miserable, fuckin' coward! You left her and Faye to try and deal with it alone, with no money.'

'You give Faye money, don't yer? Why didn't she ask you for what she needed?' Jimmy spat viciously. 'Think I don't know where she got that fiver? What you getting in return – as if I needed to ask!'

Rob leapt the distance between them and hauled his father up, using one hand on his throat. His contorted features were an inch from Jimmy's cheek. 'Fuck-all! That's what I'm getting,' he whispered against his father's rough stubble. 'And you know what? It's more'n enough. But you wouldn't understand that, would you? 'Cos you've never done anything for anyone in yer life. Helpin' a pal out in Kent, were you?' He savagely mocked him. 'Like fuck you were!' He thrust Jimmy away from him in disgust, then stooped and gathered up the ruined suit of clothes. He stuffed it in the bag and shoved it at him. 'There ... have something of Edie's to remember her by.' He propelled Jimmy so fast towards the door his father stumbled over his own feet. But he allowed himself to be manoeuvred, although his humiliation clamped his teeth tightly together and made slits of his eyes. He never liked being shown up in front of Stevie. He liked to protect the little bit of useful influence he still had there.

'Better go and see how me kids are bearing up in all this,' he muttered, ripping himself from Rob's grip on the threshold of the room.

'You ain't got any kids,' Rob sneered. 'None that want to know you, anyhow.' As his father disappeared into the hallway, he shut the door behind him.

'Can't believe it.' Stephen shook his head in bewilderment as his brother slumped down into the chair he'd dragged Jimmy out of. 'You sure about it? I mean, I only saw Edie out shopping a few days ago, 'n' she looked all right then.'

''Course I'm sure,' Rob answered dully. 'I was there with her when she died.' His head dropped forward and he raked his fingers through his hair.

Stephen paced back and forth, staring at his shoes. 'What about the funeral?' He'd finally picked a question from the many rotating in his brain.

'Not sure yet. Next week perhaps. Bound to be an inquest.'

'Yeah ... bound to be,' Stephen echoed, and glanced in the pram. Christopher had his eyes open; probably he'd been woken up by the sound of men shouting, but, on recognising his father's face, he gave him a gummy smile.

'Where's Edie's kids? They on their own in that room in The Bunk? I expect that's where he's gone off to. Might be best if he stayed away from them, d'you reckon?'

'They're all at mine. And that's where they're staying.'

Stephen sat in the chair opposite Rob and stared at the unlit hearth. 'You and Faye...?' His voice tailed off; Rob's mood was so volatile he was afraid his brother might fly off the handle at even an innocent question about Edie's daughter.

Rob settled back in the chair. 'I want us to get married, but it's not exactly the right time now to be planning a wedding, is it?'

'Have you asked her?'

Rob shook his head. 'She's cut up; can't think straight. It's not fair or right to talk about it. Michael's taken it really hard too. Little 'un's too young to understand, thank God. Aunt Til's been a diamond, helping out with the two boys.'

'Never lets you down, does she,' Stephen stated, then smiled nostalgically. 'Remember how good she was to us when Mum died?'

'Yeah,' Rob agreed. 'That's another time the git made sure he kept well hidden, in case he was expected to help out.'

'Didn't need him anyhow.' Stephen glanced at Rob. 'Done all right on our own in the end, didn't we?'

Rob grimaced wry agreement as he stood up. 'I'm off ... got things to sort out.'

A wail from Christopher brought Stephen to his feet. He went to pick up his son and rock him in his arms. 'If you need any help, you know, with anything, just give us a shout. I'll do what I can.'

'Thanks,' Rob said. 'I know you will. In fact, you might have to take over running things – just till after the funeral.'

'I'll do me best to keep things on track, for you, mate. I know without asking her that aunt Til'll do a bit of babysitting for me. No need fer you to worry about business right now.'

Matilda saw him at a distance and read from his stooped posture and trudging feet that he knew. Usually she avoided acknowledging Jimmy Wild by look or word. Her loathing of him hadn't diminished; it was as strong as it had been when he was married to her sister and regularly making Fran and her sons' lives hell. Yesterday, when Rob had told her what had happened to Edie, the puzzle of Jimmy's whereabouts had been solved straight away. She'd known then why she hadn't seen him for weeks. She'd understood too why Edie, God rest her soul, had been keen to discover where Nellie could be found. If only the woman had confided in her, she might have been able to help. But she understood why she hadn't: in The Bunk you kept your business to yourself, and sorted things out the best you could with what you had available. She'd have done the same in Edie's situation; anything to protect her family's privacy and reputation.

Jimmy looked up and saw Matilda watching him, waiting for him. It was the first time since he'd moved back here, almost a year ago, that she'd gone out of her way to put herself in his path. His steps faltered, for he understood that fierce, contemptuous stare; he'd received it from her a thousand times or more over the years. He jutted out his chin and put a jaunty spring in his step.

'How you doin', Til?' He stopped and lounged against a railing. 'Suppose you've heard then, about Edie?' He shook his head, as though mystified by it all. 'Silly of her to do that, weren't it. Why couldn't she just wait till I got back? We'd've sorted things out between us.'

'Reckon she understood you well enough to know you wouldn't be back ... not till you was sure the coast was clear.' Tilly's grim features pinched further. 'Well, it's all over with for her, God rest her. Poor cow must've been desperate and not knowing which way to turn.' She paused. 'Put me in mind of when Fran lost her daughter. Remember that, do you?'

Jimmy's features tightened and he fumbled with the lid of his tobacco tin. Once he'd got it open, he fished out a half-smoked roll-up.

'Remember it as though it were yesterday, I do,' Matilda continued damningly. 'My Alice, and Bobbie and Stevie, running up and down the road, looking for you to tell you to get back home 'cos things didn't look good. Found you 'n' all, didn't they? Up the corner gambling, as I recall. Then later my Jack tracked you down again; had yer trousers round yer ankles that time, didn't you, 'cos you was seein' ter Nellie in an alley. All them years gone by, yet you've not changed at all, have you, yer rotten, selfish bastard?'

Jimmy pushed past her with the dog-end wilting in his lips. 'Ain't got time fer no dwelling on the past, and what's done is done. Got the present to get on with.' He swung around, looking ludicrously pious. 'Got me kids to see to.' He carried on up the road, unaware of Matilda watching his back with hard, despising eyes. She knew very well that Edie's kids were all gone from the street, and she didn't expect them to ever come back. But she wasn't letting him know that. He'd go back to miserable, empty rooms and find he was on his own.

TWENTY-FIVE

'Did you tell Jimmy? And Mr Travis?'

'Yeah; saw Mr Travis first thing and he sends you his best wishes and says not to worry at all about getting into work. Then I caught up with Jimmy at Steve's.' Rob slipped off his jacket as he approached Faye.

She'd flown out of the sitting room and into the hall when she'd heard his key in the lock, and now stood close to him, trying to read in his face what had occurred when he'd confronted his father over his vile behaviour. Rob drew her into his arms and rocked her against him, closing his eyes contentedly as she immediately pressed closer and clung.

'How've the boys been?'

'Crying. Michael's not stopped and he's set Adam off 'cos he can't understand what's wrong. And I'm nearly as bad,' she admitted. Just a mention of her own grief brought fresh tears to blur her vision. 'I had a lie down on the bed with Adam to get him off to sleep. He'll wake up soon though, 'cos he'll be hungry.' She paused to let out a sigh. 'He keeps asking, "Where's Mum?" I don't know what to say. What shall I say?'

Rob understood the rawness in her voice and comforted her by nuzzling kisses against her cheek. 'We'll think of something. Got to give him a few nice things for a while. Then, when the time's right... Are you hungry?' he asked, hoping to distract her and keep the moisture in her eyes from spilling. 'Do you want to go out this evening and get something to eat?'

'I've cooked something,' Faye admitted with a shy smile. She freed herself from his embrace and pulled him towards the kitchen. She'd found a bag of potatoes and a couple of pieces of beef steak in his pantry. Not knowing how to properly cook steak – she had never tasted such rich fare – she'd cut the meat up into little pieces. She'd often watched her mother make a shepherd's pie out of leftover meat scraps and any vegetables she'd had to hand. She knew that such a meal stretched to feed a family.

'Smells good,' Rob said as they entered the neat kitchen filled with a savoury aroma. 'What is it?'

'Shepherd's pie.'

'Yeah?' He sounded surprised and impressed and opened the cooking-range door to peer in. 'Me mum would make that.' He grimaced. 'Not often, of course, 'cos that git always kept her short. It'd end up more spud 'n' bacon bits than anything else, but still it were a treat and a change from our regular bread 'n' scrape after school.' He spun the pie dish with a finger and sucked his scorched skin. 'What's in this?'

'Your steak and some onions I found in the pantry too... What did he say when you told him?' Faye blurted. She knew they couldn't avoid talking about Jimmy and the grim business of the funeral arrangements. She'd sooner get it over with. In a short while Michael would come downstairs and interrogate her again, if he could stop sobbing for long enough. Her brother had been inconsolable since he'd heard the dreadful news about their mother's death. He'd spent almost the whole day upstairs on his bed, only appearing at intervals to ask more unanswerable questions.

'He lied, as he always does.' Rob closed the oven door and straightened. 'He said he didn't know anything about Edie falling pregnant. He knew, all right; could see it in his eyes.' He leaned back against the sink, facing her, resigned to a serious talk. 'I went to see the woman he knocks about with and she confirmed what we'd already guessed: he'd taken off 'cos something had spooked him. She told me he'd probably be found at Stephen's, as he was after his job back. She felt bad about him doing the dirty on your mum. Edie'd been to see her and she'd offered yer mum some money. I imagine it was her told Edie where to go in King's Cross. She seemed genuinely worried Edie'd go to Maggie in The Bunk for an abortion and get hurt...' His explanation tailed off into a sigh. 'I think she was just trying to help.'

'Me mum went to see Jimmy's fancy woman?' Faye sounded shocked.

'Yeah; she was probably desperate to find Jimmy by then. I suppose his tart's lodgings was the first place she thought to look for him.' Rob's look turned penetrative. He'd had enough experience with women to know how their minds worked. She'd moved on from thinking about Jimmy's tart and was concentrating on his. He knew he had some explaining to do. 'Something

I need to say to you, Faye...'

'Doesn't matter...' She turned away.

'Yeah, it does, if things are going to be good between us.'

'It's all right; I guessed you said you loved me to be kind 'cos I was hysterical and upset.'

He choked a laugh. He hadn't been expecting that. 'I said I love you 'cos I meant it; but I know I should have waited and chosen a better time to tell you.' He self-consciously pressed the bridge of his nose. 'I've never wanted to say it to anyone before. But that's no excuse and I should've had the guts to tell you a while ago.' He paused. 'What I wanted to say: the other women, the ones you heard Stephen mention at Christmas – that's all done with. There's been no one else for a while now.' He stuck his hands in his pockets, gazing earnestly at her. 'I haven't wanted to be with anyone else ... only you. I was going to come round to see you before all this happened, swear I was. You said you wished you hadn't been so proud and had come to see me ... well, I was feeling the same way. I'd wanted to come and say I'd acted like a moody prat refusing to help your brother out like that.'

Faye approached him to prop her forehead against his shoulder. 'Perhaps you were right about Michael. Perhaps he should learn the hard way. And I didn't just want to come and see you to get help with Michael. I wanted to tell you I was sorry for acting like ... a moody prat...' She smiled as she used his phrase. 'But most of all... I wanted to say... I'm sure I'd like it if I slept with you.' She finished with a bright blush on her cheeks that had little to do with the heat wafting up from the oven.

'Yeah? Well, believe me, I'm gonna make sure you do like it,' he promised fiercely, and tilted up her face to kiss her. His lips swerved aside before touching as a little face appeared at the kitchen door.

'Where's Mum?'

Faye twisted about to see Adam gazing up at her, rubbing his eyes.

'You hungry, mate?' Rob asked.

Adam nodded his small fair head.

'Have tea soon, shall we?'

Again Adam nodded at Rob.

'Shall we sit in here to eat tea?' Faye suggested. She knew there was a posh dining room with shiny mahogany furniture as well as the kitchen table to choose from. She'd explored the house from top to bottom while waiting for him to come home. She'd walked from one spotless room to the other with tears dripping from the end of her nose, thinking how relieved her mum would be to know she had Rob's protection and that Michael and Adam were benefiting from his generosity too. The saddest thing was knowing her death had prompted their luck. But Faye clung to the belief that her mother was close by and contented by how things had turned out.

'Come in with you?' Adam piped up, and ran to cling to Faye's legs.

She picked him up, shushing him.

'Come in with you?' Adam repeated.

'What's he saying?'

'He wants to come in my bed with me later,'

Faye explained. 'When he's upset, he always climbs in bed with me for a cuddle. Might as well let him or he'll grizzle all night.' After a moment she asked, 'Do you mind?'

''Course not...'

A comical facial expression had denied the sincerity of that remark. It made her chuckle and protest, 'He's not three yet; he's just a baby still. It might be like this for years.'

'Yeah, I know.'

'And?'

'I'll hire a nursemaid and take you on a long honeymoon.'

Faye stared at him, a lump wedged in her throat before a desperate need to know abruptly dissolved it. 'Is that a proposal, Rob?' she breathed.

'Yeah ... it is.'

'You said you didn't want to get married for a long while.'

'So did you.'

Her melting, blue-eyed gaze made him add huskily, 'Something else I should have owned up to a while back, sweetheart.'

Jimmy's expression turned spiteful as he spied Nellie coming out of the tobacconist's. Having immediately torn open the new pack, she lit a cigarette then crossed the road. From the direction she was taking, he reckoned she was on her way home.

Something had been niggling at the back of his mind since he'd left Stevie's, and the sight of her had just helped him work out what it was. She alone had been told the tale he'd concocted about helping out a pal in Kent, yet Bobbie had thrown it back at him less than an hour ago. Bobbie had gone looking for Nellie for the same reason Edie had gone after her: they'd both wanted to track him down and had ended up poisoning her mind against him.

For an old prossie, Nellie had always been a soft touch for a hard-luck story, even though lately she wouldn't swallow any of his. And Edie, damn her, had gone complaining to Nellie about him. Even before he'd gone missing, Jimmy had guessed Nellie was again trying to separate him from her earnings. She'd left him high and dry once before, when Saul Bateman had taken over looking out for her. But that had been years ago when she was quite a looker. Now she was a blowsy old brass, and no regular pimp would embarrass himself by taking her on. Jimmy had been relieved to know it, and had felt reassured that Nellie needed him as much as he needed her. Only now it seemed she didn't, and it seemed she didn't give a toss any more whether he knew it.

When he'd turned up at The Bunk a little while ago and found their rooms empty – everything gone; even Edie's old crockery and cutlery had been cleared out – Jimmy had realised straight away there was only one place the kids would be. As he'd emerged into the street he'd bumped into Margaret Lovat, and she'd confirmed what he'd already guessed. The woman had passed on her condolences, and the information that she'd seen the kids going off in Rob's car early that morning. Jimmy had wondered how much worse his luck might get. He'd been relying on finding Faye at home, or perhaps taking refuge with the boys at a neighbour's. He'd judged she'd be too upset to be working at the bakery. And he was in desperate need of cadging a few bob as he was skint.

As Jimmy trudged along in Nellie's wake he realised, with Edie gone and her daughter now out of reach, Nellie was all he had left. He was determined to make sure she understood he was keeping hold of her.

'Seen Greavesie about, have yer?'

Tim Lovat stared coldly at Donald Bateman. He hadn't forgotten the humiliation of being beaten up by this thug and his gang. They'd not spoken since. Having given him a full blast of his filthy look, he turned around without answering, and strolled on down Campbell Road towards home.

''Ere ... you deaf or summat? I was speakin' to you.' Donald caught up with him and yanked one of his arms to spin him around.

Last time they'd clashed, Donald had had back-up; now he was alone and it was obvious he was lacking his brash confidence as well as his mates. His eyes looked shifty and he was fidgeting.

'Get lost.' Tim shoved him, sending him skittering backwards.

'Look, no hard feelings, pal,' Donald whined, swaggering back towards him. 'You only got a little smack 'cos you was interfering when I was chattin' up the girl I'm after. Now, if you like her 'n' all, that can't be helped, but it's best man wins, ain't it?'

Tim looked him up and down and sneered a smile. 'Yeah, it is, *pal*. And you've lost, 'cos she's chosen who she wants.'

'You walkin' out with her?' Donald barked.

'Not me,' Tim answered with a hint of bitterness. His smug delight in having deflated the arrogant prick melted his ill feeling. 'Rob Wild's her sweetheart,' he announced. 'Now you know that, I don't reckon you're gonna be chatting her up no more, are you?' With that he walked on, a grin on his face.

Tim hadn't been happy to discover from his mum that Faye Greaves, and her brothers, had moved in with Rob Wild and it looked like a romance might be on the cards. But he liked Faye a lot and, after the recent tragedy that had befallen the family, only a wrong 'un would hold a grudge. Ruefully, Tim realised that the turn of events had decided his future for him. He'd been holding back on taking up the offer of the job at Lockley Grange, not only so his parents would get used to the idea of doing without him, but also because, after their day out in Essex, he'd been optimistic he and Faye might become closer, and she might be persuaded to go with him. If she'd agreed to become his sweetheart, but had preferred to stay in North London, Tim would have continued working at Milligan's outfitters just to be with her. But it wasn't to be, and deep in his heart he'd known all along that he'd been kidding himself; Faye would only ever consider him a friend.

Tim took a look over his shoulder at Bateman.

He got the impression that the creep didn't even know what had happened to Edie Greaves, or that her funeral was later today. Miffed as Tim was not even to have had a chance to take Faye out again to the flicks, he graciously allowed Rob Wild his victory. He was glad Faye, and her brother, Michael, would now be protected from Bateman's bullying.

Donald stomped off furiously in the opposite direction. He'd not even realised the cow had been attracting the likes of Wild. He'd thought Tim bloody Lovat was his main rival. Added to that, he'd never have believed Wild would be interested in a girl who acted like she'd not yet been broken in. Everyone knew he had a couple of sophisticated sorts on the go. There wasn't a man who entered the Duke and copped an eyeful of Gloria who didn't reckon Rob Wild was a lucky bastard. Of course, he knew Faye's stepfather was Rob's old man, so they were bound to have known each other quite well, but... His intense brooding was suddenly interrupted.

'Got a minute, have you?'

Donald swung about, startled. 'No, I haven't, you manky old tart. Now piss off.' He shot a look right and left as though embarrassed by Nellie's company and worried somebody might see them together.

Nellie's lips tightened into a knot of crimson lipstick. 'Got yer father's charm, I see,' she muttered sourly.

Donald stuck two fingers up at her and set off again.

Nellie put a spurt on and caught up with him. 'Might just as well tell me what I want to know, then I will piss off. Don't worry, son, ain't any keener 'n you are to be seen together. Bleedin' hell, cradle snatchin' ain't my thing. What are yer? Fifteen?' She smirked as she saw his cheeks glow red.

'Just need to know where I can find your dad. Need to speak to him. It's important.'

'He won't have nuthin' to say to you.' Donald slung her a sideways look. 'You go botherin' 'im, all you'll get is a black eye to match the one you already got.' He tipped his forehead at Nellie's bruised face.

'He'll want to hear what I've got to say all right. And when he finds out he could've known about it all a bit sooner if you hadn't put yer spoke in...'

That brought Donald to a stop. He knew that years ago his father and this woman had been involved together. Once, when he'd been this side of the water, his father had mentioned catching up with Old Nellie. Donald definitely didn't want to rub his father up the wrong way. He desperately needed a sub off him now it looked like getting Greavesie to pay up soon was a non-starter. He wasn't up to crossing Rob Wild on his own and he knew his mates would never back him up there.

'He lives Peckham way,' he mumbled at Nellie.

'Yeah ... know he do ... but it's a big place, Peckham,' Nellie drawled sarcastically.

When she'd got exactly what she wanted, Nellie rested back against the wall of a shop and dug in her handbag. She fished out a pencil and an old envelope and carefully wrote down the address she'd memorised. She then took out her powder compact and flicked it open. She stared at blood-shot eyes and deep crow's feet then doggedly pressed make-up on purple skin to try to disguise the worst of it. She winced as the pain needled into her head. The bastard hadn't even had the guts to whack her while she was conscious. He'd waited until she was getting off to sleep and too befuddled to land him one back before setting about her. If she'd been in two minds before about staying loyal to Jimmy Wild, she wasn't any more. She snapped the compact shut and set off in the direction of the bus stop.

TWENTY-SIX

'Fancy a shandy?'

Michael accepted with a nod and slid on to the banquette Rob had indicated, close to the door in the Duke pub.

'Come on, Rob ... bit young, ain't he?' the landlord complained in a mutter, jutting his chin in Michael's direction, and wiping the bar with sweeping circular strokes.

'You were serving me at the same age,' Rob ribbed him. In fact, at about twelve years old he'd gone further afield for a crafty pint. This bloke had known how old all the local kids were and would always chuck out him and his friends with a flea in their ears for trying it on. 'He's only having a shandy; make it a weak one.'

The landlord moseyed off towards the pumps, shaking his head, and Rob turned to look at Michael.

Michael knew he was being watched but kept his eyes averted while his nervous hands shuffled beer mats on the table in front of him. The time was drawing closer when he'd get some hard questions fired at him by his sister's boyfriend. It didn't matter how sweet Rob was on Faye, Michael reckoned he was the type that didn't take prisoners. He reckoned Rob hadn't forgotten about Faye getting bashed by Donald Bateman, or that the incident had been all his fault. Michael suspected Rob had only been lenient so far because it'd be disrespectful to his dead mum if he started on him before the funeral was over. But this afternoon his mum had been laid to rest. He darted glances about the crowded pub, searching for Faye, unconsciously seeking her as protection. He understood that his sister was probably all that stood between him and a caning. Having glimpsed her glossy golden head encircled by the dark clothed figures of Matilda's daughters, he relaxed and again his eyes slid to Rob.

He was still leaning on the bar, every so often looking his way, and Michael knew the amused quirk to his mouth was because he'd guessed what he'd been thinking about. As Rob gave him a slow smile, Michael realised he was letting him know that hiding behind his sister might work ... but he shouldn't count on it.

'Sun kept shining for your mum. Couldn't have wished for a better day.' Alice put her arms around Faye and hugged her close. As she noticed the glitter in Faye's eyes increase, she whispered, 'She's all right, Faye ... nothing can hurt her now ... sleeping easy, she is.'

Bethany also gave her a cuddle. 'Lovely service too, weren't it? Not too long. And what beautiful white lilies you got for her!' she exclaimed. 'There were so many of them, and the lovely scent...'

Faye nodded and sniffed, using the heel of a hand against her eyes to smear away the wet. Everybody had been so kind. The funeral party had just come away from the cemetery and had now congregated in the Duke pub for a small wake for Edie Greaves. Rob had arranged for a room to be set aside for the mourners to have a buffet. Faye had asked Rob not to go overboard on the arrangements. He'd wanted to please her with an elaborate send-off for Edie, but she'd insisted something simple would be fine. As soon as they'd got back to the pub, Matilda had straight away relieved Faye of Adam. Although the toddler didn't understand what had caused their sadness, it had affected him and made him grizzly too. Seeing her distress, Matilda had led Adam away with a promise of some fancy biscuits to eat. Before she'd disappeared, she'd instructed her daughters to make sure Faye got a stiff one down her to soothe her nerves.

Faye sipped her sherry and glanced about for Rob. She noticed he was still at the bar and, as she watched, his father joined him. Rob had wanted to ban Jimmy from the funeral but Faye had made him see sense on that score: Jimmy was unpredictable; he might do the decent thing and stay away; on the other hand he might turn up at the graveside, uninvited, and cause a scene just for spite. She'd sooner those who wanted to do so simply ignored him. Most people who were aware of his cowardly defection when Edie had got pregnant had done exactly that.

'Gonna buy us a drink, son?'

'What d'you want?'

'Double scotch, if yer standing.'

'Double scotch,' Rob repeated to the landlord. A moment later, when the glass was put in front of him, Rob pushed it towards his father.

'Thanks, Bobbie.' Jimmy reached for it immediately.

'Fuckin' choke on it,' Rob muttered as he walked away.

Jimmy took a gulp from his drink and kept his eyes on the barmaid who'd just appeared behind the counter. She was taking off her cardigan, with much thrusting of her bust, and flicking glances his eldest son's way. Jimmy reckoned Gloria thought she was still in with a chance there. People knew she'd accepted having to share Robert Wild with his other women, and that she turned a blind eye to what he got up to. But Jimmy reckoned she was going to be out of luck this time. What a mug Bobbie was! Faye was a looker, but a skinny slip of a thing compared to Gloria. His lecherous eyes ran over the barmaid's buxom figure, making her preen. She sashayed over, polishing a glass, but Jimmy was under no illusions there. He knew she'd only approached him because she'd seen Bobbie talking to him moments before, and hoped he'd soon be back.

'How you bearin' up, Jim? Bad business. I'm really sorry about Edie, y'know.'

'That's all right, love. These things happen.' Jimmy shook his head, martyred sigh puffing out his lips, his eyes fixed on her cleavage.

'That your stepdaughter?' Gloria inclined her head towards Faye, who was smiling up into Rob's face.

'Yeah ... pretty as a picture, ain't she? I'll introduce you, if yer like,' he offered slyly.

Gloria shot him a look. 'Nah ... s'all right.' She wiped her hands on the towel she'd been using on a tumbler. Rob had told her it was over between them weeks ago; but she'd heard that a few times before and had previously managed to lure him back with a few tricks. But she'd never seen that look on his face, and she knew what it meant. As he raised a hand and touched the girl's face as though it were the most precious thing in the world, a sad little smile turned down her mouth. A moment later she brightened, wondering how Vicky Watson would take the news that Robert Wild had finally fallen in love.

Gloria turned back to Jimmy. 'Heard your Stevie's broken up with his wife. Coming in later, is he?' She'd also heard Stevie was back working for Rob and earning good regular money.

'Might do ... he were at the funeral. He spends a lot of his time with his kiddie,' Jimmy informed her. 'Devoted to that little lad, he is.'

'Right...' Gloria sighed and traipsed off to serve a customer at the other end of the bar.

'How you doing, Michael?' Jimmy had struggled to find himself a conversation with an adult. Most people cold-shouldered him as soon as he approached them, so he'd settled on slipping on to the bench next to Edie's son.

Michael's eyes darted hatred at him. 'Get lost,' he muttered.

'What's up with you?' Jimmy sounded huffy.

'You know...'

Jimmy frowned. He hadn't thought Michael would be old enough to take in all that had gone on with Edie, being as it was embarrassing women's stuff. But it seemed somebody had turned even a lad hardly out of short trousers against him because of the abortion.

He started ruffling Michael's fair hair. ''Course yer upset about yer mum, we all are,' he crooned. 'If only I could turn back the clock, I'd make it come right for yer, son...'

'You liar!' Michael spat, shuffling along the banquette to leave Jimmy's hand stroking space. 'You could've made it right, but you done a runner, didn't yer? And don't say you didn't, 'cos I saw you with me own eyes.'

'What?' Jimmy was feeling baffled and uneasy.

'I saw you. I was there the day you took off,' Michael hissed. 'Been up the shop with Adam, hadn't I, and when we got back he was busting to go so I took him out to the privy. We come in the back way and I saw you hiding, so we hung about outside for a bit, watching and listening, 'cos I didn't know what was going on...'

'Eh?' Jimmy stopped glancing about at people and his narrowed eyes sprang to Michael. 'What did you see and hear?'

'I saw you hiding under the stairs, and I could hear me mum and Faye upstairs. Faye was telling Mum she ought to go after you, and get some money, and heard her say to get a proper doctor.' Michael clamped together his quivering lips and shot a poisonous look at Jimmy. 'They was having a ding-dong before I went out to the shop, and was still at it when I got back, but I didn't know at the time what it all meant. But I could tell you did. Could see too that it was worrying you by the way you was acting sly. I know you reckoned nobody'd seen yer.' He paused before hissing, 'But I did. I saw Faye come down, and then I watched you creeping off out after you was sure she'd gone.'

Jimmy licked his lips. 'Yeah ... well...'

'Yeah ... *well...*' Michael mimicked viciously and sprang up. He weaved speedily through the crowded pub to the door and went out. A moment later Jimmy had caught up with him a little way along the street and had fallen into step beside him.

'See ... at the time I didn't really know what was going on any more'n you did, son, so no need to tell nobody about it...' Jimmy's slanting smile stopped short of his eyes. He stuck a hand in his pocket and pulled out a crumpled packet of cigarettes and quickly lit one. He drew on it deeply. 'All I could hear was raised voices, so I thought best not to interfere between yer mum 'n' sister.'

He laughed smoke out of his mouth. 'Knew I'd only get told to mind me own business. Bit like you, eh?' He elbowed Michael in the ribs in a matey way.

Michael distanced himself, muttering an obscenity beneath his breath. He was dreadfully upset about losing his mum, but he felt guilty too; regret had been gnawing at his insides since he'd pieced together the snippets of what he'd heard and seen. He couldn't stop thinking that if he'd told his mother Jimmy had been crouching under the stairs, things might have ended differently. She might have dashed out after the coward and done what Faye had told her to do: made Jimmy pay up so she had enough money to go to a proper doctor. Then she'd never have needed to see a doddery old bloke down King's Cross to get rid of the baby. But, that day, when he'd got back to the room, his mother had been in such a miserable mood after arguing with Faye that he'd dumped Adam and directly gone out to lark about with Tony Cummins, just to cheer himself up.

'So, you told anyone about any o' this?'

Michael shook his head. 'Wish I'd told me mum straight afterwards,' he muttered.

'Well ... never mind about that now, eh? It's good you've not gone upsetting people no more than they need to be. Your sister, for example, she's cut up, ain't she? You don't want to go making her believe things that ain't true, 'cos I've told you I was in the dark over it 'n' all...' His lie faded away as he noticed that Michael's eyes kept returning to the Weights in his hand. He offered the pack to him. 'Go on, take one.' He pulled a cigarette half out and, with a nod, urged Michael to have it. 'You're not such a lad, are you? What are yer ... twelve? Used to have a crafty smoke meself at your age.'

Michael reached out and took the cigarette and put it in his pocket. As they came level with an alley, Jimmy suddenly pushed him into it and rammed him against the wall.

'So we understand one another, don't we? You don't go telling no tales about me, then it won't be the worse for you fer makin' up stuff ... right?'

Michael nodded, barely able to breathe because the grip on his neck had tightened.

'Good.' Jimmy released him and brushed him down. 'Look smart, don't yer?' He eyed him top to toe, neatening the lapels on Michael's black suit. 'Me son get you them new togs, did he?'

Michael nodded again, keeping his lashes lowered to conceal the loathing in his eyes.

'You get yerself back to the pub before you're missed and I'll be back too and keep an eye on you, don't you worry about that,' Jimmy added softly. He ferreted in Michael's pocket and took out the cigarette. Carefully he stuck it back in the pack before he strolled off up the alley.

'Oi, Greavesie!'

Michael spun about and immediately his shoulders slumped.

Donald Bateman sprinted across the road and then slowed down so Michael could appreciate his swagger. 'Where you been? Funeral?' He mocked as he took in Michael's sombre attire.

'Yeah,' Michael answered.

'Who's died?' Bateman was still joking.

'Me mum,' Michael muttered, blinking and sniffing, but his chin went up.

Donald's jaw dropped and his smile disintegrated. 'What ... straight up?' he barked in amazement.

'Yeah ... going back to the Duke for the wake; all me family's in there.' He knew what Bateman wanted with him, so he added pointedly, 'And they're all waiting for me, so I've got to go or they'll be out looking.'

'This right wot I heard about your sister 'n' Rob Wild getting together?' Donald had caught hold of his arm as he started to walk off.

Michael nodded, curbing a smirk.

'Gone off her anyhow,' Donald announced unconvincingly. 'Girl down the Chemist's been giving me the come on and she ain't such hard work, if yer know what I mean.' He made a lewd gesture with a fist.

'Gotta go...' Again Michael stepped away and again Bateman stopped him.

''Course, it's a shame about yer mum 'n' all that, but you still owe me, and I want it. I need it so's I can take this girl out and show her a good time down the Palais. And don't go telling me you ain't got it, 'cos now your sister's all nice and cosy with Rob Wild, I reckon you can get anything you like, can't yer?'

'Can't get nuthin' out of her or him.' Michael manoeuvred his arm out of Donald's grip. 'Gotta do work in his warehouse or I don't get a sodding penny of me own,' he muttered peevishly.

'Well, don't want no hard-luck stories, just want me money, 'cos I'm off out dancing on Saturday, like I said.' Donald took a threatening step closer to Michael.

'I'll give it to you later in the week... Friday.'

When Donald renewed his clasp and gave Michael a dubious, narrowed look, he added, 'I'm doin' a bit of work in the warehouse off Holloway Road after school on Friday. I'll hang about and meet you when I've got paid, and they've all gone home. Swear I'll have it for you. Got any fags?'

Donald fished in a pocket. 'Cost yer,' he announced, handing Michael a half-empty packet.

'Yeah,' Michael said sourly. 'I know.'

'Right then,' Donald said. 'I'll turn up after seven o'clock and I want the lot: eleven shillin', and you'd better not go messing me about or you'll really get it.'

Michael opened the carton as he trudged off. He knew that come Friday he would be in for another beating. His wages, added to what little bit he'd saved for Bateman, made only about half of what he owed. He pulled out a cigarette and glanced about for a bit of shelter. He'd been hoping to have a crafty puff around a corner somewhere before he went back to the pub, but he knew he'd been gone a while now and Faye would be fretting over where he'd got to.

If Jimmy had let him keep the cigarette he'd given him, he'd not have met Bateman; he'd have been up the alley having a quiet smoke and would've missed him. Nor would he have needed to get in deeper debt with Donald; a few drags would've done him for now. He knew Jimmy hadn't taken back the fag because he reckoned he was too young to smoke; he was just a mean bastard. He was a liar too. Michael knew what he'd seen: Jimmy's expression that day was etched on his memory. The cowardly weasel had crept away looking scared because he didn't want to help his mum deal with the problem of what to do about another baby.

'What you doing around here?'

'Looking for you.'

Nellie had been hovering in Peckham High Street for what had seemed like ages. She'd been hoping she might be able to bump into Saul if she dawdled close to the top of his road. Thankfully the ploy had worked. She hadn't wanted to go and knock on his door in case he wasn't in and his lady friend demanded to know her business. Nellie had to concede the woman would have every right to do so. To pass the time, she'd looked in shop windows; she'd sat twiddling her thumbs on a bench; she'd ambled to and fro till a woman had come out of her draper's shop and glared at her, hands on hips, prompting Nellie to stare her out. But she'd moved off and taken up position elsewhere.

Saul had spotted her large garish figure as he'd been turning towards home. Immediately he'd braked and got out of his car. Presently he was gazing at Nellie across its burgundy bodywork. 'Something important, is it, brought you all this way?'

Nellie shrugged and looked a bit uncomfortable. 'Dunno really,' she admitted. 'Can't tell how you're gonna feel about him after all this time. Might be you don't give a toss no more.' She came a little closer to the car. 'But I know how I feel about him, and I know he deserves something for what he's done. Ain't right he always gets away with it.'

Saul's scarred lips twitched as puzzlement deepened his grimace; the tight shiny skin on his cheeks hardly moved. He angled his head to the left so he could examine her properly with his good eye. 'Ah ... been bashed about, have yer?' He nodded, letting her know he'd noticed the bruise beneath the powder. 'That grey-haired bloke I saw you go off with in the pub that evening, were it him done that to you?' He leaned his forearms on the car's roof and waited for her reply. After a silent moment when he could tell she was uncertain whether to properly grass the fellow up, he prompted, 'Wondered what you was doing with him, I did. Thought he looked like a wrong 'un. I reckon you told me a lie, that night, Nel. You've had someone looking out for you after all, haven't you, gel?'

'Nah ... not really, Saul,' she quietly disagreed. 'When all's said and done, Jimmy Wild don't look out for nobody but himself. Never has.'

TWENTY-SEVEN

Jimmy slunk around the corner. He'd been stalking Michael since they'd had their little talk to see if he'd frightened him enough to make him obedient. If he didn't go back to the pub, Jimmy knew he'd have to do a better job of enforcing his authority on him.

He'd been alarmed to discover that the boy had spotted him hiding under the stairs. Michael had said he hadn't told anyone about it; Jimmy knew he had to make sure it stayed that way. People might suspect him of lying, but if Michael started blabbing they'd know for certain that he'd been aware Edie was pregnant. Jimmy intended to stay around here for a while yet and, dump though The Bunk was, it had its own code of conduct. He didn't want to be shunned by the whole lot of them, right down to his old pal, Lenny.

A few moments ago Jimmy had seen Michael talking to Donald Bateman, and the sight had stirred in him old anxieties he'd thought dead and buried. He'd remained invisible to Saul so far and, as the months had passed, he'd become confident of being left alone from that quarter. It came as a surprise to him that Michael and Donald were matey, and the longer they continued talking the more Jimmy's agitation increased. If Michael was spouting off about his stepdad to Bateman's kid, word of his part in

Edie's death might spread south of the river. The last thing Jimmy wanted was a visit from Saul.

'What was you doing with Bateman just now?' Jimmy cornered Michael as he made to go back inside the Duke, sticking out an arm to prevent him reaching the door handle.

'What?' Michael stepped back, startled and wondering where Jimmy had silently sprung from. 'You been following me?'

Jimmy's fingers tightened on Michael's arm and he forced him away from the entrance as a group of people came out of the pub. A couple of things had become clear to Jimmy, and he cussed himself for not having investigated the matter further at the time. He now knew who had beaten up Michael, and he could guess the reason why. Edie's son was a regular smoker and he was getting his supply off Bateman.

'I was just getting some fags, that's all.' Michael tried to jerk his elbow away from Jimmy's painful fingers.

'You stay away from him. He's bad news. All that family's bad news. Did you tell him anything about me?'

'What?' Michael gazed up contemptuously into Jimmy's pinched features. 'Why would I?'

'You stupid little sod,' Jimmy hissed. 'He's the one beat you up, ain't he? You keep clear of him.'

'I can't. I've got to pay him what I owe him.'

That remark caused Jimmy's eyes to narrow thoughtfully. 'Well, you'll have to give me the money and I'll see him. And while I'm at it, I'll tell him to keep away from you 'n' all, or he'll have me to deal with.'

'Ain't got it.'

'Ask yer sister for it.' Jimmy's grip tightened.

'She won't give me nuthin'. She never stops going on about the trouble we had with him last time, when he punched her.'

A look of enlightenment lit Jimmy's face. 'So ... it was *him*, was it?'

Michael chewed his lower lip, cursing inwardly for letting that slip. He stopped trying to dodge past and instead shot a sideways look at his stepfather. It was obvious that Jimmy was in a lather about having been spotted eavesdropping. That day when he hid under the stairs would have been the last time the old weasel had seen Edie alive or heard her voice, but it wasn't guilt that was eating at him but the consequences of anyone finding out. As usual, all he cared about was saving his own skin. It dawned on Michael that this gave him the upper hand for once. There might just be a way he could turn the situation to his advantage and get Jimmy to pay off most of his debt. It would be even better if Donald landed Jimmy one into the bargain. It might not be much of a revenge for his mum, but it would be better than nothing.

'I've told Bateman I'll pay up on Friday, but I won't have enough to give him it all. It's eleven shillings and I've only got three bob.'

'Just give me what you've got,' Jimmy snarled, snatching at the money Michael dug from his pocket. The idea of paying Donald out of his own cash rankled, but he knew it was the only way to get the Batemans off his back once and for all.

'What's going on? Why're you out here?'

Faye, having spotted them through the pub window, had come out to investigate. Michael's guilty expression made her glare at Jimmy.

'Your brother's been after buckshee fags again. Get himself in big trouble, he will, if he don't pack it in.' Jimmy gave Michael one last ferocious look before sauntering into the pub.

Donald's face split into a happy grin. 'Didn't know you was coming over this way.' Having spotted his father's car outside his mother's place, he'd scampered up to him like a kid. His father rarely went in the house; he usually waited outside for him once he'd discovered he wasn't at home. There had been no thaw in the hostility between his parents, despite a decade having passed since their separation.

'Ow! Woss that for?'

Instead of the fond greeting Donald had expected from his father, Saul had stomped round the car to heftily clip his son's ear.

'Get in the car,' Saul growled.

Donald did as he was told, a hand cupping the ringing side of his head. His father immediately set the vehicle in motion. A few minutes later he parked at the top of Campbell Road. 'Know anyone who lives down here, do you?'

'Tony Cummins ... why?' Donald whined, gawping at his father as though the old man had lost his marbles.

'Who else?'

'No one ... why?'

'What about your pal Greavesie and his sister out of the bakery?' Saul snapped.

'They don't live here no more,' Donald cried. 'Greavesie's moved off and lives with his sister and her fancy man, down Tufnell Park.'

That gave Saul a moment's pause, but he narrowed his good eye on his son. 'And what about their stepfather, Jimmy Wild? What about him?'

'What about him?'

'So you did know!' Saul bellowed. 'You knew the bastard was Greavesie's stepfather and you never said! Why ain't you never told me something like that!'

Donald's bottom lip wobbled. 'Didn't know you was interested in him. He's only a fat old ponce. Nobody likes him...'

'*I* don't like him,' the information was ejected in a sinister hiss.

'Why ... woss he done?'

'What's he done?' Saul mimicked with a fanatical grin. 'You're looking at what he's done, son.' He gazed at his face in the car's rear-view mirror, jutting up his chin so he could examine the damage from a different angle. He knew off by heart every ridge and dip of mutilated flesh mapped on his face, yet the horrible sight never ceased to tear at his guts.

'What ... he burnt you in the war?' Donald gasped out.

'Might just as well've done.'

'I won't meet him Friday down Holloway Road then ... won't have nuthin' to do with him, Dad, promise,' Donald rattled off. He was still unsure why his father was so upset, but he knew whatever was troubling him was serious.

'Meeting him Friday?' Saul parroted.

'Yeah ... Greavesie said he ain't got the money, so Jimmy's gonna meet me and pay off all what he owes me for fags 'n' so on. He says Jimmy won't give him the money 'cos he don't trust him with it and reckons he'll spend it. Greavesie reckons Jimmy's gonna give me what for 'n' all for getting him fags in the first place.' Donald smirked. 'Some chance he's got of that! Was planning on giving the old git a dig fer even thinking about it. But I won't go. Stuff him and the money. If you don't want me to...'

'Oh, yes you will, Donnie. You'll go and meet him all right.' Saul patted his son's arm to quieten his burbling, a smile writhing over his lips. 'And when you go, I'll be right behind you.'

'When do you want to set the date?'

'Don't mind...' Faye replied dreamily, snuggling closer to Rob.

After having spent a year sleeping with the stench of a rotting mattress in her nostrils, the sweet smell of freshly laundered sheets was wonderfully appealing. But the feel of warm male flesh was equally stimulating to her and her fingertips stroked on steely muscles sheathed beneath satiny skin. She opened her eyes to see him watching her.

'Next week we could go to see the vicar and get the banns sorted out.'

She nodded against his chest. 'If you like...'

'Not too soon for you?' he asked, and dropped a kiss on her forehead.

'No,' she answered huskily, a smile in her voice. 'But the town hall will do just as well. I wasn't expecting you to book a church.' Her hand moved to touch his abrasive jaw. 'I know you're being kind and considerate because of me mum, but we don't have to wait until our wedding night, you know.' She angled her face and touched together their lips. 'It's not as though I'm going to be wearing a white dress in any case.'

In the few nights since Edie's funeral he'd restricted his lovemaking to kissing and caressing her as they lay together in bed. Faye knew he desperately wanted her. She remembered enough about her brutally quick encounter with Simon to recognise the sight of a man fully aroused. But it seemed he was being sweetly patient because of the unbearable grief that daily washed over her when thoughts of her mother bombarded her mind.

'You can wear a white dress if you want ... nobody knows about Adam.'

'They know about you,' she giggled. 'Hardly likely to be a virgin, am I?' she teased.

'People think you are.' Rob dug an elbow into the mattress and rested a cheek on a palm while watching her through twilight.

'People know that I've been living with you, and you've got a reputation as a bit of a ladies' man, I believe.' There was hardly a hint of acidity in her voice.

'Yeah, and they also know I'm caring for you and your brothers after your mum died tragically. If they reckon I'd take advantage of you in those circumstances, what sort of bloke do they take me for? Or you, for that matter?' He'd growled the last with a wolfish smile before slickly moving to cover her. His entrapment of her displayed a practised ease that made her instinctively tense. Rob swooped his lips to hers and parted them with a kiss that was gently seductive. 'You'll know what's happening to you, Faye ... you'll want me as much as I want you ... promise...'

Her hands cupped his dear face; she knew she only had to stay silent and he'd roll aside, cuddle her to sleep instead. She nodded her head then arched up to seal their lips and press breast to breast, wordlessly proving permission.

'You sure ... really sure, you're ready?' he murmured, but already his hands had traced her silhouette and were again moving upwards, bringing her nightgown with them.

'I'm wet ... where's Mum?'

Rob collapsed on to his back with a groaning curse whistling between his teeth.

'Sorry...' Faye immediately whispered and grimaced apology too. But she was already shifting towards the edge of the bed to go to her son. He was standing just inside the door, his cherubic curls haloed by a weak light on the landing.

'Come in with you?' Adam asked plaintively, but he was looking at Rob as though, even at his tender age, he understood things had changed now and Faye was dividing her attention between them.

'Come here, mate.' It had been wearily said, but Rob sat upright and opened his arms.

Once Faye had stripped Adam of his wet things the boy scampered on to the bed, naked from the waist down. Rob settled him at his side and plumped the pillow under his head.

Slowly Faye approached the bed and kneeled on it, behind Rob. Her arms enclosed him and her face buried against his neck so she could plant fierce little kisses against his musky skin. 'Love you ... love you so much ... don't deserve you ... do anything for you.'

'Yeah?' he growled mockingly, turning his head and raising a hand to tickle her cheek. 'Gonna keep you to that in a week's time, Faye. Town hall it is, then honeymoon ... just us. You'd better get in bed, sweetheart, and get some sleep while you can.'

'Not still sulking are you, Nel?'

'Yeah...' Nellie admitted sourly. ''Cos I don't take kindly to getting punched in the face fer no reason.'

'But there were a reason; a good reason, too, weren't it? Told you before, Nel, we gotta be loyal to one another or what's it all about?' Jimmy gave her an injured look. 'Never meant to upset you, but then you will go and rile me by talking about me behind me back. That ain't right, surely?' He slunk closer to her on the bed. 'Come on, gel, we been through worse'n this and stuck together.'

'Yeah ... s'pose so,' Nellie grudgingly agreed, turning away so he wouldn't see the glint of malice in her eyes.

It was Friday and she knew Jimmy would soon be getting a taste of his own medicine. On the day of Edie's funeral, Saul had brought her back home after their chat. He'd immediately driven off in search of his son, but had popped in later to see her before heading back south of the water. He'd wanted to tell her that he had a little surprise planned for Jimmy on Friday. Nellie hadn't wanted to know the details. She could guess that he was in for a beating, but she no longer cared enough about Jimmy Wild to give a monkey's what happened to him. What mattered to her was that, in some small way, she'd put right the wrong she'd done Edie. She felt guilty for having sent the woman to a blind butcher for her abortion, even though years previously the old fellow had done a job for her with no problems.

Nellie watched Jimmy fish out his boots from under the table. He sat on a chair and jammed his stockinged feet in them, then leant forward to tie the laces.

'Off out then, are yer?'

'Yeah ... but I'll be back in a while,' he told her. 'We'll have time to go out and do a bit o' business before we turn in.'

'Right...' Nellie said, before twisting away from him to conceal her satisfied smile. When he crawled back, all black and blue, she'd be gone.

TWENTY-EIGHT

Michael looked at the clock on the wall in the hallway. It was almost six thirty. He'd finished his shift at the warehouse an hour ago and, despite wanting to hang about in the vicinity, had come home so as not to make his sister anxious as to why he was late. He'd told Faye he was going off out again to the cemetery to visit his mum's grave. It wasn't a lie. But first his intention was to return to his place of work and see what happened when Jimmy and Donald Bateman came face to face. When Jimmy got the thumping he deserved, Michael wanted to be there to watch him suffer. After that he was going to see his mum and take her the flowers he'd bought with the little bit of cash he'd kept back. He thought it right to let her know that today he'd arranged for Jimmy Wild to get his comeuppance for what he'd done to her.

Rob unlocked the drawer in his desk. He'd been halfway home when he'd remembered that there was a large amount of cash in the strongbox and immediately headed back to retrieve it. He never left notes overnight in the office any more. As the dole queues grew ever longer, and men got desperate for money to keep their families, attempted break-ins at the warehouse had become more frequent. So far his range of locks and bolts, and the bobbies who regularly pounded the beat, had kept would-be thieves at bay. But he knew it was only a matter of time before he was robbed. Mindful of that, he'd recently advertised for a night-watchman. The stack of applications was sitting on his desk, waiting till he had a moment to sift through them.

He was just pocketing the roll of notes and heading for the door when he glanced out of the window and spotted a grey-haired man who resembled his father peeping around a corner just along the road. Rob squinted and realised in amazement that it *was* Jimmy. His father was peering up and down the street as though looking for someone; he then emerged nervously from his hiding place and shuffled along to rest his back against a wall. His hands plunged in and out of his pockets several times before he withdrew his tobacco tin and started rolling a cigarette. Even while his fingers were occupied, Jimmy's eyes continued whizzing to and fro.

Rob moved to one side of the window to watch him, unobserved, uneasiness worming in his guts. If his father was thinking of breaking in while it was still daylight – and he wouldn't put it past him – he was taking his time setting about it. He was about to go out and confront him when he saw another head appear at the same corner. A mix of bafflement and disbelief creased Rob's features as he recognised someone else he knew. Michael was clutching a bunch of flowers and craning his neck around brickwork. Having caught sight of Jimmy, he jerked back out of sight.

Rob tilted his head to frown at the ceiling. At any other time he might have appreciated the farce of it and had a chuckle. But something about the scenario smelled fishy. There was no reason for Michael and Jimmy to have a sly meeting; they could get together for a private natter at any time. In any case, it looked as though Michael didn't want Jimmy to spot him, and that led Rob to conclude he'd been spying on him.

When he took another cautious look outside, Rob swore under his breath as he glimpsed someone else joining the party. He hadn't forgotten what Donald Bateman had done to Faye. Months on, a red mist still descended every time he thought of her beautiful face swollen and bruised. After Faye had admitted who'd hit her, he'd arranged for Bateman to get a slap over it, but in Rob's estimation that had been a minor reprimand and nowhere near being enough punishment.

'You're Greavesie's old man, ain't yer?'

Jimmy stuck the smoke in his mouth with a shaky hand and turned towards Donald. Even before Michael had got on the wrong side of this fellow, Jimmy had known that Bateman and his crew had a reputation for starting scraps. But he was relieved to see that Donald appeared to have come alone. In any case, Jimmy could feel the comforting weight of a blade against his hip. If things looked to be turning nasty he'd pull it to scare him off. But he reckoned it wouldn't come to that; all the cocky prick was after today was his money and a quick getaway.

'Yeah, that's who I am,' Jimmy drawled. 'Here

... got something for you from me stepson.' He dug in a pocket and pulled out a fistful of silver.

'You can keep that, Jim. Let me give you something instead ...' Saul sauntered out of the alleyway from which his son had emerged moments before. He stood in front of Jimmy, blocking his path, then, with a flourish, took off his hat so his old foe could get the full dramatic force of his ghastly disfigurement.

Jimmy turned pale and the newly made smoke dropped, unlit, from his lips. It was the first time Jimmy had seen the wreckage of Saul's face close to and he couldn't suppress his revulsion. 'Saul?' he gurgled.

''Course it is, mate. You remember me, don't yer?' Saul sounded quite jolly as he strolled closer. 'I know I look a bit different, but then so do you, don't you, Jim? Otherwise I'd've recognised you before, when I saw you in the Nag's Head that evening. You knew it was me all right though...'

Suddenly surfacing from his terrified entrancement, Jimmy turned tail and bolted back the way he'd come. He didn't get far. Two of Saul's heavies materialised from nowhere and cut off his escape.

Saul followed him at a leisurely pace. 'Now that ain't nice, Jim. Why'd you want to go running off like that, 'fore we've properly said hello? Got a bit of catching up to do, you 'n' me,' he taunted. 'Remember the day we had that bust-up over Nellie, do you? Know what happened after that, Jim? I was told you'd been murdered and I was in the frame fer it. So I got meself joined up sharpish and went to war.' He stared at his hat, rotating in his hands. 'Had a bad feeling about going, y'know. D'you reckon I was right to worry? *Do yer?'* He spat the words through grinding teeth. With a final look at Jimmy, he flicked his fingers at his cronies.

They moved in fast. Jimmy had taken a forceful punch to the jaw, and one to the guts that folded him in half and put him on his knees, before he managed to whip out the knife. He swiped it from side to side, breathing hard, keeping the thugs at bay. When he'd drawn in sufficient wind, he scurried, crab-like, on all fours towards the protection of the brick wall.

'Still carryin', I see,' Saul goaded. 'Don't worry, they aren't going to *really* let you have it just yet. Still got a bit of reminiscing to do first, ain't we?'

'Yeah, ain't we just,' Jimmy shrieked, sounding hysterical. 'I've got something to say to you all right: I should have stuck you that day at Nellie's when I had the chance.' His eyes leapt aside and his lips circled his teeth in a snarl. He'd spotted Michael's white face peeking round the corner at him. He clawed his way up the wall and on to his feet. 'You little bastard!' he roared at Edie's son. 'You've set me up, ain't yer?' Jimmy's fury and fright blinded him to Michael's sickly pallor, and his head vibrating in denial.

Michael had wanted Jimmy to get a thumping, but he hadn't expected this. Petrified, he gawped at the scene in front of him. He knew this was going to be worse than a few punches being thrown; Jimmy was about to get seriously hurt.

Rob, too, had been expecting the Batemans to be content with delivering a well-deserved right-hander or two. He'd had no thought of intervening until Saul's henchmen appeared, and a wink of metal flashed in his father's hand. While Jimmy's attention was focused on Michael, Rob hurtled through the office door and out into the street. But he was too late to prevent his father charging at the boy.

As Jimmy surged past Donald, arm raised, the youth panicked and jumped to avoid the knife. Haste made him clumsy, and his feet became entangled with Jimmy's, sending them both sprawling on the ground.

The blade bounced close to Michael's shoe. He reflexively sprang back before dropping his posy and pouncing on it.

'Give us that! Give us it back, you little bastard,' Jimmy bawled. He was aware that Saul and his two thugs were close behind. 'I'm gonna kill you fer this,' he yelled, now back on his feet and lunging at Michael. Both the boy's hands shot out in self-defence.

'Give us it!' Jimmy grunted, grappling with Michael for possession of the knife.

Finally Michael's frenzied mind grasped the idea it might be safer if he dropped the weapon. Once he'd heard the clatter of steel on cobbles Jimmy landed a punishing punch on Michael's cheek that sent the boy sagging to his knees, squashing his bunch of carnations.

'You in on this 'n' all?' Jimmy screamed at Rob, bending to retrieve the blade. His son had raced up behind him, shoving him with all his might and sending him sideways before he could get his fingers on the hilt. 'You all got together against me, have yers?' Jimmy roared in frustration as the knife skittered out of reach.

'Shut up!' The barked command was for his prostrate father, but his eyes were on Bateman and his crew. 'Let's all calm down,' Rob gasped. 'No need for any of this ... 'specially as the law's on its way.' He edged towards the knife, but in his desperation to protect Michael from Jimmy he'd allowed Saul to get to it first.

Saul exchanged a look with his cronies.

'It's his son ... Rob Wild...' one of them muttered in explanation.

'Yeah, I'm Rob Wild, and I own that warehouse.' With a flick of his head, he indicated the building behind him, all the while keeping his hands in front of him, supplicating for a truce. 'Came back here this evening 'cos I got a report of a break in.' He'd rattled off the tale with plausible fluency. He hoped his next lie would sound even more convincing: 'Phoned the law to report it a while ago. They're on their way.' He gave Michael a fierce look and jerked his head, indicating that he should get himself out of danger. But Jimmy's wallop had knocked the lad senseless and he continued hugging the wall in a daze, surrounded by torn petals.

'I'm bleeding...' Jimmy announced in a voice of calm and wonderment, making everyone suddenly stare at him. He removed his palm from his side and looked, appalled, at the crimson stain on it.

Michael pulled himself unsteadily on to his feet and stood swaying, mesmerised by Jimmy's outstretched palm.

'You stabbed me,' Jimmy accused. 'You've only gone 'n' killed me, Michael,' he whined.

Saul stepped forward to have a look. His eyes swung between Jimmy and his stricken stepson. Michael looked to be on the verge of swooning in shock. 'He didn't kill yer, Jim – I did.' One of Saul's fists rammed home then jerked back and the bloodied knife was swiftly dropped in his pocket.

Rob had suspected what Saul might do once he had possession of the knife. Much as he hated Jimmy Wild, the man was his father, and he wasn't about to stand by while he was murdered in cold-blood. As Jimmy crumpled to his knees, Rob jabbed a short sharp one at Saul's profile, making him stagger; a right hook followed up to floor him before his two henchmen could spring. As Donald rushed towards him, arms flailing, Rob swung a vicious fist at his head. 'That's long overdue...' he growled.

'Can you get up?'

Rob managed to move his head to and fro to indicate he couldn't. He was lying on his back on the ground and Michael was crouching over him, yanking on one of his arms. The other was twisted to an odd angle at his side.

'You've got to get up...' Michael sobbed. 'You've got to get to hospital.' He wedged a hand under Rob's shoulders, then strained backward to try to help him move. 'You're all mangled up,' he wailed.

Rob's face was a mess of swollen, bleeding flesh; his left arm was useless, having been broken in the fight. Rob had managed to defend himself for some time, but eventually the four men had brought him down. And Donald had stayed to give him a kicking where he lay. The last thing Rob remembered before he lost consciousness was Saul talking to him in his odd, reasonable way. 'Didn't have no beef with you ... so nothing personal, you understand,' he'd told Rob as he lay gasping and bubbling blood at his feet. 'You should've stayed well out of it, son.' Saul had picked up his hat, dusted it off, then walked to where Jimmy was propped against the wall, head lolling and eyes closed. 'Right ... that's us square then, Jim. See yer in hell, I expect.' Moments later the Batemans and the heavies had disappeared.

'You've got to go and get help, Michael,' Rob forced out through his swollen lips. 'Go on ... now ... go...' He suddenly felt the heat against his profile and turned his head. 'Shit!' He screwed shut his eyes. 'Quick get help ... get the fire brigade ... d'you know where my brother lives in Playford Road?' His laboured bursts of speech faded away. He could sense a wave of blackness closing in but fought hard against it stealing his senses. He knew he might be done for, and so might everything he'd worked for, but he wasn't letting go that easily.

Suddenly finding the energy to roll over on to one side, he used his good arm as a prop to get him on to his knees. 'Fuck!' he groaned and his head fell back in despair as he saw the orange glow lighting the windows of his office. He knew that in no time at all the warehouse would catch and his stock would be cinders. 'Fuckin' bastards!' he moaned. He tried to crawl across the road on his knees but a moment later his arm gave way and he collapsed back to the ground. Michael didn't hesitate any longer; he turned and ran.

The feeling of warm salt water stinging his raw flesh brought him round. Rob opened his eyes and saw Faye's face wavering over him. She bent her head and pressed her lips to his forehead, spilling more tears to torment him. She was kneeling at his side, trembling from head to toe. 'You just keep still ... you just keep still ... you're going to be all right...' she whispered. 'Gonna stay with you till help comes. Michael's getting help,' she croaked.

'*You've* got to get help, Faye,' Rob whispered. 'Go now in case Michael's not up to it. All I've got's in there.' He tried to turn his head towards the warehouse, where smoke was curling between the shutters. 'Ain't properly caught yet. Can save some...'

'Not going to leave you,' she fiercely interrupted. 'Michael's gonna bring Stephen, and the police and an ambulance and the brigade. He will too, promise. I've left Adam with your neighbour ... she didn't mind. Stephen's on his way; he'll know what to do.' Her hungry eyes rushed up and down the road as she looked and strained for some sign of assistance, but apart from an odd passing car, and the crackle and spit of the fire taking hold, all was still in the sultry dusk.

Rob again turned his head and grimaced in despair. 'Go and get help ... gotta get the fire out. Lose too much if that goes up,' he gasped. 'Got nothing to give you ... we'll have nothing.' His own tears this time tortured his ripped flesh.

'Got everything still!' She gripped hard at his shoulders, gave them a careful little shake. 'We've got everything we need.' Despite her desperate reassurances, her face continued dripping briny tears.

When Michael had rushed in bruised and bleeding and hysterical she'd been hard pressed to make him calm down so she could understand what was wrong. But as soon as she got the gist of it she'd burst in on a neighbour and left Adam with her. Having garbled instructions to Michael to fetch all the help he could muster, she'd raced through the back streets to Holloway Road.

Her first glimpse of Rob, battered and still as death, had made her double up and retch as though she'd taken a punch to the stomach. But he'd stirred at the moment he recognised her voice, even before he opened his eyes.

'Fuck!' Rob suddenly groaned as the sound of crashing timbers made him again turn his head. A sweetish smell of burning wood wafted towards them. 'It's not insured. Fuck off! Get help!' he weakly roared at her, trying to shove her away.

Again she shook her head, making him curse and arch his back in despair. Faye licked her parched lips. 'It's all right, Rob,' she gasped through her misery. 'Look, we got this.' She fumbled with her clothes, brought out the gold necklace with shaking fingers. 'Got at least twenty pounds, see. Got enough. It'll get us a room in Campbell Road for a long while, that will. Everything's gonna be all right ... s'long as we got each other.'

He raised a limp hand to touch her face with dirty bloodied fingertips. 'Please go and get help, sweetheart...'

'If I go ... are you gonna die? Are you sending me away 'cos you know you're gonna die?' she gulped out.

'Ain't gonna die, Faye,' he promised huskily. 'Ain't gonna die...'

'Going away, Nel?'

Nellie gratefully took a rest from lugging the suitcase in the direction of Finsbury Park Station. She let her belongings plonk to the pavement and turned to Saul, who'd pulled up beside her and was just getting out to speak to her over the roof of his car. It was nearly nine o'clock and thunder-clouds had prematurely darkened the humid evening, making them squint at one another through twilight. Nevertheless she'd seen the bump on his face. She chose to ignore it; she knew he wouldn't mention it either.

'Yeah ... I'm off; too old fer this malarkey. Don't want to do it no more.'

'Where you off to then?'

'Not sure,' Nellie admitted. 'Might go up Nottingham.'

'Nottingham? Why you goin' there?' Saul asked in surprise.

Nellie licked her lips. She knew they were both skirting around what was really on their minds: what had occurred with Jimmy Wild to give Saul a fresh blemish on his scarred face. Nellie pushed it away to the back of her mind. It didn't matter to her. She was finished with Jimmy Wild and Islington.

'My old mum moved there to live with her sister, years ago, just after she was widowed fer the second time,' she told Saul. 'Ain't seen her in a long while, not since me stepfather died. Only went to his funeral so I could dance on his grave. 'Course, I might turn up and find her dead and buried. Or I might turn up and get told to piss off 'cos I'm a bleedin' disgrace.' She grimaced. 'That's what she told me last time I saw her. Long old trek, only to get told to piss off. Never mind; there's always me sister, in Walthamstow. Could try there.' A flash in the sky made her glance up with a grimace. When thunder quickly followed she picked up her case and gave Saul a rueful smile. 'Mind you, she'll probably tell me to piss off 'n' all. Caught me in bed with her old man last time I paid her a visit.' She shrugged. 'Well, best be off before the heavens open. See yer 'round, Saul – and take care o' yerself.' Tightening her grip on the case, she set off as fat raindrops started to plop on the pavement.

'Hop in, I'll take yer.'

'Nah ... s'all right. I'm nearly there.' Nellie nodded forward at the lights of the station a short distance away.

'No, I'll take you up North. That way, if you get told to piss off by yer mum, you ain't wasted your fare. And I'll bring you back.'

Nellie dropped the suitcase and gawped at him. 'You'll take me all the way to Nottingham?' she asked in astonishment.

'Yeah, why not?' he said and came round and opened the door for her.

Nellie hesitated, staring at him to see if it was a joke, but he returned her look, head cocked to one side so he could watch her with his good eye. Slowly she approached the car and got in and Saul put her case in the boot before sliding in beside her.

They sat for a moment, side by side, staring ahead, with the rain drumming on the roof of the car. Saul turned the ignition. Nellie put her hand on his arm.

'P'raps you'd better tell your lady friend first you're goin' on a trip.'

'Don't have a lady friend no more, Nel.' He turned to look at her. 'She's gone back to her old man. Knew she would. Prefers getting a thump in the guts to looking at my boat race.' His sour smile sweetened into a genuine chuckle. He put the car in gear, but Nellie touched his rough cheek, making him turn to her.

'She's a bleedin' fool then. Ain't that bad, once yer get used to it.' She stroked a chubby finger on scarred skin. 'If you'd've stayed put in London instead of doing yer bit fer king and country, you could've come a worse cropper with a shotgun stuck up yer nose, you know. S'one of the risks of the job, ain't it?'

Saul stared through the dribbling windscreen for so long that Nellie thought he might have changed his mind about taking her. Suddenly he said, 'Yeah, you're right, Nel. Hazardous old game, I'm in. Probably time I jacked in this malarkey.' He pulled away from the kerb with a jerk. 'Anyhow, law's going to be looking for me after what I done to Jimmy.'

'He dead?' Nellie whispered.

'Weren't when I left him,' Saul answered honestly.

'Know where Nottingham is, do you?' Nellie asked, settling back.

'Nah ... I'll have to stop and buy a map,' he answered with a grin.

TWENTY-NINE

'Gonna let me in, Til?'

Matilda tested the key quietly to make sure it was locked, then put her weight against the door. At the first sound of that hoarse coaxing her mind had sped back to a night when she'd been fool enough to open up to Jimmy Wild. The deadly fight that had ensued had blighted the lives of all those who'd been present

'What you after?' she snapped in an undertone. 'Ain't got no sympathy for you if you've come here for a shoulder to cry on now Edie's gone.'

'Yeah ... understand ... I know I don't deserve none,' Jimmy wheezed.

Matilda frowned against the wooden panels. He sounded breathless, as though he might be ill. After a short silence she opened the door a fraction to peep at Jimmy. He was swaying, ashen-faced, with a supporting hand propped on the frame. She pulled the door back and gaped at him. 'What's up with you, fer Chrissake?'

'I'm done fer, Til. Really done fer this time. Just

come to say goodbye.' With an effort he propelled himself past her and into the room. 'Reg about, is he?'

'Be back soon; gone to get a few brown ales.'

'Won't take long, anyhow,' Jimmy gasped out. 'Just got a couple o' things to get off me chest.'

Matilda's uneasiness increased as she noticed the way he was holding both arms folded hard against his side. She peered closely at his clothes. 'You're bleeding!' She tugged back his jacket by a lapel. Inside the coat he was pressing a bit of crimson cloth against his ribs. 'What the fuckin' hell has happened to you?'

'Told you, I'm done for fer sure this time.' He coughed a chuckle. 'I knew you'd want to know, being as you tried to see me off once before. You thought I'd been sent to me maker after Geoff Lovat stabbed me, didn't yer?'

'Never believed for one minute you was with yer maker; thought you was with the other bloke,' Matilda replied sourly.

Jimmy showed his appreciation of her remark by laughing soundlessly. 'Know who saved me that night, Til?' He paused for her to reply, but Matilda seemed mesmerised by the blood pooling on to her dirty floorboards. 'Fran,' he answered his own question and nodded to himself, pleased, despite his humour transforming to a grimace of pain. He fidgeted with the wadding pressed to his side. 'Me wife saved me,' he panted. 'Your sister, Fran, bless her, saved me.'

'What you ranting on about?' Matilda took a hesitant step closer to him. He looked on the point of collapse, as though willpower alone was keeping him upright. But much as she wanted to get him out of her room as quickly as possible, she had a gnawing need to hear what he was about to tell her. She'd spent the last year pondering how Jimmy Wild had managed to cheat death and return to The Bunk.

On the night when he'd beaten her and Fran to a pulp, and attempted to rape Alice, Geoff Lovat had been their saviour. He'd fought Jimmy off and, while trying to disarm him of his knife, had accidentally stabbed him. They'd all thought Jimmy had died of that wound; Geoff had gone to war rather than risk facing a trial that might see him accused of murder rather than manslaughter. He'd perished in France, only eighteen years old, thinking he was Jimmy Wild's killer.

'Fran hated you same as the rest of us by then,' Matilda hissed. 'You beat her up so bad that night you nearly killed her. She could hardly move a muscle she was in so much pain. She couldn't have helped yer.'

'Got to say sorry fer all o' that. Circumstances went against me that day, that's all it were ... rotten circumstances and Nellie and Saul making me crazy. Too late now, anyhow.' He sounded impatient, as though regretting apologising, and shuffled away to cling double-handed to a chair back. 'Better finish what I got to say. 'Spect Fran's cussing me up there, now she knows it were her saved me life that night.' He jerked his head heavenwards and gave his dead wife a defiant wink. 'Last thing I remember was Fran whacking me over the head with that pot. Knocked me clean out, she did. When I come round and saw all the blood covering me, I guessed you must've thought I'd snuffed it. I was getting carted off by then and knew to make me escape a bit lively or I'd end up with me throat slit. Knife had gone across me ribs, y'see 'stead of between 'em when Lovat stabbed me.' He hung his head, grinning at his shoes as though it were a proud memory. 'I knew the two clowns up front pulling the cart thought I was dead. Knew too they wouldn't go blabbing to their boss that I'd escaped. Be more than their lives was worth to upset Johnny Blake.' Out of breath, he sunk on to the seat of the chair. 'Know what's always puzzled me, Til? How d'you get him to do you a favour like that?'

'Got *real* friends, Jim,' Tilly answered in a soft voice. 'Something you wouldn't understand 'cos you've never had none; never deserved none.'

Matilda had heard enough; seen enough. A pool of blood was meandering across her floor-boards, showing the path Jimmy had weaved before he'd collapsed. She wished Reg would come back and give her a hand getting Jimmy out of her place so he could get to hospital … or die elsewhere. She realised she didn't mind which it was, so long as he was away from her.

'You had the luck o' the devil, that night.' Matilda's attention sharpened as his chin sunk to his chest. 'But I pity Fran, 'cos she's probably grinding her teeth to dust in her grave.'

'Ah, don't say that,' Jimmy gurgled and brought up his head. 'Fran were me life.'

'Yeah, and you was the death of her. Might not of killed her outright, but you wore her down over the years till she had no strength left.' Tilly's voice wobbled with emotion. 'She never properly got over losing her daughter, or the regular beatings you give her. The fool loved you 'n' all.'

'Yeah, and I loved her right back ... only you was the one I wanted.' He forced himself up and ambled to stand between Matilda and the door. 'But I reckon you always knew pretty much how you affected me, Til.'

Matilda wasn't about to bother trying to push past him. She'd only get covered in blood if they tussled, even though she was sure she could easily overpower him in the state he was in. She'd opened the window earlier because the night had been unbearably close. A jagged white light patterned the cloth covering the sash although not a breath of air had stirred it. A moment later thunder trembled the glass. If she were to take a look outside, she might spot Reg chatting with a pal. He'd been a while and she'd give him hell when he eventually got himself home. She went to pull aside the curtain and shove the sash right up to stick her head out and look ... and bawl.

'I reckon we deserve to go together, Til. When all's said and done, love ... hate ... more or less the same to me...' Jimmy had come up behind her and opened his arms. Matilda was swinging about when he fell against her with all his might and they tumbled out into the darkness, locked together in a savage embrace, to the street below.

The spike of the railing drove into Jimmy's back as Matilda's weight crushed him downwards, but his mind slowly ticked on. If he'd stayed in Kent he'd have been all right. But even when he was all those miles away, The Bunk had been an irritating scab on his mind that he'd pick at from time to time. He'd eventually have come back. It was Campbell Road that had finished him, not Saul or Michael.

'Where the fuck's Stephen?' Rob turned his head in agitation. His body was a burning, throbbing agony, yet he remained lucid enough to be oddly glad of the pain; he was sure it was keeping him conscious.

He was on his back and, as lightning illuminated his battered features to ghastly effect, Faye whimpered and then covered him with her body as though to protect him from the enormous crash that followed.

'I'll be all right, Faye. I'll be all right so long as you go and find someone.' Rob could see from the corner of a crusted eye that a couple of women had stopped at the junction with Holloway Road to fiddle with an umbrella. Suddenly they spotted the fire and began slowly approaching with hesitant steps. 'Go! Go and make them get help.'

Faye nodded and this time obeyed his pleading command. She sprang up and raced toward the women, causing them to stop dead in alarm.

Rob felt the rain on his face and tried to smile. It felt cool and clean and he opened his parched mouth to taste its sweetness stinging his tongue. 'Go on, Mum, send it down,' he croaked and closed his eyes. A hiss from one side brought his face slowly about and he blinked as flames licked around exposed rafters where part of the warehouse roof had caved in. 'Go on, Mum! Send it fucking down!' he gasped, and started to laugh.

With a sob of relief, Faye plunged on past the gawping women and towards Stephen, who had just pelted around the corner. Michael came puffing in his wake, many yards behind, and she could see his hair already plastered to his scalp and his face screwed up against the driving downpour. She suddenly stopped and swung about to scream back at Rob, 'Don't you dare die on me!'

Rob's head fell back and a wretched laugh grazed his throat. He'd just remembered something and his weak fingers patted at a comforting bump on his sodden hip. He had Faye and Adam and a roll of tenners in his pocket. Before he died he had some living to do. He wasn't going anywhere.

EPILOGUE

'It would all have been different if he hadn't died.' Michael averted his glistening eyes and gazed at the rows of headstones.

'I know...' Faye swallowed the lump in her throat. 'I know,' she repeated huskily and busied herself with arranging the chrysanthemums in the marble pot. As Michael's snuffling grew louder, Adam tilted his face to look at him. The little boy got up from where he'd been sitting on the grass and went to put his arms around Michael's neck.

'Why don't you take Adam to see the ducks?' She pointed to the right, where there was a small pond. A wooden hut, enclosing benches, was there too. A few people were strolling around the perimeter of the water, enjoying the autumn sunshine, having tended their loved ones' graves. Michael rose slowly and, taking Adam's hand, led him away.

Faye pushed herself up from the grass and went to sit on a bench stationed at the side of a path that meandered through the cemetery.

'Mum would have wanted to be here...' She turned to her husband. 'She would have wanted to be laid to rest with Dad. Wish I'd known where he was sooner.'

'They'll find each other.'

'Yeah; they'll find each other,' she echoed, and the simple comfort made her hiccup a sob. She shifted closer to Rob and he raised the arm he'd slung along the back of the bench to brush a thumb on her cheek.

'I loved me dad so much,' she said. 'More of a hero than I knew, wasn't he?'

'Yeah,' Rob gently agreed. 'You were very lucky to have a dad like that.'

She turned to look up at him but found nothing comforting to say to him about his own father. Jimmy was buried in the same cemetery as was Edie; but far, far away from her.

Faye's fingers smoothed over Rob's jaw where crisscrossing raised scars were quite visible. 'Thanks for finding out for us where Dad was. It's nice here...' She glanced about at the Kentish scenery visible beyond the boundaries of the cemetery. 'We going on honeymoon soon? You promised me, Rob...'

He grinned. 'Yeah ... just as soon as I get things back on track at work. Steve's been a diamond, keeping the business going ... or what's left of it...' he sourly said. In his heart Rob knew he should be grateful, not regretful. He'd been lucky that anything had been salvageable from the warehouse after that dreadful night, five months ago, when he'd taken a beating that had nearly killed him. Sometimes he had a private smile when musing on whether his mum, and Edie too perhaps, had been watching over them and had sent down the torrential rain that helped the brigade put out the fire.

'Get it all back for us, Faye, I will,' he said softly. 'We'll have a good house again one day, swear we will.'

'We've got a nice house,' she said, enclosing his

fingers in hers and bringing them to her lap. The neat, cosy terrace house they rented was perfectly adequate as far as she was concerned. So was the modest car that had replaced his fancy Tourer. 'Let's go. I'm ready now.' She waved at the boys to let them know they were leaving.

'Shall we go and visit Matilda this afternoon?'

Rob nodded, and chuckled. 'If they don't let her out of hospital on Friday, she reckons she'll fight anyone who tries to stop her going home.'

'What a family you are,' Faye teased and went on tiptoe to press her lips against his healing cheek. Disentangling their hands, she went to stoop and plant a kiss on her father's headstone.

'What d'you think he'd feel about you marrying into a family like ours?' Rob stiffly got up and followed her to respectfully pat the marble.

Faye smiled serenely at him. 'He'd think I'd done all right.'

This Large Print Book for the partially sighted, who cannot read normal print, is published under the auspices of

THE ULVERSCROFT FOUNDATION

THE ULVERSCROFT FOUNDATION

... we hope that you have enjoyed this Large Print Book. Please think for a moment about those people who have worse eyesight problems than you ... and are unable to even read or enjoy Large Print, without great difficulty.

You can help them by sending a donation, large or small to:

The Ulverscroft Foundation,
1, The Green, Bradgate Road,
Anstey, Leicestershire, LE7 7FU,
England.
or request a copy of our brochure for more details.

The Foundation will use all your help to assist those people who are handicapped by various sight problems and need special attention.

Thank you very much for your help.